About the Author

Ruth Hartley's first novel, *The Shaping of Water*, is a character-driven story set around a lake in Central Africa during the Liberation wars.

"With its fragmented time lines, cast of diverse characters and wonderful rendering of landscape, this is a novel of challenging intellect and big ideas," says Tanvi Bush, author of 'Witch Girl', published by Modjaji Books.

Ruth Hartley has published on Kindle "The White and Black Blues", a short story about African jazz musicians, Louis Armstrong and Tom Waller who loves jazz but is inside the 'wrong' skin.

She grew up on a farm in Zimbabwe, learnt about art and politics in South Africa and about life in swinging London. After working in Zambia for many years she returned to England to study, write and travel. Ruth now lives in France and continues to write, draw and paint.

www.ruthartley.com

The TIN HEART GOLD MINE

RUTH HARTLEY

Matador
9 Priory Business Park,
Wistow Road, Kibworth Beauchamp,
Leicestershire. LE8 0RX
Tel: 0116 279 2299
Email: books@troubador.co.uk
Web: www.troubador.co.uk/matador
Twitter: @matadorbooks

ISBN 978 1785898 761

British Library Cataloguing in Publication Data.
A catalogue record for this book is available from the British Library.

Printed and bound in the UK by TJ International, Padstow, Cornwall
Typeset in 11pt Aldine401 by Troubador Publishing Ltd, Leicester, UK

Matador is an imprint of Troubador Publishing Ltd

For John.

"Painting is not done to decorate apartments. It is an instrument of war for attack and defence against the enemy." - Pablo Picasso

PROLOGUE

OSCAR AND LARA 1985

Oscar and Lara watch the liquid heat of the day hatch out of a misty lopsided sun. It's cool and fresh on the riverbank where they sit together, shoulders touching, under a huge fig tree. Its looped and tangled roots half in, half out of the river protect them from a frontal ambush by a crocodile while behind them, its aerial roots and twisted branches mean they won't be surprised by wild creatures coming down to the water to drink. Oscar and Lara only speak to point out a bird or to identify its song. Their voices are so quiet they're inaudible half a pace away. The sibilance of whispers carries for a greater distance, but by remaining still and speaking at this low pitch, they won't disturb the most timid of wild animals.

"What a pretty creature!" Lara touches the back of Oscar's hand to draw his attention to the creature she's just seen.

"Beautiful and lethal." Oscar links his little finger over Lara's.

They have no need to tell each other that it's a *"boomslang"*, a juvenile tree snake. Oscar told Lara a while ago how he watched a friend die from the internal haemorrhage caused by its slow-acting venom.

They watch the elegant reptile wind itself down the curves and folds of the tree nearby. Its apple-green scales shimmer with turquoise light, its bright round eye is functional and pitiless.

"It's had breakfast – a bird's egg – now it'll sleep," Oscar observes.

Halfway along the snake's slender length there's an oval swelling larger than its head that doesn't impede its supple descent.

Lara looks up to see which bird's nest has been raided, which bird is fluttering distressed above her head, but there is only the long thin call of a bush shrike and the busyness of the yellow and scarlet bishop birds in the reeds on the sandbank in mid-river. In a moment the *boomslang* vanishes among the shrubs at the tree's roots. Lara makes a mental note of its nest and remembers another snake in hiding: the warlord from Angola known as General Njoka, or General Snake. He is rumoured to have burnt down villages a little way north and the local villagers are terrified. Oscar, alone, appears unconcerned.

The grip of Oscar's hand makes Lara shivery. Yesterday she made sketches of him and his men launching the camp's flat-bottomed boat into the river for a fishing trip. Though quite short, Oscar is as fit and strong as his African workers and as unselfconscious about his body. Lara can't imagine him preening himself beside a swimming pool. Oscar is different. Oscar is tough. His body tells the story of his life, of his journeys and his wars. She finds this thought thrilling. She wants to know what he knows. It pleases her that he is so much older than her. Oddly, it makes her feel powerful. Yet last night drifting off to sleep in the iron circle of his arms, Lara had noticed that Oscar's skin is softening, his flesh is slack in the hollows of his collarbones and under his chin. The hair on his chest is as grey as the hair on his temples. It made her feel tender, but it also made her a little sad. She felt something else as well. Did his mortality excite her? Last night Lara pushed the idea away and snuggled her head into Oscar's neck.

Now, sitting by Oscar, Lara is certain everything is just as perfect as it should be.

Part One

London 1997

Chapter One

Mile End

At nine-thirty the sun breaks through the clouds above Bow Church Station and tips its load of blinding light into the second floor flat. Its rays are as sharp and clean as knives. Shielding her eyes from its glare, Lara hides behind the curtain in her studio and spies on Tim, her tall husband, and Adam, her small son, as they cross Mile End Road below her.

The part of Lara that is artist observes her family with professional detachment and clarity. Her visual brain calculates the differences and likenesses between her subjects, together with their relationship to the light and colour of their environment. Yesterday Lara told Tim and Adam that it suited her very well to stay home and paint while they spent the day together.

She lied.

The part of Lara that loves Tim and Adam knows that she won't add one splodge of colour to any of her canvases today. She has no desire to paint. She feels as if she'll never paint again. It seems a pointless activity. She was working on a commission for her agent but can't decide if it is complete. She doesn't care if it ever sells though once she was proud of it. The painting is large; the brushstrokes free and confident, the colours swirl from cool greens and greys to a focus of warm red and orange. It is a painting of the wild and overgrown Bethnal Green Jewish Cemetery in a pearl-pink twilight. A bright-eyed fox sits in the foreground, its front paws neatly together under its tidy tail. Behind the fox a homeless man sleeps on a grave stone under a litter of plastic sheets and dirty blankets. Lara has made several successful paintings inspired by the wildlife and rough sleepers in the cemetery but now she is wearied by the thought of them.

She has assets sitting silently in a bank vault that free her from the need to earn her living. These assets belonged to Oscar and infuriate Tim. Lara has no idea what to do with them. The problem is driving her mad.

When a canvas is almost finished, Lara has a private ritual that helps her judge if she can stop working on it. This ritual amuses Tim and intrigues and puzzles Adam when they catch her behaving oddly outside her studio door.

"I have to catch my paintings by surprise." she explains. "I get stale – I look and look at what I've done – I need to see it with new eyes. Sometimes I turn the painting the wrong way up – sometimes I turn myself upside-down. Sometimes I go into the studio with my eyes shut and then open them fast and blink at my painting. Obviously my painting alters as I work but it seems to go on changing after I've finished. It sounds mad I know – it's actually my perception that changes. I can't immediately be certain if it's good or bad or needs more work. I have to leave a painting alone for a while – then see if it's okay. An artist I know carries on working on his paintings during exhibitions and even after they've been bought if he can get away with it."

Tim's sympathetic. "It's the same with writing. Even after publication I sometimes change my judgement of how well or how badly I've written an article."

Adam takes Lara's explanation very seriously. He turns his back on Lara's painting, bends over, hands on floor to avoid somersaulting and studies it from between his legs. "I see what you mean, Mum," he says. "That fox isn't jumping out at me today like it did yesterday. It belongs inside the picture now."

Lara is in turmoil. She has no new perspective on her life. No fresh vision. Her mind and body are wrenching themselves apart.

A sour resentful fear burns inside her. She didn't ask for any of this. She didn't want money or assets. She didn't plan wars or commit murders. She hasn't traded in blood diamonds. At least, she didn't know anything about that. Really!

Shit! Shit! Shit! Money is shit, isn't it?

She's never had much money. It's true she wanted it but does she still want it now?

Lara shivers. She's made some bad choices. Who hasn't at some point in their lives? Liseli, her old school friend, had teased her about her sun-bleached hair and her looks. "Oscar fancies blonde women," she warned. Lara is angry at the memory. She tugs a lock of hair into a twist behind her ear. There's not enough sunshine in London for her hair to be any colour but mouse brown.

"I'm first a person – second an artist. Or is it the other way around? Art comes first. Definitely! Except – I can't make it anymore." Lara is submerged in a well of self-doubt and held down by the weight of her sadness. "I'm no use to myself if I can't paint and draw."

This misery is about losing Tim when he goes to Uganda next week. He must come back so she can stop feeling this way. Tim must understand her dilemma, mustn't he? So why is he going away? Will he ever come back?

Lara twists her right hand into the shirt buttons between her breasts and thrusts her knuckles against the blade bone of her chest, but the self-inflicted pain is too minimal to counter her growing panic. It can't hold her together. It can't stop the swelling agony in her heart. Lara thinks her body will burst with the pain. If she yells out of the window at Tim he won't hear her above the traffic. He might not come back anyway and if Adam was to be distracted as he crosses the road she might be responsible for an accident and for his death.

In another week Tim will be back in Africa. Lara's left breast still tingles from last night's love making. The closer their parting approaches, the rougher their lovemaking becomes. Each of them is trying to use physical sensation to block emotional pain.

Lara continues to watch as Tim takes Adam's hand and they cross over the Mile End Road at the pedestrian lights. Neither of them looks back at the window of the flat. Lara is bitterly disappointed and greatly relieved.

The thrusting, deafening traffic below also makes conversation between father and son impossible, so they walk quickly towards the Underground Station. This is their special day together. It is the result of weeks of strategic planning. It will be a good day for Adam to remember when his father is in a distant and dangerous land. In spite of how she feels, Lara can't help half-smiling. Neither Tim nor Adam had thought to comb Adam's hair before they left home. It pokes out and up in a bird's crest at the back of his head.

Lara glances around her studio. Perhaps she'll make herself a coffee. Perhaps she won't. Most of her paintings are hidden inside bubble wrap ready to move to her new studio near Victoria Park. There's not much to see. The plan chest contains her drawings; her sketchbooks are stored in boxes. Outwardly it all appears safe, neat and bland. Some of her sketchbooks haven't been opened in years. Perhaps some of the drawings in the plan chest should remain unseen and untouched. Lara imagines the layers of paper stirring like leaves in a dry breeze or rustling like grasses in a hot wind. She imagines a whirlwind of drawings flying around the room and adding to the storm of confusion in her head. There are many drawings of African landscapes and wild animals and birds. There are also sketches of people she knows, sketches of Bill and Maria, of Inonge, of Enoch and of Oscar.

Chapter Two

Adam and Tim

Lara is present at some of Tim and Adam's planning sessions for their trip to the South Bank.

"We'll go first to Stanford's to buy guide books and maps," Lara hears Tim say to Adam, "then to the Africa Centre to see if they have anything on Somalia. Next over the Hungerford Bridge to the South Bank Centre for that jazz concert and a pasta lunch."

Lara would have liked to go with them just to stop in the middle of the Hungerford Bridge and stare out over the Thames River. The experience is always magical. The beauty of its silvered waters glittering in the slanting London light enthrals her with its poetry, romance and history. She likes to journey in spirit down the Thames all the way to the sea. Her imagination carries her over oceans and up the distant Kasama River until she comes to the rock pools gleaming in the setting sun of Chambeshi and sees again the wild creatures she had once painted from life. Lara knows however, that Adam needs time alone with Tim. She knows that Tim loves Adam and they are both excited at the prospect of their day together.

"Sure, Dad – Central Line to Holborn first – then afterwards we'll go home on the Green Line." Adam agrees. He likes to display his knowledge of London Transport. "Here, Dad, Give me your specs – they're all smudgy again."

During this discussion Adam pulls a corner of his shirt out

of his jeans and reaches up for Tim's glasses. Tim and Lara both grin. Tim loves Adam's concern about his specs even if it meant means they end up with fine scratches on them. Lara is forever pointing out that Adam also needs to wipe smudges off his own glasses. Father and son are both short-sighted but, aside from his spectacles, Adam is more like Lara, his mother, in appearance. He has the same golden complexion and pale brown hair. He doesn't have Tim's generous over-wide mouth. It is too soon to say if Adam will need orthodontic treatment, as Tim had done as an adolescent.

As she thinks of Tim, and Adam's differences and similarities that small but greedy gape of doubt and guilt grows once more under Lara's ribs. She wonders what Tim will say to Adam once they have caught the underground train. She wonders what she wants him to say about her, and then about the three of them. She wonders what dire secrets Tim might give away to Adam. Lara knows Tim is not malicious. She also understands just how easily hurts can produce spiteful words from people.

One day one of them, or both of them, Tim or Lara; or Tim and Lara, if they are still together, must confess to Adam that there was once a man called Oscar, who though dead, changed all their lives years ago and who – though dead – is changing their lives again today.

Lara imagines that on the tube train Tim and Adam will again wipe each other's specs with the clean tumble-dried hanky provided by Lara. One hanky will certainly be lost, one, with luck, may arrive back at home. Tim will grab Adam's wrist firmly as the tube train clatters in and the commuters push forward to its doors. If father and son are lucky enough to find a seat they will arrange themselves so that Tim sits and Adam stands with their heads almost level, so they can talk. Adam will want to talk about his 9th birthday next year. His 8th birthday, celebrated six months before, is still one of his favourite topics of conversation.

"Will you be back for my birthday, Dad?"

"I'll come home if it's possible." Tim will repeat the promise

Adam keeps asking him to make. "What do you want for a present, Adam?"

Lara has guessed what Adam's answer will be but Tim has been delegated to find out for certain.

"Nothing that you'll be able to get there, Dad, I shouldn't think. I'd like to see a Kalashnikov though. At school Brett said his Dad has got a proper gun he brought back from Iraq."

"I doubt that's true."

Tim would grin. He might belatedly try to flatten Adam's hair into a semblance of tidiness. Tim never had a comb with him. He didn't need one with his short-cut, tightly-curled dark hair but he is never without pens and a notebook which fill the sagging pockets of his jacket even when he isn't on a journalistic assignment.

"Why do you want a gun, Adam?"

"To shoot Brett of course – he's such a dork!"

Adam will look at Tim slyly to see if he acknowledges the joke.

"Don't think I will manage to get you a gun, but we can do the Imperial War Museum on your birthday if you like."

It was Lara who had suggested to Tim that they would both enjoy a trip to the War Museum. War and reporting on war are part of Tim's job as a foreign correspondent on a London newspaper. Adam, with the insatiable curiosity about violence common to boys of his age, always wants to know why and how wars happen and what guns and weapons are in use by the opposing enemy sides. Tim is just the best Dad for a boy the age of Adam.

"Ooh – that'd be fantastic, Dad!"

Adam makes 'fan-tas-tic' into three long syllables with the emphasis on the middle 'tas'.

Tim smiles whenever Adam does that. He had been a rather geeky kid himself but he had not had to endure the indoor life that London forces on Adam. Even the rock-climbing that Adam perseveres with, in spite of his lack of skill, and the basketball that he plays with reluctance are done inside a sports hall. It is true the buildings are large but there is no blue infinity of space overhead. Tim worries that Adam may not survive the physical bullying that is part of growing up but Adam seems unphased by his experiences so far. He is, however, not yet at middle school.

One day at home, as Adam fiddled with a model Dalek toy that no longer said "Exterminate!", he explained to Tim that he made jokes about the school bullies so that, rather than be laughed at, they left him alone.

"The power of the word," Tim had said with parental pride to Lara afterwards. "Hope it continues to work for him!"

Adam wants to know where Tim's new assignment is going to take him and Tim has promised to get him maps to cover the whole North-Eastern area of Africa as his work will probably include parts of Sudan, Kenya, Somalia, and Uganda.

"I'll let you know where I am going but sometimes I'll be off your map completely, Adam."

"Too bad – Mum will want to know where you are too, Dad."

Adam, standing against Tim's knee in the train, will push his spectacles up the bridge of his nose while tilting his head backwards. Adam has copied the gesture from Tim, who is quite unaware that he makes it in the first place.

Their plan is to leave the Underground at the frenetic Holborn interchange and wander through Covent Garden, pausing to see the performers and jugglers outside St Paul's Church. At Stanford's map shop they will look for maps and guides of the places where Tim is to work.

Once their Covent Garden expedition is over, they will cross over the Thames to the lunchtime jazz concert in the South Bank Centre that Tim wants to hear and that Adam has been persuaded he will enjoy. After that they will have seafood pasta by the restaurant window with the giant bust of Nelson Mandela on guard outside. Lara thinks the statue's likeness to Mandela is poor. Perhaps that is why she never can remember the name of the sculptor.

Her thoughts skitter back from making representational art to what Tim might say to Adam or Adam to Tim. Might Adam raise the question that his parents expect and dread? How will that go? Again Lara can only guess.

"Dad – are you and Mum fighting? Is that why you are going away?"

Will Tim take off his spectacles and rub them briskly with his scratchy paper napkin instead of his soft hanky? What would or could he say that was honest and the right thing for Adam to hear? Lara tries to breathe in and out steadily for him. She guesses how he might word it. She knows what she wants him to say.

"Look Adam, things go up and down in every family. Right now Lara and I are making adjustments to – well – our jobs are changing – we were wondering about moving house – you'll be going to a high school one day and we have to find one that suits you – yes – well – we've had a disagreement, but we are sorting it out – I promise you – "

Adam will listen attentively while spearing a prawn and twirling his pasta around it. His eyes will flick up at his father and afterwards he may ask the question that Lara wants to ask.

"Dad – do you still love Mummy?"

Tim hasn't been able to use the word 'love' to Lara for a while. Adam, however, needs reassurance. Lara feels the weight of Tim's resentment and anger with her as if she is sitting at the table with them. She knows Tim wants what is best for his family but she knows he'll never accept anything tainted by that bastard, Oscar even if it was to make them richer. Maybe Tim has come to feel that she's tainted too.

He might say simply to Adam, "I do love Lara. I love you and I love your Mummy too. I think we both need a little time to think about how we do things. None of that will ever change how much we love you, Adam."

He might not.

Lara is terrified of losing Tim's love but what is she able to do about Oscar? Everything to do with Oscar is complicated. She loathes Oscar so much that when she thinks about him she discovers that she is not breathing. When she dreams about him, as happens too often, he presses against her, a troubling but warm and intimate presence.

When Tim first told Adam he was setting off on a working trip to East Africa, Lara had seen Adam look at Tim for a moment. Then he had stood up, walked up to Tim and hugged him, ducking his head under Tim's chin so that he couldn't be kissed on his face. Tim had squeezed him and kissed the top of his head, distracted again by the hair that poked up and tickled his face.

"That's okay, then," Adam had said using Lara's end-of-conversation expression and copying her most matter-of-fact voice.

Perhaps at the South Bank Centre, Adam will get up to hug Tim again and then have to say, "Oh, I got some pasta sauce on your shirt Dad – sorry!"

Chapter Three

The School Gate

It is the divided Lara, the sad and bad Lara, the Lara who has hollowed out the artist Lara, who is waiting at the school gate on Monday afternoon for Adam. Tim has gone. He left for East Africa on Friday night and reached Nairobi the following day. They last spoke to each other by phone on Saturday. Now, today, he is on the road to somewhere else.

"Handsome boy." comments the woman standing next to Lara.

Lara knows her slightly. It is Hilda Brewer, a thick-bodied rusty-haired woman probably in her late-forties, who lives in the same block of council flats as Lara and has grandchildren at the same school as Adam.

"Looks just like his dad. Saw them together last week."

Lara turns her head rather too quickly to see what Hilda means and jerks her neck painfully. Holding her hand under her ear she tries to nod. Why does a cricked neck hurt so much? Last week it had been Tim who had collected Adam from school. This week it is Oscar who has possession of the inside of Lara's skull. She tries to mentally dislodge Oscar without physically shaking her head.

"Yes, he does, doesn't he? – I suppose."

Lara curses herself inwardly for her confusion and her guilt. She's falling apart, she's stupid, she's collapsing, she's pathetic. If only the sky wasn't so grey. If only the sun could dissolve the mist. If only she could think straight. If only thinking could provide her with an answer. If only she could answer spontaneously and say with a confident laugh, "Yes, Adam is the spit of his father."

"He can come for tea with my grandson if he likes." Hilda said, "'He's the same year as Lester – 8 years? It's Adam, innit? You ask him – then just knock at No 15. What's your name, dear?"

Lara thinks with some horror of what Adam might be fed in front of the telly at No. 15. It would probably be a bag of chips from the takeaway opposite as they watch a noisy and violent Japanese cartoon for kids and listen to racist opinions regurgitated from a florid tabloid newspaper. People keep to themselves or to their cliques in the council flats where Lara lives. There's a degree of suspicion between the older council tenants and the younger owner-buyers. If Lara ever thinks about the older working class tenants, she imagines they resent the invasive changes that herald their inevitable displacement. She personally doesn't feel a citizen of England or Britain. London, however, both contains the whole world and is claimed by it, so Lara feels safe in its boundaries even while she yearns for Africa.

Without Tim Lara is in need of an occasional child-minder. One who is a neighbour with regular habits would be convenient. Lara gives herself a mental shake and smiles at Hilda. Lara's emotions swing crazily between anger and misery every day. If Hilda can look after Adam she will be able to make an appointment to see Brendan, the therapist that her old friend, Liseli, recommends.

"Thank you. I'm Lara – Lara Weston." she says.

Weston is Tim's name and Lara's married name. It is not the name she uses currently as a professional artist. Perhaps she is truly paranoid but Lara has nightmares that somebody might connect her to the 'Lara Kingston' who had painted 'those' paintings. If someone made the connection, if it all came out, could she be arrested and jailed?

Lara gives Hilda a continuing smile.

"I'll see what Adam wants to do – I expect he would like to."

Adam and another boy are approaching. They are obviously friends and their heads are together as they laugh and tug at each other's coats in some game of unthinking natural physicality. Adam drops behind and drags at the other boy's rucksack, unbalancing him for a moment. Before they reach the gate each boy produces a length of stick harvested without permission from a school-yard tree. They begin a battle to the death with their light-sabre substitutes.

"Lester, where's Tracey? Where's your sister, Lester?" Hilda calls.

"Coming," he answers without turning to look round for her.

Lara sees a pretty child with thick hair and a brown skin wandering across the yard towards them. Both Lester and his sister, Tracey, are mixed-race. Lara sighs as she realises that she had chosen to stereotype Hilda as an East End racist. She doesn't need another proof of her own increasing misanthropy.

Hilda explains as they start to walk back to the flats together.

"My daughter and her husband work away in Essex. They've got a cleaning business. Sometimes if they are working all night the kids stay over. Lucky I'm not working. You're not working either?"

Lara gives a slight shrug. She is never sure of the reaction she may get when she admits to being an artist. It's usually blank incomprehension followed by a fatuous statement about how lovely that must be.

"I'm a painter – artist if you like – I have been using the front room in our flat as a studio – that way I can work when it suits me – and it fits in with Adam's needs. I will be moving into a new studio very soon – over by Victoria Park."

"I see you've got big pictures going in and out of your flat." Hilda grins. "Where my daughter Shelley cleans, at the office, there's pictures on the walls. Shelley says they're like patterns and not of anything – she don't understand them. What kind of pictures do you do?"

"Oh, animals – wild animals from Africa – or anywhere." Lara answers, dismissing herself, the vague, the modest artist, with a hand wave.

In her studio at the moment the paint is dry on the palettes and her brushes untouched. She has a commission to complete and if it isn't done she will be short of cash again.

"Sounds nice." Hilda approved, "Any time you want, dear – come in for a cup of tea. Don't be lonely!"

She pats Lara's arm. Lara shrinks inside. Is she being patronised? What has Hilda noticed about Lara?

They arrive on the second floor corridor outside Hilda's door at the other end of the building from Lara and Tim's flat.

"Do you want to play with Lester now, Adam?"

Hilda looks at Adam then at Lara. Lara nods and drops a kiss on the top of Adam's untidy hair.

"Till supper-time, Adam." she says.

The boys whoop and clatter their way indoors at No. 15. They dump rucksacks in the corridor under Tracey's feet with the deliberate intention of tripping her up and making her squeal. Hilda shakes her head at them and waves Lara away with a smile.

"Boys!" she says.

Lara walks back to the front door of her own flat and goes indoors to solitude. She takes off her coat, turns her back on her makeshift studio in the sitting-room and enters the kitchen to put on the kettle. The breakfast dishes are still waiting to be done. Hilda and her daughter would not have left their washing up chores till the evening. Lara imagines their expressions if they could see her loaded sink. Hilda's daughter can't be more than thirty if Hilda is, as she looks, not yet fifty. Lara feels old at almost forty to have a son of Adam's age. Her life is sliding away. She is only a jobbing artist painting in order to sell. Her art will never amount to much. All those years of wasted career opportunities while she worked for Oscar at the Tin Heart Gold Mine. When Tim talked of returning to Africa, those years that she had blocked from her memory came storming back into her dreams at night and woke her up in strangled, screaming fear.

Lara can't recall Oscar's face. Her brain has bleached him out. The flashbulbs of her memory shatter and strobe the images of him. She dares not remember how he looked, but when she shuts her eyes he is present in her flesh. She feels his heat, his weight and his size. She feels his voice vibrate against her body. It is as if she was still lying with her face resting on his chest, her lips pressing his skin. The raucous shrill of insects around them and the fierce blaze of an African sun overhead. Now she is fading into a sullen fog. Back then she had been alive. Every nerve of her body sharp and taut as the whine of mosquitoes, as the harsh screech of mine machinery or the zing of high-velocity bullets.

When a gun is fired the thud of the bullet into a body is heard before the shivered sound of its flight from the barrel of the gun. That was Oscar. Death-dealing. Impact before emotion. Fatal.

Chapter Four

Art and Family

Has Lara fitted her family around her art? Or has she fitted her art around her family? Lara doesn't really know. She knows how much stubbornness it takes to simply keep on trying to make art. She has kept on painting and drawing in the living room from 10 till 3 each weekday for years, observing strict hours like someone with a normal job. Tim often works late into the evening, sometimes at the office, sometimes at home. When Tim is busy Adam arranges his Transformers figures into an audience for his stories while Lara prepares their supper. Then she rushes around doing the most necessary or obvious of the household chores.

One evening Tim and Lara are listening politely while Adam relays to Tim the plans that Lara is making for the months that Tim will be in Africa. Lara has, of course, already told Tim about them.

"Mum's going to ask Gillian if she can also have a studio with the other artists at Victoria Park. She says it is time that we had a proper sitting room for our family instead of a stinky artist's studio."

Adam makes puppy-dog sniffing noises at the mere notion of turpentine.

Tim agrees.

"It will be nice won't it, Adam?"

"Mum says that is dangerous to be a journalist nowadays."

Adam switches wildly from subject to subject.

"Why did she say that?" Tim gives Lara an annoyed glance.

"Oh ages ago, Dad. Before you decided to go away. She says you didn't use a computer when you were in Africa first – you used phones – then you got a fax machine, then a computer with a GPS and now you use email. She also says that when you first started being a reporter – reporters only got killed by accident – like – if they got between different armies. Now she says that people are always trying to kill journalists because they don't want anyone to know the truth."

Tim is somewhat mollified but he frowns.

"That's partly true, Adam – but not where I'm going. Don't worry about me."

"Mum worries. I know. She said you are a truth collector – no – a truth gatherer – it's your nature – you don't like editing so much because sometimes," Adam puts his head on one side and squeezes his eyes shut as he grapples with the concept Lara has attempted to explain to him, "you have to change things a little bit because of the people who own the newspaper."

Lara listens to Adam's version of her conversations about Tim with her eyebrows raised but her eyes fixed on her food. Once she would have given Tim a complicit smile but now she daren't.

"And so what does Lara say about her own work, Adam?" Tim, ever the impartial, questioning journalist, includes Lara with a swift glance.

"Mum says that she invents – no, remakes the truth." Adam shuts an eye and squints down his knife's imagined cross-hairs at a potato on his plate. She paints the truth so that people can see it again – like for the first time. She says otherwise they forget what they really know."

"Wow, Adam!" Lara smiles. "You make what I do sound as useful as Tim's job."

Tim also smiles. They relax again.

"Your mum – Lara – is a special person, Adam – d'you know she's a champion driver when things get dangerous?"

"I've been driving in the bush since I was at school." Lara says. "We had a Land Rover – it was tough, slow and dusty."

Adam considers Lara briefly. Tim and Lara share an old battered car which they keep parked in a back street nearby. Adam doesn't often see his parents drive unless they are going outside London. Traffic features in his life rather than cars.

"I know Mum misses the wild animals and the bush – don't you, Mum?"

"I think it's safer to walk down a track in the veld near a herd of elephants than through traffic in London," agrees Lara.

"Can we visit Chambeshi sometime Mum – Dad? Inonge's invited us to stay with her at the Tin Heart Camp Safari Lodge. Can we, Dad?"

"Perhaps – well we should – yes."

Tim steers the conversation away from Chambeshi.

"What kind of job do you want to have when you grow up, Adam?"

"Dunno Dad. I like history at school – I want to explain things – like how we got here – like how things work in the world like with people – society and – um – in like political stuff."

Adam bats the potato with his knife and it bounces onto the table.

"Sounds interesting" Tim smiles and returns the potato to Adam's plate.

"Finish your food, Adam. Then we'll get out your school atlas out and look at where I am going again."

Chapter Five

Brendan 1997

"Tell me about yourself."

It's Lara's second session with Brendan, the therapist recommended by her old friend Liseli.

"Start wherever you like." he suggests, "Say what comes most easily and naturally – perhaps you would like to tell me about how you grew up in Africa – what first made you want to be a painter – an artist?"

Lara, with dry humour, will later tell Liseli that her first session was a complete 'washout'. She had been certain that she would be in control and her common sense and personal insight would shine out. She would be once again the charming Lara, socially confident, and a successful artist. She would give away the secrets she chose and no others. To her horror as soon as she is ensconced in Brendan's embracing sofa, looking at the cup of tea in front of her on which a wavering feather of steam is lightly balanced, she cries and cries. Not loudly but wetly. A waterfall of tears runs down her cheeks. All she does is collect balls of soggy tissues in her lap while Brendan waits quietly. At the end of that first session, Brendan says simply, "I will see you again. When would you like to come?"

It feels odd to Lara to confide in a strange man, even one who acts in a professional role. Besides, Brendan, perhaps a few years younger than Lara, is slightly built, even skinny. He slumps rather than sits in his armchair. Lara is aware of the boniness of his hips and that his physical presence is minimal.

Nevertheless here she is again, sitting on the cosy sofa with the tea in front of her. Lara avoids giving an account of the really difficult problems of her life by recounting stories of her adolescence. She is chatting, trying to enchant Brendan with her wit, to make him laugh. Lara is used to making her friends laugh but now she is acting a part. She feels shallow and deceitful.

Lara had smiled when her parents or her friends were complimentary about her talent for drawing. It was after all a gift, not something she had earned. She had understood that, even before she had learnt how much hard work it would take for her gift to amount to much. It's always seemed to her that her particular ability is too uncomplicated to be worthy of praise. Her gift is an artist's eye co-ordinated with an artist's hand. Lara can draw. Lara has always been able to make paintings which are so realistic that people who say they 'don't understand art' can still admire them.

This is Lara, named by her romantic mother after the heroine in Boris Pasternak's novel, 'Doctor Zhivago'. This is Lara, born and brought up to be the sunshiny girl who wins people's hearts as easily as she delights them with her art.

Ah – but that was Lara once.

This Lara is no longer the golden girl. That Lara has gone.

That Lara would give her heart to any man who possessed some form of gold, an element valued in its purest form for both malleability and durability.

The "gold" that belongs to Lara today remains as stone cold as the vault in which it hides.

Lara's session with Brendan made her nostalgic for her untroubled childhood.

So much luck and happiness, no wonder I'm self-centred – yes and selfish too. Mum and Dad did their best I suppose to stop me being a total prima donna. Let's face it – I wasn't that talented at ballet or gymkhanas. Just as well I suppose, not to be good at everything else. Mum always said I had a stubborn streak. Dad quite liked that in me but it irritated the hell out of Mum. She said I always wanted explanations and reasons before doing what I was told. I daydreamed a lot – it's an only child thing I suppose – or playacted – made Mum and Dad my audience.

Lara's charmed youth first glowed in the African Republic of Chambeshi in one of those small enclosed expatriate communities that appear to provide everything essential for its mostly white members to have a full and perfect life.

Lara's father, Brian Kingston, had been recruited by an international mining company in the early 70s and arrived in central Africa when Lara was almost 10 years old. They stayed longer than most of their fellow expatriates because Lara's mother, Jane, had grown up in southern Africa and felt at home there and Brian liked to go camping and fishing. To compensate Lara for being educated away from home they chose an expensive boarding school in England paid for by Brian's company. It had surprisingly ramshackle old classrooms in unfenced fields near the sea and was famous for being very progressive and libertarian as well as having an excellent art department. So Lara went to high school at Summerdales and so did her best friend from her junior school days, Liseli Ngoma Dawkins.

Part Two

Beginnings 1970 – 1980

Chapter One

Liseli and Lara

"Harry's got no sense of humour.' said Brian of Liseli's Welsh father, a left-wing academic and historian at the Chambeshi University. "But his wife is an exile and one of her brothers is in prison; the other's fighting in the bush war. Life's not secure for them."

Lara's parents, Brian and Jane, never discussed politics at home. Neither did they think the bush war amusing. It worried them both. Liseli's mother, Safina, a black Zimbabwean, made Lara's mother, Jane, uncomfortable. She felt Safina had a chip on her shoulder. In spite of their parents' opinions, Lara and Liseli had been close friends since they first went to the Chambeshi International Primary School.

Politics and the liberation wars weren't mentioned at the Chambeshi International School even though many of the parents worked with refugees or with aid agencies, or in diplomatic services and medical organisations. Whatever trouble was brewing up in Chambeshi, these children would spend their lives in large gardens behind high security fences. The photos of Lara's classmates in her yearbook included the children of freedom fighters and of American, Russian, British and Yugoslav diplomats. There were also the children of Cypriot and Asian shopkeepers from the city, English expatriate children like herself and a number of well-to-do black kids, mostly boys. They all were intelligent, seemed well-adjusted and friendly with each other even while their families' interests and commitments in Chambeshi were both varied and on occasion at variance with each other.

Then there was Chimunya Mbewe.

Chimunya wore ill-fitting unsuitable shoes with broken high heels and her cheap market-made crimplene dress was fastened at the back with a safety pin instead of a zip. She never did any homework and always lost her school books. Somebody must have paid her expensive school fees but her home life apparently did not allow her to sit at a table and study. As she did not have a television she had no idea what serials and dramas her classmates watched. The American girls would not sit next to her because she smelt of sweat and dust after walking miles to school in the summer heat. It didn't occur to Lara that one of her fellow pupils might be poor or find life troubling but Liseli went out of her way to include Chimunya and spoke to her every day. Chimunya didn't respond to Liseli's overtures with much enthusiasm. Proud and shy, she continued to keep to herself.

Lara and Liseli were at the vegetable market with Safina, Liseli's mother, when Lara saw Chimunya sitting next to a tailor's dress stall. She waved and called but Chimunya gave her startled look, made a quick crouching movement and vanished from sight below the counter top.

"What was that about?" Lara said peeved.

Liseli looked thoughtful.

"Chimunya lives here," she said, "in the shanty town behind the market. She doesn't want anyone to see her. She's embarrassed."

Lara frowned mystified. "How come?"

Liseli shrugged but Safina explained,

"Her parents are rich. They are diplomats who work in England but Chimunya has to live with her mother's sister who has no money or education. Chimunya's schooling is paid for but I reckon her aunt takes all the money that is sent for her clothes and books. Chimunya's brothers go to school in England of course. Girls don't count as much as boys in Chambeshi." Liseli grinned. "Not a problem that would bother you, Lara."

Lara was silent for a while but, as Liseli said, she didn't let Chimunya's situation trouble her for long.

Liseli was an excellent student who was admired and tolerated in spite of her rather acid comments about her peers and her teachers. She also had to find a boarding school in England and the two girls decided their parents must agree to send them to the same one. The boarding school question came up on one of the few occasions when both families met at a parents' evening. Liseli and Lara hung around listening in the hope of influencing their choices. Fortunately Liseli's parents thought Brian and Jane's choice of Summerdales for Lara was one that would suit Liseli too. Not only was it progressive but it had a positive policy towards students of different ethnicities. Liseli, was, in fact, awarded a Summerdales scholarship though Lara did not find out about until their last year there when the Principal mentioned it in his valediction to the graduating students.

She was annoyed. "Liseli – you bitch! Why didn't you tell me?".

But Lara was not angry with Liseli for long. Liseli could be quite strange and contrary on occasions, but she was Lara's most loyal and dearest friend.

Chapter Two

Boarding School

Roger, Lara's art teacher at Summerdales, was proud of her. Lara knew that. At sixteen she guessed that she attracted him sexually. She daydreamed about accidentally meeting up with him in her first year at art school and letting him seduce her. He hadn't been a highly motivated artist himself, but he was kind. Later Lara wondered if he had let her down by insufficiently preparing her for hard work and disappointment and by not informing her of the latest trends in the art world. Nobody wanted to make life hard for Lara.

It changed.

Liseli wasn't going to art school. She was going to do something useful with her life. She would study something that would make the world, or at least the country of her mother's birth, Zimbabwe, a better place.

"Economics." Liseli said to Lara, "Though my father thinks I should study law." She grimaced. "He says I can be awkward and pedantic'"

It was Lara's last few weeks in the last term of the last year at Summerdales. Lately Liseli had been a drag. She seemed always in a bad mood. Lara had finished swotting for exams and only had an art practical to complete. She had been warned by a friend that Liseli was being 'morbid'. At a loose end, partly out of concern, partly from boredom, she wandered down the dormitory corridor to Liseli's study-bedroom hoping for a chat. Liseli was still wearing the faded purple T-shirt that she slept in, even though it was mid-afternoon. It was that dead time during the weekend after exams. Liseli sat with her legs folded up under her on her desk chair scribbling at her school rough-work book. Page after page was covered with swirling patterns in black ballpoint. Lara hesitated; from the study bedroom doorway she could see that Liseli was concentrated on obliterating every white gap in the paper and hadn't noticed her arrival. Undecided as to whether to go or stay, Lara's attention was caught by a familiar children's comic book open on Liseli's pillow.

"I love Tintin!"

Lara flopped on Liseli's unmade bed and grabbed at the book. She and Liseli had long been fans of the red-haired boy reporter. Liseli looked round at Lara. For a moment she was sharp-eyed, her face alive, then she went back to her robotic drawing. Lara said with disgust, 'It's in French!'

"Hergé is Belgian," Liseli said with flat sarcasm.

"Sure he is. I'm not sure my French is good enough…"

Already Lara was engrossed in the story. Liseli was definitely in 'one of her moods'. It was easier to concentrate on the book instead of cheering her up.

"God! When was this written?"

Lara flicked the cover from inside to outside looking for clues.

"It's so ugly! Everyone is so horrible! The Africans are drawn in such a gross way. Tintin is an idiot who kills every living animal! It's…" Lara searched for the right words. "It's racist!"

"Hmm." Liseli barely shrugged. "It's so unfair to the whites – they are all villains except Tintin – but the Africans are all silly jokes."

Lara glanced at Liseli. It occurred to her that it might be an odd book for a mixed race girl like Liseli to own. Lara didn't think of Liseli as mixed race or as anything really because the school had pupils from so many cultures and countries that no one person stood out. They all were different.

"The dog's okay – Milou – Snowy – he doesn't approve of the slaughter of wild animals." Liseli contributed without turning. "Self-interest, of course."

Lara wasn't sure if Liseli was serious or ironic. "Who gave it to you? I mean – where did you get it?"

"Oh I bought it on our last French trip." Liseli replied. "It's not published in England – obviously for being racist, but I wanted to see it for myself. I read that Hergé had been a Nazi collaborator in the Second World War so I had to find out about him and his books for myself. His American books all had to be redrawn because of their racial stereotypes."

Lara was mystified. "Racial stereotypes? Hergé a Nazi collaborator?" That was a new concept for Lara. She decided on a smart and cynical answer. "I bet nearly everybody collaborated once they were conquered?"

"Don't forget about the Resistance Movements," Liseli said.

"Oh yeah?" muttered Lara.

She turned the pages again reading and thinking. Why did it matter to Liseli that a comic book published in 1946 was racist and written by a collaborator? That was all over now, wasn't it? Lara was, she admitted to herself, uncomfortable in her history class when they studied colonial history or the Slave Trade but then if she looked around her class at her friends who came from all over the world – she could say with confidence, couldn't she? – that it was all history and it was all different and okay now.

"Why does it bother you so much?" she asked slowly; for the first time she was really curious about Liseli. She turned to look at her friend.

"It doesn't bother me." Liseli said with infuriating and contradictory calm. "But Tintin is just not my hero anymore and Hergé is only another person like anybody else. It's just what happens."

"Well – there's the gold and diamond smuggling too." Liseli said a moment later but still enigmatic and terse.

"What do you mean, exactly?" said Lara, irritated.

"It is exactly the same now, you know." Liseli explained. "The United States, Russia, the West are all after Africa's mineral wealth. Any which way they can!"

Lara scowled with frustration as she walked out of Liseli's room.

Liseli's moods made her distant and uncommunicative. Had they got worse recently? Maybe it was just exam nerves. Who knows?

Chapter Three

Brendan 1997

It was Liseli who had recommended Brendan Cowan.

"He's a good psychotherapist, Lara. I know him by reputation. Just what you need my girl." Liseli pretended to sniff. "You're depressed. You haven't faced up to your past yet. You have been hiding in a conventional marriage instead of admitting what a wild life you have had – wicked woman that you are!"

Lara is at her third session with Brendan. Liseli is on her mind. Liseli is back in a private psychiatric hospital again as a voluntary patient.

"What goes on here is confidential" Brendan says. "Your friend Liseli wasn't my client. She saw a colleague for several years I believe. You are free to talk about anything you like."

"Oh good!" Lara nods without smiling.

She doesn't intend to be a client of Brendan's for very long. She will talk about Liseli though. Liseli has been such an important part of Lara's life that she often thinks of her. Especially right now. She's been thinking obsessively about the Hergé comic book 'Tintin au Congo' that Liseli gave her some time ago. Its uncomfortable coincidental plot is about a journalist hero and the trade in smuggled diamonds.

"Liseli is smarter than me. I was – am – naïve and unquestioning. I took my privileged life for granted. I think Liseli always gave me more than I gave her – I don't know why she put up with me."

Brendan's eyebrow twitches slightly.

Lara thinks – dammit – I'm beating myself up again, aren't I? She is learning that Brendan doesn't comment very often, instead he uses his eyebrows to signal coded questions at her. Hoping she has it right, Lara switches from masochism to talking about her school and about art again.

"I liked boarding school. I liked my classes. I only did what I really liked – arts and humanities – I did nothing I found difficult. I was good at art and I loved it. I tried every different medium – painting, drawing, printmaking, and ceramics. I knew I wanted to go to Art School and my art teacher suggested a School of Art in London would be the best. That's how I ended up at the Middlesex.

"I am nothing like Liseli." Lara says to Brendan, "I couldn't cope with the other students' hostility at Art School."

"You think Liseli did?" Brendan questions.

Lara grimaces. It she was honest it had probably been worse for Liseli but Liseli had understood what was happening to her and why. She had a better analytical brain than Lara. "I understand better now. Then I felt angry and hurt but it made me want to win – to show the other students I could beat them.-"

Chapter Four

Art School 1978

The thought of Art School had been very thrilling. As she said, Lara hoped to make many new friends. She also expected to do well. She imagined an institution as supportive, as forward-looking and as open-minded as Summerdales.

Art school turned out to not be like that at all.

Lara arrived friendly and eager and immediately hit a barrier. A force field that was invisible to her but she was trapped by it and could make no friends with anyone outside it. It was very puzzling. Her tutors were fine with her. Not particularly interested in her but then they appeared to keep all the students at arm's length and not to be very good at time-keeping either. They turned up late for classes and lectures and didn't seem to care if their students also wandered in half way through. It was the students in Lara's year who were odd and unfriendly. She caught the other students repeating her own words and phrases to each other as if her accent was artificial or affected. It was worse when she responded to their questions about her last school or her home. Her fellow students would cut her answers short.

"Oh yeah!" they said and turned their backs – the implication was that it was 'that sort of school'. 'Posh' was said and 'privileged.' Lara couldn't argue. Any attempt to explain how very special her school had been in its ethos and aims would have only made it worse. Lara didn't have a clue about her fellow students' lives either. They had been to comprehensive schools in towns. I easily make friends Lara thought but they've judged me by my clothes which cost too much and my accent which isn't definable. She was furious with art school, angry with the other students and with Jane, her mother for insisting that she wore a dress when she arrived at the university residence. Lara learnt fast but it took a year to break through the glass bubble of prejudice that surrounded her.

I really hated art school at first. The things I did well didn't seem to count at all. When I saw what was supposed to be 'good' art I didn't like it. I was truly shocked to find art could be plastic rubbish just in a pattern. I hated Gilbert and George – their stuff was bizarre, glossy, self-obsessed, and smug. I could draw, I understood colour, my art was recognisable but what was I supposed to do with it and myself?

Lara's first-year tutor wore a second hand tweed jacket and didn't shave until the evening and sometimes not even then. He seemed to be tired all the time – especially exhausted by his students and their inability as a group to ever spend time together for long enough for him to explain their projects or discuss their work critically. All the other students already had formed opinions while Lara couldn't think of one thing to say that would interest any of them. Steve, a sculpture student, admired the Shona sculptors of Zimbabwe and tried to emulate them. It was odd that his admiration gave him ownership in a way Lara refused to claim though she was familiar with the sculpture he raved about. Liseli's parents had work by Thomas Mukarogobwa, Joseph Ndandarika, and an artist known only as Henry; all were well-known Zimbabwean sculptors working mostly in the greenish Serpentine stone of the region. Liseli and Lara had made a ritual of stroking the smooth surfaces of their works whenever they passed by them.

Other students were into distorting photography and adaptations of graffiti.

I had the feeling that everyone thought I was – um – an intruder who was too privileged to make art –I wasn't "authentic" or something – maybe

I didn't swear enough. I eventually worked it out. It was trendy to be tough and streetwise but we all felt the same really. We're all sensitive and easily discouraged by criticism and failure. We're all afraid of having nothing to say. In the end I picked their brains about artists and exhibitions. They liked that and we got on better.

When she and Liseli were home together for their first English summer vacation in the winter of Chambeshi, Lara started to tell Liseli about her encounters with the class system. There was something in the brightness of Liseli's eye, the way her attention sharpened and a certain irony in her expression that made Lara stop.

"Shit" she said in her newly-acquired art school fashion, "It's always been like that for you hasn't it?"

Liseli made a face, then laughed and explained.

"They really can't suss me out at all. Most of the students at my University aren't working class but none of them have a clue about Africa. I told them that I did live in a grass hut – but it had gold taps in the bathroom – they believe anything you say if you are so different they can't judge you. One week I changed my accent every day – all phony and hamming it up. I did Indian, French, Jamaican and American Deep South. They related most to that – but then I switched to an Afrikaans accent and finally I did the African shanty town pidgin. Some of my class never really forgave me but I do have a few very good friends now. I am surprised it has been hard for you though – I thought it would be okay for a white student anywhere."

"It's art school." replied Lara, "It's trendy to be working class and it seems public school kids don't do art – I think their parents make them go into banking. I am the odd one out. They think Summerdales was a public school like Eton so I must be upper class – it's not even money that bothers them as much as what they see as a superior advantage. I had no idea it mattered so much. I thought that class didn't matter in modern Britain."

"That's a history teacher fallacy." said Liseli, wise after a first year in sociology and economics. "It's changed, but not gone away. The real problem is difference. People are afraid of it unless it appears exotic and then they go all smarmy over it."

"Wow – should I pretend to be exotic?" Lara had a moment's jealous pang. Liseli was exotic, and beautiful and intelligent – but sad somehow. She linked her arm in Liseli's and the two of them wandered into the garden to sit by the swimming pool where they spent the rest of the afternoon laughing and planning scenarios to shock their fellow students.

Lara realised that she wasn't in a position to apply any of Liseli's tactics and she certainly wasn't capable of hamming it up. Instead she concentrated on drawing and developing ways of illustrating her subversive thoughts. Her drawings gained the attention of Nancy, a senior painting tutor who was famous for her quiet reflective abstracts and minimal line drawings. Nancy was gently encouraging and wise in a way that Lara was reminded of years later in her therapy sessions with Brendan. Nancy praised Lara's sensitive line and ability to create drawings that seemed to breathe with movement and life. Lara felt Nancy liked her as well as her work and that was balm to Lara's hurt soul.

"Less is more." Nancy had said. "Your viewers need to do some work themselves and not be battered into submission by a bossy artist telling them what to think."

Lara borrowed Liseli's ideas to demonstrate to the other students that she was a radical artist. Remembering Liseli's book 'Tintin au Congo' she made a series of comic book style drawings. Using all her skills with line and texture Lara made lively sketches of African wildlife in the foreground of each scene. Against the flat bright landscape behind each animal, lines of men and women yoked together, marched on their dreadful journey into slavery or fell and died along the way.

Next Lara took Goya's "Disasters of War" and made drawings as gruesome as his about the liberation wars in Africa. Lara's detailed images portrayed well-armed white soldiers and helicopters as they fought and hunted African freedom fighters. They were based on Liseli's stories about the experiences of her relatives. Lara had done it to gain credibility with her fellow students – it worked – but it was manipulative of her and she felt she was a disingenuous fake. The tutors, however, commented on them and the students, naturally attracted by gore and horror, spent time looking at them and even began to ask Lara what she was trying to do. She gained some respect for being trendy and politically correct. She was neither but it did make her think.

Chapter Five

Brendan 1997

The memory of these drawings gives Lara a shudder. Looking back, they seemed to have presaged later events in her life. Too bad. She still isn't ready to talk about any of that to Brendan.

"Am I being boring, Brendan? I mean art isn't everybody's thing is it?"

Brendan smiles and dips his head slightly. He has a charity shop landscape on his wall and a faux bronze Buddha on his bookcase. Lara avoids looking at them because she is afraid that she might not trust a therapist with poor artistic judgement. It's ridiculous but right now she finds it hard to concentrate and be sensible.

"I'm no judge of what is good or bad art Lara but you're talking about your identity as an artist and a person aren't you? Art school was quite a while ago – is that still such an important issue for you?

"It was a long time ago but making art is difficult now." Lara admits. "I don't understand why I can't paint anymore. Why do I feel now that the art I try to make hasn't any meaning? I don't want to carry on making crap art that sells easily to people who just buy stuff that they think is trendy or pretty. I have wanted to change what I do anyway but now that Tim's gone I don't know if I have any ability or talent at all. I don't even know who I am – I don't know what artists are supposed to be like – I mean – if you aren't famous or your work isn't noticed or reviewed why do you keep on doing it? Artists are supposed to be different."

Brendan's eyes flicker as he does his best to follow Lara's reasoning.

"I've fallen into the trap of making art that is conventional. I thought if I made art to sell half the time – then I would be free to make my own kind of art in my own way the rest of the time. All that has happened is that I have completely blocked any creative ideas. I'm a phony with nothing to offer."

Lara sighs and continues. If she carries on talking about art she needn't tell Brendan about Oscar.

"A couple of years after Adam was born, I met an old art school friend, Gillian, at the Serpentine Gallery in Hyde Park. We both live in East London, Gillian in Stratford East and me in Mile End so we see a lot of each other. Just before Tim left for Uganda, Gillian persuaded me to rent a studio in the Art Factory. The move has made me more insecure. Gillian doesn't make art that's decorative. It's not emollient. It doesn't reassure. Gillian doesn't celebrate nature or beauty. It's the exact opposite of what I've been doing to make a living."

Chapter Six

Art School 1979

Lara's fellow students no longer presented such a unified front. She began to see them as individuals. They had never really been a cohesive group and soon split into a variety of cliques and alliances. One of Lara's closest friends, Gillian, was a shy Scottish girl who became a militant feminist by the time she graduated. Gillian told Lara that there were no famous women artists because the art establishment was male-dominated. Lara, used to being among the most talented in her class, didn't feel threatened. It wasn't until her final year when most of the few men who did graduate got higher grades than the majority of women that Lara began to think Gillian might have a point.

A solitary Sikh, Ajay Singh, was her other close friend. Ajay eventually gave up art for film and music. He became a drummer in an Asian Fusion rock band in London which led to him being much admired by all the young people on his home street and much gossiped about by their parents. Gillian, Ajay and Lara occasionally worked together on outrageous and irreligious conceptual art projects with a rag-bag of ideas purloined from American artists. They disguised and photographed themselves to make statements about gender and race like Cindy Sherman, made elaborate sexually provocative installations in a parody of Judy Chicago, employed type to make enigmatic posters as they thought Jenny Holzer did, and copied the Guerrilla Girls by going to exhibitions wearing masks and carrying banners. None of it really came from Lara's heart.

"My involvement was with the materials, with colour, line, and texture – not with politics at all."

After she graduated, it became clear that a fine art degree did not lead directly onto paid employment unless you had chosen to be a teacher. Lara persuaded her parents that she needed a break from England. She had missed her home life with them and been very homesick for Africa so she thought finding temporary work in Chambeshi for a few months would provide a solution. Gillian was going to do a teaching diploma and Ajay was to work in his father's clothes factory. Neither lasted the year out. Ajay had acquired a punk Mohican hairstyle and safety pins in his ears and ended up sharing a squat with some other would-be musicians. Gillian was living with Poppy in an openly gay relationship. She identified herself as a queer butch dyke, shaved her head, and wore a man's suit and waistcoat, while Poppy dressed in full-skirted flowery garments and very bright lipstick.

A couple of the other students said they would work part-time to start with, then go on benefits and see if they could make a living from their art. They, at least, were not going to sell out and get jobs just yet. Lara looked at her art school contemporaries when they finally all graduated with a mixture of despair and amusement. By comparison she knew she appeared wholesome and conventional. She knew that she didn't belong among them. She didn't fit in. Was it because of her childhood in Africa?

Chapter Seven

Brendan 1997

"I didn't feel as if I was really English – and I didn't want to be in England. Even Mum and Dad didn't want to stay there for long – just for the shops!" Lara pulls a face at the memory. When her parents were on home leave in London they all rushed around together shopping, going to the theatre or using one of the capital city's airports to fly away somewhere else on holiday. Lara recognised each department store by the quality of its lighting and the expensive odours of its perfume counters but none of the rented flats they stayed in had any whiff of an aroma that might suggest that it was home.

"I did like the glamour of living in Africa and having money to spend – my parents' money of course – but I felt shallow compared to Gillian and Ajay."

"I really did think that I'd just paint and draw and make a living that way – I suppose I hadn't had to think about money before – I wasn't as naïve as that sounds – it suited me to pretend I was. Just selfish of me I suppose."

Lara smiles as she explains her youthful self to Brendan,

"It didn't take long till I realised that my parents didn't really want me at home any more – well Mum wanted to make sure I behaved – that I was a 'good' girl – but she couldn't stand the strain of having a grown-up daughter around. She was worried that I would get a boyfriend or boyfriends and sleep with them all

– I might disgrace them – and well – they drove me mad too – but I think I became disgusted with myself for not being independent and not being able to hack it straight away as an artist – oh God! I was so young!"

Brendan grins.

"You're still young, aren't you?"

"Am I? Yes, maybe, and definitely still stupid!"

Lara makes a wry face, annoyed with Brendan who is, after all, a little younger than she is. She berates herself, "I can't bear the effort of selling my art any more – I don't want to make art anymore – I don't believe in myself any more – I don't know what art is for anymore!" and the easy tears run down her face again.

"You've been a successful artist, Lara." Brendan says then he asks. "What's different now? What happened to make Tim go away now? What changed for you both that has left you feeling so devastated?"

Part Three
The Safari Camp 1981

Chapter One

Chambeshi

As soon as she stepped off the plane onto the scruffy unkempt apron at Chambeshi Airport, the smell of home, like the smell of oil paint, assaulted her nostrils with viridian energy, ochre drought, indigo rain and cadmium sunshine and Lara breathed with a deep happiness.

"After art school though, Chambeshi felt less like home, too. Friends I used to know had left and there didn't seem any place that I fitted in. I was still living at home and using Dad's garage as a studio. I felt a bit like an overgrown pet dog."

The community which Lara knew best was the expatriate community in Chambeshi, but that also kept altering as people left or their children were sent off to school. Chambeshi was a vast landlocked country in Central Africa of which 70 percent was a non-agrarian wilderness. Its population was not large but, in the 25 years since Chambeshi had achieved independence, many people had shifted into densely populated shanty towns around the scruffy, urban work-in-progress known as Chambeshi City. Its government infrastructure, businesses and the farming and mining industries still depended on the skills and knowledge of a small expatriate community and the aid money attached to their services. Naturally Lara's parents had good social connections with all the wheelers and dealers who make up such societies and they knew a couple, Bill and Maria, who had recently acquired a government concession to open a safari lodge in the famous Chambeshi National Park. In fact, Brian and Jane, both passionate about the bush, had taken Lara on camping holidays together with Bill and Maria every winter for as long as she could remember. Bill and Maria's new lodge would operate only in the dry cold winter season, when it was possible to get equipment and vehicles across the rivers and into an area that would be a vast flood plain in the hot summer months of the rainy season. They could only offer seasonal work but it would be demanding. They needed to employ young people who were hardy enough to stand the heat and discomfort of the camp but who were sophisticated enough to cope with clients who had high expectations of comfort and service. Their employees would get some training but most learning would be on the job. By the end of the season they would be expected to take the clients out on game-viewing trips, to manage a four-wheel drive Land Cruiser in rough conditions, to know one end of a gun from another and to be able to use it in an emergency. They would have to recognise, identify and name birds, insects, plants and the smaller mammals. These kinds of skills could not all be picked up in one season, so Bill and Maria hoped that their employees would find some other work during the rains and be prepared to come back every year. Young people who already visited the National Park and had some previous knowledge from earlier visits and a real interest in wild life conservation would be more likely to fit in; otherwise it could be young people who had worked in other game reserves in other parts of Africa. Lara heard about the new camp during her last term at art school. She felt it was exactly what she wanted after three years in the grey of London winters. She had begged her parents to put her name up for one of the jobs even before she left London.

"I will even cook, Mum!" she said, "I've been cooking for myself for the last three years in my digs."

Jane laughed, but she did admit that Lara had made a reasonable camp cook on the family's frequent fishing trips. On one notable occasion, she had even made bread in a rough clay oven.

"I'll work for my keep, Mum," Lara said.

"That's pretty much all you can expect," Brian said drily.

Lara got her job. Soon after she returned to Chambeshi, Maria collected her from her home in the city and they set off in a Land Cruiser packed with supplies on the long day's journey into the river valley. Maria was a dusty-brown woman with blue eyes that, by contrast with her skin, seemed extraordinarily clear. Both she and Bill carried an aura of silence and spoke with the slow quietness that comes from years of solitary observation of wild creatures in remote places. Life in the bush had made them intensely practical. They accepted that nothing ever works out exactly as planned and the fine white creases around their eyes and mouths showed that they could laugh about it.

The job wasn't quite what Lara hoped. She was to look after the stores, see that orders were placed and fulfilled and help Maria plan the menus.

"You'll look after the herb garden. We'll need fresh salads too. Know something about gardening?" Maria asked.

"Mum's taught me quite a lot," Lara lied. She had watched her mother giving instructions to the two African men who kept their suburban plot trim and tidy.

Lara had imagined herself out on game trips impressing the clients with her fantastic knowledge of wild life. Instead it seemed she was to be working at the camp helping Maria with the catering and laundry side of the business. Lara tried to hide her disappointed expression but Maria grinned.

"Don't worry; you get breaks outside the camp too. Guest comfort is our top priority. The chaps who do the game trips just don't want to do this and they're no good at it anyway. This is seriously an important job. Clients spend more time in bed or in the bar than in the bush. Wait and see."

Lara hadn't seen looking after people as a job. She felt sidelined and was surprised at the feeling of fury that began to burn inside her. Why was she different from the boys? Did this prove that the grumblings of feminism that she had ignored from Gillian were relevant to her also? What choices did she have? She had been through art school imagining that she could immediately make a living as an artist, found that not to be true, opted for a job that seemed both dangerously glamorous and uniquely demanding and here she was being asked to work as a junior housekeeper. Lara was used to winning – to having things work out well for her. She had won the grudging respect of her fellow students and achieved a good enough degree at art school. She had thought that if she bided her time now she could probably get to be a safari leader too.

Maria watched her with a grin.

"Yah, you tell me. It looks like us dames get the indoor jobs and the blokes get the real work but just wait till you meet some of the clients. You'll be happy not to spend four hours in a jeep with some of them and then have to sit with them at meals and afterwards in the bar. Give it a go, girl!"

"Oh I want to!" Lara insisted and she vowed to herself that she would be the best at everything she tried to do and then still be able do what she wanted to most of all.

In fact Bill did most of the game trips in that first year. The camp was new, not yet well-known and Bill and Maria were hands-on until their new employees could prove their worth and become acclimatised. The team included two young men, Jason, a South African, who had a biology degree and had worked on game camps in Botswana and Zimbabwe, and Trevor, who had grown up on a farm in Somerset and had come straight from high school. They were enthusiastic young men, tough and physically adept. They needed to be all of that when driving out in the wild on rough tracks in vehicles that were not new and had been pushed to their limits on many previous occasions.

Lara, Jason and Trevor looked each other over on their first meeting secretly assessing each other as possible sexual partners. Physically they were all fit and Jason passed the test of desirability as far as Lara was concerned. Instinct also meant that they looked for each others' qualities and personality traits. Were they reliable, generous, intelligent, adaptable or selfish, insensitive and domineering? To discover these traits would take time. As yet Lara didn't have much understanding of her own propensities and limitations but after her art school experiences she had a better insight into her own desires.

Chapter Two

Housekeeping in the Bush

"You have to know what needs doing and – how to do it." Maria said to Lara. "That means you have to do all the jobs yourself first. You have to teach the camp staff how to clean, make beds and so on. These guys come from local villages round here. They've never seen sheets and pillows or flush toilets or detergent. They wanna work but cleaning isn't what men do around here. Give them respect, especially the older guys. Don't tell them – show them how. African men and women live separate lives. Personal hygiene stuff is private. Naked bodies – y'know – tits is okay – normal y'know – they don't mind that so much but nothing else. They work hard but they're proud – insult any of them and there's big trouble with all of them."

Maria was a good mentor. Lara remembered Jane's many house servants and thought with embarrassment of the humiliation they had been unwittingly subjected to by her mother as she stood over them while they cleaned the shit off the toilet bowls. No wonder they quit so regularly.

Lara's first winter in the valley was not as she dreamed. It was extremely hard work but she enjoyed herself much more than she could have imagined. She liked having responsibilities even if it was for housekeeping. In any case housekeeping in the bush was always a challenge. Frogs had to be lifted from the toilet pans, spiders from the basins, bats and swallows encouraged not to roost and nest among the roof joists of the bedrooms, snakes had to be caught and taken, without being harmed, some distance away.

The camp site had once been a modest and very utilitarian hunting lodge consisting of a large room with a veranda on three sides and, circling it, a scatter of round brick huts thatched with elephant grass. Bill and Maria called them *rondavels*, a South African term for a traditional single round dwelling. The separate kitchen was a lock up storeroom with a roofed area over a wood stove and a sink on concrete blocks. Maria and Bill had added a toilet and shower onto each *rondavel* and put new mosquito-proof windows and a bar and veranda into the lodge. The area was fenced and grassed and a site chosen for a modest swimming pool and a barbecue area with a good view across the valley and the river. If the first couple of seasons went well, Maria and Bill had plans to expand and improve the camp.

Maria was very happy to have Lara's companionship in the camp while the men went out exploring the game reserve, looking at the rainy season damage to the rough roads and tracks that they would use with their clients and discovering what patterns of behaviour had been established by the various wild animals in the area. Bill and Maria had first come to the National Park as research biologists straight from university and they knew it very well indeed. Maria's knowledge of the local creatures was as good as Bill's and Lara learnt from her even while she was based in the camp. She could soon name all the birds and insects and small creatures that inhabited the vicinity.

Next, Lara was employed to make the signs for the door of each *rondavel* and for the bar, then for the paths and trees. Lara made a wry face at using her artistic training and skills in this way. Experience had taught her that like many fine art students she didn't necessarily have good design skills and that the commission might prove a disappointment. A delicate line drawing wouldn't work but the drawing must be an accurate as well as an artistic portrayal of nature before she herself would be satisfied. She also knew that while she could fob off Bill and Maria with second rate work she wouldn't be able to live with it. They imagined she could do it quickly but she was a perfectionist who hated to compromise. Maria had several suggestions about names for each hut.

"Little creatures or birds I think," she said. "Not the big five – lion, leopard, rhino, buffalo and elephant – thought we'll also show the clients lizards, squirrels and frogs – any little animal specific to the camp area."

"That's a nice idea," Lara responded. "Have to think what other art materials I have that won't fade though and that also suit my style."

When Bill gave her wooden boards to use and some gloss house paint Lara could see the surface would be difficult to work on but it also gave her an idea. She would make little painted reliefs and each sign would be placed in a position on the hut that was appropriate to the creature's habitat. The surfaces she had to work on were crude. She would have to use acrylic paints and glues and simplify the images without falsifying them. The signs took much longer than Bill expected, but Lara did them well. Each rondavel had a lively patterned creature caught at the moment before it vanished from sight. A blue-headed lizard clung to the edge of the sign, a sun squirrel flicked its tail as it darted away, a bush baby stared out as it clutched the sign with damp fingers. Lara made the signs appear three-dimensional by incorporating twigs, bark and stones onto them.

She had worked from her own sketches and these earned such admiration from everyone at the camp that she was encouraged to make more for herself. Her folders filled up with paper covered in ink, brush and crayon. Hasty quick drawings based on fleeting observations. She had to keep looking, keep remembering, nothing stood still for her – the work was all about movement and change in light and shadow.

Jason and Trevor had started camp life sleeping in the storeroom with the camp provisions but then were moved into a large tent together. Lara was given the most tumbledown of the *rondavels* all to herself. She was lucky, she thought, and she cleared a space to use as a studio and improvised a table from a plank and concrete blocks and an easel from some thin tree branches. Midday in the valley was unbearably hot. After lunch the clients usually took a long siesta. Lara spent this time drawing and painting. There was no electricity in the valley. After dark a generator provided light in the dining area and guest rooms, but was turned off when the bar closed. The gas camping light was not good enough for Lara to work at night. In any case the light cast on the white paper attracted so many insects that Lara had to keep brushing them away, which meant she often smudged her work.

Chapter Three

Brendan 1997

"I was so busy I didn't have much time to make art while I was in the bush. I was frustrated by that – felt as if I was disabled somehow. My hands would start drawing at the first opportunity even before my brain knew what I was trying to do – as soon as I had paper and something to make a mark with I would scribble madly. I kept seeing things I needed to make notes about or sketch – always carried a sketch book and pen – a habit from art school – though pencils were less likely to let me down and I could always sharpen them. I carried a penknife everywhere. Drawing where people can see what you're up to is a real problem – they always want to talk about it while instead you need to have the head space not to explain or speak. You are in a different world while you are working – even grunting or going "uhuh" is distracting. Also you need to work your way into a sketch – there are so many you discard or keep only as a reference – so many lines that are tentative or light before you can make those powerful marks in the right way. I couldn't be rude to the clients – can't believe how many would ask me to draw something for them like I was a performing monkey or something. Then of course there is the flattery which is not a bit helpful."

"It was so dusty and dirty – There were lots of little creatures that walked across my paper – or ate it – termites would eat anything that you left undisturbed for a day or two. I didn't have an endless supply of materials either."

"I wasn't sure what I wanted to turn into drawings either. The skies are vast – the landscapes ever changing and huge – no creature stays still for long – there was so much observation required. The photos I took were most unsatisfactory and I didn't want to tap into professional wildlife photos – that was their personal vision not mine. Everything I attempted was very experimental. It was only when I got back to the city and shut myself into the studio that I realised I had actually begun to know what wild animals looked like and how they moved. Only then could I make my hand begin to translate my knowledge into real drawings – the paintings would come later. It was also then that I first began to look at all the smudges, the mistakes, the holes made by insects, their tracks across the paper and see them as something I could use and learn from and incorporate into my work.

"I so loved what I was doing. I so loved the bush."

Chapter Four

At Home

Lara's first season ended too soon for her. She had made no plans to look for any other work, rather hoping that Bill and Maria would take her on the following season. Her hopes were met. Trevor had decided to return to England to study environmental sciences so Maria and Bill asked her to stay on for an extra month and then return a month earlier the following year. They said that they might need her help for part-time jobs over the rainy season if she felt able to stay on those conditions. Lara said yes, of course. Then she told her parents that she wanted to spend Christmas with them and stay on afterwards until the next safari season. Jane raised her eyebrows a little but Brian looked pleased.

"It's only for the time being", Lara reassured them.

Brian had a quiet chat with the manager of the main hotel in town and arranged some temporary work for Lara over Christmas but she found city life dull and lonely after the aggravation of art school and the delights of the bush camp. Lara persuaded Brian to turn one end of his garage workshop into a studio for her and she became absorbed into reworking her sketches from the valley into paintings. An irritated Jane reminded Lara that she had offered to do the supermarket shopping and help with the catering for the Christmas parties at Brian's office. Lara sighed, started to pack up her sketch book, decided to make a small alteration, then forgot where she was, and ended up being too late for the shops.

"Honestly Lara – how did Maria put up with you? Did you daydream all the time there too? You've forgotten to go to the butcher again." Jane stopped scolding as her eye was caught by Lara's work.

It was a series of ink and watercolour drawings of young animals playing, turning, scratching, leaping, and feeding. Each captured a brief moment of action particular to that creature. The drawings concentrated on the instant of life rather than being a detailed representation.

"Those are lovely, Lara!" Jane said, her voice alight with surprise and pleasure. "Why don't you have some of them printed – they would make lovely Christmas cards and you can donate the sales to the Wildlife Charity"

Lara shrugged, but after thinking about it she agreed. The cards could also be sold at the safari camp to visitors during the season. She wouldn't make any money after the printing costs but it would be a validation of sorts for her art.

"I'll phone up that woman who runs the art gallery in the city centre – whatever her name is – something Greek that I can't say – Helen Yannu, I think – maybe Ioannou?" Jane promised.

Lara found Brian and Jane's dinner parties dull. Brian's male guests liked her and some even tried to come on to her. There was a restless need for entertainment that expatriate men seemed to succumb to in the evenings that was not so manifest during their working days. She felt that she didn't own herself when they were around and that they mentally pawed at her.

The wives looked her over in a different way then asked her if she had a steady boyfriend yet or was engaged. They laughed.

"Young women," they said to each other, "have it all, don't they? When I was that age I was married."

"Are you going to have a career?" said others, "Are you selling your art yet?" "What kind of art do you do? Landscape? Still life?"

Lara felt as if she was being chopped up and sorted into different parcels, wife, girlfriend, career woman, artist, but they didn't join up and where and what was she? At the camp with Maria she had felt useful. Drawing or painting took her into another dimension that was sufficient in itself. Should she go back to England as she had first been advised to and get a teaching diploma and then a job? She had never really had to think about money but her holiday work had given her pocket money, not independence. The thought of leaving Chambeshi and the seasonal work in the bush was depressing and when and where would she find time to paint? Artists need studios and above all time – hours and days, weeks and years of time.

It was only one year since her graduation. Her parents were tolerant and well off. Lara didn't want to face the harsh reality of earning a living. She wanted to make art. All the same she was ashamed to be still living with Jane and Brian. She was exploiting her parents but what options did she have if she was to be an artist?

"No one thinks that making art is work, because it's solitary and silent and sometimes it's just about being still and looking and thinking. I can't instantly be a good artist. I have to go through a sort of apprenticeship," Lara told herself.

Chapter Five

Jason

Towards the end of the rainy season Maria and Bill contacted Lara.

"It's going to be a good season," Bill said. "We are building more guest chalets and reckon we can use your artistic expertise."

"Of course Bill – but you know how slowly I make arty things," Lara answered.

"You're a fast worker at everything else," Bill said. "We'll get our money's worth from you."

"You've the gift of making things look nice," Maria said. "We've got to keep to a tight budget. We want to use local crafts but it has got to look special – not tatty."

Lara reluctantly promised to do her best and was rewarded when Maria told her that Jason was coming back early too.

"Bill needs Jason to get the Cruisers and equipment working properly. We reckon we'll need both of you to help check out the game drives in the reserve. We think the game has moved this year after the poor rain in January," Maria continued.

Lara nodded. Many animals returned to the same locations each year with fairly minor variations but there would always be some changes especially if the river had altered its course or there had been a bush fire or major depredation of game from poaching.

This year there had been poor rainfall and some animals,

hippo mostly, had died from anthrax poisoning, a natural event that was caused by lack of good fodder and the lowering of the water table.

Lara was delighted to be back in the bush and working very hard again. By ten at night they were all exhausted and knew that they would be awake again and working at sunrise, which every day happened slightly later. Very soon they found themselves responding to light rather than alarm clocks, just as the Chambeshians did. Lara loved the way everyone in the wild, people and animals together, responded to the lunar calendar as well. On moonlit nights Chambeshians would visit friends and stay awake chatting till the moon set. Wild creatures, even some who were not nocturnal, were always more active at full moon.

National Park requirements meant the camp team had to take armed and uniformed game guards with them every time they took guests into the bush. Bill was planning to train Chambeshians to take on some of these duties.

"I'm now a teacher as well. So is Jason. So is Maria. You too, Lara. These guys have to take qualifying exams in everything from first aid and basic vehicle mechanics. They must have a comprehensive knowledge of animals, reptiles, insects, arthropods and birds, as well as their habitats and habits. It's all hands on deck," Bill said. Lara smiled at the naval metaphor. Chambeshi was a landlocked country. The camp was far from the sea or even from a large lake.

Maria had employed an experienced camp cook but she was training a man to work in the bar who had never seen a gin and tonic in his life before.

Maria's father had been a hunter.

"A crocodile hunter, in fact." Maria said with a mildly ironic smile. "It was a different world then. Now we really have to stop so many species becoming extinct. Our main job here is to get the Chambeshians to see what a valuable resource they have in their wild animals."

"Hence our training programmes and work with government,"

agreed Bill, "and of course the safari business – raising the profile of the tourist industry here."

Their first guests turned up before the camp preparations were complete. They were friends rather than clients and quite happy to set to and help with the final arrangements before the camp opened properly in a fortnight. It was a relief to have a test run with people who were both tolerant and sympathetic, who could laugh when the towels had been forgotten or when the toilet paper left on the floor ended up housing a scorpion. The camp site was not a place that offered much privacy. Bill and Maria had some bad moments when tiredness and worry meant they lost their tempers and shouted at each other. Jason would look over at Lara with a grin and they would offer to go and see if the pool had been chlorinated or if there were jackals or honey badgers raiding the garbage bins outside the kitchen. They were easy in each other's company during the working day but walking around the camp at night with Jason made Lara's skin prickle. Her senses were heightened in any case by being outside in the dark of an isolated camp in the middle of the wilderness but she knew that she was more intense and aware of the physical presence of Jason that of any danger from the bush. The evenings were cool but Jason's body gave off a heat that warmed her even when they were not close. The smell of him was exciting too, a mixture of sweat, sun, dust and engine oil even after he had showered. She delighted in her own physical being when she was at the camp. The golden brown of her tanned body and the sun-streaks that lightened her hair gave her a pleasurable feeling of physical strength and health. She enjoyed being outdoors using her muscles as well as her brain but was quite unaware that Bill and Maria were watching her and Jason with tolerant smiles.

Bill had plans to take clients into the game reserve on overnight excursions. Permanent camps were not allowed in the confines of the National Park but the Nature Conservancy authority had agreed that temporary camps would be allowed inside the reserve if they were made of either canvas or the sustainable local materials of grass and wood and dismantled at the end of each season. Bill reckoned that a safari that offered an authentic rough bush camp experience would, contrarily, attract richer punters.

"Hey Jason, hey Lara!" Bill said, "How would the two of you like to make a *recce* into the park for me? You would need to spend a night there in the bush. I have sussed out some likely sites – nice trees – good views over a loop on the river but I need to know all about the problems – the local game and if we can get good enough drainage for some temporary long-drop loos. I know you'll both be good on the practical stuff but Lara will see it from the tourist angle as well. We are down on guest numbers this week. If I need to I can send out a safari with Kunda – his training is now complete. The two of you can look after each other I know – but how do you feel about it?"

Maria turned her back ostensibly to attend to some accounts, but she was listening carefully to what Lara and Jason decided to do. Lara didn't notice. She was looking at Jason and he was looking at her. They would have a night and two days alone together in the bush. Lara felt her body lurch a little dizzily towards Jason. She knew her attraction to him was reciprocated

Chapter Six

Camping Equipment

It didn't take long to kit out the Land Cruiser for Jason and Lara's recce into the bush to find a suitable summer camp site. They needed only the most basic equipment, plus binoculars, camera, a gun and a radio for contact with the main camp when the generator was on at night.

"Radio contact needs the right conditions. No electric storms, no large hills or geological formations." Bill explained the workings of the camp radio against the hiss and crackle of its static in the badly lit camp office on the evening before their trip.

Jason was put in overall charge as he knew the area they were to explore and he delegated Lara to organise the food and the sleeping gear. That made him slightly awkward towards Lara. She knew, and she was sure that Jason knew, that once they were alone in the bush they would make love, but, Jason didn't appear quite as sure of himself as usual. He had joked that girls could be 'tricky' and needed to be handled in ways that didn't upset them, but it was clear that on the whole he found relationships with women easy. Lara guessed that her self-assured manner both challenged and provoked him. For once he wasn't over-confident. Lara smiled to herself. The electricity that fizzed between her and Jason made her super-aware of his moods and slight anxieties. She chose a moment when the camp staff were briefly off duty.

"Do you want to take a tent, Lara?" Jason asked. "I usually

fix myself a bed under a mosquito net in the back of the Land Cruiser but – it's up to you -"

He left his suggestion unfinished.

"Come and check out the stuff I've put together," Lara said, looking directly at Jason with a smile. Then she set off towards the Land Cruiser without a backward glance, but with her hand held out towards him. He caught her wrist and loosely circled it with his hand as he followed her into the shade where the car was parked.

"Wasn't sure about how to arrange things," Lara said, leaning into the back of the vehicle. Jason, standing close behind her, put his right hand on her shoulder and his left on the door frame. With a simple twist of her body, Lara turned into his arms and found his tongue searching greedily for her open mouth. Jason's skin around his lips was salted with sweat, a little roughened by slight stubble. Lara could taste his last cigarette. The burning-hot metal door frame curved against the flesh of her shoulder. Jason's hand enclosed her breast and his fingers squeezed on her stiffening nipple. The firm swell of his erection pressed against the bones of her pelvis. Lara's body began to melt and strange sounds came from her throat.

Sleeping arrangements in the park were decided.

Much too soon the clang of the struck ploughshare summoning the camp staff back to prepare afternoon tea and the evening meal recalled them to themselves. Lara was trembling with delight, Jason's eyes hard and bright as they returned to the camp office. Bill and Maria pretended not to notice Lara's reddened cheeks and the love bite blotched onto her neck.

"We'll just *braai* some meat and take bread or mealie pap for supper." Jason said. "Let's keep it simple. Brew tea at dawn and eat brekker after we've had a good scout around. We'll spend the first day looking along the river at the places Bill thinks are okay. Sleep at the furthest possible site and then come back and see how things look at a different time of day. Bill wants us back before dark so we'll need to be back outside the park before the gates shut – about 5-ish I think."

Lara had already thought of what was needed and naturally packed it up with a couple of extras. She knew Jason liked pickle with his meat while she would need the clean taste of cucumber and maybe some oranges as well. The camp cook on Maria's instructions had made a rich moist fruit cake and given them a substantial slab to take. They would have drinking water and a cool-box with beer. Maria secreted a half-bottle of white South African Grunberger wine into the cooler as well.

"Us girls like a little sophistication." she said with a smile at Lara.

Lara carried the cool-box out to the Land Cruiser. Kunda was there checking the tool box with Jason until Bill came to find them.

"Kunda's rather busy with organising game trips right now Jason," Bill said. "You can manage to get things ready on your own, can't you?"

It was a reproof.

"Sure." Jason's eyebrow flicked up for a second. Lara had noticed that Jason still treated Kunda as a subordinate though Kunda was now qualified and they were on equal footing at work. She pushed the insight away. What mattered was the fantastic trip that she was about to take up the river with Jason.

"This could be the start of something real," Lara thought. "Jason and me working in the bush together. God! I want this life to last forever."

She imagined herself a few years hence, partnered with Jason but running the safari camp while Bill and Maria were on holiday somewhere – or retired. She would of course, still be painting and probably famous.

Chapter Seven

A Night in the Wild

Lara and Jason were ready to leave before the sun rose. Bill and Maria's camp, though outside the National Park, was on the banks of the river that made its southern boundary. Each day the camp clients would be taken on a safari into the Park and return each evening before nightfall. Lara and Jason were making the same trip but on this occasion they had permission to stay overnight in the Park. Accordingly Jason and Lara would drive to the only bridge across the river, arriving, they hoped, at approximately the same time as the Park guards opened the gates into the Park. Their exploration was to take them back along the opposite side of the river to Bill's camp on roads that were poorly maintained and into an area that had not, as yet, been exploited for game-watching safaris.

"It's a really good time to be going along the river banks. We'll see plenty of game – should see lots of elephant and antelope – you'll need to estimate numbers and make notes, Lara."

"Yes, Boss Jason!" Lara teased. They had been locked in a long and passionate embrace when Bill arrived to check their arrangements were complete. A shy man, Bill was discomforted by their intimacy and he said farewell to them with some irritation.

"Your report will have to be thorough." he said, "Don't let me down."

Lara smiled at him and he softened.

"Enjoy yourselves. *Yendani bwino*. Go well."

Early winter mornings are bitterly cold in the bush. The temperature can drop below zero but the extremely dry air means that no white frost crystals form and tender green plants just blacken and die. Pools of still water along the river may ice over but only until the sun reaches them. Lara dressed in several layers of light clothing under a wind-proof jacket and wound a cotton sarong, scarf-like, around her head for the start of the trip. Before midday her trouser legs would unzip into shorts and she would strip down to a tee shirt. At dawn even Jason was wearing a fleece. Lara had never heard any Chambeshian complain about extreme weather conditions but she knew they appreciated the comfort provided by their camp uniforms. She hunkered down behind the vehicle windscreen as they drove off to avoid the chill breeze. It was dark enough for headlights but the bush was still and quiet. The changeover between nocturnal and diurnal creatures happened with great stealth. This was a time of dangerous transition. The waiting silence of the bush filled Lara with trepidation and thrilled excitement. In the wild no one could predict what might happen. It was always an absolutely new day.

When they reached the bridge across the great river, the guards were half asleep, warming themselves at a smoky fire by the sentry box. They waved Lara and Jason across, and in those brief moments the river surface was transformed from shadowed grey to opalescent pearl. The first birds began to call and the first water creatures made the river's edges ripple and the reeds stir. They savoured the smell of the river, moist and fresh, the rank stench of decayed plants on its banks, the sweetly powerful and comforting odour of animal dung, the taste of the dry dust of the road rising up in yellow-grey clouds behind them, the clarity of every sound, the increasing sharpness of every sight around and about them. Early morning in the bush was to Lara a song of praise, a precious gift of life. This was a moment of such beauty that no artist could capture it. That it existed at all was sufficient. The two of them, herself and Jason, were the only humans in Eden and it had been made for their delight.

They journeyed very slowly. The rough surface of the track needed frequent gear changes and constant attention. The spoor imprinted in its surface, the dung along the way told them what creatures had passed, how long ago and in what numbers. They stopped often to check how fresh the tracks were, how moist the dung, what it indicated of the food ingested by the animals. Jason was an expert tracker. Lara a fast learner. They competed as to who could recognise and name the most species of birds. Lara had the edge on Jason in this field. Working most days at the camp had not prevented her from developing her birdwatching skills. Jason however was more forceful in claiming first sight of individual birds and, as their score was so close, Lara let him win the count. She was too happy and engrossed to mind.

Antelope were prolific on the open grassy plains. Elephant crossed the road ahead of them on their return from the river to feed among the forest trees. They saw zebra, waterbuck, wildebeest and warthog, their ears pricked, tails up, as they danced and leapt away from the Cruiser. There were also the quiet creatures, a tortoise, snakes, a swift sun squirrel ducking behind a branch on the tree above and below in a gully, a honey badger, its head down in an anthill, oblivious to them, its silky fur gleaming and rippling in the windy grass.

Before midday Lara and Jason watched a family of hyena on guard over the anteater burrows they had taken over. Their spotted hides were almost invisible under the dappled shade of a thornbush. Soon afterwards, Jason parked where they could observe a pride of well-fed lions resting in a circle around their kill. Lara had seen the circling vultures overhead and Jason had eased the Cruiser up onto a ridge and as close as it was safely possible to go.

In the early afternoon the two of them turned back towards the river bank to eat sandwiches and have a beer. In the hot sun, sweat on their upper lips and foreheads, they kissed, licked the salt off each other's lips and ended up on a sandy patch of ground by the Cruiser making love.

"Shush, Lara!" Jason warned. "Too much noise and you'll attract predators."

"Only bugs and insects!" Lara said, standing up naked to brush off sand and flies.

"You're not shy, are you?" Jason said half in admiration, half to admonish.

"We're all alone – oh Jason – you are so beautiful! You have such a gorgeous body. Look at you!" Lara said smiling, her hands held out to Jason. It wasn't new for Jason to be admired, but it was new to have a lover who expressed herself so directly. He was aroused and annoyed at the same moment.

"We must move," he said, "We have work to do before we set up camp for the night. We still have to find the site for the new camp."

Jason took the Cruiser down to several different places on the river bank and up to various higher places that were wooded. One site afforded good access to the river but might be vulnerable to flooding, from another it was possible to see both upstream and downstream. Here road access might be more awkward. There the trees were too dense. At another place the river would eat away at the bank each year. Here was a watering hole that they did not want to disturb and there a hippo path or a nesting site for bee eaters. Eventually they decided they had found the ideal place, close enough, high enough, and on the inside curve of the river, and they set up their camp for the night. They had brought some fire wood as they would not cut any trees but they also found fallen branches nearby. When night fell they would light the fire, but first they sat together in the serenity of the evening, watching flocks of birds gathering for the night, hearing the baboons call to each other from across the river, listening to the noise of a pod of hippo downstream, in the distance the hyena laughing and the occasional sound of a distant lion's roar. Bats dived over the river to drink where, earlier, swifts had skimmed. Crocodiles' eyes reflected red in the light of Jason's torch. The magnificent sweep and spread of the billions of stars in the Milky Way arched overhead in an unending slow spin.

It was time to light the camp fire and cook the steak. To drink wine and beer and kiss and make love, once and then again, and at least once again. Passion and desire made the night-time into a wonderland. Jason did not understand foreplay but Lara's receptiveness and his virility were more than enough to satisfy them both. The night was alive with movement and sound as hippo trampled heavily towards their night time grazing and splashed thunderously across the river shallows on their way back into the water. Elephants passed by in silence except for their internal body conversations with each other. Lara heard nightjars and owls and watched as the stars spun a slow circling web over her head. The waning moon made the bush visible once more so that Lara could see a single bush-buck and an alert genet pass by her camp. She could even identify the beetles and spiders leaving their tiny trails in the sand under the Cruiser. When the dawn light whitened the sky ahead of the rising rosy sun, Lara had hardly slept but she knew that this was the best, the most perfect day of her life. The whole world had come into existence just for this moment of time and especially for her.

Chapter Eight

Wildlife Art

Lara's sketches attracted the attention of Bill and Maria's clients. She was pressed into selling some of her drawings. At first she was reluctant. They were, after all, notes to herself rather than finished works of art and she wasn't yet sure how she would use them. She found, however that what she valued and what she could sell were not the same. The clients wanted souvenirs of their trips – recognisable animals that they had seen for themselves – mostly lion and elephant. Occasionally they would ask Lara to draw animals from imagination or memory. Sometimes Lara did as they asked then found that the buyers claimed they had been drawn from life. This curious conflation of creativity and fakery puzzled Lara and made her smile. What was art after all? She did not want to cheat, however, though she still did not know what the purpose of art was, either for herself, or for its viewers.

Lara learnt to hide the drawings she intended to work on later. Those were slighter, more suggestive, much more uncertain, a search for something glimpsed, something moving, half-hidden, in flight, in half-light, perhaps even sensed not seen during the night. On the whole the clients liked detail. Spots, stripes, feathers and fur carefully inked and coloured. Drawings that Lara thought lifeless; where her determination to get something right had stolen the soul of the creature she was drawing, where she had worked for hours, and as she thought done the animal to death, those were the choice of the tourists. They had taken hours to do and did not fetch much money but Lara did not in the end regret parting with them.

A couple of the clients were also wild-life artists, one rather well-known. Each had come to spend some time refreshing their skills and replenishing their portfolios. Lara found them generous with advice and information, with ideas about techniques and how to transport materials into the bush, how to work *en plein air*, and bring the results back safely. The most famous of the artists insisted on leaving Lara most of his materials, water colours, inks and beautiful sheets of Fabriano handmade paper 360 grams in weight. Lara was both humbled by his kindness and proud that he considered her work good enough to encourage. The attention she received appeared to Lara's surprise to annoy Jason but there was a more subtle edge to his jealousy. Lara knew Jason was by far the better at knowing and recognising game in the bush. What was strange was her ability to capture in a sketch more than should have been possible from her learnt knowledge alone. It was as if the artist in her saw with a third eye. Jason was empowered by her drawings to explain the nature of the creatures she illustrated and they each wondered, but did not discuss, how she had managed to draw what she understood but was not yet able to explain verbally.

"My Ma paints, you know." Jason said to Lara, "She paints watercolours – landscapes of the bush – they're nice but she doesn't spend so much of her time doing it as you do."

Lara looked at Jason. They were both occupied in different ways in the camp. Finding much time together wasn't always easy. They were late to bed and up early. She swished her paintbrush clean, stuck its handle down in the water jar and went to kiss him. Maybe when Jason was occupied with clients on a night drive there would be time when she could finish her work. She wasn't going to give up her evenings making art if she could help it. There were dangers, she acknowledged. Jason was a sexy and handsome young man. Lara knew very well that some of their female clients, regardless of age and sometimes regardless of husbands, partners or children, came for the glamour and the erotic thrill of the safari camp and that Jason was the embodiment of both.

She could see that he was sensible enough with the married women, but she knew that he enjoyed it when the single women flirted with him. Maria had hinted that before Lara's arrival, Jason had helped a number of the single women fill photo albums with romantic memories. Bill shook his head, recounting the stories as if they were all past history.

"Honestly, Jason – remember how I had to tell you to stick to girls who had careers and return tickets – you nearly got yourself married off several times."

He scratched his chin. Lara wondered who he was warning, her, or Jason, or both of them together.

"The camp needs you both," Bill said.

Maria said nothing. She wiped her hand over the top of the bar. It was dusty. If the weather was windy everything would be covered with a filmy cover of finest sand.

Lara felt confident about Jason in spite of Bill's comments. She was good-looking enough not to worry about her appearance. That freed her to focus on the world around her and not on the impact of her appearance on others. When she stopped to look in a mirror in one of the guest chalets she saw that she was slim, that her breasts were full, but not too large. Her buttocks were more curvaceous than she personally would have wished and her hips heavier but who was perfect anyway? She had always preferred the fleshier life models to the skinny ones at art school. She tanned easily to a warm dark honey. Her light brown hair, thick and slightly waved, had sun-bleached blond streaks because she was outdoors so often. Life was a delight. Jason was fun. She had so much pleasure with Jason. Loving him made her body glow with satisfaction. She could feel that she was attractive to men, and also to some women. She was like sugar to ants. Lara knew her power and was sure that she and Jason were made for each other.

Okay – Jason needed to assert his independence from time to time – she did too. It was the same for both of them, wasn't it?

As their third season at the camp and their second as lovers drew to a close, Lara saw, but did not take notice of the small creased ridge that hooked Jason's brow down when her drawings were pulled out to show to clients. She saw, but did not take real notice of, Jason's look of relaxation and relief when Maria decided that Jason and Lara should leave the valley separately when they completed their different tasks.

All the same, separation fed their sexual desire. Jason and Lara even found time while clearing the camp to make love on the bags of linen piled in the store.

"You and me – we're together right?" Jason said, "Got this Christmas at Hluhluwe rhino conservancy then I'll be back for next winter. No messing around Lara – you promise don't you?"

Lara promised easily. Jason promised the same.

"No messing around for me either, Lara."

She had heard that, hadn't she?

Chapter Nine

Helen

Back in Chambeshi City Jane dragged Lara off to the small art gallery in the centre of town to sell some more of the cards that had been printed from Lara's drawings. Jane had met the owner, Helen Ioannou, at a cocktail party and even been to a preview of an art exhibition at the gallery. Tutorials at art school had not included the business of selling art or finding an agent. At the camp, selling her art made Lara feel false. She was uncomfortable with the praise she received. It had been fulsome rather than critically appreciative. After three years working in the bush, Lara could not imagine herself having an exhibition. She hadn't talked to other artists or been to exhibitions during that time apart from the wildlife artists'. She recognised their skills but could not relate their work to anything she had seen at art school or even to what she wanted to do with her own wildlife sketches.

Helen Ioannou was a dumpy woman with thick wavy hair dyed to an indigo blue-black. Large amber and blue and white trade bead necklaces bounced off the broad soft shelf of her breasts. She was squared off by her long shapeless kaftan in bright African colours but her clear voice had the modulated accent of an Oxbridge graduate. She was divorced. Her ex-husband was a Cypriot and a wealthy businessman in Chambeshi. Her divorce settlement had included a well-frequented grocery and bar near the town market and a luxury flat in a good suburb. Helen employed a good manager for the shop and bar. Her passion was art. She looked Lara over with calm dark eyes and then looked Jane over with the same ruminative glance.

"Let's see your work, shall we?" she suggested and spread the cards out on the reception desk.

"The cards will sell – they are quite commercial. Your choice?" she asked Lara and nodded when Jane said that she had helped select them. "I like to see where the images are taken from," she explained. "Here in Chambeshi so many artists make excellent copies of the work of other artists and see no harm in it. We try to encourage and explain professional standards in art and insist on intellectual copyright."

"But this is Lara's own work!" Jane said, offended.

"Did you bring your sketch book and portfolio?" Helen asked Lara.

Lara smiled.

"I did bring it. It's in the car – I'll get it"

Helen Ioannou placed herself between Lara and her mother as she reached over the portfolio, her jewelled and weighted bosom smoothing away the dust of the bush from the plastic envelopes holding Lara's drawings. She looked in silence every now and then raising an eyebrow or pursing her lips so her lipstick wrinkled. At last she turned to Lara who was feeling more and more uncertain.

"What do you want to do with these? Where are you going with your work?"

"I don't know." Lara confessed. "I love doing them but I think they are only beginnings – ideas but for what – I don't know."

Helen examined her shrewdly for a long moment.

"Right – this is how it is at the gallery. We choose not to exhibit wild life art here. My artists are all African, mostly Chambeshian. For them, wild animals are what they eat – even lion if necessary – or what they can sell – skins, bones, ivories, horns, teeth. I see bush meat from every species for sale everyday outside my store at the market. My artists will happily make copies from well-known wildlife artists even down to the signature because they know it is big money from tourists – that won't stop them eating bush meat if they are hungry. They know I don't approve of plagiarism or fakes. If I exhibit the work of a white wildlife artist then it looks to my artists as if I have double standards – but you – what are you Lara? Is this really your chosen genre?"

Helen waited a moment while Lara hesitated, tried to answer, then stopped.

"All the same I think your drawings are exceptional and I would like to show them here. They have a different quality to most wildlife art. They suggest the elusiveness of wild animals, the spirits of the creatures, they have movement – they have more life. Some wildlife artists are very skilled but they concentrate on biological accuracy and knowledge – you don't."

Lara worried that Helen saw this as a fault or a weakness.

Helen continued, "I would like to take some of your work, Lara, but no pictures of the Big Five – no elephants, rhino, lion, buffalo or leopard. The small creatures, sun squirrels, the mongoose, jackals, and the birds and actually for the moment I will take those that are most sketchy and experimental. Think about it and come back to me."

Jane was furious.

"Dreadful woman! Dreadful taste!" she said as she swung the car round the busy roundabout near the gallery. "Don't go back, Lara! We can do an exhibition for you in the hotel lobby in Parkside. People will love your work. They will buy the lion and elephant paintings, I know!"

"I'll go back Mum," said Lara, "I think Helen's okay!"

Her mind was already moving and shifting, creating new drawings in different ways.

Part Four
London 1997

Chapter One

Tintin au Congo

Lara's therapy sessions with Brendan are all going quite smoothly, or so Lara thinks. She has enjoyed talking about her childhood, about Liseli, about art school; she is in the driving seat with Brendan. She is in control, isn't she?

The therapy sessions are also proving useful in making her think about how and why she makes art. Lara chews sideways at her lower lip.

It is not enough, though, is it? I'm avoiding the real issues aren't I? Don't even really know what they are. I miss Tim so very much. Will he come home and want to live with me?

Adam calls downstairs from his bedroom.

'Mum, read this book to me.' He adds 'Please.' just in time to forestall Lara's reminder.

'When I've finished. '

Lara is on automatic response as she puts clean crockery away. A moment later she catches up with the question.

"What book do you mean?" Adam doesn't need help reading.

"It's a Tintin book, Mum, but it's not English."

The wine-glasses seem jumpy and irritable.

Blast! Lara thought. *I should have thrown that ugly book away. I should have used a tray instead of making my fingers into cup-hooks and risking dropping them all.*

"Read another book, Adam." The wine glass she pushes into

place in the cupboard knocks another two over. They make a clear sharp sound, one breaks into shards and the other cracks. Lara gathers up the slivers with one hand and picks up the glass stems with the other.

"That's a horrid Tintin book. You won't like it."

"Why have you got it then, Mum?"

Why indeed?

'Tintin au Congo' had not been published in English because it was considered too racist both in content and illustration. Ownership of it would have put Lara high on the hit list of the Animal Liberation Front. Lara doesn't know why she has kept it. She doesn't like the complex reaction it arouses in her. Liseli gave it to her as a joke of sorts very many years ago – perhaps 15 years – maybe less – maybe more. Lara isn't sure.

Lara remembers her sly look as she handed over 'Tintin au Congo'.

"Here. It's a good luck charm. It'll protect you," Liseli had said.

"From what?"Lara had asked, puzzled but smiling.

"From colonial exploitation and sugar daddies."

Liseli and Lara had been laughing about the rich older men who bought Lara's paintings and who seemed ready to consider ownership of Lara as part of the purchase. Lara had explained that she might be asked to paint some commissions for the famous Oscar and she had confessed to Liseli that she found him both fascinating and frightening.

Liseli had laughed wickedly.

"It is sure to end with you sleeping with him!" she said.

Lara had given her friend a shove and made a squirmy, shuddery movement of her shoulders. At the time she had not been displeased by the joke.

Now, standing by the empty dishwasher, Lara's world begins to implode in slow motion. She feels an immense pressure on her body, her limbs are weighted down and exhaustion overcomes her. Her guilty dreams and the horror of her long-suppressed memories crowd around her. She can't possibly read or explain to Adam a comic book that takes such gruesome pleasure in the slaughter of wild animals and that ridicules the people of Africa. She can't read a story to Adam in which a journalist hero uncovers and defeats a Mafia boss who has instigated tribal wars in order to exploit the diamond wealth of the Congo. She cannot let herself think of Oscar.

The winter darkness leans in and breathes on the windows. The electric lights dim as the neighbours turn up their heating. Lara collapses heavily on the chair beside the kitchen table. She tips the broken glass from her hands onto the scrubbed pine surface and stares at the shards of glass lying between her wrists. The kitchen lurches, spins dizzily and turns upside down. The reckoning has arrived. The past reaches out for her and enfolds her in its pain. She wants so much for the terrible unacknowledged hurt to shift from inside her chest. She wants to cut herself, to see the lines of beaded red appear against her skin so that all the pain can surface and bleed away. She wants to crush her forehead onto the glass fragments so that her memories will die. She wants to take the sharp curves of glass and slice her ears off, stab her eyes out, slash at her tongue. She wants to destroy all her senses so that Oscar, the Tin Heart Gold Mine and all the events of that time can never be recalled. She wants to be dead as Liseli wanted to be dead. She understands at last why Liseli sometimes finds life intolerable. Lara wants not to exist so that Oscar can never have existed. So that Oscar could not ever have been born.

Tim has gone.

Lara has been abandoned.

Her throat makes an involuntary wrenching cry. She must not abandon Adam.

She must not leave him. She must get up. She must make supper for him.

She must burn *'Tintin au Congo'*.

But what is she to do with herself?

Adam calls out.

"Mum, what's wrong?"

Lara can tell from his tone that he isn't worried and he doesn't want to leave his room and come downstairs if he can help it.

"I'm okay," she says twice. The first time her voice is feeble – a mere croak. The second time it is audible and firmer.

"I'll get us supper Adam. Won't be long. Hang on."

Chapter Two

Nightmares

Lara starts to have her nightmares again soon after Tim leaves for Uganda. They always follow the same pattern. She dreams she is back in the wilderness in Chambeshi. At first she feels so free, so happy. It is as if she has just come home after boarding school, then the dream would change and she would wake sweating and horrified. Last night she had dreamt again almost the same dream as the night before.

At the start of the dream Lara feels safe. As safe as if she rests in the neutral comfort of her bed. Underneath her the golden sand is washed cotton-soft. Over her head a laundered sky is neither hot nor cold. Her left hand props a book open at a page of print that is even, regular and unreadable; her right hand supports her weightless head. The shore on which she rests is grooved and ridged with horizontal exactitude by the retreating water until it is reflected in an isolated pool left in a quiet meander of the river. Minute particles of grit suspended in the clear water reflect motionless light. There is no current, no movement at all. It seems the ideal place for a picnic.

Without warning or explanation, Lara flies through the air until she flops like an escaping fish into the oxbow pool. As the still surface shatters into sparkling rain, her belly's expectant cringe changes to instant delight at its pleasant warmth. The water caresses her with the intimacy of a traitor or a lover. From her new viewpoint with her eyes level with the curved meniscus of liquid Lara sees that she is afloat in an elliptical pool surrounded by soft steep banks of collapsing sand. Immediate and total terror overcomes her. It is the same shape as the long red laterite oval of bare earth that surrounded the Tin Heart Gold Mine.

Help me! Help me!'

Her voice sounds strange and outside her control, panic makes it deep and harsh. She knows she must not scream or splash. Eddies from her own desperate doggy paddle encircle her, obscuring her view of a river bottom that she is afraid to touch with her feet. If she attempts to scrabble her way out, the sandbank will collapse onto her and hold her down in the water. Underneath its golden fragility is a curving shadowed hollow that is a perfect hiding-hole for crocodiles. Lara's head twists round this way, that way, her eyes stare through the clouding water. She sees for the first time in the sand above her the indented lop-sided stars and plough marks of crocodile spoor. She knows yellow-green eyes have blinked open at the sound of her voice; she senses the surge of powerful armoured muscles thrusting through the river to her unprotected flank. Oscar was stretched out reading on the bank above her. Lara can make out the familiar round of his solid skull, his loved short-cropped grizzled hair against the sky. She calls his name, hope increasing her buoyancy.

'Oscar! Oscar, help please!'

Oscar turns his head towards her. Lara sees his chin lift, his cheek crease with the quizzical smile with which he always greets her but he does not rise to help her. He seems to miss seeing her at all. It is then that Lara realises that his eyeballs have the thick grey opacity of lizard skin.

Chapter Three

Therapy

Though Lara's thumb has been hurting for fifteen minutes she only becomes aware of the pain as she nears the zebra crossing. She is on her way once again to her routine rendezvous with Brendan. Her wrist aches with the tension of forcing her hand into the front corner of her pocket. The exposed stitching there slots into well-worn grooves in her ragged nail. Now the thread cuts into her flesh. As yet she hasn't managed to push her constricted thumb through the lining. The coat is of too good a quality. It is warm and the only one she owns at present. With an effort, Lara shrugs her arm loose, twists her wrist free then flaps it about as if it doesn't belong to her. There is a sharp stab at the junction of her scapula and her shoulder as she does so. The pain continues as persistent small shocks. Lara sighs and thrusts her hand back. Then the dusty grey pavement requires her attention. A sweet wrapper obscures some frail grass next to a cement step. It invites her to lie down next to it. Lara tries to balance her need to place her cheek on the hard cold paving stones next to the wrapper and the grass against the effort required to shift her body from the vertical to the horizontal. After a moment she turns away fretfully to concentrate on crossing the road. At this point the road goes downhill and it is a little easier to keep on moving.

Walking is good for her, according to Brendan. It is therapeutic. Someday, or one day, Brendan says the grey clouds will lift. Now

Lara is an ambulant corpse, a ghostly nomad on grey streets, among grey houses, on a grey autumn day with a long winter ahead of her. She continues to walk about the streets at weekends. Adam is spending weekends with Hilda and Lester, or with his grandparents Sydney and Gwen. She continues to walk to her studio each weekday to stare at her static dull canvases under the constant grey north light of her studio window. She walks to Brendan's every Thursday evening. She talks to Brendan. Brendan's personality is of a quality as good and warm as Lara's winter coat. Brendan has a common sense that Lara can push against with her stories as she pushes against her common sense coat pocket with her thumb. She tells Brendan about the bright white light that burnt above the rivers of the bush veld. She tells Brendan how Oscar's blue eyes had turned to grey lizard skin in her dreams. She doesn't tell Brendan yet that she considers herself as morbid and mad as her best friend Liseli Ngoma Dawkins, but she is afraid. She is afraid that she will never get better, that she will never escape the grey sludge of depression; never make a good life again for herself or for Adam.

When Tim left she had been angry.

"I'll take a lover," Lara had thought, stalking off to stand at her easel, "why should I do without sexual pleasure?"

Half an hour later she was scrubbing at the canvas trying to remove a daub of the wrong colour. Nothing was working for her.

"The trouble is that lovers are so demanding – they take time and work – not like husbands. Marriages may also be work but they are convenient for sex. Besides there's Adam to think about – Adam belongs to Tim – not to any lover – it's time away from Adam – not time shared.

"I'll spend more time painting – that's what I'll do."

It wasn't working out like that, however. A lifeless weight of heavy cloud occupies her brain. She lacks the energy to lift her paintbrush. Her thoughts go in descending circles. She is listless, dull. It is certain she will never paint again. There is no meaning in that activity.

"How did I ever believe that I was able to paint? How could I ever have visited the Umodzi gallery and felt full of confidence about my first ambitious solo exhibition?"

Lara sighs, remembering the first time she visited Helen Ioannou at the Umodzi Gallery. That was when she had once again met Chimunya Mbewe. Years before Chimunya had been an unhappy girl whom Lara and Liseli had known at school. Now Chimunya, under Helen's generous patronage, had become a well-respected Chambeshian artist.

Part Five

The umodzi Gallery
1983 – 1985

Chapter One

Chimunya

Lara wandered around the Umodzi Gallery looking at the paintings on the walls while she waited for Helen. It was a mixed exhibition, some woodcuts and lino prints, a few paintings of scruffy landscapes outside the city not chosen for their scenic value, but nevertheless atmospheric, and some super-realistic market scenes of humorous incidents. She hadn't thought much about art as part of life in Chambeshi and she wasn't sure what to make of these works. They certainly were not avant-garde in any recognisable way. They were nothing like the work of Damien Hirst and Tracy Emin and the Young British Artists who had rocketed to fame so recently in London.

"What do you think of them?" Helen said smiling at her, "Most of the artists are self-taught – or teach each other – you can see some replication of Congolese art styles and even Senegalese abstract styles. Artists from Senegal and the Congo consider themselves the masters of African art. I try to encourage our artists to develop in their own way but also to learn to understand painting techniques and use art materials properly. The first paintings that artists brought to me were made variously with sand, coffee and house paint. Men take up art because they can't find other paid employment. There are no women artists yet – except for Chimunya here – who also works for me as my receptionist."

"Chimunya?" Lara looked around in surprise. Could it be the Chimunya she and Liseli had known at school? Lara saw a handsome woman in a loose cotton dress of a bold African print with an embroidered bodice. Her hair was plaited and beaded, her earrings dramatic and heavy. Her smile was shy as Lara remembered, but it lit up her face.

"Oh, Chimunya! It is you! Hello – how are you doing?"

Chimunya was still as hesitant and seemed as unwilling as ever to be recognised but with encouragement from Helen she relaxed and became friendly.

"Hello, Lara." Chimunya's voice was soft but she carried herself with a proud dignity. "I am an artist too now. Do you want to see my paintings?"

She led Lara into the storeroom at the back of the gallery where she pulled out a stack of canvases and turned them around to face Lara.

"Gosh!" Lara said, "These *are* different."

"I try to paint our traditions." Chimunya said in her quiet voice. "I don't paint the dancers like the men artists do. I paint the spirits of the dancers and the spirits that we believe in."

Helen had followed them into the store room.

"Chimunya draws well too." she said, "I showed her the work of some Australian Aboriginal and Maori artists, also some by Inuit people but she has taken off in her own direction. People like it and buy it. Chimunya also earns a living by making Batik wall hangings"

"Your paintings are really interesting – and lovely too. They do make me wonder what I am doing with my stuff," Lara agreed.

She bit her lip thoughtfully, then continued.

"I don't know what to think about art at all at the moment. I didn't expect to find artists here – I haven't really thought about where my own art is going. The more I draw the more I feel as if I have nothing to say that's new and I don't even know if that is what art is supposed to be – endlessly new all the time or representational so that people will buy it.

"I stopped liking the art I saw in England because I didn't know what I was supposed to feel about it. In fact I didn't feel anything for an awful lot of it."

On an impulse she asked Helen to have a look at her work from art school. Helen smiled.

"Sure." she replied, " Don't know if I'll be useful – I did History of Art at Oxford – among other things but I am not an artist myself – I just love it – that's all. Do let's have a look at what you are doing."

"Would you like to be included in my next group exhibition, Lara?" Helen asked.

"Oh gosh, yes! Please – I'd love that!"

"I'll probably call the show something like 'Chambeshi: The Artist's Eye.' or 'Aspects of Chambeshi' – I'll show your work and that of Pascal, Chimunya and two other artists. It's already planned to follow the current show but I can include you easily, as you'll fit in with the theme, which is local life."

Helen had other plans as well and she wanted to enlist Lara's help in running some workshops for local artists.

"The artists are keen to learn. They teach each other but some of the techniques they have picked up are rather dubious, to say the least. A little art history would give them more of a perspective on what they are doing. I'll see if I can get some cultural association to fund it but there won't be much in it for you financially."

Lara hesitated at first. She had never considered teaching art. Could she analyse her own methods and explain them to other artists? A little self-reflection would be useful for her own practice but what would be the best way to go about it? The more she thought about it the more she liked the idea.

"Chimunya, what do you think? Is there anything or anyway that I could help you with your art?" Then as she saw Chimunya's doubtful expression she added, "Chimunya – perhaps you can help me with my art – perhaps we can help each other – Pascal as well maybe?"

It was the first time Lara had considered sharing what she had learnt about making art. How could she share her knowledge? What did she know that might be useful to Chimunya and Pascal? How should it be done? Chimunya was her age and Pascal older. In fact, most of the Chambeshian artists were older than she was and were working in very different ways. They knew things she didn't, had lives and experiences that she could never have had or known. Suddenly humble, Lara understood that they would politely resist any suggestion of patronage from her. She recalled her art school tutor Nancy's words.

"You can be taught skills and techniques, but learning doesn't make you an artist. Making art goes on inside the artist. It's for you to search inside yourself – to question yourself. To make art that is true for you. It is your personal journey and your exploration. When you show your work to an audience you are exposing your own entrails for people to feed on."

Here in Chambeshi, if she was to be useful to artists, if they were to share their work with her, then she would have to be open and share equally with them.

Chapter Two

London 1997 Gillian

It is years later that Lara tells her friend Gillian at the Art Factory studio about her fellow artists in Chambeshi and how much she learnt from them.

"They turned all my ideas upside down. It didn't happen immediately because at first I did think that my art degree must amount to more than what they had taught themselves. It wasn't what they said that changed me but what I gradually began to see as we worked together.

"I started to reconsider my preoccupation with two-dimensional easel art. Why did art have to be in that form? It does have to be like that to sell easily, I know. All the Chambeshians wanted to sell their art so they made it that way just as I did. What they believed in, however, was making art. For them that was most important – much more important than selling art."

Gillian looks sideways at Lara.

"Sure, making art is the most important thing," she agrees, "but what do we do with art when it's all stacked up here in the studio and nobody even looks at it? Shall we burn it?"

"Maybe we should burn it to make space." Lara answers more than half-seriously, "I think that's what I began to grasp – the spirit of the art, which is what we are really making, can only come into existence when the art is looked at – when its seen – art is an interaction – a communication. For the Chambeshian artists the survival of the art form itself isn't essential – it can always be made again – and again if necessary – but it absolutely has to be used."

Then Lara laughs. "And it was made again and again. Some Chambeshians made many copies of their art and plagiarised and imitated other artists unashamedly. Copyright wasn't understood exactly. I guess that's how art was before printmaking changed everything?"

"Jee-sus!" Gillian shakes her head. "That's fucking marvellous! It devalues art though, doesn't it? But then I suppose nothing makes more nonsense of art than collectors hoarding art from a few stinking rich artists -"

" – or loads of impoverished dead ones!" Lara interrupts.

" – for a futures market that is of no use to most artists like us."

Lara and Gillian look at each other and recite in singsong unison.

"And how are we going to market this year's studio show?"

They had just attended their studio's monthly planning meeting and the artist who chaired the meeting had spoken in a rather stilted way in her effort to enlist the studio members.

"Pascal was fascinating to work with." Lara goes on. "He came with me when I went to the city markets to take photos. That was Helen's idea. She said otherwise the marketeers might get rather aggressive with me and demand money when I used my camera. Without Pascal I would never have been able to do the visual research for my paintings for the Sakala Bank.

"Pascal is also a traditional healer. He explained to me how the spirit exists in some essential linkage between the mask, the dancer and the dance performance. When the dancer takes off the mask, the spirit departs. The dancer becomes an ordinary person, the mask is just discarded clothing, the dance has worked its magic and is over.

"When an art collector buys an African mask he buys worthless rubbish – just detritus left behind after a performance – litter after the show."

Lara adds, smiling at the memory. "At exactly the same moment Pascal offered to sell me a mask – "just like the real antiques," he said. "They make very good masks in the Congo today. Tradition is something new we make every day in our art. It's always changing."

"Pascal must be some helluva person to know." Gillian says. "Lucky you, Lara!"

Lara nods in agreement.

"Yup!" she says.

Chapter Three

Preview

The preview of the 'New Perspectives: Art of Chambeshi' exhibition was very successful. It was also Lara's first group exhibition since her degree show at the end of her final year at art school. That 1981 degree show had been a silent and serious affair which felt as if it was scripted with only a walk on part for Lara. A couple of agents did appear but only looked at the work of one or two students they already seemed to know. Gillian, her girlfriend Poppy, and her artwork attracted a lot of unsmiling stares.

"My work is funny! Laugh – damn you!" Gillian hissed loudly.

Ajay at an early point in the evening threw a half-empty can of strong brew at his tutor's head but missed him by such a wide margin that the tutor didn't flinch. Ajay scowled at Lara and left the venue.

"I thought you'd come to the pub with me," he said.

"How was I supposed to work that out?" she said affronted.

By contrast the Umodzi threw a noisy party.

Everyone was there to meet everyone else and prepared to do it at the same moment. This was done by standing in a tight circle, talking to the person facing you, while glancing constantly over your shoulders to see who had just arrived. No one appeared to look at the art on the walls but round red sold stickers went up by every painting and the woodcuts acquired long tails of red dots as every print was bought.

Someone was smoking marijuana, probably Pascal. Lara wasn't sure if she was pissed or high but she did know she and Chimunya couldn't stop laughing. She had sold most of her paintings. So had each one of the artists. It would be good to have credit in her bank account on her return to the National Park. Towards the end of the evening Helen came up behind her and took her firmly by the arm.

"Lara, do meet Mr Jeff Sakala. He's managing director of the new bank here. He is interested in getting you to do some large paintings for the lobby of the new main branch."

"Why did he choose me?" Lara asked Helen in disbelief next day.

"I recommended you Lara, especially." Helen said, "Not entirely for flattering reasons though. Mr Sakala feels a modern bank needs a more sophisticated style of art that he would get from a Chambeshian artist. He thinks you have that extra polish. I also know that I can rely on you to both deliver the work on time and be consistent in style. You have less financial pressure on you than Pascal and Chimunya. The bank won't pay for six months and the work must be completed first. I'll work on Mr Sakala later to support Chambeshian artists, but now we'll give him what he wants. Okay?"

Lara, nodded, smiled and pulled a face.

"You mean that my drawings are representational enough for him?"

"That's part of it, Lara – but you are good too – you know."

Helen reached up to pat Lara's shoulder, "It's a start, you know!"

Chapter Four

The Poachers

Lara returned to Bill and Maria's camp filled with enthusiasm and self-confidence. Jason had arrived a week before her and was busy setting up the summer camp inside the National Park.

"Things don't look good this year." It was unusual for Bill to look tired at the start of the season but the day was unseasonably hot and the dusty wind irritating. "The rains were very poor. River levels are much too low. The best water holes are drying up. Bush cover is sparse. We are going to have to go further afield before our clients see any game. It is going to be hard work."

Bill stomped off to see his mechanics service the Cruisers. Lara turned to Maria, who shrugged and sighed.

"There's a big increase in poaching this year. We found elephant carcases everywhere. Machine gunned indiscriminately. They haven't only killed the tuskers – they take out whole families and juveniles. Threatened elephants are dangerous. When we did come across a big herd they were aggressive and we had to drive away very fast."

She smiled at Lara.

"Well I'm glad to see you – that bad boy Jason will be, too."

Jason, however, didn't seem as pleased to see Lara as she was to see him. While she was bursting to tell him about her exhibition, Jason was more reticent about his summer. He had learnt a great deal at Hluhluwe with the rhino project but it seemed to have congealed in him rather than opened him up. He said he was pleased that Lara had done well at the exhibition but he didn't want to talk about her commission at the bank.

"How are you going to manage to paint and do the work we need you to do here?"

His words made Lara's chest constrict.

Jason's not my boss – she thought angrily, *Bill is okay with how I arrange my time. Besides I am a painter – it's what I do! It's what I am.*

A dull sense told her that Jason didn't much care what she was or did. With that realisation a hard ridge of resistance grew inside her just as, outside the camp in the shrinking river, a band of rocks was being exposed.

Lara and Jason still made love or, as it was beginning to feel to Lara, they had sex. It was more businesslike, over sooner and less satisfying. Lara began to understand that without love and consideration the sexual act didn't amount to much and was quickly forgotten. It was jarring to hear a noisy drunken group of men and women guests at the camp bar laughing and teasing each other about 'ball-breaking nymphomaniacs' and men with 'little dicks'. Lara was quite certain that, as a woman and a lover, she did not fit into any category.

A plump white envelope arrived at the camp for Jason.

"Stuff about Hluhluwe," he said casually and took it away to read it.

Another one, fat as a small pillow followed.

"Pwah! Something here is a bit scented!" Bill said, handing it over.

The grass had died away on the nearest plains and the mupane trees had suffered heavy depredation by elephants. The antelope had moved on in search of new pastures. Bill called in a pilot who made a reconnaissance flight over the park and located more antelope further to the north-east. After consultation with the camp team, Bill sent Jason and Lara out together to explore new game trips that might make it possible to take clients closer to the ever-diminishing game herds. The weather was unpleasant and cold, the sky concreted over with stiff grey clouds, a spiteful wind flapped about, blowing spirals of dust and grit into their eyes. The wind and the Cruiser with Jason and Lara in it were the only things moving in an empty and deserted landscape. There wasn't even sufficient fresh animal dung to attract dung beetles. Without insects there were fewer birds. It was a dismal trip. Jason and Lara hardly spoke to each other. Their words would make too much noise in such an empty world. Soon after midday they parked out of the wind in a sheltered gully to brew some tea and eat sandwiches.

"Let's take a walk – I need to stretch." Jason said after half-an-hour. "We'll have a look around from the hilltop."

Leaving their vehicle they walked up onto the crest of the hill above and raised their binoculars.

"That's a vicious east wind – nothing is likely to scent us from that direction – or hear us either." Lara said pulling her jacket shut.

There was a sudden rigid alertness in Jason.

"Quick, Lara!" he hissed, "Get down flat on the ground," and he too dropped down beside her.

"It's poachers, Lara! I swear to God there's a least fifty of them all loaded up with meat and ivory. They are trekking south-east. If they see us we're dead. We can outrun them in the Cruiser but they'll have long-range bullets and AK 47s so it will be a risk."

Supporting themselves on their elbows, they looked out at the distant line of men. Against the dull sky, a long line of misshapen black silhouettes trailed slowly across the high ground to their east, some 50 metres distant. They humped great burdens on their shoulders. Some carried loaded litters between them.

"They're moving away from us, thank God!" Jason said.

"You're right – there's forty-three that I can count." said Lara, "but some of them are very small – just children – I think. There are about six men with elephant tusks. The guys at the front and back of the line have guns and aren't carrying anything."

"Bastards! They go into isolated villages and get the old men and the young children to porter for them. Sometimes the villagers benefit from the poaching – get some meat maybe – but these kids and old men will walk 100s of kilometres and then have to walk home again. I expect there will be lorries waiting for this meat where the road enters the south-east of the National Park."

The poachers moved very slowly. They were not expecting to be seen and fortunately for Jason and Lara did not bother to look around themselves at all.

"We're bloody lucky!" Jason said, "They're not doing any more poaching so they haven't sent out scouts to check out the bush."

"I expect they know they've driven everything away that they haven't killed." Lara said.

Lara admitted to herself that she was afraid and fear was enervating. It was strange how fear felt like boredom. She would remember this time years later when boredom and fear seemed the total of her experience.

The poachers trudged on. It was an hour before they vanished from view and another half-hour before Jason risked driving their vehicle out of the gully and turning it for home. They had to race back to arrive at the Park Gate before sunset. The Cruiser jolted and bumped. Lara and Jason did not speak. They both had to concentrate on the road. Jason, in order to not damage the Cruiser, and Lara, so not to be flung about and be herself damaged.

Bill was stony-faced when he heard their news. The camp guests, nervous and thrilled. The necessary action was taken and the poachers were met by Game Guards when they reached the South-Eastern Park Gate. The haul totalled twenty boys, nine old men, some rotting game-meat, three poachers and the six ivory tusks. A number of the poachers had escaped. Most of those caught would hang around the Gate under police guard for some weeks and then be allowed to drift home when there was no more food.

The whole business took up time and energy. It was several days later than scheduled that Bill and Maria sat down with their camp staff to discuss their plans for the coming month.

"Ah, Jason." Bill said, putting on his reading glasses and taking his pen from behind his ear. "We've received this application for work from um – from Leone Cilliers, your friend from Hluhluwe Game Park. She wants to come here next summer to work." Bill looked at Jason over the top of his reading glasses. "You know we have a full team complement at the moment, don't you?"

"That's okay, Bill," Lara said and coughed to clear her throat. "I'll be painting full time next year so I won't be coming back -" She looked at Maria. "I don't think so anyway – sorry Maria."

Part Six

Chambeshi City 1985

Chapter One

The Bank

It was a hot evening. The huge entrance lobby of the bank was solid with round-faced, smiling black businessmen packed into tight dark wool suits and with discreet unsmiling grey diplomats in loose light-weight suits. The plump appetisers piled sweating and gleaming on large tin trays were carried round by ample waitresses who had squeezed themselves into tight white shirts and very short skirts. All the guests laughed and talked, ate and drank, so did the men serving at the two bars which had been set up for the occasion in front of the manager's office.

Lara and her parents arrived together.

"Everybody is here," Jane said, bright-eyed with excitement. "Lots of people have asked me where they can buy your paintings."

"At the Umodzi Gallery, like I said, Mum, Helen's acting as my agent. It's such a relief. She has asked me out for dinner after this, you know."

"Brian and I are invited to the Chambeshi International Hotel by Mr Sakala – so that's fine, Lara," Jane said. Then she made a little pout of disgust. "Oh God! Oscar Mynhardt's here! Oh God! Lara – do not let that man buy any of your art!"

Lara, distracted by the whistling screech of a microphone, had stopped listening to her.

The Managing Director of the new bank, Jeff Sakala, made a speech which was surprisingly short. He praised his bank, the new building, joked about the architect's fees and then, very briefly, he introduced Lara and her paintings.

"We hope," he said, "when Miss Lara Kingston is famous, to sell these works of art for many more dollars than we paid for them."

"We have paid you haven't we, Miss Kingston? You know what our African banks are like with money. We are waiting for the value of our currency to drop and for the value of your art to go up before we pay you! "

There was a roar of laughter and then the guests returned to their drinks and their friends. Lara, flushed with heat and embarrassment, was able to step down from the platform. She had yet to receive the final cheque for her work. Helen, acting as her agent, had insisted on a down-payment for Lara when she was commissioned to do the work and Lara had seen her heavy eyebrows twitch at Jeff Sakala's joke.

Bill and Maria were smiling at her from across the reception hall. Bill gestured with an inviting glass of white wine. Lara's parents were occupied with a British diplomat, so she wriggled, wangled and excused her way through the crowd to join her friends. They had cornered a space by the French doors that opened onto a central courtyard. A fountain splashed and gurgled in its half-finished garden next to a stack of cement and scaffolding under plastic sheeting. Maria, dressed in a white kaftan with a bead-worked yoke, looked by contrast thinner and more sunburnt than when she was in the bush. Bill was wearing a new safari suit that had become rumpled and stained with grease in the short journey from their town flat to the bank. Lara thought they looked out of place in the air-conditioned metal and glass environment but they appeared not to mind and were enjoying an animated conversation with two men whom Lara had not seen before. The group of four stood out, an eccentric group, noticeable by their lighter skins and informal attire among the dark suits, richly embroidered African outfits and glittering jewelled cocktail dresses. The younger man was curiously attired in a casual jacket over jeans, together with a bush shirt and tie. His nose and wide mouth were rather too large for his thin face and he had a small red graze on one side of his temple. One earpiece of his spectacles had been fastened back onto the frame with a piece of sticking plaster. Lara noticed that, while he had none of Jason's physical beauty, his expression, alive with interest in his companions and in the surroundings, gave him an attractive gracefulness of manner.

The older man wore an immaculate light-coloured linen suit over an expensive pink shirt. A handkerchief peeked from the top pocket of his jacket. He had no tie but its lack added to, rather than diminished, his air of confident authority and quiet good taste. He was perhaps fifty, his well-cut hair grizzled at the temples. Lara imagined that her mother would think him handsome. Something in his regard put her on her mettle. She wondered what he did – what line of business he was in.

"Lara, this is Oscar Mynhardt." said Maria, waving at the older man.

The man Mum says I mustn't sell to! Lara thought, amused.

"And this is Tim Weston." Bill grinned at the younger man.

Tim turned to meet Lara, holding out his hand.

"Hello," he said smiling, "Nice to meet you. Congratulations on your work. Looks good!"

"Sorry about this -" his hands waved around brushing his clothes.

"The minibus I was in crashed and in the confusion someone nicked my rucksack. What I am wearing is going to have to cover every situation for me in the next few days – it's all I have."

Lara laughed.

"Its looks as if it will do just that – perhaps you can even start a new fashion trend!"

Oscar too held out his hand towards Lara but he also leant forward and kissed her lightly on both cheeks.

"Oscar!" Maria tipped her head at Lara, "Don't be so continental! This is Chambeshi not France!"

"He's a dreadful ladies' man, Lara." she warned with a teasing glance at Oscar.

"It is lovely to meet you, Lara." Oscar said, smiling first at her and then at Maria. His rather fleshy mouth was flexible with a humorous twist at its corners. "Tim and I have heard all about you from Bill and Maria – I like your paintings very much. Please will you tell us about them – as soon as you have a chance that is – do relax first – these social dos are hard work."

"Thank you and – of course I will."

Lara shot him a quizzical look. He did not appear to find social events taxing. She had several different levels at which she explained her art to casual acquaintances. How likely was it that Oscar or Tim would have any grounding in art appreciation? A few minutes, an indeterminate 'ah' or 'ooh' and the business would be over, but as the bank lobby was so crowded, that brief moment could wait.

Lara smiled and glanced at Oscar. She wondered why she hadn't met him before. He was about the age of her parents and they knew pretty nearly every white resident in the town. He wasn't particularly good-looking but in a subtle way he radiated an energy that made it hard not to feel that he was the centre of the group.

She turned deliberately to Tim.

"Why are you in Chambeshi?" she asked.

"Journalist – trying to write about mining and economic development in this part of Africa. Contacted Oscar – friend of a friend – he offered to put me up and – introduce me to people – that's why we came – to this do." Tim was struggling to cope with an over-full vol-au-vent and a bottle of beer. At even the grandest occasions in Chambeshi men drank their beer from the bottle.

"Oh," Lara was surprised. She thought her father knew everyone in Chambeshi who had any connections with mining. Why had she not heard of Oscar?

"Are you with the Chambeshi Mining Company too, like my Dad?"

Oscar's face creased in a smile.

"Oscar owns a gold mine." Bill interjected, grinning. "Small and defunct I believe."

"Yes – worked out pretty much." confirmed Oscar, "I keep the machinery in working order but the seam is exhausted. It's not economic to develop it further – it's close to the Kasama River and is always in danger of flooding.

"I am busy with other more interesting projects for the area around it. Bill and Maria are telling me how to go about setting up a base camp for a safari business."

"Competition for you?" Lara widened her eyes at Bill.

"Not really." he said, "It's a different part of the National Park in any case. In fact we all do better when there are more choices for tourists and we share some advertising and other related costs."

"We would love you to come back and work with us again, Lara." Maria said, "What are the chances now you are doing well with your art? Jason's left us you know. He's moved to a bigger safari outfit in Zimbabwe."

"If the bank does actually pay me I should be able to concentrate on my painting, but I will need to keep coming back to the bush for inspiration. Would you have me work with you for a shorter time or wouldn't that work?"

"You could choose" Bill said, "Come and help set up the camp when we don't have guests – or come and work with guests at the peak period. Either would suit."

"Right, here we go." said Oscar, "there's a space. Come and show us your paintings. Go ahead, Tim." He deftly nudged Tim ahead of him and with his hand lightly on Lara's back, he steered her through the thinning crowd to the paintings.

"Ah well -" Lara smiled at the two men, "Here we are – but first tell us what you make of them yourself." She had become used to discussing these particular paintings at the bank and felt relaxed.

Tim stepped up scanning the three canvases with quick movements of his head and eyes. Oscar studied them more slowly, the corners of his eyes slightly crinkled, his chin up a fraction. Once or twice he looked at Lara. Brief as his glance was, Lara felt the intensity of his regard and it angered her and made her feel exposed in some intimate way that was not to do with nakedness. Lara waited. Instead of immediately asking her for explanations both men spent time really studying the canvases. That made it feel important that they should each like her work and think it, at the least, good enough.

Lara, standing behind them, could at last manage to look at the three paintings with a sense of detachment. She had titled the three together "Chambeshi Triptych" and each painting dealt with the themes of Farm, Wilderness and City. Yes. She could feel proud of them but they had given her lots of problems with both the context and the techniques she had chosen. Tim turned to Lara. He said in admiration

"You can draw. You've captured the movement and the life of the market, the animals in the bush are wonderful, and the farmer ploughing with oxen has a very interesting viewpoint. Obviously the bank wanted positive images of Chambeshi. How much freedom did they actually allow you in the way you treated the subjects? It doesn't look too censored and all three have tremendous energy."

With a quick look around to see who was listening, Lara answered. "I didn't get censored because no one expected me to do anything that might need censoring and no one really has a clue about art or what I was doing. I did get lots of suggestions from Mr Sakala at first. Instead of the wilderness he wanted the President's Zoo – and the President." She grinned. "Helen saved me. She pointed out that the President was very proud of the National Game Reserve – she also told me to be careful how I portrayed people – idealism rather than realism would be expected of me – all commissions must be a bit like that I suppose. I thought I would hate it but I enjoyed the challenge and artists can always find a way to say the things they want to in the way they want to."

A sudden thought occurred to Lara. She put her hand to her mouth. "Oh God! You're not going to print what I say in your paper are you?"

Tim shook his head and grinned at her. "You're safe from me – unless your paintings are used for money-laundering."

Oscar looked sharply at Tim then spoke to Lara.

"Helen says that you do a lot of your work in ink and watercolour. This is oil – and some acrylic isn't it? I like the way you have kept the liveliness of the drawn line – is that oil stick? Even with the intensity of your colours you have a sense of light and air in all three paintings. It reminds me of some German Expressionists – and the Fauves. Tell me about your process here."

Lara had attempted the wildlife painting last because she expected that it would give her the fewest problems but it turned out that the market scene had been the easiest to finish. The scale was human and full of life and colour, but then she often visited the market. Lara needed to connect the paintings to each other with visual and colour relationships. The traditional farming scene had been completely new for her as a subject but she had enjoyed that challenge. The market and the farm related back to the wilderness, but the horizontal wilderness was vast and the vertical city huge. The scale of the city against the farm and the market might appear disproportionate. In the end, returning to the wildlife painting had been hardest of all. How could she make the wilderness fit in with the modern world Mr Sakala wanted to see?

Finally Lara had resorted to repeating themes in each painting to give them visual continuity. The city scene and the wilderness were connected by the same stormy sky of towering thunderheads and brilliant light. The city and the storm appeared in the distance of the farming scene. The farmer's wife stood centre in the market with the produce of her garden. She explained all this to Oscar who listened intently while scrutinising the paintings.

"All three paintings have the same sky but from different

viewpoints. I imagined I was sitting on a hill or hovering in the air like an eagle and able to see for miles. As I turn from the south through east, north and west the light and shadows change direction but the rainstorm and the thunderhead are always there, though seen from a different angle."

"For the farming scene I drew a farmer guiding an ox plough, his wife hoeing the maize in the foreground. In the middle distance is a combine harvester on a commercial farm. On the horizon the skyscrapers of the city are white against the iron grey of the approaching storm. I was worried that the storm might look as if it threatened the city. I meant it as renewal and hope and thank goodness Mr Sakala saw it that way too. The city painting I centred on the farmer's wife at the market with the skyscrapers close behind and I did sneak in a beggar, a thief and some street kids though they appear as part of the crowd. I struggled to avoid making the wildlife painting trite and obvious by having the obligatory elephant and lion. I focussed on the way the wild creatures are part of their environment and how the whole environment makes all human life possible."

"Well Jeff Sakala is happy with it." Oscar continued to look at the work. I told him he had done well to commission you. It works very well in this space too. Made for it."

"It was made for it." Lara laughed, "I was expected to fit in with the architect's plan for the colour scheme."

"Was that Ahmed Patel by any chance?" Oscar asked mentioning the name of an architect in Chambeshi with the best reputation and the highest fees. "I hope he was sympathetic and helpful."

"Yes – luckily for me – he went to Helen Ioannou to discuss which artist to recommend to the bank and both Ahmed and Helen were really kind and supportive. They suggested me to Jeff Sakala and helped me with my portfolio for the job. I had no idea that a commission could be so demanding."

"Ah – Helen is the art doyen of Chambeshi. Without her we would only be a Wild West frontier town!"

Oscar turned to look directly at Lara. "Perhaps you will make some paintings for my new office."

He smiled, "It will be a demanding commission too."

Lara smiled back. She expected that she would cope with his commission if she had to, and in any case it would have to interest her before she accepted it.

"Who are your influences?" Tim wanted to know, "Do you like African artists and traditions? Have you seen Malagantana – the Mozambican artist – and the Nigerian artists like Twins Seven Seven?"

"Let me guess." said Oscar, "I think your influences are more European – I think you must like the Fauves for colour, Matisse and Joan Miró for line perhaps? Your use of colour is lovely and it looks as if you understand its abstract qualities. These are lovely, Lara – you must be proud."

"Oh thank you!" Lara was delighted, "Thank you – honestly – I really worried that that the work was becoming rather superficial with all the fuss about the bank's concerns and the colour of the carpet – I worried that if my paintings worked for the bank they would feel too commercial to me."

"No, they aren't at all." Tim said, "Is this what you usually do?"

"It's what I have usually done since leaving art school." said Lara laughing, "I think it is too soon at my age to have a fixed style or even be sure of where I am going."

"We are booked at the Kudu Grill for a meal. My partner, Enoch Njobvu, is already there." said Oscar, "That's Tim, Bill, Maria, me and now of course you and Helen as well. Let's get going. We can make plans to see your studio when we are all sitting down and relaxing."

Tim grinned and raised his hands in a gesture of acceptance.

"We are organised then! Let's go Oscar!"

Chapter Two

Jane and Brian

At home the next day, Lara told Jane and Brian about the restaurant meal.

"Oscar and his partner Enoch paid for everyone. Oscar said he was taking Bill and Maria out as his business consultants, Tim was his guest anyway and he wants me to make paintings for his new lodge at the Tin Heart Camp, so I was also there for business. The food was fabulous – giant tiger prawns and smoked salmon mousse."

"Are you going to the Tin Heart Camp to make the paintings?" Jane asked, her face unusually stiff. Brian avoided Jane's eyes.

"Has a few too many fingers in too many pies, does Oscar." he said and changed the object of the discussion to Tim. "What's that chap Tim doing here? Strange outfit he was wearing. Must be your age I suppose."

"Being my age explains his weird clothes, does it?" Lara answered, "Tim's suitcase was stolen off the minibus he was on when it crashed. He's working for a London newspaper. He is a bit too tall to find his size in the shops here – have you got something to lend him Dad?"

Unaccountably her father's words about Oscar made her remember the feel of his hand on her back. She had been aware of his hands again as he refilled her wine glass at the table and offered her the cheese board.

"At home I like to have cheese before the dessert – as the French do." Oscar had said.

Oscar's hands were not soft and white like Brian's or thick and work-damaged like Bill's. They were long-fingered, smooth and hard and moved with an exact and delicate precision. She had avoided looking at them and avoided looking too long at Oscar's face also. Strange – it wasn't as if he had touched her again or looked more at her than at the others in their group.

"Oh I don't know if Oscar will follow up on paintings for Tin Heart Camp." Lara said, "But Bill and Maria say I can work for them in town before their season starts – I would like that!"

Later that day Lara heard her parents arguing. She thought Jane shrieked out Oscar's name but Brian was making shushing noises so she walked away quickly. She didn't want to know more.

Chapter Three

Tim

Tim came around to see Lara the day after her exhibition opening. He had phoned first, spoken to Jane and made her laugh as he explained his lost clothes.

"Oscar's flown off to somewhere in Europe – long-standing business meeting he told me. But he's so generous – he's lent me a vehicle and told me I can stay on in his guest wing. Fantastic – Oscar has a fax-machine and phones that work – I am made – I really am. I get so sick of having to stay in hotels. I can work from Oscar's place."

Over the next few weeks, Lara found that Tim was great fun to have around. He was so interested in everything and was so good at drawing people out and making them talk and divulge interesting and surprising facts about themselves and their lives and their work. He even increased Lara's interest in African politics. It was not a surprise that Tim's perspectives were wider than those of Lara's parents. Lara loved complexities and problem-solving so when Tim talked about all the confusing conflicts of Africa, Lara could relate them to the problems of development that she had become aware of in Chambeshi. Her commission for the Sakala Bank had been complex.

"The bank commission I did for Jeff Sakala was an eye-opener for me" Lara said. "What I depicted in the actual paintings had to please everybody from the President's office and cabinet to the bank workers. There were various diplomats and aid agencies that had to be soothed because the bank wanted their accounts. Everybody's uncle, brother and auntie wanted the bank to commission an artist they knew who had connections in trade or exports. Luckily for me I had Helen to do all the wheeling and dealing – I had to paint, that was all. I'm beginning to get the "picture" of how things work in Chambeshi."

Lara wiggled her fingers by her ears as she said "picture" and they both smiled.

Tim had made no secret of the fact that he wanted to interview her father, Brian, about his job. "Do you think your Dad could get me introductions to the big-wigs here? The important Chambeshians who are in the mining business? My special field of research this trip is mining and economics and how that pans out politically."

Lara liked Tim's open acknowledgement of his own motives for what he did and want he wanted. She hadn't encountered many people who were that frank and fewer people who had much insight into their own personalities. Liseli tried to be honest but she was so complex that she often confused Lara by her self-analysis. With Tim, Lara felt that she didn't have to pretend that she was a nice person. Even while he understood how selfish her personal artistic ambitions were he would still remain a friend.

Tim's conversations with her father taught Lara facts about her father's life and work that she had never known or been told. She also discovered that Brian and Jane had once known Oscar socially though it was clear that they didn't have anything to do with him now.

"Interesting man, Oscar," Tim said, "Self-made. Arrived here in Chambeshi from South Africa, had a job in the Rand mines there, served a short time with the Police Force over the Independence period, worked here for a chap who imported cars and ran an upmarket garage. Took it over in a very short space of time, made it even more successful, became good friends with Marcus Chona, the current president of Chambeshi, got these mining rights and does 'Business' of a rather nebulous sort. Entertaining and charming though – don't you think Lara? And very cultured – likes music and art."

Lara put her head on one side and considered the idea of Oscar and culture.

"Cultured! What does that mean? I don't think I am very 'cultured' even though I paint. I don't know all that much about art and music really. How is Oscar cultured? It kind-of sounds as if he has been all smoothed over in a tasteful way and always does the right thing."

Tim shook his head at Lara.

"Wow – you sound defensive! Yes I guess it's sloppy of me to use such a cliché to describe Oscar. I suppose I meant that Oscar is a discriminating person and appears to really enjoy beautiful things – he is definitely not smooth though – suave – I don't know – likeable – yes – manipulative – maybe."

Lara wished she could think of Oscar in the same detached fashion that everyone seemed to judge him by. She felt as if he had put a special mark on her that connected the two of them. Did she think him attractive? No, she didn't – yes, she did – he was an old man – as old as her parents – but he wasn't creepy like James, the operations manager in her father's office. Oscar was just too old and too experienced for her somehow. She felt he knew things about herself that she didn't know and that she didn't want him to tell her either. She had liked Oscar when she met him and he had not singled her out from her friends on that evening. Nevertheless something very tiny stirred just below her breastbone when she thought of him – a soft almost imperceptible moth-like flutter under her heart. The light touch of his hand on her back had left an imprint that had seeped through her skin and entered her bloodstream. She was glad he had vanished so suddenly and that she could relax in Tim's company. She could see that Tim liked her and found her attractive. That was flattering, but she felt safe with Tim. He was so unselfconscious and indifferent to his very ordinary appearance. He was also very outspoken about his hopeless inability to make relationships last because his work did not let him stay in one place for very long.

"I'm a travelling man." he said, his eyes alight, his grin wide. "Will you be my girlfriend when I'm here Lara?" "Got a girlfriend in every city in Africa. You can be mine here in Chambeshi City if you like Lara – but I wouldn't advise it – we journalists are heartless people."

"I'll make a decision on your next visit, Tim." Lara offered Tim lightly. "In the meantime you can take me out to the club barbecue tonight. There will be lots of interesting people there to give you the low-down on Chambeshi politics."

So their relationship continued. Tim came around for lunch and a swim fairly regularly but he worked hard writing up his many interviews and filing his reports for his editor back in London. Lara spent time in her studio working for the one-person show in the Umodzi Gallery that Helen had promised to give her. She was not working on any commissions so she was free to develop her own ideas for her paintings. Helen pursed her lips a little at Lara's plans to make fewer paintings of wild-life.

"No and yes." she said. "It will be lovely to have original work that's different and good if it is a bit more challenging but also promise me some drawings that are easy to sell. I still have to pay rent and staff salaries from the sales, you know."

Tim took Lara round to Oscar's home for lunch one day.

"You should see Oscar's Kasenga Ranch, Lara. He has quite a collection of paintings – some German expressionists and a couple of naïve Yugoslav artists as well as a good selection of local artists. It's a beautiful house – I think that architect, Patel or whatever, designed it. He has a small farm. He also has his own runway and his own light aircraft."

"He won't be there, will he?" Lara asked, and was both relieved and disappointed to hear that Oscar was now in Berlin.

"East Berlin, would you believe!" Tim grinned. Lara needed to be reminded of what that meant.

"Communist East Berlin," she repeated, "Why? What possible business can he have there? Isn't he a really successful capitalist businessman?"

That much she understood about the difference between East and West Germany.

"No idea," replied Tim, "I mean to find out, though! Come to his place and you can get to know his partner and business manager – Enoch Njobvu – he's a really good bloke. You'll like him."

Lara found it strange to be shown around Oscar's living room. She felt as if she was an intruder into a private space. At the same time she had a curious feeling that she was being given a preview of a future life connected with Oscar and she gave herself a quick admonishing shrug.

Stupid Lara! she told herself, surprised.

She had as yet no ambition to marry and had never thought about being rich and living in a big house with designer furniture and art everywhere even though that was her mother's deepest desire. Jane was always planning makeovers for her home and exclaiming over home and garden magazines. Odd, but seeing Oscar's house made Lara feel closer to him in a way that she couldn't understand. Was it his taste in art that made her feel sympathetic to him? At the same time she resented the feeling of being manipulated by something outside her experience and control.

Tim, Lara and Enoch Njobvu had a lunch of salads and cold meats outside on the big veranda overlooking the pool. They could see in the far distance to the north-west the first swelling slopes of the lower escarpment riding up into a ridge of rugged hills before it fell away into the great river valley and the Chambeshi nature reserve.

"You can't see so far to the escarpment in the winter months when it is dusty and hazy," Enoch said, "Beautiful now though, isn't it – and so green."

Enoch turned politely to Lara.

"You must meet my wife, Inonge – you would like each other. She's on a shopping trip in London right now. My son is at medical school there."

Enoch was a quietly spoken man with a gentle manner. His skin was so dark that it seemed to absorb light. When he sat on the veranda with his back to the sun it was hard to distinguish his features but Lara noticed that he had the heavy brows, straight nose and thin lips more common in the north of Chambeshi. Lara found him very likeable. He spoke of Oscar as his friend rather than his partner.

"You have known Oscar a long time?" probed Tim.

"Yes," Enoch answered, "We served together in the 1966 emergency just after Independence. We became friends then. Oscar saved my life."

"Oscar told me you saved his life – what actually did happen?" Tim asked.

Enoch smiled. "It was perhaps mutual – one good turn deserved another. The two of us were on a reconnaissance mission and were ambushed and cut off from our unit. I suffered a spear wound in my leg and Oscar refused to leave me. The people who surrounded us were poor rural people armed with traditional weapons but they were a very numerous group. We could not have shot our way out of that situation and in we were trying to negotiate a peaceful solution by traditional methods. We had to do much talking –"Enoch shook his head and his voice went higher as he did so. "Much, much talking and only I spoke the language. It was a very complicated situation. Since those days I know I can trust Oscar with my life."

"What was that fighting about?" Lara asked, "My family wasn't in Chambeshi then."

"It was a religious sect led by a woman priestess with a large tribal following that threatened to disrupt the handover from Britain to President Chona. It was a messy business – a compromise couldn't be reached. Religious fanaticism made it impossible. I don't know what else could have been done." Enoch shook his head again slowly and sadly.

"That kind of unrest is long gone, isn't it?" Lara asked.

"It seems so." Enoch said, "Since independence Chambeshi is not so troubled by those kinds of tribal rivalry. Further north in the Congo there is still a lot of fear and conflict."

"Impossible to exploit the mines there as a result." Tim said, "I understand they have much richer resources of precious gems there as well as cobalt, caesium and platinum."

Lara raised her eyebrows intelligently and bit her tongue in case she said anything silly. She might learn by listening. This was Tim's area of special interest. She had never been told anything by her father about the mining industry in Africa and didn't think her mother had been either.

Tim, with his engaging interest in everyone, was good at drawing out confidences from the people he met. He loved to gossip and laugh about what he learnt from them too. He would give long amused and amusing explanations but he never seemed to dislike his sources or to judge them very harshly. Lara was fascinated and intrigued. As they drove back to Lara's home after their visit to Oscar's ranch Lara asked him about the risks that gathering such knowledge posed for Tim.

"Ought you to say that, Tim? Isn't it also dangerous to write about it? Won't you be sued for libel – or barred from coming back to Chambeshi?"

"Oh – don't worry." Tim replied, "I do censor what I write – and so does my editor. I have a personal interest in leaving every country I visit alive, but then one day – who knows – I'll write that book – or that history – or that memoir. I'm not employed to write personal stories – I just enjoy knowing them. I am supposed to write about economics and politics, you know, mines and banks and how in Africa everything fails."

"Does it really – always? Is it so bad here?"

"Right now the West has a vested interest in Africa either failing or staying as their allies. They would rather have failing allies than successful enemies obviously – but with Africa's immense problems and lack of infrastructure, who knows if it isn't all down to chance? Journalists, I am ashamed to say, get more approval for reporting the negative stories than the positive ones. It's safer to do that in this cynical world."

Tim shrugged, then ventured, "Oscar is rumoured to have been a very influential person during the early days of President Chona's government but no one will say exactly how or what it was he did. Maybe they were just friends? President Chona is a sociable sort of chap."

"You should go to Tin Heart Camp, Lara, and have a look around – invite me too; I would love to see it. Do you know that it is actually like a little separate state inside Chambeshi?"

"What on earth do you mean?" Lara demanded. Oscar sounded more and more interesting to her.

"At the start of the new Chambeshi Republic there was a small working goldmine there. The owner, a really unusual Afrikaner called Jannie Oosthuizen, was totally committed to African independence, and he financed Chona during the Freedom Struggle – as they like to call it. Actually, after relatively minimal resistance the colonial powers were desperate to hand back power they couldn't exploit or control. After Independence Chona rewarded him with full land rights and exemption from tax in perpetuity, a tiny tax haven if you like, a mini-Andorra in Africa. It didn't mean anything in real terms – the mine was failing – you couldn't run casinos in the middle of nowhere when life itself is a gamble, but it was what traditional Afrikaners have always dreamed of – a stateless state answerable to no one but God."

"What an incredible story!" Lara squeezed her eyes shut and opened them wide again. "How did Oscar get to own it then?"

"Murder probably," said Tim, then seeing Lara's shock, he laughed, "No. I made that up! I don't know, but I do mean to find out!"

Turning to Lara and momentarily serious, he said, "Lara – do be careful of Oscar – really careful! He is so likeable and you can see Enoch trusts him but there are stories – many stories. I think a lot of the stories may be jealousy – or because he is the apocryphal outsider – he has a German name and in a community of British expats that makes him an object of interest. That bitchy woman who runs the Sports Club says things about him and his sister that you wouldn't believe."

"His sister! I didn't know he has a sister. What things?" Lara knew Jacqueline, the Sports Club manager so appropriately described as a bitch by Tim. Jacqueline had implied things about Lara and Jason and the Safari camp clients that had caused a row between Lara and her mother.

"It's sad," Tim said, no longer smiling, "Oscar's sister died of cancer about 13 years ago. She never got rid of her German accent and she seems to have been very reclusive. Jacqueline implied that her relationship with Oscar was too close by half by which I suppose she meant incestuous – Jacqueline is very poisonous."

Lara was silent.

As time passed by, Lara could not help but think of Oscar. She was often at his house with Tim. By the end of a month she knew where in his kitchen Oscar kept both the local coffee beans and grinder and the imported leaf tea and teapot. Both she and Tim counted Enoch as a friend and Lara had spent some hours studying the paintings in Oscar's collection and she knew which ones she liked and why. Lara had also gained an education from both Enoch and Tim about Chambeshi's history and its current political situation. Tim said there was increasing discontent with the economic situation and cost of the staple food. President Chona was being blamed for the corruption rife among Chambeshi's bureaucrats.

She wanted to return to the story about Oscar's sister but learnt little from Tim and did have enough courtesy not to ask Enoch about her. That would have seemed like prying and she would have been ashamed.

Chapter Four

Friends

"Tim is so intelligent." Jane said to Lara one day over breakfast. "You do like him more than Jason, Lara, don't you?"

"Mum!" Lara was mildly exasperated, "They are such different people – you can't make a comparison." She knew what Jane wanted to know and had no intention of telling her. Jane persisted, this time more directly.

"So is he your boyfriend then, Lara?"

"Mum!" Lara was irritated. "Tim is only here for a few more months. He spends his whole life travelling to quite dangerous places and he doesn't even have a place of his own – he stays with friends all the time even when he is in London! We are not getting engaged! We are not girlfriend and boyfriend – we are just friends! That's all!" Then she added sarcastically, "I am surprised that you think he is right for me!"

"Oh!" Jane was hurt and angry, "You are old enough to settle into a proper relationship, Lara – you are almost 25 now." Jane pushed her plate of toast aside then suddenly she was shrieking at Lara and stuttering. "Don't – Don't – don't ever get involved with Oscar Mynhardt – just don't!"

Lara stood up, picked up her cup of coffee, and, without looking back at Jane, she stamped off to her studio in the garage. Of course she could not settle down to paint after that exchange. What was it about anyway? Was Jane jealous of her? Was that really likely? Was it about Oscar? Her parents didn't seem to know him that well so why?

What did she want from her life?

She knew that if she gave Tim any encouragement they would end up sleeping together. She missed having sex. It had been such exciting and satisfying fun with Jason and she had been so blind and so in love with him and with the bush. Jason wasn't an experienced or subtle lover, but mutual desire, sexual energy and physical stamina had been all that they needed for pleasure. Lara had felt humiliated by the end of the relationship but hindsight taught her that it would not have lasted. If Jason wasn't talking about wild-life and conservation he was rather uninteresting. She had grown up and grown out of the relationship before it ended.

At school and art school her contemporaries had discussed marriage and sex and decided that the two didn't necessarily go together. Children might be another thing, but no one could imagine what it would be like to have a family and to be responsible for it. Though her girlfriends said they were feminists, most of them secretly hoped to get married to someone decent and stable so that they could bring up children who would be 'better' and 'happier' than they felt they were. None of the boys planned on settling down while sex was apparently so easy to come by. Well – easy for their friends, if not for themselves. If a boy had a girlfriend, he felt possessive about her while their sex was new. Then he felt uncertain about her as soon as the balance between the emotional relationship and sexual desire altered. At least it seemed to Lara that that was how men and boys behaved in their relationships.

Lara's body ached for sex but, as she did not feel that her desire was for any particular person, she felt she was somehow betraying her idea of herself. Women, she understood vaguely, did not have unfocussed sexual feelings. That at least was the wisdom of women's literature and magazines and what girls quoted to each other under the guise of their own experience. It was what Jane, her mother, hinted at constantly. Men on the other hand were given to such strong sexual urges that they could not easily be contained. Women had to avoid arousing men's passions unless they wanted to suffer the inevitable consequences that would follow – whatever they might be – rape or pregnancy? Sexual feelings for a woman, she was led to believe, were supposed to arise from an emotional and physical attraction to another person who would, of course, be a man. Lara's friend Gillian didn't fit into any of these scenarios – or did she? She was the dominant 'butch' and Poppy, her girlfriend, was submissive, so presumably women could be one or the other. Lara sighed at the idea of being either.

It was inconvenient to have a body that ached to be touched, ached obsessively for orgasm and then left her ashamed when she masturbated. Her body's demands made it hard to concentrate on her work in the studio. Maybe it was irrational but she was afraid that overwhelming sexual desire would gradually make her into some version of a man.

Tim's friendship mattered a great deal to her and while she did not want to risk losing it, she knew that their relationship was close to tipping over into a physical one with all the risks and complications that that must bring. To avoid what looked otherwise to be inescapable – another sexual relationship that could not possibly last, she allowed herself to indulge in unrealisable and undefined sexual fantasies about Oscar. That helped until she became afraid that she might have discovered another problem. One secret night she masturbated until she achieved an exquisite long-lasting orgasm. As she reached the agonising thrill of climax, her body astonished her by a burst of fluid from her vagina that perfected and completed the sensation. She knew that it was the best orgasm she had ever had. She even understood that it was normal, right and not perverse, but at the same time it didn't fit with all her received knowledge about women and sex. As her breathing slowed, she noticed she was lying on a damp sheet so there must have been a significant amount of liquid. What was that wetness from? What did it consist of? Lara put her hand down into the moisture and then sniffed at it. It wasn't pee. It smelt clean. She licked her finger – it tasted of nothing particular. She rubbed at her sheets. It would have been embarrassing to have to change them but luckily it was summer and they would dry easily on the bed and it seemed likely that they would not smell of anything.

There was still the question of how she, Lara, was to understand herself and her body?

She was sorry, not for the first time, that she hadn't accepted Gillian's invitation at art school to join her women's group and discuss the intimacies of the female body and female sexuality. At the time she suspected that the discussions might have led on to more practical experiments and even emotional commitments to some female person or some feminist cause that she didn't feel was all that relevant to her. It wasn't only a lack of curiosity and even some prissiness that had stopped her, but also a desire to keep her focus on her art. There was something too demanding and personal in the way in which Gillian, her eyes hot and intense, had looked at her when she had tried to persuade her to come to the group. Lara sighed. She knew that if she had joined Gillian's group she would have probably taken other decisions on leaving art school but all she had wanted then was to get back to the heat and familiarity of Chambeshi.

If only she could ask Gillian now. Or Liseli.

Some of the women's group discussions had continued on into the shared space of the student kitchen. Had she not heard one of Gillian's more attention-seeking girlfriends mention G-spots and female ejaculation? Was that what she had just done? Ejaculated? It wasn't even a word she liked though perhaps she could get used to it as it had been so pleasant. Most of the group's conversation however had been about male exploitation of and domination of women. That part hadn't bothered or interested Lara much. It didn't enter into her personal experience of life. She had never felt dominated or exploited. Lying stretched out on her bed, guiltily but delightfully relaxed, Lara spared a moment to think of her mother, Jane. What did Jane know about sex that she had not told her daughter – or perhaps would not tell Lara? They had discussed menstruation and pregnancy and, of course, contraception. Lara had continued to take the pill after she and Jason had stopped sleeping together. Lately she had begun to worry if it was bad for her. She could ask Jane but if she did then Jane would know that though she didn't have a boyfriend she was still hoping to find another. Did Jane even have sex? Children were supposed to be disgusted at the idea of their parents having sex but the abstract idea of that did not bother Lara. It was more difficult to imagine her parents approaching each other for intimacy after the cool bitchiness with which they rather often spoke to each other at mealtimes. What did any other person think about sex anyway? You could not tell by looking at people's faces. It was extraordinary to think that every person was the result of a sexual act and that everyone surely, or nearly everyone, was at some moment in their lives going to be engaged in the rhythmic pumping with another body that would end in the gasping climax of the sex act.

"God!" Lara thought," I am really fixated on sex aren't I? Why does sex interest me so much? Am I normal?"

"No," she added to herself a moment later. "Of course I am normal – and actually rather a boring self-centred person."

With a little embarrassed groan Lara turned on her stomach and buried her face in her pillow as she remembered the sex that she had shared with Ajay in their second year at art school. It hadn't been great but then they weren't in love or even very attracted to each other. It was more a relationship driven by curiosity about difference and a need for sex without social complications or commitment. It wasn't Lara's first experience of sexual intercourse. That had taken place in her last year at school with a boy called Floyd. It had been a surprise to Lara. The immediate experience was so physically wonderful and exciting, but it had been so brief and left her at the end unfulfilled.

"That's because you didn't have a proper orgasm." Liseli had explained later.

The affair had ended by being annoying because Floyd did not know how to behave afterwards. Neither, Lara conceded, did he know what he felt. He no longer looked her in the face when they spoke to each other but Lara knew that he stared at her when he thought she wouldn't notice. When he moved on to another relationship Lara found herself relieved rather than humiliated. Afterwards she and Liseli had agreed it was better to sleep with a man who was at least 25 years old and a great deal more grown-up. Lara pulled an ugly face at herself in the mirror.

"Fancy imagining that any man would be grown-up at 25."

She was almost that now and though she didn't feel very grown-up she had a good idea that she was a great deal more mature than most young men her age. Jason had not proved too wise about relationships, had he?

"If only Liseli were here now." wished Lara, feeling alone. "I need a girlfriend who knows all about sex and knows the men I know."

At art school she had avoided sex at first because she had felt alienated from the other students. One morning Lara and Ajay had found themselves in the residence when there were no other students about. Lara invited Ajay into her room for a mug of coffee and they perched awkwardly side by side on her bed as her desk chair was covered with a pile of Lara's intimate laundry. They found themselves silent and unable to speak a word. Somehow the unspoken words expressed themselves in actual kisses then abruptly, Ajay grabbed at Lara and with a helpless cry fell against her knocking her backwards flat onto her bed. Lara had no idea what it was for a man to ejaculate prematurely but she understood Ajay's desperate need and embarrassed shyness. She took him gently in her arms to comfort him and in a remarkably short time he was erect again and they were lying naked together on Lara's bed enjoying a much more successful sexual encounter.

They had continued for quite a long time afterwards to have sex with each other as secretly as possible. Again by another unspoken understanding they did not go out together socially where they could be identified as a couple. Ajay was not ready to confront his family and Lara did not want to explain to her friends that their relationship was primarily sexual. Nevertheless they liked each other and were tender in their sexual intimacy.

Lara had told Liseli about it when they were on university vacation in Chambeshi. Liseli was approving.

"It's really good to have a relationship that is just about sex if you can. The trouble is that most guys like to own you and show you off – or slag you off – one or the other!"

Yes – Lara wished Liseli was around to offer advice and support.

Unexpectedly Liseli arrived back in Chambeshi but she was in a rather fragile and excitable state having apparently quit her well-paid job. Lara was at first delighted to have her friend and confidante close by again and they soon had their heads together over long glasses of cola and ice on the Hotel Sunshine Everyday veranda.

"Oh yeah!" Liseli said in answer to Lara's questions. "Female ejaculation does happen for some women but you need to be a randy woman and uninhibited – but stuff men – I mean honestly – just do it to yourself and then you don't have to pretend to please a man!" She added, "But I thought by now that you and Tim would be living together or something – he's much more your type than Jason. Jason well – he is dishy maybe, but dim in ways that matter. You're an artist Lara for God's sake – aren't you supposed to be promiscuous and unfaithful and just taking your pleasure wherever you want!"

"That's men artists!" Lara said attempting to be sardonic, "This is Africa remember – you have to look out for AIDS and disease – can't just enjoy yourself. Look at my mother – there is so much work in pleasing men – you have to keep cooking meals and dressing yourself up – they just wander round in shorts and casual clothes and eat."

"And fuck." said Liseli.

"Well – it's true." Lara admitted a short time later. "I do like Tim but we just don't seem to want it with each other – it would have to be so part-time – and if everything keeps changing I can't concentrate on my work."

"Have you met Oscar again?" Liseli raised an expressive eyebrow. "I could fancy a rich sugar-daddy like him – but you do wonder about men his age who aren't married – something wrong or weird or just different? He doesn't seem to be gay – at least he isn't a bit camp but I think you can tell by the way a man looks at you as a woman don't you? I think Oscar has hot eyes when he looks at a woman."

The idea of Oscar's hot eyes made Lara and Liseli giggle like schoolgirls.

Liseli continued.

"Well maybe he's got a girlfriend in Europe somewhere – my father said he saw him in a restaurant in Berlin with a gorgeous blond girl. He is supposed to have had affairs with all the expatriate wives here -" Liseli stopped and gave a quick glance at Lara before continuing, "but that is just a rumour – maybe he is gay or like the priest Abelard – you know castrated because of his love for Heloise."

Lara attempted to speak in a bass register. "His voice is too deep for him to be castrated. I haven't met him since that first dinner – but he does interest me -" Lara pulled a face. "I don't know why. Perhaps he just seems different – like he might know about things that I don't – I do want to have experiences and learn about life and strange things -"

"God! Pain and broken hearts stuff, you mean! We all have that anyway without asking." Liseli's face was very still for a moment. "I expect Oscar could give you that – men with his big nose and thick eyebrows can look really cruel don't you think?"

"No-o – can't say he seemed cruel to me." Lara reflected. "But maybe it's cruelty I want to understand – you know – in the bush – life is cruel and dangerous. We say it's beautiful but its more than that – it's dangerous and raw. I mean – even here with all the people dying from AIDS – life is cruel, isn't it? Sometimes I think that my paintings are just so bland and nice – I want to get to -" She searched for the right words. "I want to get to the heart of life – to the part where it all begins – you know what I mean Liseli?"

"That's sex isn't it?" Liseli said "The little death – *la petite mort* – is what the French call an orgasm. I bet Oscar could show you that – he does look as if he understands death!"

"Do you suppose he has killed people? I mean when he was in the police and there was that rebellion in the north?"

"Probably." Liseli said. "I, for one, wouldn't be at all surprised."

Chapter Five

Liseli

Having Liseli around again meant an adjustment to Lara's social life. Lara and Tim would no longer be a twosome. They would be a threesome and soon after Liseli joined them Lara was surprised by an unexpected and overpowering feeling of jealousy. Liseli had arrived looking gorgeous, exotic and expensive in the latest outfits. She was brimming with confidence and insisted on going to as many parties as possible. If there were no parties then everyone had to accompany Liseli to the most popular and heavily frequented bars in town. Tim and Lara were introduced to a new crowd of young Chambeshians of their generation who were back from acquiring first degrees and busy settling into new jobs in top positions in Chambeshi.

It was on one of these occasions that they met Enoch's son.

"Hey, meet Enoch Njobvu Junior." Liseli took Lara and Tim each by the hand and pulled them across to a young man standing in a group by the bar at the Hotel Sunshine Everyday.

"Don't tell me, but you must me related to the Enoch Njobvu who works for Oscar at Tin Heart Holdings," Tim said. Lara's mouth gaped for a moment.

"Yeah!" Liseli was talking too much, too loudly and interrupting everybody. "Enoch Junior is training to be a doctor – on a Tin Heart Foundation scholarship that Oscar has set up."

"Wow – that's great!" and Tim was soon plunged deep into an information-gathering conversation with Enoch Junior.

Liseli had whisked Lara off to another group of young people to whom she was explaining why she was back in Chambeshi.

"My boss made a pass at me and the secretary told his wife. I just couldn't be dealing with that shit! Besides, the job wasn't interesting enough for me. I need something more stimulating. I went straight in there to the boss's office and demanded money in lieu of notice. Then I walked out, went straight to the airport and here I am!"

The way Liseli spoke seemed odd and exaggerated to Lara – she was off-kilter spinning away like a detached helium balloon in a breeze. Lara could not find any way to tether her.

Later Tim wanted to know if Liseli was high.

"Is she on drugs, or something?" he asked Lara, frowning and serious.

"No, absolutely not!" Lara was adamant, "Liseli is just a brilliant person, very intelligent and talented and cool. She is just too bright for her own good sometimes – but no, she would never take drugs. She has just been through all this shit with her job."

Tim seemed relieved and Lara relaxed. She had done the right thing by Liseli.

At Liseli's insistence they all went to a new Disco that had been created inside an abandoned warehouse in the light industrial area of Chambeshi. It was down a wide, ill-lit street with plenty of parking. The disco attracted not only well-to-do clubbers, but hordes of beggars and street kids who promised to protect the clubbers' cars from thieves. The street kids also offered blow jobs and anal sex, though their participation was not always voluntary. Inside the disco the steel walls reverberated with booming music and rebounding ultra-violet strobes. The heat was tremendous. Lara sought temporary respite in the wash rooms. They were surprisingly and pleasantly clean. A team of modestly dressed young girls under 15 years were busy wiping and cleaning up after the women had used the basins. Lara gave the youngest child a smile and a thank-you while she searched for a tip.

"Would you like to have sex with me?" the girl said.

Lara stopped. Sex had been on her mind but not this way.

"You won't believe what happened to me in the Ladies room." Lara said to Tim outside.

"Yes, I would!" he answered. "It's far worse in the men's toilets. You can't get into the cubicles. Sex is the only way some people can get food in Chambeshi."

A few days later she drove around to Oscar's house for what had become a regular lunch with Tim and Enoch. There were a number of cars in the drive and a group of young people including Enoch Junior were lounging in the easy chairs on the veranda. Lara recognised some of them from the evening out with Liseli and Tim. The table already held a large number of empty beer and cola bottles. She was about to ask where Tim was when she turned her head and saw him approaching from his room in the guest wing. Liseli was with him. Tim's arm was around her shoulders and Liseli's arm was around Tim's waist, their faces close enough together to make a single lop-sided heart shape.

Lara's heart imploded and her throat filled with the bitter acrid taste of old smoke.

"Tim! Liseli!" called Enoch Junior, "My father says that Oscar is back on tonight's flight and he wants us out of here so he can get the place cleared up for his return. *Tiyende!* Allons-y! Let's vamoose!"

Chapter Six

Madness

It was a long week before Lara saw Tim again. He phoned her, he sounded miserable and uncertain.

"Lara – I must see you – there is something really wrong with Liseli. Please can I come and see you? Have you seen Liseli this week? I don't know what's going on."

A few moments later Liseli's mother, Safina, called Lara; she sounded cold and distant.

"Liseli has asked me to phone you. She says she must tell you something very important – it's urgent, she says – do you mind?"

"I'll come right around if you like." Lara said. She didn't know who had upset her most, Liseli or Tim, but she thought there was a better chance she would find out more from Liseli and within 20 minutes she was sitting in Liseli's bedroom staring at her dramatically altered friend. The room was dark, the curtains drawn, Liseli had pulled her beautiful carefully styled plaits to bits and her hair stood out around her head in a scruffy frizz. She was sitting hunched up in bed against the wall with a look of terror on her face plucking at the bedclothes. Both Liseli's parents were at home; they looked tense and worried but something about their demeanour told Lara that this was not a new experience for them. Liseli's father had been sitting with her but as soon as Lara arrived he left the room with a look of relief that he couldn't quite hide. Liseli's desperate plucking at her bedding intensified.

She also started pulling at her hair. Lara was shocked and puzzled but Liseli was so distressed that it was clear that anger was an irrelevance. Lara reached out to hold her friend's hands and to still their manic twitching.

"Liseli what is it? What is wrong? Tell me!" but for a while Liseli remained speechless. She began to rock herself back and forwards drearily shaking her head. At last she spoke.

"Forgive me, Lara!" she pleaded, "Forgive me! I am such a terrible person. It wasn't Tim's fault – tell him it was my fault – tell him I am sorry – tell him! I am so bad."

There was very little else that she said. Her mother came in ostensibly to offer Lara a cup of tea but in fact to try to persuade Liseli to get up and eat. At this invitation Liseli lay down and pulled the blanket over her head. Eventually Lara got up to leave. She touched Liseli's shoulder through the coverlet.

"Can't I do anything to help you, Lise?" she said using the shortened names from their school days. "Please can Lar help you?" but Liseli just rocked herself harder.

As Lara reached the door, Liseli turned over and muttered at Lara just loud enough for her to hear.

"I am mad! I am mad! I should be dead! I am bad, Lara! Sorry! Sorry!" and she flung herself back into the bed and rocked even harder.

"Thank you for coming." Liseli's father said.

"What's wrong? Can I help?" Lara repeated uselessly. He shook his head.

"No, the doctor's been. She has been like this before – she'll recover eventually we hope but we may go back to England with her. It started this time when she was sacked from her job."

Tim and Lara went into the garden where years before Lara and Liseli had gone to plot ways of surviving their university education. They were both awkward with each other, Tim most of all. Lara took the initiative.

"Liseli is very ill I think." she said, "I went to see her – she asked me to come – she wanted me to tell you that it is not your fault and that she is sorry

"What does she mean?" Tim was also distressed, "What has she done? What have I done to her? I don't understand!"

Poor Tim. Lara felt for him and once again anger and hurt pride seemed irrelevant and unhelpful.

"Honestly Tim, I am sure it is nothing that you have done. She seems to have arrived back here in a terrible state because she lost her job. I didn't realise – and she didn't say. From what her parents say she seems to have had a breakdown. I mean when she arrived she was so over the top and wild that I didn't altogether recognise her – she didn't seem like the Liseli I knew."

The Liseli who had been her friend would not have had sex and gone to bed so quickly with Lara's own best friend. How could she put that to Tim?

Tim said slowly, "I was surprised too how fast things happened between us. I thought you must have had an idea – sorry – this is probably wrong – but girls talk to each other – so I thought you would know somehow – and that it was okay – that you didn't mind?"

Lara, silent, shook her head but after a moment she touched Tim's shoulder. It seemed to reassure him.

"No, I didn't know. It still seems out of character for Liseli. She did seem – well – high I suppose – but she wasn't on drugs – at least that would also be out of character for her."

Tim said, "There wasn't anything weird while we were sleeping together – that seemed normal – except that Liseli couldn't sleep at all afterwards."

Lara found herself laughing.

"Oh Tim, when and how is sleeping together and sex and love ever just normal and easy – how would one know? It just always seems so individual and sometimes too complicated to explain, even for me who isn't that experienced!"

Tim gave Lara a look of relief and they both smiled. When he got up to leave they hugged each other and Lara gave Tim a kiss on his cheek. Tim wanted to go and see Liseli but Lara said to wait till she had spoken to Liseli's parents and to Liseli. Liseli did not want to see anyone, Lara was told, and within a week Liseli and her family had left for England.

It was Junior who explained what was wrong with Liseli to Lara. Junior and Liseli had been friends since primary school and had also dated while they were studying in England.

"Liseli is a manic depressive – nowadays the medical term is bi-polar disorder – I haven't done my psychiatry training yet but Liseli told me of her diagnosis a while ago when we were still going out together. She made me go through some text-books with her."

"What does that mean?" Lara asked, "She isn't mad as far as I can see and I didn't think she was depressed till the last time I saw her – that was horrible – she was so desperate!"

"It's a pretty miserable illness to have." Junior agreed, "When you are up you think you are invincible as far as money and sex and life goes – when you are down you are in danger of committing suicide – the medication isn't great either."

"Will she get better?" Lara asked, wanting to be hopeful, but Junior rocked his head while making a face.

"Kind of depends – I think you have to learn to live with it."

Lara asked no more questions. That Liseli might kill herself seemed horrible but after the last week not impossible. Lara wondered what to tell Tim but it turned out he had found out about it by asking Junior himself. Lara remembered how good Tim was at getting information. Somewhat hesitantly at first but soon as easily as before, Tim and Lara resumed their friendship and spent time together again. As Oscar was now back, Tim was more circumspect about using his house as a base. Even so he always had some new piece of information or news about Oscar to discuss with Lara and she was always ready to hear it.

Chapter Seven

History and Politics

"Oscar's German and originally from Dresden as I thought," Tim said. "Came to South Africa in his teens."

Lara said surprised, "He sounds so English – well – he has no obvious accent – but everything about him seems English and looks English – his manners and his way of doing things – I was sure he must have lived in England for a while even if his sister didn't. How did you find out?."

"He tells you if you ask him directly but then he doesn't give away too much. I still like him but I am beginning to feel more and more than there is a lot that he keeps hidden – he is consistent with what he says but it is so little. Enoch also knows surprisingly little about Oscar's past but then he is such a polite man that he can easily be deflected from being too pushy."

"Now there's another interesting person – Enoch's father, Samuel, served in the Second World War – in Burma, Enoch says. Many Africans served with the British Army, you know, in the worst places too and without much recognition for their bravery and their losses. Battle of Arakan mean anything to you, Lara?"

Lara shook her head. Where had she seen that name?

"Samuel arrived back committed to the idea of freedom from colonial rule and determined to educate his children when he had them. I like the idea that Oscar's and Enoch's fathers were on different sides in the war but that Oscar and Enoch became friends! Don't you?"

"Oscar grew up during the war – in the region that's East Germany today but somehow or other he arrived in South Africa from West Germany as a boy of about 16 – with his sister Hanne of course – she was older than him by 3 or 4 years. He must have been – well he still is – very clever and determined – he worked down the Rand mines for a bit but he told me it was tough and had no future so he quit as soon as he could."

Tim and Lara were lounging in the shade in the International Hotel garden as they talked about Oscar. A press conference on a new regional economic policy was to take place in the ballroom following a summit. That kept being postponed as the various leaders had not agreed on their final statement. Tim, bored with waiting, had persuaded Lara to leave her studio for a swim in the hotel's Olympic-sized pool and to get a taste of the hotel's new poolside lunchtime speciality – a toasted ham sandwich. A first for Chambeshi.

"Oscar must be the same age as your Dad, Lara – wouldn't you say?"

Lara had wondered if Oscar and her father were contemporaries. She didn't like that idea much.

"That old!" Then she laughed for no obvious reason.

"Go on." she said.

"Well – I work out that he must have been about 9 or 10 at the end of the war – old enough to see and understand really horrible things were happening – but he never talks about it. What do you know about that time, Lara? Anything?"

"History stopped in 1945, didn't it?" Lara grinned, "At least my history lessons did, but we did get the feeling that history had concluded as something that was capable of being analysed. I think my teacher quoted something smart like – um – '*Santayana said, History is always written wrong and needs to be rewritten*'. At any rate I am still waiting to learn about modern history because so far it hasn't been written 'right'!"

For a moment a dark shadow crossed her sight and she looked up to see if a cloud had passed overhead. What might Oscar have seen as a boy? She felt a moment's coldness but sunshine was Lara's element and the sun was shining. She shivered the feeling away and smiled again. Tim gave Lara an amused look.

"We are living our history, if you hadn't noticed!" he said, then he continued, "At the end of the Second World War my darling Lara, it wasn't the good Doctor Zhivago-types in love with Lara, the heroine, who marched on Berlin. It wasn't Pasternak's righteous army of Russian men finally winning a just war – it was a rough and ready disorganisation of an army using old trucks and cars and horses to pull their guns. Some were serious communists, most were soldiers who had been brutalised by their experiences of war with Germany. They had been fighting in appalling conditions for four years without a break, their numbers halved, tens of millions dead, unthinkable stuff – and it was payback time. Europe was an extraordinary and enormous mess of refugees and devastated cities and revengeful Russians bent on rape – on at least two million rapes in fact – that was probably the Europe of Oscar's experience at the age of 9 or 10."

"Anyway Oscar doesn't talk about it – he just smiles and changes the subject so I don't think I'll find out from him."

"How come you are staying with Oscar when you seem to be so suspicious of him? I mean how did you get to know him?" Lara wanted to know.

"One of my editors had met Oscar and thought he would be "a mine" of information about mines. My editor likes to pun! He gave me a letter of introduction. I did some research but didn't turn up much. Oscar seems to have been one of the key advisors to the President at Independence – a rather unlikely person for that role in some ways – but I guess President Chona felt in need of advice from people who weren't part of the colonial government and Oscar was for a time useful for his business expertise. Possibly that was when Oscar and Jannie Oosthuizen got to know each other. The Tin Heart Mine seems to have changed ownership without much documentation – so perhaps Jannie adopted Oscar as his son and heir?"

Tim smiled at his invented scenario.

Lara was quiet for a while thinking. At last she asked,

"What about Hanne? What was she like – as a person? What does Enoch say about her?"

Tim raised quizzical eyebrows at Lara.

"You really think I am capable of anything in my search for information, don't you Lara?"

Lara grinned, rather ashamed.

"Well you are, aren't you Tim? Actually I am the one who is curious – I suppose – I would love to know."

"Be careful Lara!" Tim warned, "I think you fancy Oscar – not only is he too old for you – but I think he may be quite dangerous – and I still haven't worked out where he gets his money from and how – to me his businesses all sound a little far-fetched and unaccounted for."

"I'm not all that interested in Oscar." Lara lied.

Tim shrugged without looking at her, so Lara decided to cloak the reasons for her questions with some literary guff from Charlotte Bronte.

"I just think there is a bit of a mystery about Hanne though. She didn't seem to have much of a life or many friends and people always look strange when she is mentioned – like Rochester's woman in the attic in 'Jane Eyre' or something."

It was absurd of her to be a little jealous of the only woman who apparently featured in Oscar's life.

"As long as you aren't going to be the Jane Eyre in that scenario and marry the corrupt older man." Tim was sombre as he looked at Lara. Since his disastrous one-night stand with Liseli there had been a degree of physical awkwardness between Lara and himself. They both regretted it but did not know how to make it right.

"Have you heard from Liseli?" he asked, but he and Lara had spoken simultaneously. "I need that painting commission from Oscar," she said.

They both stopped, laughed, started again at the same moment, interrupted each other.

Finally Lara explained, "Mum and Dad are going to retire in 6 months or so. They don't plan on living in England and are thinking of settling in Cyprus. I can't bear the thought of going back to England – my art is about Africa – I need to rent a flat but if I can't sell my work I can't afford one."

"Dammit!" Tim said, "I am also going – well not exactly leaving for good. My editor wants me to do more travelling in Africa – I am to base myself in Chambeshi – they have found me a flat here but I won't be living in it very often. You'll know where it is – a rather grotty area with lots of small industries and warehouses. The flats above those units are reasonably secure as the premises are all under guard at night so I can leave my stuff there safely while I travel. It is fine for me. You could stay there if you wanted. Not very nice for a single girl though – a bit lonely and quite far away from the posher part of town."

"Thanks, Tim." Lara was touched, "Helen says she knows places I can stay if I house sit for people on leave. Mum and Dad would prefer that for me – but I won't be able to paint in those kinds of homes, they are too – well – 'Homes and Gardens' posh – so it's a dilemma for me."

"Well," Tim looked more cheerful, "You can use my flat as your studio – there's a spare bedroom there that would do – and you can sleep – well – live in the places that are more salubrious that your parents would like."

"Oh Tim – you are a darling!" and Lara leant across and gave Tim a sideways hug and kiss. Tim caught her hand as she sat back in her chair.

"Lara," Tim said, "I am so sorry about that business with Liseli – I liked her but not half as much as I like you – I'm still this travelling journalist but I wish you could come with me – I wish you wanted to."

Lara looked at Tim.

"Everything is so uncertain right now." she said half-apologising and squeezed Tim's hand back. She liked him so much, her bespectacled, beaky-nosed, gangling, tall friend with the too-large ready smile and the intelligent eyes. In fact she was very fond of him but everything in her life was starting to shift and move. Her parents, Liseli, Tim, the elusive jet-setting Oscar. She wanted to stay in one place and paint and draw, live the imagined life of some artist in a bohemian community and perhaps have a lover one day. What was on offer was a studio in a spare bedroom and to keep moving from one house-sit to another. It would do for the moment. At least she wasn't shut away like Liseli.

"Liseli has been admitted to a psychiatric ward for 3 months." she told Tim. "They hope to get her stabilised on medication." She had heard this phrase from Liseli's father.

"It's not the first time she has been in hospital, Tim. Apparently she did the same kinds of things the last time too. She got high then, slept with her boss, got the sack and almost killed herself. At least, she took an overdose of sleeping pills, I think. It was not your fault. None of us realised what was happening and even her parents didn't see it until it was too late. Honestly Tim – it isn't any more your fault than it is mine."

Tim and Lara looked at each other. It was a moment of intimacy but neither of them felt they wanted to, or could, risk making that moment last too long.

Chapter Eight

Oscar's Art Collection

Lara felt the discomfort of a sneak who has looked uninvited at a private letters and who is faking ignorance about them. Oscar was showing her the paintings in his library and Lara needed to explain that she had already seen them.

"I have already spent quite a long time looking at your paintings." she said, "You have an amazing collection – Enoch and Tim showed them to me when I came here to have lunch with them."

Is Oscar offended by the freedom with which she and Tim had made themselves at home in his house?

One day she had spent almost two hours alone in Oscar's study not only looking at the prints and paintings but also running her finger along she book shelves and taking out the books that most aroused her curiosity. She had seen both novels and non-fiction about Africa by writers such as Wilbur Smith, Laurens van der Post, and Robert Ruark. There were also books by Norman Mailer, Jack Kerouac, Hammond Innes, Alex Haley and Kurt Vonnegut and whole shelves of twentieth-century histories including all those by Winston Churchill. There was Adolf Hitler's *'Mein Kampf'* and *'Kapital'* by Karl Marx. Lara had first noticed a recent copy of 'Capital' in English then saw old and rather battered copies of the same books in German on a higher shelf. Lara's neck prickled. She hadn't read them and didn't have a clear idea of what they contained but something about the place they occupied in the mythology of her parents' lives suggested they signalled danger.

Lara ran her finger along the edge of the shelves tapping the spines of those she wanted to remember or already knew. There were also books by Sigmund Freud and Carl Jung.

"Dreams and desires and the secrets of human experience. Will I ever really truly know myself and understand what my motives are?"

Of course all those disquieting names and books had been current in art school conversations. They might be names used to conjure up ideas, but who at art school had done the hard work of reading the literature?

None of my art class, had lived long enough or experienced enough to really understand it all.

For a moment Lara felt her confidence diminish. She was on the brink of new excitements and achievements. What would happen to her?

When Tim had shown Lara around the bookshelves before Oscar's return he had pointed out some books about the Marquis de Sade including those written by him with women's names, 'Justine' and 'Juliette' as the titles.

"Strange taste for a man who runs a business in Chambeshi." he had commented.

"Very strange." Lara agreed, "Do you imagine Oscar is an admirer of Sade?"

"Well" Tim said, "The Marquis was a revolutionary, feminist, sodomite, erotic writer, the original sadist obviously, and spent most of his life in a madhouse, some of it with a woman who loved him till he died. That would make him one helluva role model?"

Lara shrugged. Madness was actual and revolution possible in Chambeshi. The erotic? Well yes, perhaps. The erotic is fascinating. Lara stared at the bookshelf avoiding Tim's eyes. She kept seeing Oscar's smile. Artists were often interested in such things. Well – male artists were weren't they? What about herself? Was she different? Among Oscar's books was a Dover Edition of erotic drawings by Pablo Picasso of bulls and satyrs and naked females. The drawings were clever, amusing and suggestive. There were also books of Audrey Beardsley drawings and Gustav Klimt paintings of a perversity that was eerily disturbing. Lara was intrigued by the Japanese and Mughal paintings of couples explicitly engaged in unlikely couplings with each other or with octopuses in physically impossible variations of sexual intercourse but she preferred to look at those when she was on her own. Tim's company made the two of them complicit in some way. They aroused her and she assumed they must have the same effect on him. Did this mean they were engaged in a literary version of consensual sex? She had to stop and think about sex and morality. Sex seemed more and more to pervade her life and her thoughts.

Weird sex and any version of sex and sex just for pleasure seem okay for artists – at least men who are artists – but what about women artists – or me? Lara thought.

She had made some pen and ink sketches herself. One was of a the bare back of a man looking at a naked woman spread out asleep on the bed in front of him. The other was of a naked woman looking back over her shoulder in a provocative invitation. Lara had hidden them away under a pile of unused paper not sure what her purpose was in drawing them. She had portfolios full of life studies of nude women and men but they were technical exercises quite different to her drawings about sex. She wasn't sure why she had made them or if she had a future purpose for them.

Tim however, noticed her interest in Oscar's selection of erotic art.

"Beware!" he grinned. "Rabelais says that to speak of love is to make love – I think that might apply to looking at drawings of love-making too."

So Tim had sussed her out.

"It does feel kind of voyeuristic doesn't it? Go away Tim – I don't want a voyeur watching me being a voyeur!"

Tim laughed.

"Let's go eat! I thought that's what all artists are – voyeurs of a sort!"

"Yes," countered Lara, "and so are journalists."

During Liseli's period of madness, Lara had completely forgotten about Oscar's erotic books. Now, some weeks after Liseli had returned to England and psychiatric treatment, Lara was back in his house and Oscar was asking her opinion of the art in the library.

"What do you think of the paintings? Are there any that interest you particularly?"

Lara recognised the Käthe Kollwitz at once. She knew that the prints and paintings were from the German Expressionist period between the two world wars but she hadn't known who all the individual artists were apart from Otto Dix. Seen up close enough to touch, the work seemed so extraordinary that she wanted to find out more about it. From her knowledge of art history and visits to museums, Stanley Spencer's war paintings appeared to be the closest comparison she could make to these, but Spencer's work was so gentle in its emotions and its colour and rhythmic forms that it suggested to her England and hopefulness. She had used Goya's passionate and horrifying etchings about the Spanish Peninsular Wars to inspire her final exam work but though they had moved her she had thought of them as past history like the Slave Trade. Nothing, however, matched the despair and cynicism of these, or the brilliance of the colours and power of the brush marks. Oscar had both art catalogues and art history books of the period and Lara soon had all the information she wanted.

"I recognised the Käthe Kollwitz immediately – are they really original prints? How wonderful! I love her stuff but it is so painful – women – mothers crying over their dead children – I didn't really know all the others. I'd heard of some. I couldn't believe that you own original paintings by Otto Dix. I'd never heard of Conrad Felixmüller – so I did look through your art books to find out about them both – hope you don't mind?"

Lara turned to look at Oscar's face. He smiled without turning to her and replied, "What else should be done with books and paintings except to look at them and use them?

"I keep these paintings in my study rather than display them in the lounge because not many people here in Chambeshi would understand them or approve of them. They are terrible and tragic. It is also more secure here and they are valuable. Your mother hated them by the way."

"My mother's seen them! She never said!" Lara was surprised and silent for a moment. When had that happened and why was it never mentioned at home?

She looked again at the art. It was even more interesting. The first time she had seen these paintings she had been repelled by them but her art school liberation war work based on Goya's 'Disasters of War' had not been dissimilar in nastiness so she forced herself to study them more closely. It was only honest to do so. Nancy, her tutor, had suggested that Lara look at the German expressionists who had been through the 1914 – 1918 World War as well as Goya.

"They probably all suffered from post traumatic stress disorder," Nancy said.

Lara knew Dix had painted murder as well as war.

"Murders did take place after the war." Nancy said. "The killers must have been driven insane by the ferocity of the fighting and the thousands of mutilated, bloody corpses."

One of the Dix paintings in Oscar's library showed a disembowelled prostitute whose vagina had been slashed by the maniacal knife-wielding figure rampant above her body. Another was of a group of card players all hideously disfigured without eyes and limbs.

"The Otto Dix subject matter is really awful – how did people carry on living after their war experiences – these deformed crippled men – these open bloody wounds – the made-up eyes of these women – so hard and cruel – and damaged. It is all so cynical and upsetting. What was the artist saying and feeling?"

Lara looked at Oscar again but his expression was stern, his face closed up, hard, as if he reflected the faces painted by the artist. Lara almost reached out to touch him and break the spell of the framed pictures. After a momentary silence, he relaxed again and turned towards her.

"Let's get back to the other guests." he said and put his hand lightly on her shoulder as he guided her through the study door.

"Wherever did you get these paintings from?" she asked. She really needed to know why he owned them.

"Ah!" Oscar said, "Family stuff, you know."

Then he expanded again into the genial party-giver as he joined his other guests on the veranda.

"How are the drinks?" he asked, "Time for some more aperitifs – or wine instead?"

Part Seven
Oscar 1985

Chapter One

Tim's Farewell

Oscar was giving a farewell party for Tim on the front veranda of his ranch house. Helen was there with an admirer of hers from the French Embassy, a diplomat called Michel Landes. Also among the diners were Chimunya and Pascal, Enoch, his wife, Inonge, and Enoch Junior, Maria and Bill, plus several acquaintances of Tim's including Ben, a local newspaper editor, and William, a satirist who wrote critiques of the Chambeshian government under an assumed name. There was also a house guest of Oscar's, a man so quiet, so buttoned up in his suit, so carefully shaven, thin-lipped and unsmiling that Lara assumed he was foreign and did not speak or understand English.

"Ah Lara – you have seen Oscar's wonderful collection of paintings and prints have you? What did you think of them?" Helen asked with interest.

"I can't say I loved them – they aren't likeable – the subject matter is so dreadful – but I don't think I will ever forget them. The colours and the paint in the Otto Dix are rich and beautiful. It is strange to be so attracted to them in one way and to find them so repulsive in another." Lara turned to Oscar, "Please, Oscar – do show them to Chimunya and to Pascal – I know they will find them so interesting – won't you Chimunya – Pascal?"

Oscar smiled. He shook his head lightly.

"Lara please you show them to your friends if you like – you know more about art than I do – Chimunya and Pascal – you are welcome to go and have a look – perhaps after we've eaten lunch."

Lara was flattered at being singled out to have a unique relationship with Oscar's art collection. She nodded at Chimunya and Pascal who looked pleased. Maria pulled a face. "I've seen those paintings and I think they are really horrible – I said so didn't I Oscar? Honestly Lara – your own work is so beautiful and – well – I just think that animals are so much nicer and much more suitable subjects for pictures – don't you Bill?"

"No comparison, I'd say," Bill agreed, "but then I think it's about the difference between animals and humans and the way they behave. Humans are so immoral and destructive. Animals aren't like that at all."

Tim was listening with interest. He grinned.

"Humans have to be moral – or have an idea about morality to be immoral. Animals are neither – they are amoral."

Pascal's eyes widened.

"What are all these words – amoral, immoral, moral – don't you just mean that some people are good and some people are bad? I don't know about animals unless the spirits of very bad dead people and killers have gone to live in them – that's when animals become bad and come back to kill more people."

Chimunya shook her head, clicked her tongue and shut her eyes.

"Oh this man Pascal! He is so full of superstition."

"But isn't that what your paintings are about, Chimunya? Don't you paint the spirits and the beliefs of the Chambeshi people?" Lara asked.

"Yes I do." answered Chimunya, "but I am also a modern person. I go to a medical doctor not a witchdoctor. I fly in an aeroplane. I know when someone dies that the death isn't always caused by magic."

Pascal laughed.

"Old people die because they are old but when a young person dies it is the result of a curse and somebody else made the curse and that person is responsible."

"Perhaps there is something in the concept of responsibility for a young person's death – why do young people die after all? Wars, accidents, famines, disease – it is a bit of a long shot but I suppose you could argue that if we were all moral and responsible perhaps there would at the least be fewer unnecessary deaths." Tim was enjoying playing the devil's advocate.

"Don't understand that at all, Tim," Bill said, "and I don't understand why this man – Otto – Dickson – Dix – painted these dreadful things. What was he trying to do?"

"He was warning people about war. Maybe it was a catharsis for him – an exorcism of his hideous experiences? More than that, he was containing the pain and the suffering," Helen suggested, "by identifying it, making it, then putting a frame around, it he was keeping it in a safe place – rather like putting an evil genie in a bottle."

"*Iyii*!" said Pascal, "Yes – we do that too – but not in paintings – in our rituals. We put an evil spirit in a kind of container – rather like a fridge that you keep meat in, Maria – so that they can't get out and hurt us."

There was general laughter at the idea, led by Pascal himself, then Lara asked, "But what was Hitler trying to do with all this art that he removed from art galleries and labelled 'Degenerate Art'? He must have thought it had immense power if he destroyed it."

Helen said, "Of course he may just have been jealous – he thought of himself as a great painter who was hated by the critics. He blamed the Jewish press for his bad reviews. He did the same thing to art that Goebbels did to literature with the Nazi book-burnings. No free thought – no terrible visual images of how dreadful war is and then it will be possible for you to start another war – can't make people fight for no good reason unless you only let them have a part of the argument. One reason given for not exhibiting Dix's work was that it would spread despair and despondency in the armed forces and that was a treasonable act.

"Dix included a portrait of Hitler in his Seven Deadly Sins painting you know. Hitler's forces may have wreaked havoc throughout all of Europe and most of the world but Dix saw him as a tiny worthless figure – well -" Helen stopped, then said. "A creature who is – yes – so reductionist that he is disappearing up his own arse!"

Helen's comment produced shocked amusement and bewilderment among Oscar's guests but Lara could see that Tim was seriously considering the idea.

"You really think art has so much impact, then?" she asked him. The things that interested Tim always challenged her to think harder about her choices and her work.

"For God's sake, Lara! Of course I believe in the power of the image, of the word, of artists and of writers! Why else would I be a journalist?" Tim shook his head at her and Lara shook her head back in apology. After all why else did she make art?

"Do you like Dix's work, Helen?" Lara asked.

"Oscar let me write a paper for an art journal about his collection." Helen replied. "Dix's work is extraordinarily powerful. It feels to me as if he became possessed by his subject matter. It inhabited him and then boiled up out of him into his paintings. He didn't observe and judge his sitters – he became them – he knew them and their lives. He was the soldier who killed, the crippled veteran, the amputee, the prostitute, the sex murderer and his victim. Somehow he knew what it was to inhabit their flesh and suffering. He hated all ideologies and he resisted any political analysis that would diminish one of his portraits. They are all just of human beings."

Helen's boyfriend, Michel, turned to Oscar, "So come, my friend, please tell us how you acquired these paintings that were once so dangerous to own?" and with a meaningful sneer he added, "What is the actual provenance of this, your so famous art?"

Oscar smiled but his eyes creased up angrily for a moment. He looked, Lara thought, quite dangerous himself.

"The paintings belonged to my grandfather. He was a doctor in Dresden in the early part of the century. He knew Otto Dix personally and some of the other artists and he bought work from them at a time when they weren't well known. As things got harder some of the artists paid him with their paintings. He was a shrewd old man and usually got a receipt acknowledging his ownership from the artists. Once the artists were labelled 'Degenerate' they lost their teaching jobs and some went to prison. He helped some of them out by buying their work then. Of course it was also not a good idea for him to own such art. He and his brother found a hiding place for the paintings in a cellar at his brother's farmhouse outside Berlin before the war. Eventually I recovered them – and the letters of ownership!"

"I have met Otto – Otto Dix – since. In Vienna where he received a prize for his work, I told him of my tiny collection." Oscar smiled at Michel, "And by the way – they travelled out to Chambeshi in a Diplomatic Bag – I am also indebted to the diplomatic community for giving them safe passage so I can have them in my home."

Michel made a small bow back at Oscar and smiled too.

"Discreetly managed, I am sure."

Lara pursed her lips together. Her mouth had almost dropped open at the idea that Oscar could have met Otto Dix.

"So you are originally German, then Oscar?" Tim's journalist friend Ben, asked Oscar. "I thought Mynhardt was an Afrikaans name?"

"I'm originally German, yes – my father's name was Meineke but when we arrived in South Africa my sister and I decided to adopt a Dutch version of it. It was still not so long after the war and it made life easier. Now – time for our desserts and I have a sweet wine – a Sauternes – for those of you who wish to have it."

Oscar deflected the conversation away from his past and Lara determined that she would find out more about that time in history. Perhaps her father would know. Tim didn't approve of her interest in Oscar and though he could probably tell her all about it he would also subject her again to warnings about Oscar which would bore her. In any case Tim was leaving for Zimbabwe at the weekend and would be working from there for at least six months. There probably wouldn't be enough time to have those kinds of conversations before he left.

William, the Chambeshian satirist, was amusing Tim with a story about a dinner he had been invited to at the home of a white hunter.

"Trophies on every wall and leopard skins on the settees!" he chortled, "but the best part of the evening was eating our steaks under this huge painting of a male lion devouring a kudu bull. Every bite I took I could see into the lion's maw with all its teeth and red blood and flesh and gore. I nearly got to my feet and roared at the end of the meal! Such a nice gentle lady the wife was too!"

Amid the general laughter Helen said that she knew the hunter, the artist and the particular painting.

"Not your style, I think Lara."

"Well I suppose it is no less or more horrible in its own way than the Otto Dix painting," Lara replied, "but I guess it is a question of the artist's intention and what the artist suffered – and well – also felt and wants to express – I don't suppose the hunter felt sorry for the kudu bull! I do wonder sometimes if I paint too romantic a version of wildlife. After all, animals that are wounded or not killed outright do suffer pain."

Abruptly and unexpectedly, Oscar's quiet secretive guest broke his silence. Lara did not know his name but he spoke with an unusual richly-guttural, Arabic-sounding accent. Perhaps he was Lebanese or Israeli. Certainly he was from the Middle East.

"Death and suffering aren't the same for animals and humans. For us humans our own death is total negation of the self and we view it with the utmost fear and horror and loathing and we will do anything to avoid dying."

"Animals do not want to die either. They fight like hell to avoid it." Bill interjected.

"True enough," the Middle-Eastern man said, "But they do not suffer the psychological and psychic pain that humans do. We can suffer despair at the idea of death even when we are not in danger, not in captivity and not in pain."

Maria did not agree and shook her head so hard that her hair whipped around her face.

"Animals die in captivity – they pine and die of sorrow too – quicker than humans do!"

"You are correct, but we are different." the Middle-Eastern man said. "We live because we have hope. We suffer and despair. Animals suffer neither hope nor despair. They fight to survive. It is all they know."

Lara found herself thinking of Liseli. She had never seen anyone suffer as Liseli had suffered on that last day. Not even Lara's own broken heart over Jason's betrayal had reached that height and that depth of misery.

Who was this intriguing man, she wondered, and why did he speak with such authority on pain and on death? Oscar listened, his eyes averted.

"We have to have our revenge on the bad people," Pascal said. "Bad actions and death must be avenged to stop the bad growing stronger."

"We are most human when we do not take revenge." Again it was the man from the Middle East who spoke. "Justice must go together with mercy. Payment for bad acts is not and should not be revengeful. Revenge will only go in a circle of pain."

"You are right, Natan. You are right – but it is hard not to take revenge when you're angry." Oscar said.

Natan shrugged and returned to his self-contained silence.

"So that's his name," thought Lara. "Is he Israeli? I must ask Tim about him. What is his business here, I wonder?"

"Talking of revenge – what news does anyone have of the trouble on our north-western border?" It was Junior speaking. He had been having an animated private conversation with his father. He continued, "I've heard in the bars of Chambeshi City that some breakaway rebels from Angola plan an attack on our mines in that area. I understand that they say the attack would be in revenge for the help President Chona gave to the legitimate government of Angola? Any opinions anyone – any useful information?"

"I don't think it's anything serious." Enoch Senior contributed. "They're an isolated bunch – not very numerous, led by a man called Njoka – Njoka means snake – quite fitting for him except that he's fat. He was born in Chambeshi near the border and says he's a General – General Snake! I think he may have been trained by the Cubans as a freedom fighter but he became a renegade and his group was funded by South Africa to destabilize Angola. So far they have had no success, but they have done a lot of raping and killing."

"Honestly, Dad, I hope you're right about this – Oscar – all this trouble is rather close to the Tin Heart Mine isn't it? I don't want my Dad to be taking any risks at his age! He's done his share of fighting for Chambeshi." Junior made his plea sound like a joke and he put out his hand and rubbed the top of his father's head. At this playful patronising gesture, Enoch gave his son a friendly shove, a pretend smack on his cheek and a hug that ended in a brief wrestling match.

Lara saw Natan cast a swift sharp glance in Oscar's direction.

Why was Natan bothered about the Tin Heart Mine?

She looked at Enoch and Inonge and their son with envy for their apparently close and happy family life and thought about her own parents. *Everything's changing for me. I suppose Mum and Dad were happy together? Who really knows about anyone else's relationships even if it's your own family? Mum and Dad retire very soon and they aren't all that old. Dad's not sixty yet.* Jane and Brian had plans to travel and to buy a holiday home in Cyprus. *Will Mum like that? She's never seemed that pleased with things in her life. I thought that Mum was irritated by me but how would I know? Perhaps she's menopausal?*

Lara had heard her mother's friends mention hot flushes

and depression. Obviously that had nothing to do with her. Lara wasn't really interested in her mother's physical state but now she wondered about Inonge, Enoch's wife and Junior's mother. Enoch and Inonge always referred to each other in formal terms as Mr Njobvu or as Mrs Njobvu.

"Even when they're at home in private," Junior had said with a grin. "These old types who grew up in the village – they are so conservative!"

Lara did not find Enoch and Inonge conservative. Yes – they had traditional manners and some traditional beliefs but their approach to the modern world was – well – modern. It seemed odd that if she asked Enoch how Inonge was he would say Mrs Njobvu was fine and if she asked Inonge a question that concerned Enoch she would be told what Mr Njobvu wanted. At the same time their relationship with Enoch and his siblings seemed both informal and respectful. Tim had said to Lara how much he admired the way Chambeshians adapted to every event and problem that their new independence threw at them. Technology doesn't bother them. They learn to use it faster than British graduates do. Business – well – they just go and make it happen. Politics – well again – that is much more of a mess – but at the same time every Chambeshian is certain of his right to self-determination and expects to voice his opinion and be listened to. It is really interesting seeing how ready they are to grasp every opportunity that comes their way.

"Take Enoch," Tim had once said, "He is one of the most adaptable people I have ever known and he has such a strong sense of duty, such loyalty to his friends – he is such a moral person – and he has had to work it all out for himself, learn the hard way and – well – I really like Enoch – and trust him."

By which Lara knew that Tim meant, but did not say, that he did not trust Oscar.

They were an interesting partnership those two – Oscar and Enoch.

Chapter Two

Oscar

"Well Lara – we must arrange to have a meeting at my office very soon to talk about that commission I want you to do."

The long luncheon was over at last and Tim and Lara were heading back into Chambeshi City before the sun set. Oscar had shaken Tim by the hand and wished him luck for his trip to Zimbabwe. Now he turned to Lara and took her hand briefly. As usual he kissed her on both cheeks in what now seemed a formal gesture.

"May I phone you tomorrow to make an arrangement?"

"Yes please do. I will be working from Tim's flat most days and I can take incoming calls there."

Oscar nodded. "I have Tim's number. Tomorrow then."

"Best before lunchtime." Tim said. "Lara's running me out to the airport in the afternoon."

Lara was relieved. She needed the commission to see her through the end of the rainy season. At the moment she was working for the exhibition at the Umodzi Gallery which was to take place in April and so was not selling any of her work. Her small income from her last winter with Bill and Maria was diminishing each day and she had not yet decided to take another job with them over the next winter safari season. Her parents planned to stay until the opening of her first solo exhibition. By then they would have packed up their home and be living in the company guest house until their final departure to England en route to Cyprus and retirement. Brian would be leaving Jane's car for Lara's use. It was a small four-wheel drive jeep but fortunately light on fuel. Even so Lara was unashamedly bumming lifts off her friends and off Tim to save herself money. She wouldn't be paying any rent while she was house-sitting but if Oscar gave her a commission she would not have to worry about food and fuel expenses.

As promised, Oscar's secretary phoned the next morning and a meeting was fixed for the following day. It gave Tim another opportunity to discuss Oscar with Lara when she drove him out to the airport that afternoon.

"The thing is Lara, no one seems to know exactly where he gets his money from. His gold mine must give him very little income if it's not producing, as he says. When he first arrived just before Chambeshian Independence he joined the colonial police force as a commissioned officer. Enoch served under him – that's how they met and how they came to be ambushed together in the rebellion. Soon after that he took his discharge from the police but stayed on in Chambeshi. He was employed as the manager of the Herman Levy car import firm and garage but Levy was looking for a fast exit from Chambeshi. Lots of whites left around then – the rebellion had scared them shitless. I gather Levy hadn't played by the book anyway and didn't fancy prison under a black administration. Somehow Oscar put the money together to buy him out but against all expectations that the luxury car market was finished both Levy and Oscar did well out of the deal. Somehow Oscar brought in all the cars for the new Chambeshian administration – Mercedes dealers generally do very well out of African governments and Oscar had good connections in West Germany."

Tim shook his head with a wry laugh. The new class of Mercedes owners in Chambeshi, known locally as the *WaBenzi*, were the source of both hilarious jokes and bitter complaints.

"It doesn't add up, Lara," Tim said. "Oscar did make a fortune from the garage before it was sold. Now he runs an enterprise office in Chambeshi City that supports odd business ventures. It is easy to be a millionaire in Chambeshi but to compete financially in international business? I don't know. He has a beautiful house, a light plane, a tiny mine and a safari camp that's not very well known. Enough to be very comfortable – yes – but to keep flying off to Europe? He is almost never in his office – I have never seen him actually working at his desk!"

"Well I'll make sure he pays me before I give him any paintings." Lara said feeling some frustration at the negative portrayal of her new patron-to-be. "What else can I do, Tim? I will watch out for him. I am not a complete idiot you know! I really wouldn't like to be taken in by someone who is dodgy – especially here where it is no fun to be hassled by the police. I'd be mad to. In any case I don't like cheats and crooks – but he does seem to know about art. Helen trusts him and he supports the gallery – what more can I do?"

Tim looked at Lara for a moment.

"You're right, Lara. He may well give you the break you need – and I know that you can look after yourself – take care though – and there's my own new fax machine at my flat – keep in touch and send me drawings by fax, won't you – so I know you're alive and okay!"

Lara laughed. David Hockney had been the first artist to send a drawing from the USA to Britain by fax and she and Tim had occasionally faxed each other drawings rather than letters.

"Oh you'll hear from me, Tim! Often! Who else can I talk to about what is happening here who will also understand my peculiar and personal take on it all? You know I'm hopeless about politics and only interested in becoming a famous painter."

"You don't kid me." Tim said, "You're much more shrewd about politics that you let on. Beware of the rich though. Don't let fame ruin you –"

"More than it has already, you mean," Lara interrupted, smiling.

Tim shook his head and continued, "Keep your ear to the ground – or the listening post – or whatever – about this second rebellion in the north of Chambeshi. The rumour is that it isn't going to go away and something is stirring in the heart of Chambeshi too. I'll let you know what the journalists in Zimbabwe are saying about it."

Chapter Three

Oscar's Commission

In spite of Tim's criticism, Lara did see Oscar working at his desk the following day. The phone call from Oscar's secretary had invited Lara to Oscar's town office at 11 o'clock on Wednesday to discuss the paintings he wanted to commission from her. Perhaps because of what Tim had said, Lara decided to go casually dressed.

"I'm not applying for a job with him." she told herself. "I'm an artist and should dress as I please – or should I? What does an artist look like in any case? Arty – like Helen with dramatic clothes, heavy jewellery, and exuberant hair? Scruffy, like Gillian who would wear paint-stained jeans and two t-shirts with holes in overlapping places? Or like Ajay, who as a punk musician, had outrageous pink hair and hobbled his thighs together with chains?"

She plaited her hair from the crown of her head to the nape of her neck leaving a loose pony tail down her back and put on a cool cotton shirt over a bright vest and a swirly skirt. It was hot so she put sandals on her feet.

"Safari camp clothes – what I usually wear." she thought. "But it's what I like and when I work at my art I am in the bush. Anyway – Oscar knows me and has seen the kind of person I am. What is in my portfolio ought to be more important."

Oscar's office was in a long white building set back from the main road. Palm trees and a large metal sculpture outside the front door distinguished the building from its neighbours. Inside it was quiet and tasteful with a selection of art that Lara recognised from the Umodzi Gallery. A young man at a reception desk stood up to greet Lara and after a phone call she was taken into the secretary's office. Oscar's secretary was an elegant and efficient Chambeshian woman with a pleasant smile. She invited Lara to sit down in an armchair to wait and offered her a coffee, which Lara refused.

"Mr. Mynhardt is on an overseas call and will soon be free," the secretary said. "He apologises for keeping you waiting."

The secretary, Lara noticed, was very busy with both phone calls and fax messages. In between she typed on an electronic typewriter at a great speed. It did indeed appear that Oscar was doing business. After studying the art on the walls, Lara amused herself with tourist magazines advertising safari holidays in Chambeshi. There was an article about Bill and Maria with a photo of Jason taking a group of tourists out in his jeep. Lara sighed. In Chambeshi City's business world everybody knew everybody else and all about their businesses too. Big fish in a small pond was how her father Brian had described Chambeshian businessmen. Did she really want to go around the city touting for commissions, particularly from someone like Oscar?

"God! What is it I have to do to make a living from my art? Am I selling myself 'the artist' – or selling what I make?"

Lara felt a moment's disgust with herself for spending so much time and thought on how to dress for her meeting. She was scowling at herself when Oscar opened the door in front of her and invited her into his room.

He grinned at her and raised one thick eyebrow. "Is it that bad?" he asked.

Lara could not help but smile back. Her shoulders relaxed and she shook her head.

"No! It's not at all bad but – I think that I am probably just bad at selling my work. If you don't mind I can't fake it. I have never done this before."

"Your art will sell itself – or not. Just be who you are Lara. Let me have a look at what you have brought."

Oscar carried Lara's portfolio over to the large polished mahogany table in the centre of the room. He opened it out and began to take out her work and look over it slowly. He had put on spectacles for the task and Lara thought they made his face look more ordinary and his nose appear larger and more irregular. He was dressed for work in a suit but he wore no tie and his jacket hung over the back of his chair. Lara noticed the detailed tailoring of his shirt, the designer stitching on the collar and cuffs, the coloured buttons holding them in place.

"Is he vain about his appearance as well as using an expensive tailor?"

She wondered if Tim had noticed Oscar's dress sense. Probably not, judging by Tim's own inelegant style.

Oscar seemed unhurried as he looked at Lara's drawings. He glanced up at her.

"I have set aside plenty of time for this." he said "No need for us to rush."

Standing by him ready to answer questions, Lara was able to observe the room and also look over at Oscar without seeming to stare. He wasn't a very tall man. Not much taller than Lara. He had wide shoulders and a broad chest without carrying any fat. Lara decided he could crush her easily in his arms if he chose, and then wondered why the idea had occurred to her. Perhaps women always measure men in such terms just in case it was necessary to escape from them. He moved lightly on his feet too. Could she outrun him? She smiled to herself at the possibility that she might need to run from Oscar. No man had ever chased her, in that physical sense at least. The hair above Oscar's ears was greying, but his thick eyebrows were dark and so was the faint stubble on his chin. She felt the rasp of it when he rubbed his hand slowly over his chin as he concentrated on one piece of her work. His skin was that of a man of fifty years, just starting to crease and slacken in ways that exposed a person's nature. It had always been interesting and more rewarding to draw older people at art school. It was a long time since Lara had found the soft pale pinkness of Renoir's female nudes or Titian's smooth ivory women either pretty or attractive. She loved the painful honesty of Rembrandt's later self-portraits. What did Oscar's wrinkles tell her about his nature? She stopped herself from studying him just in time. He was looking closely at her.

"Now come and explain your work to me and I will tell you what I want – maybe would like – you to do for me."

"Right," said Oscar over an hour later as Lara replaced carefully her artwork in her portfolio. "That has made me very hungry. How about you? It's almost one o'clock now. Shall we continue our conversation at the steak house down the road? We still have plenty to discuss before we begin to think about contracts and payments. Also – I do need to know more about your own plans for your art before I tie you down even temporarily, in a direction that makes you uncomfortable."

Instead of eating a proper supper, Lara had spent the previous evening arranging and rearranging her portfolio and her CVs. The idea of lunch at a restaurant filled her with pleasure. She seldom planned or prepared meals for herself even when she was alone. In Tim's flat the fridge was empty and the small sink loaded with cereal bowls and spoons.

"That would be good." Lara was smiling and relaxed. "It has been great to look at all of this with you. I think I can do what you want me to do – and yes – I am hungry too."

Chapter Four

Lunch with Oscar

Oscar was good company. Nothing he did or said made Lara feel either condescended to or patronised. They discussed a wide range of subjects from game management, to politics in Chambeshi, to current trends in art in Britain. Never once did he imply that Lara's lack of experience or knowledge invalidated her perceptions and opinions as a young adult.

"I wouldn't think of it in that way myself," he said with a smile in response to her criticism of one of the current art trends in London, "You know more about it than I do, but I guess that I have seen a great deal of changes and adaptations and art will never stagnate. Everything must and will change. Do you know when I first arrived on the Mines in South Africa it was a hotbed of radical labour ideas mainly stirred up by immigrants, many of whom were Jews from Eastern Europe. There was every shade of opinion from Nazism to Communism and everything seemed possible. It began to change after the Afrikaner Nationalists took over the government in 1948 and made their ideology of racial segregation and apartheid into law. I arrived in the early 50s soon after that started to happen and I reckoned it was bad news. Coupled with that, work on the Rand gold mines was dirty and dangerous work for everyone. I left as soon as I could."

"Why did you come to Chambeshi?" Lara asked.

"I had seen enough of war in Europe when I was a child,"

Oscar said. For a moment his eyes flickered, then he smiled again. "I rather fancied being on the side of the victors you know – British colonial traditions seemed rather reasonable by comparison with the direction that the South African Nationalists were going in. I really wanted to be my own man and start over again. Chambeshi was without question attractive. Besides they were recruiting for the police force and the terms of employment were bloody good. It was that or join the South African army." Oscar's face lit up and he smiled. "I didn't know I would see the end of colonial rule and the start of the Rebellion. It was, however, an education and an opportunity – and of course I got to know Enoch."

"But how come you are so interested in art – and – well – also you know a lot about it. My parents haven't a clue really and that goes for most British expatriates," Lara persisted.

"People of my age and generation?" Oscar grinned at Lara. "It's also class and generation Lara – your generation may have escaped from class considerations. My generation didn't."

"Really!" Lara leaned forward with a shade too much enthusiasm. "You mean you came from a class that cared about art?"

"I was born in East Germany – well my family came from Dresden – Saxony – art and music was part of the life of middle class people in a way they weren't in England. We weren't upper class in the English sense or intellectuals in the Oxbridge sense but it was woven into our lives along with politics. We were not insular like the British, you know!" Oscar smiled at Lara and she laughed.

"Well – perhaps living as an expatriate makes you change some of your attitudes." Lara puzzled about it for a moment. "It doesn't necessarily integrate you into another culture though – it puts you into a different group." She grinned and continued. "At art school at first I was seen as upper class – and I was so offended. I hated being seen as different from the other students – though of course – I did – and do want to be distinctive and among the best!"

"Mm, how do you see yourself as an artist then, Lara? Where do you fit? Is it a competition or a race? What do you want for yourself?"

Lara frowned, "I suppose that every artist is different but I think first of all you have to want to make art and that process makes its own individual rules – but then – it is hard to believe in yourself and to keep on driving yourself forward all on your own. I want people to see my art and to tell me that it matters – but selling it – well – that's a pile of shit!" Lara had spat out the last words, something she would have said to Tim without a thought. Now she wondered about their impact on Oscar. She looked at him, widening her eyes for a moment.

"Sorry." she said, "Probably shouldn't have said that! If it wasn't for Helen and the Umodzi I would be very unhappy – she is fantastic."

Oscar regarded her seriously but without offence.

"The business of making money in order to survive is a pile of shit!" he agreed but then he smiled, so she did too.

"We must get on with making a pile of shit out of your art, Lara!"

Oscar seemed to Lara to hesitate for a brief moment but almost at once he went on with a lengthy explanation. He wanted, he said, to put capital into the development of a safari camp at the Tin Heart Camp which his partner Enoch would both own and run.

"We want it to be small but exclusive. Personalised safaris. People could choose to bring their own guides with specialized knowledge – say of birds – maybe of plants or insects. We would provide expert local guides for game and fishing, but the emphasis is on luxury and quality of the wilderness experience. Bill and Maria see many more clients and their safaris can't be beaten but they don't often get the same people coming back year after year. We would hope to attract regular clients. What I want from you, Lara, is a series of paintings of the area around the camp – obviously with the animals in their habitat as far as possible. These paintings would be for the safari camp and the town office. I also want a range of varied drawings – or sketches – of every possible subject – portraits of the workers at the site, the guides, the village people and traditional dancers, the safari camp, the river, different fish, animals, birds, big small and insects, trees, flowers and butterflies and so on that I can use in brochures advertising the place. Of course the clients like and need to see photos but as you know – a good photo of a lion in the bush could be in any part of Africa – I think your drawings will give the place an individual and unique identity only possible because the artist made the paintings at that place. What do you think, Lara?"

"It sounds like a huge amount of work," Lara said hesitantly. "Rather as if it could take a lifetime to do."

"Oh yes indeed it might." Oscar agreed. "But my brief requires it to be deliverable within strict time limits so that I can get the brochure to the press for the next season. What I suggest is that you go to the Tin Heart Camp with Enoch and Inonge for a three to four month period while they finish equipping and setting up the camp. All the construction work is complete and the supplies are all there. You will be there and be free to do your drawing and painting – all your materials, food and accommodation, expenses, everything all found, though you will be camping and it will be rough at the start. At the end I will give you a lump sum which we will agree before you begin work. It will cover holiday pay, pension and period of notice. I will also buy from you all the art I want and the price will be agreed by Helen as your agent, yourself and by me.

"How does it sound?"

"It sounds very interesting," said Lara. "I need to know the amounts though, as holiday pay and a pension sum as a percentage of four months' low pay could be very little money indeed. I also need to know how Enoch and Inonge feel about this arrangement. I don't want to be the outsider artist who is seen as a free-loader and a liability"

Oscar considered Lara's idea for a moment then he nodded an approval.

"Good, Lara. I'm glad you've got your head screwed on and are sensible. I'll set up a proper meeting with Inonge and Enoch so you can discuss expectations together. My secretary has drawn up a draft contract with figures that you and I can talk about and I expect you will make your own arrangements to discuss this all with Helen. We would be planning on making our first trip to the Tin Heart Camp in early April – you are busy with your solo exhibition at the Umodzi before that, aren't you? It should work out well for us all I think."

"There's another thing about the Tin Heart Camp." Lara said "I probably will want to finish the paintings here in Chambeshi City or even have to wait to begin them till I am back. Working in the bush has problems – never mind the difficulty of transporting large canvases back to town. I also won't be able to work so well at night even if you have electricity generators and cooling fans. I think I might need another role besides being the camp artist. Inonge and Enoch need to feel they can get on with me. I have to fit in with them so I'll see what they want and if I can do it."

"Very practical of you, Lara." Oscar again approved. "What extra work do you have in mind? Inonge said pretty much the same thing about you."

Chapter Five

Enoch and Inonge

When Lara first met Inonge she immediately liked her. Inonge had a friendly manner that was unassuming and kind. She had the polite African way of not looking directly at Lara when she spoke to her but Lara trusted her at once. It was clear that she was very practical and used to working hard as indeed she had done all her life. Inonge's proud father had somehow managed to pay for her education as a school teacher. Lara found it hard to believe that Inonge was Enoch Junior's mother. She appeared far too young to have a son who was a medical student in Britain.

Oscar had arranged the meeting with Enoch and Inonge for himself and Lara as promised. It went well. As Enoch said, Lara's experience with Bill and Maria meant that her excursions to draw and to sketch would tie in with the camp wildlife guides as they explored the bush to set up bird hides and view points and decide on the routes for safaris. When Lara said she had looked after the camp stores and the housekeeping for Maria, Inonge nodded in appreciation.

"Good. You can help me in the evenings with that side of the business. Enoch will be supervising the building of the store rooms, kitchen, bar and lounge. We are providing tented accommodation along the river bank. Oscar wants it to look rather like a film set from the 30s I think."

Inonge smiled at Oscar. She had obviously teased him about this before.

"Oscar is the Great Game Camp Pretender, Lara!" Inonge said.

"Most safari camps are run by white people." Enoch explained. "It is still the age of romance about the Great White Hunter turned Great White Conservationist. To succeed with overseas clients Chambeshians like us really have to be the best."

"One day we will have Chambeshian clients who can afford to come on safari and who also want to save wild animals – I know." Inonge ducked her chin in a little stubborn mannerism that would soon be familiar to Lara.

Once Jason had said right out in front of his Chambeshian colleagues and the other African workers, "Well – what can you expect from Africans – they have no interest in wildlife conservation and their leaders are all corrupt, you know."

Lara still remembered the horrid uncomfortable silence that greeted his words. Jason had not blinked. He was quite unaware of the impact of his statement. At the time Lara was in love with Jason and it was easier to have double standards than to be critical of him. She slept with him with the knowledge that he would be shocked to find out that her previous lover had been Ajay, a brown-skinned Sikh.

Bloody hell! Lara thought remembering Jason, *Sex is never about sleeping with people who have enlightened opinions or are 'good' people – supposing you could know for certain who was 'good' before you kissed them!*

Who might be a 'good' person to sleep with? Tim probably was – but would he be a good lover – he was a good friend – did that mean he might be a good husband? Now Oscar…

Lara's gaze shifted momentarily to Oscar as he and Enoch pored over some maps of the Tin Heart Camp. Her instinct told her Oscar – was not 'good' – but – was he sexy?

Lara made her mind turn away from sex with Oscar though her pulse had already quickened at the idea.

Enoch was definitely 'good' and obviously a very good husband and father too. Inonge clearly believed so. Would Enoch Junior be like his father and be a 'good' person to sleep with and then to stay with for all one's life?

Oscar looked up at Lara and smiled. She smiled back. It was a small complicit smile as if they had shared something.

Did Oscar guess she was thinking about sex?

Lara put her head up a fraction. She was no pushover – that she felt confident about, but the pit of her stomach tightened with excitement all the same.

Chapter Six

Making a Living from Art

Lara had enjoyed talking to Oscar about painting and why she made art. Though he said he would help her make money from her art and he was clear that making money was a necessary objective for any person, he seemed to feel as cynical as she did about the art market. Curiously and contradictorily he supported her in the idea of making art for herself even if she remained worse off for it. They had only too easily wandered away from a discussion about Lara's pay-and-conditions at their first meeting.

"I'm not being romantic about art and the bohemian lifestyle artists are supposed to want," Oscar said. "The world has a way of not turning out as one expects and there is no morality in the way it works. Of course you need to make a living but it is not the same thing as making art. I have seen artists whose work was at one time considered subversive and politically dangerous so they were prevented from making art in their own personal way. Those artists couldn't change their way of seeing the world and making art – oh yes some did give up and try to paint differently but they were the ones who usually suffered most because they lost their souls. You mustn't betray yourself Lara, even if you betray other people."

Lara couldn't imagine a world that wasn't ruled by morality in some degree and she could not imagine betraying anyone else either. Her expression must have given her away because Oscar laughed at her, though not unkindly.

"Well", he continued, "I am ready to do pretty much anything to make money. I expect you have been told that about me – but I would say, Lara – don't sell out yourself to make money. You will become a factory unit producing identikit art. If you are heart and soul an artist then you will always be changing and exploring. You will need freedom from commercial considerations to do that. Some artists make it big and get rich but they lose their freedom – and they lose time – you need time to explore what you are making. Don't worry. We'll do our best to make money for you from your art. If not we'll make money for you anyway and anyhow – so you will have the freedom to make art."

"I can't see how you can do that," Lara said, outspoken as ever. "What about the paintings that I do for you at the Tin Heart Camp, Oscar? How much freedom do I have to experiment or will you want standard conventional wildlife art?"

"We'll talk about it together over those four months," Oscar replied. "The drawings for the brochure have of necessity to be clear and descriptive but the paintings – well we will see as they progress. I like the idea of seeing work that is new and not derivative. I think you are very gifted, Lara, at seeing things in new ways."

Lara's thought returned to the present and the problems of the Tin Heart Safari Camp.

"Your project does worry me," she said. "I think that you will have problems getting clients. Bill and Maria get clients who seem very conventional and some are rather racist. I think they place more trust in white-run safaris."

Oscar shook his head.

"We're looking at new markets. There are Afro-Americans from the States now who are looking at visiting wildlife reserves and there are also people from the Middle-East and even Latin America. Yes – it's a small market but it is there."

"Don't some of those people also like hunting – isn't that a problem?"

Once more Oscar shook his head.

"I myself very strongly draw the line at hunting and killing wild animals," he said. "Maybe some of our clients will also want to go onto hunting camps but there won't be any direct connection between Tin Heart Camp and hunting, I promise you. I don't need to tell you that if the hunting safaris are well organised and ethically run they help to protect game reserves like ours but it is often a complex and fluid relationship. There is too much emphasis on the importance of the 'Big Five' – lion, elephant, buffalo, rhino and leopard – we should encourage safaris to see insects, birds and trees – in fact the whole ecosystem. They, after all, sustain the bigger wild animals."

Lara looked at Oscar with admiration. She liked the sound of his plans. It struck her suddenly that it was odd that he had no pets at his ranch.

"Why don't you have any dogs and cats at Kasenga Ranch?" she asked

"It wouldn't be fair to have a dog when I am away so much," he answered. "And I cannot stand domestic cats."

Chapter Seven

Helen

"It feels like the last place on earth."

Lara pushed her hand forward, palm out, fingers flat against an imagined resistance as she explained her painting to Helen.

"There are no roads, no visible human tracks beyond this line of trees. Even the game paths can't be seen crossing through the tall grasses of the plains. The ground rises at such a slow and constant angle that your eye gives out before it can see the far horizon."

"Here, at this latitude, you stare northwards at a distant light-filled infinity that is not interrupted by sunrise or sunset."

Lara hesitated and stopped, engulfed by memory. She felt the immense aloneness surrounding her. The deaf sky humming over the resonant grasses. She was back in the bush alone working at her easel.

Helen's glance was sharp as she angled it briefly away from the painting towards Lara.

"So this one is also going in the exhibition?"

"Yes." said Lara, "I am ready to let it go. Really! It is finished and I have lived with it long enough."

She dropped her hand onto the pliant canvas and stroked the painting upwards from the impasto of the olive green shaded grove of trees to the thinning scumbled silvery brush marks of the wind-lit shifting grasses of the Great Plain.

Readiness is all, some poet said – Lara had felt ready for a while. *God knows it's taken me a long enough time to reach this point and to bring these paintings to completion. Hard to let them go too. Each one is a child sent out to face the world. It takes a long time to feel that I can let even one go with some confidence.*

Helen said, "They'll sell, I think – but not to your regular customers. They may feel betrayed. They don't like their favourite artists to change style or to challenge them with new ideas."

Lara shrugged thinking first of herself and Jason, then of Tim and Liseli.

Betrayal is not new to me. Believe it! The people who buy my art don't own my soul. I am tired of people who think they have bought a controlling share of me when they buy one of my paintings.

Reading Lara's thoughts, Helen smiled and her giant jewelled earrings flashed and shook noisily.

"We need your regular buyers, Lara. It's hard work building a new clientèle.'

"Oh Helen – you wonderful woman – what would I do without you!"

Lara bent to kiss Helen on both cheeks and to hug her short solid body.

"Without you, Helen, all my art would be stacked in my studio and lost to the world – and you still manage to stay my friend in spite of all the trouble I give you!"

"There you go, Lara." Helen smiled, "It's all about love of art, love of money and love of hard work! What else makes the world go round?

Chapter Eight

Flying

Three weeks before her solo exhibition Oscar flew Lara up to the Tin Heart Camp on a one day trip.

"Natan and I have got some business to sort out with a local headman at Busanga," Oscar had said when he proposed the trip to Lara.

"Natan can't spare much time so we'll fly up to the camp site at Kasama and he and I will drive to Busanga from there. We'll leave at first light from the airstrip at my ranch, arrive at the camp about 8 a.m. for breakfast – that gives us six hours in total. An hour plus to reach the village and chat to this chap – that'll take most of the time – then back to the camp – another hour plus. We have to be back in Chambeshi City before the sun sets. Curfews and flight permissions all sorted."

"If you like you can come up with us – we'll have to leave you at the camp site. No uninvited guests allowed at our meeting I'm afraid, but it will give you a chance to look around the camp and see how you feel about it and the paintings you might want to do."

Lara, surprised to feel uncertain and shy about the invitation, said yes in her most positive way. She felt a strong antipathy for Natan. It was unusual for her to dislike anyone so much. Was she glad not to be making the trip alone with Oscar or was she a little disappointed? Oscar had made her feel special, as if she was the centre of his attention when he had been with her before. On this trip though, she was just to be the hanger-on, the spare part.

Reasonable enough, Lara thought, *I am rather in the position of an employee.*

Well, she was used to being independent. It would be lovely to be back in the bush even if it was just for a day and she had never flown in a small plane before. That would be exciting.

It was.

Lara, dressed in her light slacks and bush jacket, arrived in good time, with her camera, binoculars, hat, insect repellent and sketch books all packed in her rucksack. Natan ignored her. Oscar greeted her with a kiss on both cheeks and then gestured at the tray of coffee on his desk.

"Help yourself. Use the bathroom. I'll do the flight checks. We're off in 10 minutes."

The plane felt small and fragile when Lara climbed into it. She knew it had to be light to take off but the thin materials of its fabrication and its delicate struts filled her with doubt. The engine, however, proved both powerful and deafening even with ear protectors on. Surely the plane must rattle itself to bits very soon. Conversation was obviously impossible but Lara was isolated in the back seat behind Oscar and Natan. Oscar turned to her, smiled and gave a thumbs-up sign. Natan just stared ahead. The plane shuddered and bumped its way down the grass airstrip. Lara felt heavier with every dragging judder then there was a sudden lift, a momentary weightless sensation, the engine note changed and they were flying above Chambeshi towards the Tin Heart Camp. Lara was entranced. She could view her beloved Chambeshi from the perspective of the red-tailed kites and snake eagles who had circled above her when she had been in the bush with Jason.

The light aircraft banked away from Chambeshi's grey shanty towns. The ramshackle huts lay low, hidden under dust and smoke and surrounded by webs of broken pot-holed dirt tracks on which ant-like people journeyed in search of work and food.

Clumped at the edge of the tarred roads were beetle-sized coaches and squat maggot minibuses that flicked out wing-like doors to swallow up those commuters who had paper money for fares. Behind Lara in the rising sun, Chambeshi City's few skyscrapers glistened with a deceptive, but enticing beauty. The plane climbed steadily, its route taking them over ransacked vegetable gardens and empty fields prickled with the stalks of old dry crops. Further out, the ochre earth was smoothed and flattened by the sun or blackened by fires that had been lit to flush mice and rats into traps for food.

At last they reached their maximum height and the plane levelled out. The first half of their flight would follow the power lines on their northward march to the copper mines. Next they would turn north-west to fly up the Kasama River as it twisted over rapids on its sheltered journey through hills and valleys. Finally the plane would reach the start of the endless flood plains above the escarpment, the site of the safari camp and Oscar's gold mine.

Away from the city Chambeshi was all green and gold, its yellowing grass still thick and high. Under the trees, Lara saw long dark shadows first point south-west towards the camp then gradually rotate south and grow shorter. At midday they would hide themselves under the leafy crowns of the brachystegia forest. She gazed in wonder and delight, her eyes devouring the terrain below her, absorbing and learning its geography. She saw country roads, a satellite station, large irrigated farms, little settlements, thatched villages, earth dams and small streams all relating to the physical logic of the landscape. From her viewpoint above Chambeshi she could understand how and why people had chosen to occupy particular places in the natural world. What swelled Lara's heart with pleasure was the thought of the enormous stretches of wilderness that lay ahead of her. Wildernesses where perhaps wild animals could still live untrammelled lives without fear of humans and guns.

Oscar, turning to Lara, pointed out elephants and large

herds of springbok, antelope and zebra. Lara realised with a sense of exclusion that he and Natan had been talking to each other through communicating headphones but the immediate excitement of seeing the game below her put that feeling out of her mind.

They were approaching the camp much too soon for Lara and much too fast for her to take it all in as she would have liked. The first thing she saw was an ugly man-made structure and a huge raw oval wound in the green of the woodland. It was the jagged headgear of the mine poking up at the sky and the scarred red gash of bare poisoned earth of tailings below it. Next, Lara had glimpses of the broad river gleaming among rocks and trees. As they banked over it she saw the horizon open up northwards into the vast treeless Kasenga Plains. Immediately below was a cleared space with a circle of thatched buildings that must be the camp site. Instead of floating peacefully in a muted sky, the Cessna had begun a noisy pell-mell rush towards the ground. Oscar made two low passes over the grass airfield to clear it of wild animals. As they turned for their final approach, Lara saw that a Land Cruiser had left the camp and was making its bumpy way towards them. A man waved from the driver's seat. Lara held her breath while the plane slowed, seemed to hesitate, landed, lurched awkwardly, then jolted and swayed over the rough ground towards the tree line and the approaching vehicle. Oscar cut the engine and the vibrating silence and stillness of the African bush engulfed them. Glad at last to stretch and move, Lara climbed out of the plane into the bright sunshine and a hot scent-laden breeze and knew this was where she belonged and this was what inspired her art.

Mainza Mbala, the camp manager, had come to meet them. A breakfast of egg and bacon was being cooked right now and would be served in the dining room overlooking the river, he said, smiling and shaking hands with each of them in turn. The Land Cruiser was ready for Natan and Oscar's expedition and an armed game guard was waiting to accompany Lara if she wanted to make any excursions beyond the camp perimeter during the day. Oscar had arranged for everyone's needs to be met. Hunger made the excellent breakfast taste more delicious and disappear rapidly. Oscar and Natan wasted no time in leaving on their mission; the camp staff returned to their chores and Lara was soon alone. It was strange being left to her own devices but Lara had already talked to Oscar about the camp and the places that he wanted her to paint the week before. First she asked Mainza to show her the camp and explain its situation and what animals would be found in its vicinity. Then she familiarised herself with the immediate river bank and established how it fitted into the local geography from her memories of what she had seen from the Cessna. She took photos and made notes and sketches. Her Polaroid camera would give her instant images but the quality would be poor. Better photos from her Nikon would have to be developed and printed back in the city. She observed places where hippos had left the river at night, noticed the dung and the spoor of wild creatures who wandered around the camp, made notes of the birds she saw, and delighted in the bird calls. The sounds of cicadas and crickets, the movements and rustles of grasses and leaves under the sun's dry heat and the wind's secret forays through branches and bushes provided the familiar background sound texture to her wanderings. Lara came alive, all of her senses sharpened. Even inside the camp fence it was necessary to take care, not only to avoid disturbing a snake, but in order not to miss the opportunity of seeing a leguvaan, turning its beady slitted eye on her before sliding into a hole in search of prey, or of glimpsing a sun squirrel skip behind a branch on its way to find food high above her. She tried sketching birds, but a crested barbet flew off too quickly. Following the sound of its call, she had walked a short distance off the road and come again to the river bank. She was watching a pied kingfisher dive into the river when her skin prickled, she turned her head very slightly and then kept very still as three elephants entered the river only ten metres downstream from her. Their leader was a giant bull whose huge asymmetrical tusks made his appearance quite distinctive. The river was deep at this point, its surface smooth and unbroken by ripples yet the elephants walked steadily and unhesitatingly at an angle across to the opposite bank. Lara saw the lower part of their limbs and the ends of their trunks darken and gleam in the water. The three stately beasts apparently walked on the deep river's surface but they knew, and had always known, that a sunken ridge of rock made a ford for them at that point. They went without haste, without a sound and vanished into the thick riverine forest opposite.

"Thank you, God thank you!" Lara said. It was a gift, this beautiful visitation. Had she seen them or imagined them? The water was smooth again. The rocks where the elephants climbed out of the river were already drying. Elephants move through a forest without a sound. These three were once again silent and invisible to her. Minutes later Lara heard the ripping and tearing of the upper branches of the Ilala palm trees as they fed on the leaves. Of the elephants there was no other sign.

Back at the camp, Lara told the camp manager Mainza about the leading elephant.

"That is the one that Mr Njobvu calls the 'Old Chief'." Mainza said smiling with pride. "Mr Njobvu says that he is very special, that bull, and that he brings blessings to the Tin Heart Camp and our camp here. Mr Njobvu's ancestors are the people of the elephant. That is how it is."

Chapter Nine

The Tin Heart Gold Mine

It was midday and very hot. Normally this would be a time to rest but Lara had to be ready to leave when Oscar and Natan returned from their trip so she knew she would have to go out sketching in the heat. Mainza had arranged a light salad for her lunch. Tembo Chulu was standing ready to drive her out of the camp to take photos of the mine and then a short way from the river to a viewpoint above the camp and last to some rapids beyond the camp. Lara didn't know if it was the deadening effect of the heat and the beer shandy she had rashly indulged in with her food, but she found the mine site thoroughly oppressive.

The heat of the African bush is oppressive at midday but it is green and still without obvious movement. All living creatures hide in the darkest shade they can find. They are followed by flies and biting insects whose incessant hum and buzz quieten as they settle down to feast on animal blood. The mine site, however, was an organised monster of rusted metal rearing its hoists and gears up over the grills and boxes that guarded the pumps and mine shaft. It stood menacingly in the midst of a great open sore of bare and empty earth that ate its way into the surrounding forest. Lara felt it might move, that it was alive with some vile and sinister spite. On the tree line skulked two grim grey shapes made of concrete blocks and roofed with corrugated iron sheets. The heat and devastation of the place, intensified by its burning hot metal structure, made Lara's head ache. Oscar wanted a painting of it nonetheless. How would she interpret this place? Would he like the way she painted its harsh ugliness? A pump was still working at the mine, pumping a thin stream of orange coloured froth into the milky-blue lake in the bottom of the bare blood-coloured oval hollow that lay between the mine and the river.

Tembo shook his head, fattening out his bottom lip expressively. His loaded gun rested casually against his shoulder, pointing safely upwards.

"It's been like that always." he said. "Always since the mine was here. Nothing grows – the earth is too sick – too poisoned. It used to send all its badness into the river – but not now. Not anymore. Now the land here is just dead. The plants stay away and so do the birds."

It was true. The demarcation between the gravel of the poisoned earth and the bush surrounding it was as sharp as if it had been ploughed and harrowed the day before.

Had the mine ever produced enough gold to justify the damage it had caused? Sadness grew in Lara, then fury. Could the land ever be healed? She took photographs, made some scribbled sketches that almost tore through the paper of her sketchbook then shoved a handful of red stones into her bag as markers of the colour of the place. As she turned to leave Lara passed close by the old grey cottage and its concrete block shed lurking by the road out. For no reason they filled her with foreboding.

"They are locked!" Tembo said. "Storerooms for Mr. Mynhardt."

"It's all so ugly." Lara said. "And it'll be here forever – longer than I'll live!"

Lara's lunchtime drink of shandy made it necessary for her to stop and find somewhere private for a pee. As soon as they left the area of the mine, she asked Tembo to park the Cruiser for a moment. He insisted on walking into the bush ahead of her to make certain there were no lion about. Lara didn't let him see her smile but she did get him to return to the Cruiser while she ducked behind a wild hibiscus. As she stood up to adjust her trousers Lara looked around and behind her. That was when she first saw the cemetery. It was so overgrown, its iron crosses so rusted, its concrete graves so stained that it was completely camouflaged. She would not have seen it except that a soft rustle and an odd unnatural sound drew her eye to a rusted and creaking sheet of tin fastened to one of the fence posts that protected the site.

Chapter Ten

The War Cemetery

The tin heart swung gently in the breeze.

It was made from a half-metre-square sheet of galvanised tin that had been shaped with a pair of snips into a large heart. The tin heart was fastened by wire at its centre top and bottom to the trunk of an old dead tree that guarded the tiny cemetery. With time and wind it had become creased so that it folded down the middle into a half-open book, a book that had once carried a painted message on its surface but the words had faded and rubbed away. As the soft wind rocked it, the tin heart creaked and scraped out an arbitrary, meaningless dirge. Who had fastened this token of love to the edge of the cemetery? Was it a mother, sister, wife, lover, friend or nurse? For whom had the faded words been painted and by whom? Someone bereaved or their agent? No one would ever know and no one would ever ask.

Lara, open-mouthed, stood staring and wondering. Perhaps if she listened long enough over hours, days, weeks, months, seasons and years, a rhythm or a pattern or music would gradually emerge and be heard. It was very hot in the bush by the cemetery but the painful little groans of the tin heart froze her own heart. Here in the bush, was a symbol of undying love that was no longer remembered or seen by anyone. The vanished words must surely refer to one of the occupants of the graves but there was no obvious clue to make a linkage with any of the dead.

Oscar had told her that the mine had taken its name from the tin heart at the cemetery but given no details. Jannie Oosthuizen had decided on the name apparently. Lara had not expected to find the overgrown cemetery and Oscar had not suggested she visit it. She had found it by chance and because of her need to pee. Strands of the fence were broken and sagging in several places but it still more or less enclosed the cemetery. Possibly the wire had not been stolen to make animal traps because it surrounded burial sites and was believed by local villagers to be the home of ghosts. Ghosts of white men, as Lara could see from the names on the eight iron crosses on the eight concrete rectangular graves. No chance of jackals and hyenas digging up the bodies from under that weight of cement. They were all soldiers – all British, all but one were non-commissioned men, all were young, most not twenty, none over thirty. All had died, the iron plaques said, after long illnesses, all after November 1918, most in late 1919.

Why – and how – in such an isolated place – how extraordinary it was that British soldiers were here – so many thousands of miles from the fighting in northern Europe. Why was this war forgotten? Lara was held at the cemetery by fascination but inside her chest, against her heart pressed an irrational and paralysing fear which made her want to run away. Death by illness in the bush miles from anywhere. How desperate, how lonely and who had cared for these sick boy soldiers, who had buried them, who had made the crosses that bore their names?

Back at the Cruiser, Lara asked Tembo if he knew anything about the cemetery.

"You can ask the father of Mr Enoch Njobvu, Mr Samuel Njobvu, if you go to make drawings in his village – it's near here. He knows the stories about the graveyard. He was a *'mwana',* a child then – about six years old maybe," Tembo answered. "Mr Njobvu perhaps will take you to meet him when you come again."

There was a pot of strong brown tea waiting for Lara in the dining room back at the camp. Mainza had asked the cook to make a jam-filled sponge cake in her honour. It was not Lara's favourite treat but she ate two slices out of politeness while she waited for Oscar and Natan to return. She saw Mainza walk to the camp gate and talk to Tembo, who was on watch there while they both looked down the road. It was getting very late. Oscar had said they should leave by 4.30. It was already after that time. At 5 o'clock the sound of a vehicle could be heard from a distance away. Lara heard it shift gears and the engine note change as it negotiated a steep incline. It turned down a gully and seemed to go away in a long circuit before it could be heard finally approaching the camp. When she saw him, Oscar was already talking to Mainza. He waved at Lara to come over. Natan was not with him.

"Sorry, Lara. I'm much later than planned but we just about have enough daylight to get home. We'll talk when we are in the plane. Are you okay?"

"Where's Natan?" Lara asked, puzzled.

"Gone with his friends. Change of plans." Oscar shot a quick glance at Lara.

What on earth! Lara thought.

She couldn't imagine Natan walking through the bush. He had only carried a minimal amount of stuff with him in a back pack.

Yes he was tough! He had probably been a soldier in the Israeli Army. But why was he here? And who would he have met and gone away with in this isolated part of Chambeshi? Had Oscar done something to Natan? Shot him and dumped his body for the hyenas to tidy up? Oscar looked so sane and relaxed and he had no motive that Lara could think of. What a ridiculous idea!

They were in the Cruiser bumping along the track back to the airstrip. Conversation was impossible. The windsock half way down the airstrip was limp and hardly moving. Oscar looked at it, licked his forefinger and held it up, made a quick study of the few soft stationary clouds above. Mainza was already driving down the airstrip ahead of the plane hooting noisily. Lara saw a bush buck start up, begin to run across the airstrip and then turn and flee into the forest. Oscar raced through the flight checks, swung the propeller and finally the plane bumped down after Mainza's Cruiser to turn and take off into what little wind there was. They were airborne and flying into the sun. Oscar banked and turned the plane south-east. They climbed slowly over the river. A tiny excited Tembo waved from the camp gate and they were on their way back to the city.

Oscar had given Lara the headset with the intercom that Natan had used but neither of them spoke much. Lara had important questions for Oscar but judged that she couldn't expect proper answers mid-flight. By the time they reached the airfield at Oscar's ranch, the sun was a red sphere on the west horizon and lights had come on all over Chambeshi City, except in the shanty town where there was only an occasional orange fire burning. Pascal had told Lara that people in the shanty towns barricaded themselves into their shacks at night to escape thieves and marauders. That was a life that Lara could not imagine.

"You must be tired, Lara," Oscar said as he helped her out of the plane.

"You look pretty tired yourself," she said. Oscar shrugged.

"I am – but do stay for supper, Lara – I want to hear how your day was and what you think about the paintings I want. Stay for a drink, anyway."

As Lara turned to go into the house, Oscar put an encouraging but too-familiar hand on her buttock. Lara leapt forward enraged.

"Don't do that ever!" she said turning to face him.

Oscar's eyes widened in surprise, but then into amusement and contrition.

"Sorry, Lara. I didn't mean anything by it."

Lara was embarrassed to have lost her temper so easily but still angry at being touched in such a way.

"It's such a -" but could she explain to someone of Oscar's age how it made her feel?

"It's demeaning!" she said emphatically.

"I know." he acknowledged quietly. "I'm old and badly brought up. Sorry I offended you. Please come in. Let's just sit down and relax – it's been a long day."

Lara had not one, but two gin and tonics. Oscar offered her olives and salted nuts. She was suddenly loquacious and reckless.

"What did happen to Natan, Oscar? Whatever did you do to him? Abandon him? Murder him?"

She stopped, shocked by what she had said but Oscar seemed unfazed. He grinned.

"Lara – you have a wild imagination as well as immense creative talent. Natan had arranged to meet a contact at Chief Sanga's village who was to drive him to the Congo border. He has business there and will fly back from Kinshasa. He is sourcing gemstones for business partners in Europe. That's all I know. It wouldn't be worth killing him until he returns with his loot, don't you think? Okay – shall we eat? I think you're a little tipsy from hunger."

"Oh shit!" Lara said. "I am a bit pissed and I have to drive home."

"My driver can take you home, Lara. You can collect your car tomorrow – or you can have the guest wing tonight and lock yourself safely in there after supper."

Lara thought of the empty fridge in Tim's flat. She was increasingly curious about Oscar. Curiosity was probably dangerous.

"Thank you, Oscar." she said. "Supper and the guest wing sound perfect."

Oscar's cook served them steak and salad and Oscar opened a red Boschendal wine from South Africa. They talked about the Tin Heart Camp and Lara's ideas for her paintings.

"I want to paint the mine and the cemetery," Lara said, "but perhaps as they are seen by the people who live near them – you know – with the ghosts of the dead people and wild creatures around them – floating – perhaps a bit like Chagall's paintings."

"Well – you might scare away both my workers and my clients,"

Oscar responded, "but I do want you to use your imagination and skills freely. Show me your rough sketches and ideas – possibly there will be room for different interpretations. We'll see."

Lara was falling asleep.

"Must go to bed, Oscar." she said dozily. "Thanks for everything."

Oscar stood up. He accompanied Lara to the door.

"Lara," he said smiling gently, "When I am not tired and when you are not pissed and – if you want to – I will make love to you."

Lara's mouth fell open.

Without touching her with his hands he bent his head and kissed her lightly on each cheek, then he kissed her on her lips at first tenderly then harder.

Lara saw the sharpening stubble on his chin, the softening skin under his eyes, the puckering of his full-lipped mouth and shut her eyes. She had intended to speak but said nothing more. Oscar tasted of wine and garlic and maleness. His lips were fleshy and muscular, the bones of his face solid, his teeth sharp, his tongue searched and explored. Lara's body turned to liquid fire. A strange passionate sound like no wild animal she had ever heard came from deep in her. She wanted this moment to last forever, but Oscar lifted his head.

"Goodnight Lara. Sleep well."

He stroked her nose lightly with a finger and turned away.

In the guest room, Lara locked her door, unlocked it, locked it, decided she must think about things – about Oscar – about sex – about how curiosity killed the cat – about unlocking the door again or was it locking it properly at last. She took off her clothes, climbed into bed and fell fast asleep.

Chapter Eleven

A Pact with the Devil

Lara slept most of the next morning. She had woken before sunrise, thirsty, needing to pee and hating the sour wine taste in her mouth. She had no toothbrush but saw when she got to the bathroom that Oscar provided new plastic-wrapped toothbrushes, toothpaste, and hotel packs of soap and shampoo for his guests. It was a mistake to wash her face and brush her teeth so early because when she got back into bed she thought that she would never get back to sleep again. What was she doing here? What had Oscar said about making love to her? What did he mean? Wasn't it madness to consider an affair with someone that old and someone who Tim thought might be bad? She was now sober. She could dress, get into her car and drive away before breakfast – just leave a note. Nothing had happened in the night and in the end she had left the door unlocked. How humiliating was that? She wanted Oscar's commission and she was fairly sure that he would honour his promise even if she didn't sleep with him. She wanted to have sex with Oscar. She thought of his kiss. It aroused her. She put her hand on her clitoris, started to masturbate and fell back to sleep at once.

It was embarrassing to wake up so late but the day was not going to go backwards. Lara showered and dressed in yesterday's clothes. She was hungry. Time to go and find Oscar and say a possibly embarrassed goodbye. It was a peaceful Sunday morning.

None of Oscar's staff were around. The house was quiet, then Lara heard the sound of music from the sitting room. Teasing orchestral music, a mix of jazz and lyrical folk, magically light and dark. Lara followed it and found Oscar stretched out on the settee, spectacles on his nose, a book in his hand. A tray of coffee and box of chocolates on the table by him. Lara looked at them greedily.

"Would you like some coffee?" Oscar offered, sitting up to pour her a cup.

"Yes please. What's playing? It's lovely." Lara asked.

"Stravinsky's 'Soldier's Tale' – it's a fable about a soldier who makes a pact with the Devil. He wants money in exchange for his violin and his musical ability. Of course he regrets it and the Devil takes his soul and his freedom. Never give up your art for money, Lara!"

Lara smiled. Of course she wouldn't. She knew that.

Sipping coffee and munching chocolates she asked, "What about you, Oscar? Weren't you once a soldier? Would you make a Faustian pact with the Devil?"

Oscar leant back on the settee again.

"Perhaps I already have – but not in exchange for Helen of Troy. Instead I want you, Lara."

Lara looked at her coffee cup. She could still leave. With his book on his lap and his specs on his nose Oscar was relaxed and not threatening.

"So you haven't run away from me." Oscar said.

"No." Lara answered. She put down her coffee cup, stood up and walked to Oscar's side. She picked up his book and put it on the floor, lifted off his specs and sat beside him. Her hip against his.

"You're old, Oscar." she said. "Too old for me!"

"Yes." he replied with a smile. "And I am bad. Too bad for you." Lara's heart went thud so loudly that he heard it too and he pulled her face down close to his and they kissed until Lara was gasping and moaning.

"You're wicked too, Lara!" Oscar said.

"Oh I am! I am!"

Lara, guided by Oscar's hands, swung her leg over Oscar's prone body hearing his groan of pleasure with satisfaction. However did she know how to behave so badly? She pulled off her shirt and undid her bra so he could reach her breasts and suck and bite them which he did with thoroughness. Now she herself was wild with desire but she understood that Oscar was in no hurry. He held her upper arms firmly and pushed her upright. She flung back her head, living in that moment of the sweet and terrible sensation of sexual passion.

"Let me look at you." he ordered. "We will do it my way slowly – very slowly. I want you to come when I am ready."

"Oh God!" Lara said. "Oh God!"

Chapter Twelve

The Solo Exhibition

It was the opening of Lara's first solo exhibition. Nervousness meant she hadn't eaten all day and anticipation had made her drink two large glasses of wine faster than her usual rate. She felt alone. Thank God Brian and Jane weren't there to add to her tension. Oscar had jetted off to America which was in some ways a relief because she had been able to focus on her work.

Helen was soothing and supportive. "It's a really good show Lara. Nothing for you to worry about – it'll sell well."

Lara found she missed Tim. The quality of his friendship provided her with something special. What was it exactly? He's reliable, steady, more than that, Tim is constant. "I'm not constant." Lara thought. "Up and down and emotional – neurotic about my art and me. Selfish too." She hated the time before exhibitions. "Why did I do this? Why do I make art and expose myself to scrutiny by strangers?"

Lara was returning from another unnecessary journey to the gallery storeroom. She'd lost her wineglass again and her face felt stiff from smiling at people she didn't know when she heard Tim's voice.

"Hello Lara!" he said smiling his wide smile.

Lara was so delighted to see him that she flung her arms around him. She might have chosen to be less demonstrative if his appearance hadn't been so unexpected and hoped-for. She pulled back as she sensed Tim's real pleasure in her affectionate greeting and tried to crack a joke. She mustn't give him the wrong idea.

"Oh gosh! I really need an international reporter to write about my exhibition – thank God you're here, Tim!" then seeing his eyes shadow she softened and added. "I have so much to tell you! You must tell me how are you and what your news is, Tim, but first come and tell me what you think of the exhibition and which paintings you think successful. I have saved a painting for you in lieu of rent for my studio. I hope that you like it."

"Oscar's not here?" Tim looked over one shoulder then the other.

"No. He is in America this time touting his safari camp. He's back in a few days."

"So have you succumbed to his charms, Lara?"

"Well – to his money, Tim. Well – I have a job with Enoch and a commission from Oscar – it is such a relief! I have another year paid for in Chambeshi with this exhibition and I can stay as long as I don't spend everything I've earned – hey – look Helen needs me – I have to talk to my buyers – Tim – lets go out afterwards – can we?"

Afterwards, of course, there was a large party which went out to the new Manchurian-style restaurant. It meant that everyone was constantly up and down from the table as they selected new bowls of meat and vegetables to be grilled and spiced by the busy cooks. Lara felt obliged to speak to everyone there: Helen and Michel, Enoch and Inonge, Maria – on her own as Bill was busy at their camp – Chimunya and Pascal. It meant that she didn't get to have a private conversation with Tim till the end of the evening when they were finally left alone together in the bar. By then, Tim, with his information-gathering skills, had found out about Lara's plans to work at the Tin Heart Camp over the winter from Enoch and Inonge and he had heard from Helen about Lara's commission from Oscar and the estimated success of sales of paintings at her Preview.

Lara had noticed that Tim was engaged in what seemed to be a very serious discourse with Helen's boyfriend, Michel, in which the mouth of the Cultural Attaché turned down with even more disapproval than usual for a French diplomat. Later Tim and Pascal had an animated discussion. Pascal's hands and head agitated emphatically as he laughed. Lara wondered for a moment about the ability of Chambeshians to smile and laugh while describing sad and bad events. What could be the subject of their conversation?

"Well that's over – thank God!" Lara said with a smile at they leant against the counter, cigarettes in hand and a bottled beer gleaming with moisture in front of each of them. She looked at Tim properly for the first time and saw that he was very tired. The skin around his eyes was mauve, a muscle in his jaw tensed and jumped. He drew deep on his cigarette and closed his eyes for a brief moment.

"That's better." he said exhaling slowly. "I have pretty much had it tonight. I will have to crash soon or I'll fall over."

"What's happening, Tim? How come you're so stressed?" Lara asked in concern.

"Developments, my dear Lara! Things are building up in the region – and especially here." Tim glanced suspiciously at the barman in case he was eavesdropping on their conversation but a heavily made up Chambeshian woman in a tight shiny red dress had the barman's full attention. It was too early for her to start her night's work of visiting the hotel bedrooms of lonely businessmen.

"I don't suppose you know what's going on here in Chambeshi, do you Lara?"

"Sort of," Lara said vague and defensive.

Tim raised an eyebrow at Lara then explained.

"The President's support for the liberation struggle in Southern Africa has wrecked Chambeshi's economy – you know that. Unrest is building up and money is coming in to support the dissidents here – there is even talk of money to fund a coup. General Miyanda, the head of the army, is tipped as the possible coup leader. The trouble further west in Angola has spread across the borders into Chambeshi and the rebel leader from there – General Njoka, as he styles himself – is talking of taking over the whole of the Western province of Chambeshi and setting up a breakaway state. Anyway it's all happening on at least two fronts at the moment. I am here to try and get an interview with President Chona this weekend and then I am off to explore the Angolan side of things on Monday. It's very serious, Lara – Michel was dropping big hints about the sources of the money that is coming into Chambeshi and Angola – Russia one side – CIA the other – Israel has Mossad agents in the region and it has also been buttering up President Chona – wish that strange friend of Oscar's, Natan, was not so close-mouthed – bet he knows a thing or two."

"But why, Tim? What is the reason to cause all this trouble? Who stands to gain and what do they think they'll achieve?"

Lara was not unaware of the situation but, being single-minded about her exhibition, she had chosen to ignore it and to avoid even buying the local paper. Perhaps it was now time for her to give Chambeshian politics some practical consideration.

"Oh well – it's all rumour and gossip right now." Tim continued with a tired sigh. "The CIA wants simply to destabilise the whole region rather than let it become socialist or communist. They are terrified about South Africa being run by Reds – God – dare they allow Africa to develop at all? Anyhow the mines are immense and valuable sources not just of copper but of plutonium and uranium and there's possibly even oil – whoever exploits these resources could tip the balance of world power – so better no power in control than the wrong power – it's very cynical. Israel and Holland between them manage the precious gems market and that is probably the easiest trade for smugglers to exploit in a war situation. The Cold War is very hot in Africa believe me!"

"So what should I look out for then – what should I do? I don't want to leave – I don't have to – do I?" Lara asked slowly.

Tim shook his head.

"It all may come to nothing Lara, but you are well-placed to keep abreast of any developments and get out of Chambeshi if there's a coup. Chimunya and Pascal, Pascal especially, both have their ears to the ground – Helen probably knows an awful lot too. That's the reason that Michel is so friendly with her – I think he really prefers young black boys to women. Helen's bar is the place to go to get the latest on Chambeshian politics and Helen is still friends with her ex-husband – he's a wheeler-dealer if ever I saw one. You though, are the one, Lara, who can find out about things -"

"Me! How?" Lara felt indignant and confused.

"Why – through Oscar of course – I think he must know exactly what is going on in Chambeshi and I am sure he has a finger in every pie."

Lara's face creased in distress.

"Tim – honestly – I just don't think he is a bad person – he's kind – and he has a sense of humour – besides don't you like him yourself?"

Tim's face relaxed and he smiled.

"I guess we all go on instinct in the end. I guess Hitler didn't have a sense of humour. Maybe it's good that Oscar does have one. Yes Lara – I like Oscar too – maybe I'm just jealous of him!"

"You don't need to be Tim – you are my very best friend!" but Lara knew that wasn't what Tim meant and she also knew she wasn't being quite truthful though she wasn't quite sure in what way she was being dishonest.

"I'm so tired I no longer make any sense." Tim said. "I could ask you to sleep with me tonight Lara and it wouldn't be a euphemism. I don't think you'll see me for 24 hours at least. I hope I don't fall asleep in the taxi going home because I won't wake up."

Lara hesitated. Right now she wanted to put her arms around

Tim and invite him to come home and sleep in her bed at the latest place where she was house-sitting. That would be all – just friendship – but there was tomorrow to think about and the week after that Oscar would return from Berlin.

Enoch, Inonge and Oscar were planning to drive up to the Tin Heart Camp I the next week. Lara was to travel up with them and stay there on for several months.

"It's time to move, Tim." she said. "I could use some rest too."

Part Eight

The Tin Heart Gold Mine 1985

Chapter One

Buffalo

The National Park was opening for the winter season. The rainy season was over except for occasional light showers and it was time for the various safari businesses to set themselves up again. Oscar and Enoch were to be among them for the first time. Their Cruisers had been packed up ready for the trip the night before. Enoch and Inonge would go on ahead leaving right after breakfast and arriving at the camp in the early afternoon. Following his trip, Oscar said he had office work to do first and would leave later.

"You'll travel with me, Lara." he said. "You're okay about that? If you can get here about 11 o'clock we'll set straight off."

So she wasn't being invited to his bed the night before they left then? Would she be invited again? She refused to feel bad about her behaviour that Sunday a month ago. It had been wonderful even if it only happened once but what did it mean for her relationship with Oscar?

Since the day they had spent making love to Stravinsky's music, Lara had not been alone with Oscar and he had not shown by words or manners that he remembered it or that it had changed their relationship. He greeted her as he always did with a continental kiss that now seemed cool – even indifferent. He wasn't in love with her. They had had sex. For a while she had had to fight back her feeling that she was in love with him. That was how sex made you feel. You became so aware of someone – so attuned to them, so wired to them physically and emotionally that it seemed like love. But Lara knew she couldn't be in love with Oscar. They had nothing in common except maybe an interest in art and not the same art either.

Lara swallowed hard. She found it difficult to appear neutral and unmoved when her body became electric in Oscar's presence and remained that way for hours after. She willed herself to keep focussed on their discussions about the first rough paintings she was developing from her sketches of Kasama.

"Sure!" she said and smiled directly at Oscar.

"Good!" he confirmed and returned her gaze as directly.

I'll show him that I'm his equal in sex at least. Lara thought. *But, of course, I can't be. I don't know what he knows. Maybe I don't even want to know. I do like the sensation of my body burning up and fizzing with sexuality though – but what do I do with this feeling –* .

Lara noticed that her heightened awareness of herself had an impact on all the men she knew. Whatever they did or did not understand about her, they all reacted to some degree at least by noticing her more.

Lara arrived promptly for the trip as she had promised. She parked her small jeep, lifted out her rucksack and the sketchbook and materials that she liked to keep to hand, and went to stow then in the space behind the passenger seat. The larger part of her studio equipment was already in the back of the Cruiser. She waited for Oscar by the Cruiser and watched as he left the house and came to greet her, trying to see him dispassionately. She saw again the physical ease with which he moved, his alertness, the way he exuded energy and zest for life and how his cropped grey hair was thinning. She was surprised to feel anger building up in her.

"Lara! Hello. You should have come inside." he said. He put down his bag and took both her hands in his. As usual he kissed her on each cheek but she didn't smile in response. Oscar folded her hands up palms together and kissed each upward-facing thumb. Looking up at her face, he turned his head sideways.

"You are angry with me, Lara."

Then he bent and kissed her at the base of her throat.

"Can I make love to you again, Lara?"

"You are a bastard, Oscar!" Lara didn't feel in control of her voice. She coughed a little to clear her throat and smooth her words. "Do you think you can just make love to me when it suits you? You bastard! What about me? What about when I want to make love? Do you think you can just leave me and pick me up when you want? I am not just a convenience! Suppose I want to make love to you, Oscar!"

She stopped, suddenly uncertain.

Was Oscar appalled by her? She was appalled by what she was saying. She hadn't even known it was what she thought. Should she take her case out of the Cruiser again? It must be his turn to be angry.

"Lara, my dear Lara!" Oscar said looking straight at her. "As long as you promise never to fall in love with me – I will make love to you as often as you want."

Lara was silent.

"Now we must leave – are you coming?" and he stroked her cheek once again with a soft swift touch.

Lara stared at him, hesitated, then turned and climbed into the Cruiser.

Oscar climbed into the driver's seat. He turned to Lara. She saw again that his eyes were blue but she could not read his expression at all.

"Lara – don't feel you have no choices. You can still make the paintings for me without coming to the Tin Heart Camp. You are free to go, you know. You can come if you like and we won't have sex if you don't want to."

Lara looked away. No sensible course of action suggested itself. She wanted to be in the bush. She wanted to paint.

"Okay. Let's go and let's not have sex any more, Oscar. It's impossible not to care about the people one has slept with – at least that's what I find – so it's better for me not to have sex with you."

"You find that do you Lara? I don't have that problem." Oscar said. "That's the deal then – no sex – and no hard feelings?"

Lara glanced at him quickly. If she could have killed him with a look she would have done it right then. Anyway Oscar wasn't staying long at the camp. In a few days she would be shot of him.

"Yes!" she said. "That's definite."

Lara had the feeling that Oscar was laughing at her but she wasn't going to give him the satisfaction of looking at him to check his expression. She stared straight ahead as Oscar manoeuvred his way out of Chambeshi past the illegal street markets, roadside stalls and crowds of buyers, sellers, thieves and beggars on the fringes of the shanty towns. They were facing a 5 hour long drive to the camp site. For the journey to be endurable she would have to pull herself together and at the least appear to be relaxed.

After a time Oscar began a conversation about art.

"When did you know you wanted to be an artist, Lara?"

"I didn't know I wanted to be an artist." she answered giving in to her need to chat in a normal way with Oscar.

"It was just how I was – how I am. It was like – well – I was carried by a river that I didn't choose. I had to learn to swim in it – or float – or make a raft and paddle – I just had to 'go with the flow' – sounds a bit crap I know – I think there is a lot of debris in the river and I do get pushed into back currents and eddies sometimes -"

"As long as you aren't trapped in a stagnant oxbow lake that's drying up – there are plenty of those around the Tin Heart Camp." Oscar contributed, smiling. Lara smiled too.

"There's a lot of rubbish that I don't want that seems to be part of the river -"

Would Oscar take what she said personally? Did she care at this moment?

"I need people to look at my art – and – and respond

somehow – but every time I have an exhibition I feel as if I have taken off all my clothes and people are looking not just at naked me but inside me too. Maybe that's part of the river – some of it I really hate!"

That was how she felt but should she have said that to Oscar when she had taken her clothes off for him? She felt an uncontrollable desire to laugh and shot a quick glance at Oscar. He was smiling too but with her not at her. They were friends again. It felt good.

Oscar looked serious for a moment.

"You are very hard on yourself, Lara. Sometimes you are too honest – too outspoken. That makes you a better artist but it can make your life more difficult."

"Mmmh. I don't know. What can I do to change anything? Anyway I just want to paint."

Oscar nodded.

"When I was 9 years old I wanted to be a painter. My grandfather encouraged me but that kind of future wasn't possible after the war – I lost a few years of schooling in my early teens too."

"What happened to your family then, Oscar?"

It was not a good question. Oscar's expression hardened, a jaw muscle twitched, but he answered calmly.

"Both my parents died in the war. My father fighting on the Russian front. My mother when the Russians advanced on Berlin. My grandfather looked after me and my sister. He made all three of us walk south-west to a camp for displaced persons in the American occupied sector. It took us weeks. When Grandfather died, Hanne and I immigrated to South Africa. Art wasn't possible for me in South Africa either – but it is for you here, Lara. Tell me more about what you want to do with your art – how about a trip to sell art in America?"

"Oh well – dream on Oscar – but how would that help me and the kind of art I want to make?"

"It would give you a substantial income Lara."

"I'm not going to get there, am I?" Lara said throwing up her hands. "What would I have to do to get that kind of money?"

"We'll find out." Oscar replied.

They were a good three-quarters of the way to the Tin Heart Camp when the Cruiser began to sound as if it was choked for fuel. Oscar checked the fuel lines and injectors.

"Can't see any problem. We'd best just get on. It's as far to the camp as it is to the last village and there's no mechanic that I know in that area. I wonder if the last lot of diesel was slightly adulterated. Can't trust the guys at the petrol pumps these days."

Whatever Oscar had done or not done, it was true that the Cruiser did run better for being checked. They were almost at the camp site when it stopped abruptly. Nothing Oscar could do made the engine fire up again. Lara had got out of the Cruiser and found a thicket dense enough to crouch behind for a pee. As she returned to the vehicle she could see from the position of the sun that they had perhaps an hour before it set and maybe with luck another half-hour of poor light after that. It was not yet winter but the African twilight became shorter with every passing day.

"We're a couple of kilometres from the camp by road." Oscar, a little distracted by some tsetse flies, was beside her pointing out the route. "It's only half a kilometre from us as the crow flies across this valley where there's also a bit of a swamp during the rains. The road has to make a long curve round to the east here to avoid the steep rocky hillside in front of the camp and straight opposite. We are going to have to walk, Lara."

Lara shook her head in wonder at the sight before her.

"Look!" she said. "Can't you smell them and see them – there are just hundreds of them! That's why the tsetse flies are so bad here."

"See what?" began Oscar then said astonished. "Damn! What a bloody nuisance! What an absolute bugger! I didn't see them – too focussed on the Cruiser!"

From her acquaintance with Oscar, Lara knew that he almost never swore and seldom repeated himself. They both stood in silence watching the buffalo herd spread out on the valley plain below them. It was the biggest herd that Lara had ever seen. There must have been almost a thousand buffalo. They were moving very slowly and grazing quietly on the rich vlei grass of the dambo. As Lara stared, more and more of them became visible. At first their dark hides and the dust they made had helped to obscure them among the light woods that dotted the valley but the longer she looked the more there were to see. They filled the valley between them and the Tin Heart Camp and spread out into the bush on either side and over the road that would take them into the camp. It was amazing that so many animals could be so quiet. They could hear them breathe and snort gently, hear them chomp and tear the grass, but their great bodies and hard hooves made little noise.

Oscar grinned at Lara then shrugged his shoulders.

"Well that is some sight isn't it? But Lara – what are our options here – what shall we do? What do you think? I can leave you with the Cruiser and walk to the camp, but it will be dark before I get back."

"If you walk I'll come with you." Lara responded. "We've only got one rifle between us. I don't fancy being left without it in an open Cruiser and you'll need it if you're on foot. We're not going to get to the camp in what's left of daylight if we take the long road around the valley in order to skirt the buffalo. I think that this herd of buffalo will have every predator in the area prowling around it and we will be just in the right place in the dark if they want a change of diet."

"It's a risk." Oscar agreed. "Right now the buffalo seem quite settled and it's hard to judge without spending more time watching them where they came from and where they're moving to. They may be moving across our route anyway. If predators attack and they stampede while we're out on foot – well!"

"They're quite relaxed and spread out aren't they?" Lara observed. "If we go straight across the valley where the herd is thinnest how long will it take us and how serious a risk is it?"

Oscar drew in his breath and let it out slowly.

"My thoughts exactly, Lara. If we do walk straight through the herd we'll have to go very steadily and slowly – no faster than they move when they are grazing and without sudden movements or sounds. We'll go together but not too close together. Be like an innocent young buffalo calf, Lara, but without any frolicking."

Oscar's hand was dusty and smeared with engine oil. He used the back of it to lightly touch her face. He raised his eyebrows in question. Lara nodded once.

"Let's go girl! Sorry about the smudge on your cheek." he said.

Oscar collected his rifle and Lara took the heavy rubber-encased torch from the Cruiser. They made their way down the slight incline to the point where they judged the buffalo herd to be least dense. It was also where the ground was hardest, the grass sparse and the dust heaviest.

"Don't look at any one of the buffalo for long." Oscar said. "Try and use your peripheral vision. Buffalo can't see straight ahead but they can see on both sides of themselves. Most animals have an extra sense of being watched and they will look back at you and realise you don't belong among them. As it is they rely on each other by listening as well as watching. They act as a group – if one of them is spooked they will all react."

I should be terrified. Lara thought. *Why aren't I?*

She walked slowly and carefully keeping her gaze low but using every nerve of her body to feel any changes in the behaviour of the animals around her. She was aware of Oscar half a pace behind her and to her side. He varied his step so the two of them did not move in unison. The dust floated around her head, out of the corner of her eyes she saw tails flick at the tsetse fly, heavy lashes blink over dark liquid eyes, heads lift as they made little tugs at grass clumps, hooves stamp and hides twitch. Ox peckers with bright red beaks hung on the sides of the buffalo. White black-legged cattle egrets among the buffalo's legs tilted their yellow beaks up to watch her from one eye. The rich smell of the beasts and their dung filled her nostrils. She and Oscar were buffalo too, making their quiet and certain way to the other side of the valley.

It took half an hour to cross the valley and begin the scramble up the steep rocks below the camp site. Half way up they turned to look back. The herd seemed quite undisturbed by their passage through it. The Cruiser was just visible under a distant grove of mupane trees before the road began to curve around the valley.

"Lara – you wonderful, beautiful girl!"

With his left arm, Oscar gathered Lara and pulled her against his chest. His right arm cradled his rifle in the safe position. Its butt pressed into her hipbone. Oscar put his face close to hers so their noses touched and with his tongue he tickled her dusty lips. She put her arms right around him and the gun and squeezed him tight. Then they kissed until she had to pull away to get her breath back.

By the time they reached the camp Enoch was arranging to send Mainza and Tembo out to look for them. Instead they all met at the main gate. Enoch flung his arms around Oscar with a huge smile of relief and patted out a rhythm on his back with both hands.

"Oh my friend! Glad you are fine! What's happened to the Cruiser? Did you see the buffalo?"

He clasped Lara's hand, his left hand supporting his right wrist as he did so and made a short bow.

"Welcome to the Tin Heart Camp, Lara. We are so happy you are with us!"

Inonge appeared from the kitchen and the two women hugged each other.

"The sun is well down." Oscar said. "Double up on the sundowners and we'll tell our story."

An hour later and delightfully woozy from several gin and tonics, Lara bathed under the hot water bucket shower in the enclosure behind her tent. The air was cooling and the night sounds of the bush were all around her. She was hungry for supper.

She could smell the wood smoke of the kitchen mingled with the flavours of a meaty stew. There would be wine and company for supper. Oscar would come to her bed and they would make love all night until she feel asleep with her head on the dark wiry pelt that covered his torso..

Chapter Two

Samuel's Stories

Lara sat on a traditional stool while she sketched. A Kasama village craftsman had shaped the stool for her from a pale light-coloured wood, probably – Lara thought – a fig tree trunk. Following her instructions he had carved a hand grip on one side of its solid single leg, then burnt a decorative black pattern onto it with metal adze heated on a fire. It was low but comfortable to sit on and allowed Lara to balance a large lightweight drawing board on her lap. Two spindly folding legs held the board at a convenient angle and a shoulder strap allowed her to carry it around easily when she had to move. All her tools, pencils, knives, watercolour pans, brushes and palette and a plastic bottle of water went into a sturdy flat-bottomed basket together with cans of personal insect spray and pastel fixative. Lara had always to check to make sure that she had picked up the correct can before she used it. So far at least she had only glued some mosquitoes to her shins with the fixative but had not yet put insect spray on her drawing. She found it was almost always the better drawings that suffered accidents but she had become used to working in a rather rough and ready way, trusting to her ability to reuse or remake any damaged work and to have a large number of sketches from which to work on her return to the city. It was almost the end of her first safari season at Enoch's camp.

At the moment she was seated in the middle of the village near the ramshackle grass-walled church with its left-leaning crucifix of twisted branches. Behind her the boys of the village played football on a dusty sloping patch of beaten orange earth. Their lop-sided football made of plastic bags was held together with odd knotted bits of string. Their goalposts were rickety sticks.

The old man, Samuel, sat outside his mud-brick house on a low home-made bed, its frame strung with bark strips. He was thin and shrunken. His hair was tiny white hailstones, sprinkled thickly over his dark head. His cheeks were hollowed and his mouth sucked in over a few yellowed teeth, but his eyes were bright with life and he chuckled often. Inonge, his daughter-in-law, sat respectfully on the ground close by his side. Samuel spoke good English but his mumbling voice was difficult to follow and Inonge repeated his stories in answer to Lara's questions as she worked on his portrait.

"Three wars," the old man said. "There have been three wars in my life. Soon there will be another war. It is coming."

"We hope there won't be any more wars, Ambuya, Grandfather." Inonge reassured him. "Lara wants to hear about the first war and why there are graves of white men here."

"There are many dead among my people in the first war." Samuel said. "Many, many, too many – but my people were not buried – they were left in the forest for the animals to eat.. The British army was defeated right here by the German general and his Askaris."

"General von Lettow-Vorbeck," Inonge interjected.

Lara nodded. She had heard of him.

Samuel moved his head slowly sideways and back again, considering.

"He was a great leader but a hard man to his Askaris. The British died from malaria. My people died because they were used like animals by the British and the South Africans to carry guns and supplies. There was fighting here. When we heard the guns my mother and my sisters and brothers left the village and ran to hide in the hills."

"For four years all our crops were destroyed or stolen along with our cattle. First by the Germans – then again by the British. All those years there was famine and hunger and many people starved and died. The last battle of the Great War was fought near here. Von Lettow-Vorbeck was not defeated, he surrendered. Only when the white armies made peace were those of us left alive able to return to our villages."

Lara knew that the regional rains produced only one crop a year. Often the stored grain didn't last very long and people were hungry before the next harvest. If enemy soldiers also stole or destroyed crops and animals local people would die of hunger.

"Huge numbers of people starved." Inonge said. "The estimated figure is of many, many thousands."

"So is that why there's a cemetery and soldiers' graves at the mine?" Lara asked.

"The white soldiers too sick to travel were left here. It took them many months to die," Samuel said.

"Missionaries nursed these men," Inonge said. "Black-water fever comes from repeated attacks of malaria. It kills slowly by destroying the red blood cells and turns the urine black. Oscar says it's because the kidneys stop working."

So that was the reason for the war graves in the cemetery with the tin heart. These images and Samuel's accounts of his life must be used somehow in her painting of him. Lara looked up again from her sketchbook at Samuel. She wanted him to keep on talking.

"What about the Second World War, Samuel? Why did you join up – why did you enlist?"

Again Samuel chuckled and again shook his head.

"They told us we had to go. We did not choose to go!"

"Really!" Lara was concentrating on her work but she was shocked.

She looked again harder at the subject of her drawing. What extraordinary experiences he had had and all to do with the wars that she had thought were centred in Europe. She supposed that Tim would know all about how the world wars had impacted on Africa.

"I was about 30, I think. The District Officer came here and looked for the strongest men who had been to school and could read and write. They made me sign papers – I was the teacher then – and two other men from my village also signed. Then we went far away for training to another part of Africa. After that they took us by ship across the sea – that was a long journey across much water. Most of the soldiers who went there to Burma were from Africa – only our officers were white. They said that Africans knew best how to porter heavy loads through the jungle without getting malaria."

"The rationale was the same as in the Great War." Inonge said pursing her mouth.

Lara frowned. This wasn't the war that she had watched on television and in the cinema where even black American soldiers were seldom on the screen.

"And the fighting – what was that like?" Lara wanted to know. This time Samuel did not give his beguiling chuckle. He looked down at his knotted lumpy fingers.

"It was very hard fighting. The Japanese were like wild ghosts from the forest. Always they waited in hiding and then surprised us and killed us. They did not like us black-skinned people at all. If we were captured they would only take the white people as prisoners. They killed all of us Africans."

Inonge made a snort of angry derision and sucked at her teeth.

"The army barracks in Chambeshi City are named for the battle of the Arakan that took place in Burma." she said with a grimace. "The same name has been given to other army barracks in other African countries where the British once ruled. Did you not know that, Lara?"

Lara scratched her cheek with the end of her paintbrush.

"No, I am ashamed to say, not until Tim told me. Years ago, when my grandfather came to Chambeshi on a visit, Dad took him to that run-down club – the 'Memorable Order of the Tin Hats' but there were only old white ex-army men in the bar. I had always imagined that Africa was pretty much untouched by the last war. I mean I know Oscar arrived in Africa as a refugee from the war but I hadn't realised that so many Africans took part as soldiers."

The stories that Samuel and Inonge told were already changing the ideas that were forming in Lara's mind about her paintings. She couldn't wait to get into her studio and start to explore ways of depicting and exploiting them. Though they were tragic and shocking, they mattered. She was filled with excitement and pleasure at the thought of how she could use them – how she would work them into her canvases. Lara knew that she wouldn't sleep – she would spend her nights in wakeful dreaming until these new ideas found form and expression. She had already made a large number of preliminary canvases of wild life subjects and filled a folder with drawings and watercolours of wild creatures but these images from history and from the intervention of humans into the wild environment would be challenging. How did she feel about them? What was her angle to be? Lara thought of Tim. It would be nice to talk to him about her plans. She didn't want to report on events though. Or to be sentimental about the suffering of those inadvertently caught up in wars. Perhaps her work would centre on a portrait of Samuel? It was odd but here she was thinking of making paintings about war. At art school she had invented her Disasters of War drawings. Now she was making a portrait of Samuel who had lived through wars himself. Lara thought of the Otto Dix paintings in Oscar's library. She wouldn't want to make such art if it meant personally suffering trauma as he had done.

Oscar had also asked her to do a series of paintings of birds and these had occupied a good part of her time.

"All quite small and to a standard size," he had said. "I have a client in the United States who is a collector of bird paintings from Africa. Do them in oil so they don't have to be framed under glass."

Lara hadn't been too keen on the commission at first. She felt that birds needed a freer style of expression. This had sounded rather too commercial but in the end she had enjoyed doing them and was proud of what she had achieved. Making the birds look alive and not like studies for a bird book was a challenge.

"I'll frame them here in the mine workshop using local hard woods – ebony and mubanga. The client is a bit obsessive but he is ready to pay for the freight charges even if the frames are heavy. It's not a bad deal," Oscar said.

Lara raised an eyebrow at the cost of the air freight for her work, but Oscar was talking about taking her on a trip at the end of the safari season. He had promised to show her the biggest art exhibition of wildlife artists in the world. It would be at the Jackson's Hole Wildlife Foundation in Wyoming in the United States of America and it would be Lara's first real opportunity to see a wide range of wildlife art. She would learn a great deal and she would make good contacts. She was very interested to see how her own work compared with world famous and reputable artists. Oscar had promised five star hotels, business class seats on their flights and good restaurants wherever they stayed. Living and working at the camp was demanding and much as she loved it, a change would be wonderful. Lara felt fit, she felt engaged, both creatively and physically. Her body was alive and a source of great pleasure for her and for Oscar. From her toes to the top of her head, Lara was delighted to be alive. A few things did niggle at her. Oscar's secrecy about his business, for example. His insistence that she must not become fond of him and that they must never talk about love between them. He was intelligent company, however, supportive about her art and a lover who made her shiver with anticipation. Just thinking of the feel and smell and girth of him made her body melt and her joints loosen.

Lara yawned and stretched. When Oscar was back at the camp she didn't get much sleep and she didn't get very much work done either.

Chapter Three

Fred and Bernie

The first time Lara met Bernie and Fred she was rather put out at the idea of sharing one of her precious evenings with Oscar with two old men, both over seventy.

"We have an arrangement to play chess together." Oscar told her. "Sometimes Bernie takes Fred and me on together in the same evening on two boards. He's very good. I didn't think you'd want to play chess so I've arranged for us all to play bridge."

"I'm not much good at cards." Lara tried not to seem peeved. "Why these two men, Oscar?"

"Bit of shared history." Oscar looked amused by Lara's expression. "Fred's wife is German. Bernie is Polish and speaks Russian and German."

"Won't they disapprove of us – of me, I mean?"

"Should they?" Oscar asked. "Do you mind if they do?"

Bernie and Fred were both short men but quite different from each other. Lara was conscious of how far she had to bend down to shake hands with them. Bernie wore a neat grey three-piece suit with grey shoes so polished they shone like enamel. Fred wore a jacket over a patterned sweater and corduroy trousers. His shoes were brown suede and his tie of faded wool. He was somewhat more reduced in height and every other way than Bernie. Bernie's smile and manner were charming but Fred kept his mouth clamped shut. He tilted his head up to talk to Oscar and Lara which made his clenched jaw look even more forbidding.

Bernie immediately started a conversation while Oscar organised whisky and ice for the men and white wine for Lara.

"My name's Solly Berman – but call me Bernie – everyone does."

In answer to Lara's question, he said, "I was taught to play chess in the army. The Russians had some idea that chess showed strategic intelligence but no! If you're good at chess – you're good at chess. Doesn't mean you're good at anything else. Not at all!"

Bernie confided that he and Oscar liked to get together and talk German to each other on occasions. Though he was a Jew, he had enlisted in the Polish Army before Hitler invaded.

"Many of us soldiers ran away when Poland fell." Bernie continued his story. "We ended up with the Russians – then I got taken prisoner by the Nazis but because I spoke German and Russian I managed to escape again and join the Polish 2nd. Corps who fought with the British."

Lara was fascinated. "How did you end up living in Chambeshi?" she wanted to know.

"It was a British Protectorate that took in refugees after the war. In fact before the war it accepted German Jews who were refugees from Hitler."

"It must have felt very strange and dangerous coming to the centre of Africa from a city in Europe!"

"After what we left behind?" Bernie said, his eyebrows going up and down in sequence. "Here was good, let me tell you!"

"What about you, Fred?" Lara turned to the smaller man with his suspicious eyes.

"Have you got a story too?"

Fred chuckled, his face relaxed momentarily, then, in a broad Yorkshire accent, his face dour again, and he began his story.

"It was t'Depression. No work, no money. I went to seek a fortune in South Africa. They said it were wonderful. Didn't like it a bit. Me – I'm a union man meself. White people carrying on like lords and slave owners. Treating Blacks like dirt. I got back on the boat not sure what to do next. Any road the boat sailed via New York – land of opportunity and equality they said. I had no papers so I jumped ship. Lived rough for a bit then got a job with the Consolidated Edison Company in New York. Married – the wife's German – lass had immigrated to States afore the war. We had kids. Then McCarthy got going chasing Jews, spies – immigrants – communists – us in Trade Union – you name it – I was still an illegal so we decided to leave. All the news from England was bad. No way we're going back to Germany. So we tried South Africa again – me thinking to go north. They needed electrical engineers in Chambeshi – so here I am."

"We're flotsam and jetsam – all washed up here – war debris. Living the good life." Bernie nodded at Oscar. "Same as Oscar – only he's the one who made it big."

Oscar grinned as he set up the card table but Fred was dissatisfied.

"It's not the good life any more. Not for the whites now colonial rule is finished. We'll all be gone soon – or dead." Fred jutted his lip out. Lara assumed he referred to his own life expectancy rather than a general possibility of life ending for all white people,

"But colonial rule finished ages ago." she said. "About 25 years ago wasn't it?"

Oscar handed round oily amber whisky and brittle ice in cut-glass tumblers.

"There's still lots of opportunity here." He disagreed. "It's a better place since it's been run by Chambeshians for Chambeshians. It's just now that there are worries about who will succeed President Chona,"

"Maybe, Oscar – but you like to keep in with all those people – all on the make – all wanting to be top dog. No – politics is not for me. I want my pension. I want to feel safe. Monika and I – perhaps we will end up in South Africa after all."

Fred raised his glass. "*Slainte Mhath,* Oscar!"

Bernie answered, "*Na zdrowie!*"

"*Prost!*" Oscar responded.

"Oh well!" Lara joined in. "Cheers then! Aren't we a gathering of polyglots here?"

Bernie smiled, Fred ignored her and Oscar clinked his glass against hers.

Bernie turned to Oscar, his manner deceptively mild.

"Oscar, do you know this man – Natan, I think he's called. Not a good person in my judgement. You don't do business with him do you? Funny fellow that one – came to our Passover meal this year – sat there all night but didn't say a word to anyone. Why? Can't see how he can be an observant Jewish man when he is mixed up with those Angolan dissidents. Bad men – very bad – arms dealers I'm told. One of my language students is an Angolan refugee – saw Natan hanging out with this rebel scum – reckons he's dangerous but loaded with money. His advice – have nothing to do with this Natan! You don't, do you Oscar?"

Lara hoped her face was neutral and natural. She glanced at Oscar. His expression didn't alter but she thought he blinked once. She stood up. The way this game of bridge was going she was going to be dummy yet again.

"I'll get more sandwiches – okay everyone?"

When she got back the three men were relaxed and laughing. They were talking about a local car dealer who had been apprehended for selling a stolen car back to its owner. Fred had tears running down his face and was coughing. Both he and Bernie smoked. Oscar was smoking a cigar.

"So why are you wasting your time with this man?" Bernie asked Lara. "Beautiful girl like you? Must be able to do better."

Lara smiled. It was such a trite line but Bernie was shrewd and he didn't seem to mean it unkindly.

"I like Oscar." she said. "He knows about art and he helps me promote my art too."

"Ah." Fred said, turning his sharp gaze on Lara.

"We like Oscar too, he's a good mate, but he does owt for nowt. Be sure of that Lara. He never loses at bridge, do you Oscar? Only at chess against Bernie and then he doesn't bet."

"Pity you can't get lowdown from Hanne no more. She and Monika they used to talk German to each other. Monika knows all about Oscar – Hanne told her."

"You must be good at art if Oscar is helping you." Bernie said slapping his cards down on the table with a quick glance at Lara.

"Lara's good." Oscar said unfazed by the conversation. "She'll make money from her art."

When Bernie and Fred had gone home, Lara tried to bring up the subjects of Natan and Hanne with Oscar. Oscar flicked a shred of cigar off his lip, wrapped his arms around her and squeezed her so hard that she couldn't utter a word.

"First of all, Lara – before we get into the business of talking about business, I want to fuck you! Right here. In the dining room. On the table. Now!"

"Why on the table?" Lara asked breathlessly. "Isn't that uncomfortable?"

"Probably for you." Oscar said. "And it's cold. Let's go to the bedroom and I'll tie you up instead."

"No you won't!" said Lara.

Lying in Oscar's arms after they had made love without rope or ties, Lara, sleepless and yawning, frowned to herself. Why did the idea of being in bondage to Oscar give her a sexual thrill? She was far too impatient and self-determined to really want to be at the mercy of another person. It must be something to do with the way sex is – a surrender – a loss of control – or was it to do with the emotional enslavement of falling in love? Would she trust Oscar if he did tie her up? Should she allow him to imprison her for sexual pleasure? The idea made her shudder, not exactly with fear but with a thrill that was excitement. Sexual fantasies were supposed to be okay, weren't they? Or did they betray your weaknesses and secret fears and give them power over you? Why when they were pleasant did they also make her feel guilty? No matter who her lover was she could not bear to give that person ultimate power over herself. Nevertheless the idea aroused her, sleepy and sated as she was. In any case half the pleasure that she and Oscar had in each other was in their difference and opposition. Perhaps she ought to be more afraid of the imbalance between them in money and resources? Wasn't she too dependent on Oscar? Also – and this was much harder to answer – she could only make guesses – what did Oscar get from his relationship with her? What did Oscar really want?

Could either Bernie or Fred have advised her about Oscar or told her something useful? There were too many questions without answers or the possibility of answers. Lara yawned again and drifted into sleep.

Part Nine
London 1997

Chapter One

Adam

Lara had already given Brendan a short and simplified account of her life after she and Tim arrived in London. She remembers it as a smudgy time as if she was working on a charcoal drawing in a badly lit studio.

"I was pretty traumatised, I suppose." she tells Brendan. "The real problem was the way the days became shorter and darker and colder. I had lived through English winters at art school but this time I felt that I was being buried alive – it was as if I was interred like Persephone in a gloomy Hades."

Brendan and Lara both smile at her exaggerated description. Brendan, Lara has discovered, had begun a novitiate as a Catholic priest and had a classical education.

"Being in bed with Tim was the best thing about it. I was warm there. We talked a lot – made love – became better friends – and laughed – but Tim had a job and when he wasn't around I was afraid of everything.

"It did get better though and when Adam was born in the summer – we were both so happy."

In the first trimester of Lara's pregnancy her physical body had steadily ripened and swelled while her mood fluctuated as wildly as Liseli's had when she was at her most ill.

"What if it's Oscar's child? What should I do? How can I know?" she cried.

"Lara, Lara – it's not a problem." Tim squeezed her stiff shoulders.

"Let's just take it slow! It's your baby and that's what matters. We have to wait till the baby is born. Then we can find out the baby's blood group – but that may not tell us anything for certain. Even if I am not ruled out we still don't know Oscar's blood group so we can't know definitely who the father is."

There was much more they did not say and more they dared not say at that time.

Life was not slow, however, as Tim and Lara rushed around finding accommodation and settling back into London before her due date. They started by squatting together in the basement flat of one of Tim's newspaper colleagues and had to move twice before they found an affordable flat with a spare room for a nursery.

Lara didn't want to tell her parents about her pregnancy till she was settled one way or another. Neither did she want to live with Tim and be a burden to him but she had to accept that she was incapable of coping on her own. Tim knew it was possible that he might be the baby's father but he did not think it wise to lay any claim to that while Lara was so distraught and traumatised. He shrugged away the idea and concentrated on their survival in London and his change from a risk-taking foreign correspondent to a senior desk editor. When he was with her and they were eating supper, Lara talked on and on endlessly about setting up a place for herself and the baby but they both knew that wasn't practical. Lara had left Chambeshi with a suitcase and no money and she refused to ask her parents for financial help. In any case Brian and Jane were living out a dream retirement in a villa above the sea in Cyprus and it was easy not to give them any real facts.

At night Lara would burrow into the bed next to Tim, shut her eyes tight and try and exclude all memory of the past months. Inevitably she woke up crying aloud and begging Tim to hold her tight. Inevitably they made love. Lara obliterated the past, burying herself in Tim's smell and Tim's arms, in the different feel and texture of Tim's harder, thinner body until the struggle for orgasm released her into a drugged sleep.

At last, after 20 weeks, Lara's pregnancy took control of her. Protecting and providing for the baby became her focus. She stopped telling Tim that she must look for a place of her own. Providing for the baby became her excuse for not leaving Tim and her life took on a dreamlike quality. The flat they had found had three bedrooms, a little one for a nursery for a baby, a large double room for Tim and Lara, and another for guests or for a study. The flat was convenient for the hospital, for Tim's work, for shops, friends and even for galleries. Lara pottered about in the flat, visited an art exhibition or two, showed her portfolio to a few agents and doodled in her sketch books but spent most time drawing up lists of baby clothes and painting a mural in the nursery. It was a mural about wild things, not wild things from fairy stories, but from Africa – night apes, pangolin and honey badgers. Shy hidden secret things, but small creatures, not large predators.

When Adam was born the very thought of questioning his parentage seemed sacrilegious. Such a perfect creature needed no proof of legitimacy. Tim and Lara were both in love with, and enslaved by, Adam. Tim had been with Lara at Adam's birth. Lara's labour had not been long and the delivery had been straightforward. The miracle of birth was sufficient for both Lara and Tim to know that they were now a family. When Brian and Jane arrived to meet their grandchild they could see nothing to worry them in their daughter's life or choice of partner. They thought the baby took after Brian's side of the family and that was definitely not a problem. Brian's father had run a successful small business.

"When are you going to get married?" Jane asked Tim with a meaningful look at Brian. She was careful not to catch Lara's eye.

"Oh soon, probably." Tim said lightly, glancing at Lara and

she nodded back, a hint of wryness in her smile. They had both agreed it would be the best thing for Adam and knew they would like it too. Adam's birth had to be registered very soon. It was almost two weeks since his arrival. Lara insisted that Tim should be registered as Adam's father. She needed to put a secure barrier around Adam and exclude Oscar, whom she obstinately refused to discuss or mention after Adam's birth. Neither would Lara let Tim even try to find out where Oscar was or what had happened to him.

Besides it might still be that Tim was Adam's father.

"I so want you to be happy, Lara!" Jane said, her eyes moist with longing. Lara understood for the first time how much her mother loved her. She also saw that her kind, hard-working father had perhaps been a rather disappointing husband and that Jane had done her best not to mind too much.

Lara's world regained its light, its promise and hope. The Tin Heart Gold Mine was forgotten or not mentioned. On rare occasions Lara found herself trapped by her unwashed London windows in a beam of sunlight and a drift of dust motes and her heart would stop as she listened for the screech of cicadas above the Mile End traffic. As she either had the washing or baby Adam in her arms, she would have sooner or later to move on. In any case she still had the irrepressible youthful rubbery quality that allowed her to bounce back. Even post-natal depression only took hold of her very briefly. Tim and Lara knew they loved each other and knew they both enjoyed sex. They talked, they argued, they made up and they laughed. They made love before they ate supper while Adam was a babe and when he became too aware of what they were up to, they went to bed to have sex as soon as he slept and then got up later to watch the late news and documentaries on TV.

It was Helen Ioannou who finally made a difference to Lara's circumstances. Soon after Adam was born, Helen sent over the contents of Lara's studio and some of her personal possessions.

They came hidden away as part of a consignment of art for an exhibition in London. Helen also managed by some not quite legal fiddling of accounts to empty Lara's bank account in Chambeshi and transfer the money to her at a rate that was not too punitive. Lara's gratitude was profound and her self-esteem improved as a result of her improved financial status. Helen said that Chimunya was now running the Umodzi Gallery.

"She's doing a great job," Helen said. "But it is rather at the cost of her own work."

Chapter Two

Lara

After Adam was born, Lara's career also picked up again in a way that was very satisfactory for her finances. The last frugal years spent in the bush that she had found so frustrating creatively began finally to pay back. The hundreds of small drawings, notes and observations in small black sketchbooks that had been done hastily and at the time felt so trivial, formed the basis of a new series of romanticised wild animal paintings. These sold for a decent price. There had been a proliferation of galleries in Covent Garden around that time and Lara's work hit the jackpot.

Lara had managed through an artist friend of an artist friend to get a part-time teaching job at the art school in Whitechapel. It was only two evenings a week teaching fashion students to draw figures that were not just headless and handless garments. These appendages to the human body are apparently 'difficult to draw' or so the students would wimp at Lara as their jewellery clacked and swung with their pencil strokes. The classes, however, had the unexpected benefit of informing her of the fashionable colours predicted for the coming year so she could design her paintings to match the curtains and clothes of young people in city apartments. Lara's paintings probably went out with the old sofa when the latest one was acquired but she did not care or at least said she didn't. She was paying her way in a commercial world and often repeated to herself that she was only being realistic about her value as an artist.

"I did – and do – feel rather chewed up about it if I am honest." Lara explains to Brendan at one of their sessions. "In Chambeshi I was considered a bit of a star in the art world along with Chimunya and Pascal and a few others but we were a small group in a small society. There wasn't too much competition. I took my status and the money I made from art for granted. Here in London – well – I do sell – but what I do is rather commercial and I'm not very proud of it."

Over time and with the birth of Adam, Tim and Lara's flat altered to suit their changing life requirements. Then their lives adapted to their different living arrangements and soon they couldn't remember how things had been when they started.

In the ordinary way that these things are done, Lara, the woman, was the one who instigated most of the changes, but then Lara was the one who lived and worked the longest hours at home. At first Adam had the little bedroom for a nursery and Tim and Lara a king-size bed in the biggest, quietest room next to the bathroom. At two years Adam needed a playroom as well as a bedroom. Lara put Adam in the big room with his toys and books and swapped the king-size bed for a three-quarter bed that she could squeeze into the one-time nursery.

The third very tiny room became Tim's office – he could do his editing from home on the nights when Lara was teaching and he was baby-sitting Adam. Journalism and computers meant he was always on call. Tim had left Chambeshi in the furore after the coup against president Chona. He had predicted it would take place and reported on its convolutions rather than its revolution right to the last moment. The outcome was that his newspaper had rewarded him with safer work as a desk-based African editor. Newspapers, however, were given their final edit late at night for the early morning press.

The nursery-bedroom felt rather cramped for Lara and Tim to be in together unless they were lying down but that, oddly, reduced their interest in sex. The nursery mural survived on their bedroom wall for a year or so but at last Adam allowed Tim to paint it out – not an easy job as it took several coats of emulsion and much muttering as he barked his shins on the dust-sheeted compromise that was their bed. Adam's room was no longer decorated with art, but with posters. Thomas the Tank Engine and later Dr. Who became his night-time companions, not strange and nervous fauna from his mother's past.

Lara wasn't particularly sad to lose the mural of the wild creatures of the midnight. She was working on a series of paintings about the wildlife of London and her foxes, cats and owls were selling very well. Africa was far away and that part of her life was over.

It had all vanished, as Oscar had vanished.

Chapter Three

Brendan 1997

Lara doesn't want to talk about Oscar any more. She sits silent in Brendan's armchair looking down at her lap and observing the way her blue denims have started to thin and lighten in colour above her knees. Why is she so afraid to talk about her affair with Oscar? Is she afraid of exposing herself as a sex-obsessed fool? Was that what she had been? Is that what she is? Several times she almost speaks and several times she hesitates. Brendan sits, occasionally glancing at Lara's face to see how she is. Eventually Lara has to speak and opts for honesty.

"I can't bear it if you disapprove of me, Brendan. Do I need to talk about what happened with Oscar?"

Brendan answers quietly.

"Lara, perhaps it is you who disapproves of yourself. I am not here to make any judgements. What are you asking me to do for you and why?"

"I am ashamed of myself but it's complicated." Lara says.

There has been a storm in her head for so long. Broken bits of self-knowledge and experience fly around in her brain like leaves in a gale. There seems no chance of them falling into a pattern. Suddenly it is calm. The leaves become birds. They flock upwards into the branches of her mind and she begins to understand herself a little better.

"I think my mother must have had an affair with Oscar some

years before I met him. When I told my parents that I was going to work at Oscar's Tin Heart Camp she had this weird screaming fit. She accused me of being an ungrateful daughter and burst out crying. She was really upset. Eventually Dad took me aside and tried to explain – he was embarrassed – said Oscar was a bit of a Romeo – his words – and had made a pass at Mum. I tried to make out that my relationship with Oscar was really only business. I could see that Dad was relieved but didn't entirely believe me so I said -'Oh well Dad, you know and I know, that Oscar will always stay single and not be faithful – I won't fall for him. Do reassure Mum that I won't be stupid.'

"I didn't realise that I could be so dishonest and co-opt Dad into lying for me. I was lying to myself also. Poor Mum. I would have felt the same I suppose."

"Dad did visit Oscar's camp – on his own – Mum wouldn't come. I think Dad wanted to shame Oscar into treating me decently but Oscar went off on a business trip at the last moment and they didn't meet. Anyway it doesn't matter – I knew what I was doing."

"Yes, indeed," Brendan says, "but did you know what Oscar was up to and understand how dangerous he was?"

Lara stares down at her worn jeans. After a while she shakes her head and remains silent.

"There is no need to talk about Oscar if you don't want to or don't feel ready. Would you like instead to tell me about something else – perhaps you want to talk about Tim and why he has gone away."

"Oh, God!" Lara's head is in her hands, "It is such a mess – such a mess! I don't think I can talk about that yet."

"You have told me a little already." Brendan says. "You and Tim flew back to England together and ended up living with each other. Tell me about that time if you like."

"I never stopped taking the pill those last weeks in Chambeshi," Lara explains. "But it was a mini-pill and I was sick and had diarrhoea. The obstetrician told me afterwards it could explain how I became pregnant. My body didn't have time to absorb the pill before I vomited. In any case I was in such a state when I first arrived in London that when I missed my period the doctor put it down to stress. Very soon my breasts became sore and my body felt different and then I began to panic. I knew what was happening to me – but there was no way I could know exactly when I became pregnant. Tim and I had made love fairly soon after we met again – but then Oscar -"

Lara's voice fades, then she looks up directly at Brendan.

"I still don't know for certain if Adam is Oscar's child or Tim's. The only thing I thought I did right was telling Tim at once. Now I wonder if Tim and I would still be together if I had been able to convince him that Adam could only be his child. I don't know any more what is or was right and for the best."

"You have all had blood tests haven't you?" Brendan asks.

"Yes." Lara replies, "It doesn't rule out Tim as Adam's father but as we can't test Oscar's blood the doubt remains and complicates what we tell Adam.

"I want Adam to be Tim's child but suppose he's not? How will that be for Adam? What happens when it becomes easy for him to get a DNA paternity test? What will he feel?"

"Do you think Tim left you over Adam?" Brendan asks, "Was there another reason that was not to do with Adam at all?"

"Oh, God, yes!" Lara weeps again, "Tim left *me*. He didn't want to leave Adam! It's my fault!"

Again her mood changes.

"We were fine Tim and me – we were fine!" she says shooting a defiant glance at Brendan. "Then the money and the paintings arrived from Oscar. And we had terrible rows."

Chapter Four

Two Brown Envelopes

"So how did Oscar vanish?" Brendan finally asks Lara. "What exactly did happen and how did you feel about it?"

Lara looks at Brendan in silence for some moments before she answers.

"I have never spoken about it." she says. "Not even with Tim. Oscar just did vanish – well disappear – as far as we knew or could tell. He came back to Chambeshi City about three weeks after Tim and I had left. He was seen at the ranch and in his office over a period of a few days. Then he flew off again in the Cessna. It was rumoured that Natan was with him then. That was it. After that no more sightings.

"I didn't want to think about him – I blocked any thoughts of him at first. Everything in Chambeshi was chaotic and for a while there was no news or facts – just rumours. Tim kept in touch with Junior so we knew that he was okay and that Inonge was safe but not much more. It was Junior who told Tim about Oscar's disappearance. Junior and Inonge had to disassociate themselves from Oscar for political reasons and for personal safety. Once Oscar's crimes were known, it was easier for them to do that. The difficulty was that there was no trace of Oscar and no way of finding him. Oscar's office, the ranch house and the safari camp were just left under guard, but empty, and unused for several years."

In answer to Brendan's raised eyebrows Lara shrugs. "I was very busy and so was Tim. There was Adam and there was work for us both."

"And now?" Brendan repeats his suggestion, "Perhaps taking anti-depressants would be helpful. They are recommended and they do work, Lara."

"I'll stick to self-medicating with wine," Lara says, attempting a joke.

Though Tim and Lara hardly noticed it happening, both their lives and the flat had changed. The living room had metamorphosed into Lara's studio. When at first she began to draw again she used a small table in a corner of their living room that she tidied up before Tim came home. As her income increased, her canvases grew larger and she worked for longer periods. Lara began to leave her palettes and brushes on display and ready for use at any moment and stopped turning her paintings to the wall. Tim also stopped asking Lara about her work. He could after all just look and see what she had done before going into the kitchen for tea or – if it was later – for the gin and tonic that they were both addicted to from outdoor African evenings.

The comfortable settee remained in the studio but it was mostly used by Lara when she flopped down in it with a coffee to scowl at and reassess a painting. Occasionally and grudgingly a couple or a guest were allowed to pull the settee out into a bed so they could stop over for the night.

Luckily for Lara and Tim's relationship, the kitchen was quite large and became their main living space with a fair sized table for entertaining and the TV for when they were just family. They had always used it that way to watch TV. Journalists and artists like to do a lot of talking and networking. Tim's life had been adventurous and Lara's had been romantic and exotic, or so it had appeared. Successful artists, even rather commercial ones, are believed to have charisma so Tim and Lara had reasonable social clout and spent many long and fascinating evenings with friends having excited discussions accompanied by many bottles of wine. That was the one aspect of their life that survived with the least change for the longest time. A few of the friendships endured too – those people with whom they had shared experiences and passions – the other acquaintances recycled themselves casually into newer and trendier social groupings.

Tim and Lara were settled into a routine mostly arranged around Adam. By comparison with him they didn't seem to alter much in appearance, personality or habits. They were old friends and good friends, each of them ambitious and hard-working about their chosen careers. Though they rushed around on separate tracks all day, they always went to bed together and there they talked, laughed, made love and slept. On the whole they were practical and adaptable. Their relationship was solid. They were a couple who had been friends for fifteen years and lovers for ten.

Whenever necessary, Adam had been looked after as an infant by a licensed child-minder in the next block of flats. Adam went first to nursery, then reception class, started proper school and was happy and adjusted with a circle of friends mostly with ambitious, high achieving parents. He was growing, he was healthy. He didn't look particularly like either Tim or Lara but he was too young for the differences to be remarked on. Sometimes Lara caught Tim looking at his son with a puzzled air as if he didn't recognise some aspect of him. If Lara asked him what he was thinking of he simply looked surprised as if nothing had yet surfaced fully in his mind or as if his thoughts were elsewhere. In that way Tim was uncomplicated. Adam was his child and Lara's child. That suited her too. Lara set her jaw. The Tin Heart years were shut out of her mind and her heart and Adam was safe. Occasional ghostly images from the Kasama region manifested themselves as she painted and a few imprinted their ether on the canvas but they moved out to galleries and sold. Tim's puzzled alienation still made occasional appearances and Lara knew that someday something would materialise and she would be surprised by it. So it turned out.

Tim craved the independence and the risks of his work as a foreign correspondent. It had taken Lara a long time to work that out about her dear friend and lover. She thought at first that it was her independence of mind and artistic success that bothered his security; that perhaps he had regrets about accepting Adam as his own without question. The problem was neither of these things. Boredom and safety meant that Tim did not feel alive or confident. His work showed signs of suffering too but fortunately before it became an obvious problem, his chief had the insight to recognise what was happening and took the first opportunity to offer Tim work abroad. It was also true that Tim was the best person for this particularly unpleasant assignment. He was to go to Uganda to investigate the Lord's Resistance Army.

"You love someone and therefore you believe that you know them," Lara says to Brendan, "but the reality is that your knowledge is as mutable as the person you love and as you yourself are."

"I think that Tim is afraid. He's afraid of one day not existing, of being meaningless. It's worse when his life is too secure – too certain. When he was out on a job in Africa facing actual danger, and really afraid for himself physically, then he felt that he counted in some existential permanent way. Now he feels uncertain even while he is successful and well-paid."

Much as he craved excitement, perhaps, Tim would not have left very easily as his life had come to be given significant meaning by Adam and Lara. As Adam grew older and as he and Tim shared more activities and hobbies, they formed a closer bond. Tim's weekends included rock-climbing with Adam at the new sports centre or sailing on the Docks at Canary Wharf, exploring the Dinosaur and the Volcano sections at the Natural History Museum, or looking at the Great Fire of London at the Museum of London in the Barbican. Activities that brought them both home to a relaxed and paint-spattered Lara. Bright-eyed and full of anecdotes about their varied achievements, they would set out together to the latest family restaurant for a pizza or a hamburger or a dish of chilli con carne.

Then two fat, official-looking, foolscap-sized, brown envelopes arrived. They were addressed to Lara and came from a lawyer in London. They might as well have been packed with plastic explosive, because they blew Tim and Lara's lives apart.

Chapter Five

Questions

For the most part the years Lara spent at the Tin Heart Gold Mine had passed smoothly. After four years she was becoming rather dissatisfied, it was true. The business side of the safari camp was eating up more and more of her creative energy and her precious time in the studio. She was fed up with the need to supply her American patron with the small commercial bird paintings. They had become repetitive and uninspiring to do.

She also couldn't see how the safari camp remained in the black. They simply did not have a sufficient turnover of paying guests. It was sometimes completely empty. On other occasions Oscar invited his business contacts to the safari camp for free parties. At first the parties, though very hard work, had been fun but after a time they were just hard work, rather boring and had little to do with the purpose of the safari camp. These particular guests were nearly invariably flown in by Oscar in his Cessna. They were almost always men and if there were women among them they were decorative and young. Lara resented the girls and despised them – feelings she would later be ashamed of when she understood more of the powerlessness of these women. Meals were always five courses instead of three and champagne and wine were on the house and consumed in large quantities. Many times the guests did not even venture out to see the wildlife. They sat on the veranda overlooking the river and kept the kitchen staff busy all day. At first Inonge and Lara had taken pride in offering food that was sourced in Chambeshi. It was plain and simple, often grilled on a barbecue, but it was fresh, of good quality, and full of taste. In order to stretch the menus to the five courses expected by these business associates, Lara had to ask Oscar to bring in imported cheeses and smoked salmon. It also meant that the kitchen staff worked longer and later and were not treated with the usual friendly politeness that marked those who came to see the National Park.

Once or twice Natan used Oscar's Cessna to fly in his own small groups of tourists. Lara noticed that he almost always picked days when she was in Chambeshi and not at the camp. His guests were air stewards, male and female, who because of restrictions on their flying hours were grounded in Chambeshi City for several days. Inonge pulled a face as she described their behaviour in a low voice to Lara.

"Natan gives them *chamba* and *ganja,* I mean marijuana." Inonge used the local words. "He gives them some other drugs too. They stay up all night. No wild animals would dare to come near the camp when they are here because they laugh and scream so loudly."

"I'm afraid Natan makes them take parcels back to London for him – you know – drugs as well. Those pills from India – Mandrax I think. Do you think Oscar knows, Lara? Enoch refuses to ask him about it."

"I'm sure Oscar doesn't know." Lara said firmly. "I think Natan does it all on his own. I'll find out from Oscar." She was troubled though and became more afraid when she tried to think what words she might use to tell Oscar about Natan. Inonge was looking at her with concern. Lara wasn't certain for a moment whether Inonge was warning her or asking for her help.

"Lara – I don't know who is in charge here anymore." Inonge continued. "Is it Oscar? I think it's Natan!"

"What are Natan and Oscar trying to do with these people? Where is the money coming from? What is it for?"

Lara did try to discuss some of these issues with Oscar. That was most often when they were in bed together but Oscar would only want to make love. He was an exceptional lover who always aroused her fully and brought her to climax. Lara always wanted him too and afterwards, of course, they both slept. There was both danger and delight in submitting to the pleasures of sex with Oscar.

If Lara raised her worries during the few moments of privacy that they shared, he was always pleasant to her but seemed to disregard them. He would look at her with a smile, but his eyes would be expressionless and flick over her face as if he was just checking whether or not she was too bothered because he had another more important consideration to deal with at the same time.

Chapter Six

General Snake

Then there had been the horrible business of the incursion into middle of the National Park by the self-styled General Njoka and his gang. Rumours had reached Lara while she was shopping for camp provisions in Chambeshi City that he had attacked a couple of villages north of the camp. People had fled and their homes had been burnt down. He was considered to be responsible for a recent increase in poaching in the area. Oscar and Lara were returning to the camp one day when they heard the sound of gunfire ahead. Oscar slowed the Cruiser down and they continued carefully down the road until they saw another four-wheel vehicle on its side in a shallow gully a few metres in front of them. A tree and branches had been pulled into a rough roadblock.

"Out!" Oscar ordered, "Get out, Lara! Lie down in the bush away from the Cruiser!"

He took his heavy shotgun and made his way up to the road block using the tilted car ahead as cover. He seemed to vanish from sight though Lara couldn't see easily from her prostrate position. Next she heard shouting and thought it was Oscar, then more shouting, at first angry, then commanding. In a surprisingly short time Oscar was back with Lara, annoyed but calm. Some Chambeshians in ragged uniforms appeared and heaved the fallen trees and branches out of their way. Oscar and Lara were waved past to continue their journey to the camp. As they drove by, Lara glimpsed a white man in among the group of men. She thought from his height and stance that it must be Natan. Next to him was a solid black man in an army cap decorated with a red band.

"What was that about, Oscar?" she asked.

"Poachers!" he said tersely. "It's under control. Tell you later."

He never did explain but that evening he insisted on teaching her how to use his pistol and showing her where he kept it hidden under the passenger seat of his vehicle.

"Can you use a handgun, Lara?" he asked.

"No – I've never held one. Bill taught me how to use a shotgun and a rifle. I can hit a target but haven't shot anything moving or living." Lara answered. I've always had a game guard in the bush if I needed that kind of protection."

"Right." Oscar said. "I'll show you how as soon as we're back in camp."

Oscar taught Lara how to hold the pistol steady and reload it immediately. She learnt fast. Oscar approved but immediately afterwards he was very busy at the camp and early the morning he set off back to Chambeshi City taking Mainza with him. Mainza returned in the Cruiser the next day but Oscar did not. There was no explanation. Oscar flew in a week later unannounced. That was the day when General Njoka's body was brought into the camp. That was one of the most grisly experiences that Lara was ever to have.

The disgusting smell of Njoka preceded his body and the cortège carrying his makeshift litter. Lara had smelt dead and rotting animals before. Death was part of life in a National Park but the sweet and foetid stink from Njoka was worse than she could have imagined. Usually the first thing that scavengers do is to eviscerate the bodies of their prey which helps reduce the stink a little. General Njoka's guts hung out of his belly wound. It was even more hideous knowing he had once been human.

He had been killed 80 kilometres away from the camp four days previously.

Executed, probably, Lara thought, trying not to retch. She was standing as far away as possible from his corpse with her nose and mouth covered.

The litter was borne by six of Njoka's men. They had been captured with him and as part of their punishment were being forced to carry him from village to village so that the people of the district would know that he was, without any question, absolutely dead. Lara could see from the wretched misery on their faces that everything about their task was both totally repellent and utterly terrifying. A group of armed men in scruffy unidentifiable uniforms stood on guard, but not too close to the captives and their dreadful burden. Njoka's body was swollen and shapeless; his blood had dried on his bullet wounds including those that had made holes in his collapsing sagging face. The identifying army cap with its red band lay under his head. Gleaming blue flies swarmed around the body. It crawled with glistening maggots which hatched inside a day and then joined their parents in the odious cycle of laying eggs in his putrid flesh. This was the murderer, robber and would-be overlord of the region – the Lord General Njoka.

Oscar watched for some moments with a face of stone. He turned to Tembo with instructions.

"We'll give them fuel and transport to Chambeshi City. If they don't get the body there soon it won't be recognisable. People must know Njoka is dead. So must President Chona. Give the bearers and the soldiers some food and water and get them away – fast!"

"Who's responsible? What happened? What do they say?" Lara asked.

"We'll never get the truth." Oscar said "People will be warned by this. They won't forget."

Lara thought of the old man Samuel's prediction of another war.

Was that what he meant? What did the death of Njoka mean for this region?

By mid-afternoon the spare Cruiser had left with Njoka's body on board. Normality of a sort returned to the camp. Lara was busy with menus and shopping lists in the office when through the office window she saw an unexpected vehicle drive into the camp. It was Natan. Oscar went to greet him, had even expected him Lara thought, with surprise. She jumped up, impelled by a need to find out what was going on. Natan had left his Jeep's engine running and neither man heard Lara approach.

"That's the end of the trouble-making snake." Natan said. Oscar's head moved in agreement as he spoke.

"We'll have only to deal with Miyanda then on his own. Have you arranged the transfers, Oscar?"

Natan looked up at Lara as she approached. She saw his face darken in suspicious anger. Oscar spun around. Some extra sense warned Lara. She smiled a bright welcome at Natan.

"Hello! Are you staying for supper, Natan? It's a special fillet steak treat tonight for Oscar."

Oscar's face was hard. He said nothing for a moment while he studied her face.

"Sorry, Lara." he said, "Natan and I are flying off immediately back to the city."

He stepped up close, took her head in both hands and gave her a bruising kiss on the lips.

"Be very good!" he said.

He was gone before she could ask more questions but Lara knew there was something very wrong with what had happened.

Why do I have such a sense of foreboding? The bad man is dead and killed justifiably?

Why do I feel that this is the start of something terrible and not the end it seems to be?

Why does this feel manufactured and in some devious way part of the Tin Heart Mine?

Where was Natan when Njoka died?

Who carried out his ambush and capture?

Chapter Seven

Monika

Every time Lara saw Fred at Oscar's ranch, he had appeared to hint at something dark and secret in Oscar's past. Lara had tended to dismiss Fred as simply jealous of the position she had come to occupy in Oscar's life. It was years later that she realised he had been trying to tell her from the first moment they met, that all was not as it seemed and the problem was not only the past but the present too. On each occasion when Fred visited the ranch, he would wait till Oscar had left the room or was out of hearing and then he would mention Hanne's friendship with his wife Monika and what she had said before she died.

"Ooh – she had a hard life that one. Never a moment's peace. Always felt guilty and sad. Never got over the war and what it did to the two of them. Never forgave herself."

Lara thought he was just a spiteful old gossip so she didn't follow up his cues. It never occurred to her to ask why Monika didn't come with Fred to visit Oscar and why she had never met her. It was only at the travel agent a few weeks later when Lara was booking her flight out of Chambeshi that she finally met Monika. Monika was tiny, white-skinned, white-haired, and frail, but with an expression of almost ferocious alertness in her raisin-coloured eyes. She reached out and took Lara's hand in both her small ones.

"At last we meet, *meine Liebe*. *Mein Mann* has told me all about you but he has not, I think, told you to be careful of Oscar. No, that is hard for you to believe, I know. Oscar and Hanne – they had no childhood. That makes it difficult to be good. Hanne always wanted to change, but Oscar – well – that is a man's way, I think. They keep going even after it is time to stop. Oscar – he does not stop even for the people he loves. Friedrich here, he says that you do not know what Oscar does to make money. No one does – only Hanne told me before she died. She was sorry and so sad. *Meine liebe* Lara, you must leave this man Oscar if you want to be safe and not go to prison.

"We are going now to our daughter in South Africa before things get too bad here in Chambeshi. You too, I hope."

Lara looked from Monika to Fred and back again. Her throat was dry and constricted. She tried to nod and smile. Monika had let go of Lara and the elderly couple were hand in hand again. Lara could see that Fred was full of proud affection for his wife.

"She's a good old trout." the old Yorkshireman said, smiling at Monika. "Kept me on the straight and narrow these 60 year. Take care of thyself Lara. Be a good girl now."

"I will." Lara said with difficulty. She had been living with the fear and knowledge of what she was implicated in for weeks. The truth was she did not know how to escape. She did not know if Oscar would just let her leave or if he would blackmail her into staying. Maybe he also killed people who endangered him.

"Had she been wilfully blind? Yes – but also no. Oscar had friends who liked and trusted him, people that Lara also liked and trusted like Enoch and Helen. True her mother hated Oscar and her father had expressed reservations about him but wasn't that the fallout from her mother's supposed affair? He was well-thought of in Chambeshi in the business community but then people with money and power are always admired sometimes even when they are known to be corrupt. Lara could feel that cold black wormhole, a tumour of fear and doubt, growing ever bigger at her body's centre. It had been there for how long now? A year ago perhaps, it had been a stealthy prickle of uncertainty. She had tried

her hardest to ignore it. Oscar, the Tin Heart Gold Mine, the wilderness surrounding the safari camp, the people she loved, the art she was making were all bound together in an indissoluble marriage of passion. It was all or nothing. If she left Oscar, she would have to leave Chambeshi and the sources and inspiration for her art, the things that gave meaning to her whole being and her whole life. She could not do it. She loved her life. She loved Oscar.

Everything was changing though and very fast – every breath she took marked a difference in her world. It's not always an advantage to have a wild and vivid imagination," Lara thought. "*In my mind I have been through all the possibilities of what might happen and I really think Oscar is capable of murder. Chambeshi is full of crazy rumours at the moment – but maybe it's me who has gone mad? I need to speak to Tim and tell him what I have found out about Oscar. But do I know what Oscar is really like? I need to get Tim's advice, but Tim will hate me forever when I ask him. I need to warn Enoch and Inonge. I am sure that, like me, they are an innocent cover for Oscar's crimes, but I really don't know how to do that and or to make them believe me. What proof do I have after all? The trouble is that I cannot make anyone believe that I am not a willing partner in all that Oscar does."*

There had been a car accident outside the goods depot at the airport. Damaged vehicles and unlicensed drivers meant car accidents were frequent and often fatal in Chambeshi. The result of this particular accident caused Bernie to phone Lara one morning. Bernie did the accounts for Oscar's art exports.

"Bloody car crash near the airport!" Bernie said. "One of Oscar's shipments is slightly damaged. Normally he deals with anything like this himself – absolutely insists, he does. Right now things are complicated in Chambeshi. If this shipment doesn't leave it may be stuck for weeks and Oscar is not in the country. It's one of your bird paintings Lara – it may just need a little touch up with paint on the bird's wing. The frame I can glue, I think. Please could you have a look? Do it here, please, if you can. You know what a fuss Oscar makes. I am not to let it out of the office."

Lara agreed, collected some paints, tools and glue from her studio and arrived at Bernie's office. She rather dreaded the thought of patching up one of her least favourite paintings.

"Thanks, Lara." he said. "Fix yourself some coffee. I'll leave you to get on with things."

Bernie hadn't taken the painting out of its damaged wrappings so Lara lifted it out carefully. She was reminded by its weight that Oscar had insisted on using the heartwood of an ebony tree to make the inner frame. The whole frame was dense and heavy but even so the mitred corner had taken a hard sharp knock through the cardboard and bubble-wrap and it was bent slightly backwards. As she lifted it, the frame rattled and a bit of black gum came loose from the mitre joint. Lara turned her attention to the painting first. She painted in both oil and acrylic on canvas for these commissions. The acrylic dried swiftly in the bush and she could touch them up with the slow drying oil paint back in Chambeshi if necessary. She needed to use acrylic to repair any damage otherwise the painting would not be able to be packed up for many hours. The problem was that acrylic doesn't bind onto oil. Oil, however, could be used over acrylic. Fortunately the damage was slight and in the corner only. It was just a matter of laying a little more undercoat over the marked canvas and patching up a leaf and her signature. Lara looked at the frame and very gently flexed it. If she could just push it back together with a spot of wood glue that didn't show that would be best. It seemed that the black gum that had been dislodged was holding the frame apart. Lara poked at it with her penknife and a pencil-shaped piece of black gum slid out of the carved decorative insert in the frame. It was followed by a tube of dark-yellow beeswax embedded with green, red and white crystals.

Lara's heart stopped. She thought she was falling. She was choking. She was going to die. Time stood still. The world stopped. The next few moments lasted forever.

Lara, in fact, reacted in an instant. She reinserted the beeswax and rough gems into the inner frame, shoved back the black gum that locked the gems into their hiding place, covered the separated surfaces with wood glue and pushed the frame back into shape, jamming her tool box against its side to hold it until it set. Only then did she reach behind her for a chair to sit on, her hand holding her thudding heart in place behind her breastbone. Only then did she see Bernie standing watching her silent as a cat. This time Lara did stumble and almost fall. This time her gasp of fear was audible as she collapsed onto the seat.

"You didn't know? You didn't know?"

Lara kept shaking her head. Her body was also shaking.

"You mustn't say a word! You mustn't tell a soul! Nobody must ever know!"

Bernie, normally so suave and well-spoken, sounded strident and East-European. Lara grasped in the midst of her extreme fear that Bernie too was terrified. No one must ever know that Bernie had accidentally allowed Lara to find out Oscar's secret. Bernie had made the mistake of believing that Lara already knew about the gemstones. Bernie was at risk as much as she, Lara, was in danger. They both had to keep this secret or die. Lara knew at that moment that if Oscar found out that she knew she was in real trouble. Oscar might kill her, or blackmail her, or simply shop her to the police as the guilty party in the illegal export of gemstones while he made an easy escape.

She had been used.

Chapter Eight

The Plane Crash

Oscar was dead.

There were questions about exactly how and when it had happened but there seemed to be no doubt about the fact. Tim was given a detailed account by Enoch Junior who was one of the first to hear what was assumed to have taken place. Tim and Enoch Junior remained good friends and often phoned each other. Lara made Tim tell her word for word what he knew. Oscar must have died within a year or so of the failed coup against President Chona but nothing was known about it for around six years. He had taken off in his plane one day with Natan beside him. No flight plan had been registered. The plane and its two occupants simply disappeared.

It was a second plane crash that led to the discovery of Oscar's plane and the two bodies in it. A couple of wild life conservationists, co-pilots of a small plane, were making a study of game movement in the north of the National Park when they had engine trouble about one hundred kilometres north of the Tin Heart Gold Mine. They managed to send out a mayday call before they crashed into the hills. They were found alive and very thirsty, the following day, one with a broken collar bone, the other just badly battered and bruised. However the search and rescue team sent out to find them had first spotted the remains of a second small plane. It hung rusty and broken, suspended on a shattered tree against a steep rocky cliff where the northern escarpment dropped into a river valley. The registration on its fuselage identified it as Kilo Golf Tango 132, the Cessna 172 that had belonged to Oscar Mynhardt. To their relief it was obvious that this more deadly accident had happened a long time before and was not anything to do with the aircraft for which they were hunting. When the searchers circled above it they could not see bodies or movement but neither did they expect to given the state of the plane. As their first task was to arrange the rescue of their injured colleagues, they flew on until they located them. They dropped water, food and first aid supplies, then radioed-in the vehicles sent to pick them up. Though they reported the sighting of Oscar's plane it was some months before anyone felt motivated enough to make an expedition to the crash site and then only in response to a rumour that there might be diamonds or emeralds stashed in the Cessna's hold.

The same two rescuers set off again. They first reconnoitred by plane, then having located the crash, they landed at a rough airfield used by the flying doctor service, rented a battered truck from the local chief and drove through the bush to the top of the escarpment from where they climbed down to the crash site. The plane was balanced precariously on a large tree growing at an angle out of the hillside. This had kept it out of reach of scavengers like hyena and explained why they found the two skeletal remains relatively intact. One body was jammed in the cockpit and quite clearly had been shot. A round bullet hole was apparent in the right temple and a large jagged hole behind the left ear. The men who had climbed down to the wreck took photos and searched the plane and the dead man's clothes for any proof of identity. There was none and the photos taken on an instamatic family camera were not of good quality. They reckoned that this man, seated as he was, was too tall to be Oscar. The second person had either been flung from the plane or had managed to climb out. The body lay face down stretched out on a sturdy branch a little lower down. The men could not be sure if its leg was broken or if it had just adopted a strange angle with the passage of time. Identification was complicated because the skull had become detached and fallen further down the hill.

"Poor bugger!" the adventurers said to each other. "I hope it didn't take him too long to die."

Tim did not tell Lara this part of the story but she understood its likelihood and asked him about it anyway. Tim could only shrug.

The two men reckoned that the plane must have been close to the limit of its fuel. There was a metal jerry can in the back of the plane that amazingly still had some fuel in it but it was jammed into the twisted body of the plane so they did not try and lift it out. A passport was buttoned in the second corpse's shirt pocket. The name in it was Oscar Mynhardt.

"Where's the pilot's passport gone?" one of the men asked. The other shook his head and frowned.

"Do you think there were only two people on board?"

Again they took photos and returned to their camp-site for the night. They were up early to the smell of smoke from a bush fire. The fact that they had explored the crash site the day before had led other creatures to do the same. Perhaps a leopard tracking their scent had disturbed the plane. It had shifted, rocked and fallen further down the rock face taking both bodies with it. Some spilt fuel, broken glass the heat of the rising sun – who knows? The angry flames around the jumble of metal and bones were a transparent red. The quick smoke curled upwards black and choking. It was the end of a very dry season. The two adventurers had to turn their truck around and drive away from the bush fire as it roared up the rock face out of the valley towards their camp site. They never went back. Instead they took their photos, their story and Oscar's passport to the Chief of Police who informed Junior Enoch about it. They hadn't found any gemstones, which they thought was disappointing – and odd.

It took Oscar's lawyers two more slow years before they decided they were sufficiently empowered to carry out his will and settle up his estate. It was then that Lara received the two fat brown envelopes informing her that she was one of Oscar's legatees. The other legatee was Inonge. Inonge became the sole owner of the Tin Heart Gold mine and the Kasenga Safari Camp site. Half the proceeds of the sale of Oscar's ranch house went to Lara, half to Inonge. The Otto Dix paintings and the Käthe Kollwitz prints now belonged to Lara and were in a London bank vault.

"Worth a lot of money." The lawyer said. "Real gold!"

"How did you feel about Oscar's death?" Brendan asks Lara.

"After so long? Relieved and indifferent I think." Lara says hesitating at first, then with a half-smile at the way Brendan phrased his question. Her feelings, complicated and so changeable for so long seem to have settled. Maybe into an emotional sludge. Does she want to have them stirred up?

"I knew he must be dead. If he wasn't, I think he would have let me know in some way. I mean he could have blackmailed me into seeing him again if he had wanted to – he could have said that I was an accomplice of his. Could I have proved otherwise?" Lara watched Brendan's reaction to her words then carried on. "I couldn't understand how he could be capable of loving me and using me. I couldn't understand how he could be both -" Lara searches for the right words. " – a crook – and – and such a good and loyal friend to Enoch and also to me – and then do what he did to us both – betray us – and then? How could he use my paintings to smuggle out diamonds? It incriminates me! I don't know what happened to the paintings." Lara glances up at Brendan and manages a grin. "The idea that my paintings have been junked makes me absolutely furious even if I am safer for it!" She stops smiling abruptly. "He didn't appear so – damaged or so exploitative but I guess I knew he couldn't change and he wouldn't stop doing what he had always done in Chambeshi."

"What was that? What was it he always would do?" Brendan persists.

"Oh I don't know really." Lara says crossly. "Be an opportunist always – looking to survive – like a wild animal on the hunt always."

"When did you begin to realise that?" Brendan asks.

Lara shakes her head slowly and soberly.

"I don't know exactly – the knowledge gradually seeped into me somehow. I began to see that he was not quite in control of himself – he was driven always to take chances – like someone canoeing down rapids in a deep, steep-sided gorge – there was no way out for him and he didn't know whether he would be drowned going over a waterfall or finally reach the sea.

Part Ten
London 1997

Chapter One

Gillian

When Adam goes back to school the week after Tim's departure, Gillian and Anne help Lara move the contents of her studio from the flat into her new, much larger, and very much colder space at the Victoria Park Art Factory Studios.

The abandoned living room is a dismal mess now that it is empty.

"Mum, you haven't cleaned your studio ever, have you? Wow!"

Adam is so impressed by this idea that Lara has to laugh. She had been thinking gloomily of the time and money she would have to spend to get the room into a usable condition. It's time, rather than money, that she is most reluctant to give to the task but as she doesn't want to touch Oscar's money, time is what the task will need.

"It's certainly got the dirtiest spider webs and biggest dust-balls in the East End of London, hasn't it?" Lara says. "Bedrooms aren't the same as artist's studios though. You still have to clean yours and I still do always keep the kitchen clean. How about you give me a hand with this room, Adam? Maybe the spiders will defeat me and I'll end up wrapped up in spider web cocoon like a dead fly."

Adam hesitates a moment in case he is being tricked into housework, but racing around this newly discovered space with a broom and batting at webs with a duster proves too tempting. Lara has to call an end to their game when the air fills with dust and makes them both cough.

"This is great, Mum. Can you leave it like this for a bit?" Adam asks.

Why not? Lara thinks, happy and breathless from their shared exercise.

"Okay, until I get the curtains down and cleaned and start to paint it."

Adam brings down any of his toys that still have wheels and sets up competitions to see which of them would crash most spectacularly into the opposite skirting board after travelling the furthest distance.

Lara is pleased to put off cleaning and decorating the living room and instead concentrate on settling into her Victoria Park Studio. She is paying for a half-share of a large space but as the other half is still unoccupied she lets herself spread out a little. It is lovely to be undisturbed as she works and she has almost three clear days a week to concentrate on her own work.

Lara paints steadily, using the twilight greens of the soft shadowless English countryside and blurring colour through mist.

Behind her, last year's unfinished canvasses of hard dark edged grey, robotic city forms are stacked facing the studio wall.

On her work-table, the sketch books are still in piles, but now their pages are jammed open with any convenient or appropriate object and Lara constantly refers to them. Boxes of pencils, crayons, stones, feathers and leaves collected from the bush sit uneasily on their awkward upended lids ready to give up information or to provide memory markers.

Hidden for the last ten years, a huge blood-red canvas still wearing a skirt of bubble-wrap glows in the late light of the window right where Lara can see it if she dares to confront it. Lara is determined to find a new direction and a new meaning for her art. The red painting was from a previous life. Maybe she will strip it off its stretchers, tear it into shreds and put it out with the rubbish.

Tim has been gone several weeks now. She can redefine herself. Lara decides that she needs to find a new way of rooting her art in the place where she lives. She will start with English paintings and perhaps make them more abstract and less descriptive. The idea frightens her. She begins to feel as if she is floating rootless above her own life. Will she be able to find meaning for herself in isolation in England? Tim phones her regularly and always speaks to Adam but their conversations are all surface chat. They always seem to cover the same territory.

"I'm fine. You're fine? Yes me too. No life's fine. Adam's good. Aren't you Adam? Yes work's okay. I'll tell you about it? I'll write and I'll fax you. Is your fax private? Adam wants to fax some drawings to you. Okay?"

They exchange letters by fax machine and Lara always includes something that Adam has written or drawn or occasionally dictated if time was short.

Lara knows she needs other artists. It had been a good move to reconnect with Gillian and get back into a different, more avant-garde, perhaps a more extreme art coterie. It was proving interesting but would it was also disruptive and maybe it increases her sense of displacement and uncertainty about herself and her work.

She has to give it a try but her feelings of detachment are accompanied by a growing sense of desolation. Then the dreams start again and turn into nightmares.

Chapter Two

Rape

Lara had encountered her old art school friend Gillian by chance at an exhibition at the Serpentine Gallery. At first they were wary of each other but to their mutual surprise found their old art school friendship was built on a the depth of passion each felt for their own work together with a readiness to laugh at their mistakes. Gillian is more relaxed than Lara remembers and her appearance is more ordinary. She still has a stud in her nose and another in her eyebrow but she wears no make-up and her hair, though very short simply looks fashionable. Her tattoos have faded slightly but are now mostly covered by her T-shirt. Gillian has a new partner, Anne, a red-haired woman with a friendly open face who dresses like a school-teacher and, in fact, is one. Lara immediately feels comfortable with her unchallenging manner. She meets Gillian and Anne at their small Stratford East house which is pleasant, comfortable and well-maintained with a tiny but pretty garden.

"Anne never minded being gay." Gillian says. "It was just how she was and what she wanted to be. I had problems about being a lesbian – you'll remember. I felt I had to go on a journey to become what in fact I already was. I had to join a club, choose to belong, change myself and show I was different by my appearance. Mad really. I wasn't the only one who felt that of course."

They are on the bus heading for Gillian's studio near Victoria

Park. Gillian had invited Lara to come and see what she was working on.

The studio was in an old factory with large spaces, wide stone stairs and iron frame windows. Heating was obviously a problem. There were boiler suits and thick sweaters hanging behind the doors of the studios.

"Horrid aren't they? At least – I hope you think they are." Gillian says.

Gillian and Lara stand together in front of six enormous black and white photo-montages.

"My God yes – they are awful. It's you isn't it? What made you do them? I mean I know what they're about, but why did you do them? What happened? They are about you, aren't they?"

"I was raped." Gillian says matter-of-factly. "It happened a long time ago when I was living with Poppy after art school. You know how we looked – we were both so into punk then. There was a pub we used to go to near where we lived. We used to chat to some blokes who hung out there. They seemed okay with us, I thought. They seemed to accept that we were weird and they used to rag us about being punks and being gay but they didn't seem aggressive or anything – I thought they liked us and we were almost friends. Anyhow I was there one night on my own and after I left the pub they followed me. Seems they had decided to educate me into being a heterosexual so they pulled me into a side road and all had a go at showing me what I was missing. I fought like hell which was probably a mistake – I lost my front teeth." Gillian clacks her fingernail on the bridgework in her mouth.

Lara is aghast. She stares at Gillian open-mouthed. How does she manage to be so calm about it?

"How awful!" Lara repeats in shock. "What did you do? Did you go to the police? What happened?"

"Oh I did. The case went to court. On my lawyer's advice I even dressed in ordinary clothes for the court appearance but of course the 'boys' got off. A punk unemployed artist in a gay relationship is asking for it apparently. With my lifestyle what could I expect but to be raped?"

Lara looks around for a chair to sit on.

"Hey" Gillian says, "I'm okay now you know – but you don't look so good."

She pulls out a high stool for Lara and makes instant coffee in stained and chipped mugs that smell faintly of white spirit. Lara stares at the photo-montages.

They are horribly explicit. Gillian's agonised and distorted face is pasted in each montage. In one her body is pressed into the shape of a Spanish ham in a metal cuff on a bar counter. A maniac butcher slices at her rump with a long knife while her distorted face screams in protest. In another there's a butcher's display of carcasses of meat and each piece carries Gillian's face. In this image the man serving the meat is wearing a judge's wig and the customers all have the faces of four young men taken from newspaper cuttings. The art works are deliberately made to seem crude and blurry but they are also beautifully produced and executed.

"I shall probably paint over the men's faces in some way." Gillian says, "I don't want the exhibition to be closed down for reasons of slander or whatever. A friend of mine posed as the judge for me."

"How do you like the one where I am being weighed on the scales with the judge's hands on my breasts? I don't know if I will use them all. I am talking to the gallery about how far we can go without being sued or visited by someone like Mary Whitehouse – though I wouldn't mind the publicity of course. I don't expect to sell these easily."

Lara puts her hands over her eyes and rubs them.

"Am I upsetting you, Lara? Some people can't bear to have rape mentioned. There are a lot of us women who it's happened to – but we never talk about it, do we?"

Gillian is watching Lara.

"Hey girl! Take it easy. We needn't look at these."

Lara can see Gillian is concerned for her. She makes a great effort.

"No!" she says. "I want to see your work. It's important – it has impact though."

"I hope so – I want to counter that patriarchal crap about women asking for it."

"Rape isn't only physical, Lara." Gillian continues, "I was also raped mentally and emotionally by the press – and the court – and the judge. It's the way women are used and perceived. It isn't over when the chap removes his dick – though he may think it is."

"Oh Gillian! How have you survived?" Lara asks.

"Turned the experience into art of course – what else? If you don't you just end up in a vicious spiral of self-hate."

As they walk back from the studios Gillian tells Lara the rest of her story.

"I can laugh now – most of the time – at what happened afterwards. It really screwed my relationship with Poppy – my first girl friend – you remember her? She didn't want to testify on my behalf. She was really frightened and left London very soon afterwards. The other women in the commune where we lived wanted me to make a stand as a feminist. To go to court dressed as I had always done – punk you, know. I think I had already started to want to move away from that commune and that group though. It had got very incestuous and controlling. I wanted to identify myself first of all as an artist and then as a woman. It was all very complicated and nasty. I survived because I got a good therapist and support – I eventually met Anne – she made a huge difference to me because she has a sense of humour."

"Hey Lara – on the subject of sex – are you planning on taking a lover while Tim's away?"

Lara laughs at Gillian's directness.

"Not with Adam to look after –it would be too complicated!"

Gillian looks over at Lara questioningly.

"Well, then – I'll take you to my sex shop in Hoxton if you like – there are other things a woman can do."

Part Eleven
The Coup 1989

Chapter One

Riots

"I have to collect Tim from Chambeshi airport early tomorrow." Lara said. "Do you think the riots are over now? Nothing has happened all afternoon in the city centre."

Inonge's mouth turned down at the corners. She shook her head.

"Who knows? Things are quiet in town but the students are holding meetings at the university right at this moment. Enoch Junior says that there are some very radical ideas being put forward. In any case the students haven't been getting anything but maize meal to eat for weeks and not much of that! With the latest price hikes for maize meal they won't eat at all."

"I think I'll go down-town to Tim's flat and see that it's ready for him and maybe do some painting while I am there."

"No! Don't." Inonge said. "Until things are safe in the city you should bring Tim back here to Oscar's ranch when he arrives!"

"Don't think he'll like the idea of any association with Oscar's business or friends!" Lara muttered quietly to herself. It would be safer than Tim's down-town flat of course, but Tim was returning to Chambeshi to report on the riots and the political troubles that had befallen President Chona. He would want to be where events were taking place in the town centre and outside the Parliament. In any case his antipathy and distrust of Oscar had increased over time. Lara blamed herself. He had been right about Oscar. She knew he was right, she had proof, but what could she say to him about it now?

"No news from Oscar?" Lara said by way of passing time and changing the object of the moment. She had come to see Inonge and Enoch with the half-formed intention of telling them about the smuggling of the gemstones. Perhaps they already were in on the deal? She didn't think they could be but how did one know for sure? The trouble was that tension had been increasing on the streets of Chambeshi with the exorbitant price rises in the staple food. Now there were crowds of angry people in the streets. Riots had started and spread.

Was this the right moment? What should she do or say?

Enoch, hunched at his desk with piles of papers in front of him, shook his head slowly and for a long time. Finally he looked up at Lara.

"No news and I have still no idea what he is doing. All the US dollars have gone from the safe – there were several thousand I think – and he has flown off in his plane but made no flight plans and said nothing to me. I don't like the look of these accounts either. A lot of money has been moved around and then vanished."

Lara's guts already felt hollow. Now she felt sick. She did not know who to tell about the last time she had seen Oscar and she still was not sure what to make of what had happened between them. There was a cold heavy lump behind her breastbone and a sense of desolation possessed her.

It was after she had seen the dead body of Njoka and before she had discovered the precious stones being smuggled out of Chambeshi in her paintings that Lara attempted to confront Oscar in his office. She stuttered out her question about Natan's role at the Tin Heart Camp and how it was being financed. Oscar stood up, his face expressionless. He moved like an automaton, gripping her by her upper arms and pushing her back against his books. She felt each shelf like a ladder's steps against her spine and the back of her head.

"What do you think is happening here? Can't you see it's over for President Chona? Chambeshi is falling apart. The region is on the point of collapse! I stay afloat as long as I stay on top. I will be the king-maker. I will finance the changeover. That's how I will survive! That's how you will survive! Do you understand? Do you see?"

Oscar gave her a last hard shove backwards. Then he released her. Her arms were circled with bruises for days later.

"Yes, I see." she said submissively. She did not really understand him, though, or believe him. She thought he might be mad.

"Kingmaker! Could he really mean that? Had he delusions? I've left it all too late." Lara said to herself. "Chambeshi is disintegrating fast. I've got my plane tickets for ten days time – if the planes are still flying that is! I must – must – tell Enoch and Inonge what I know – but I want to find out more – I want Oscar to tell me more. Did he ever love me at all – was I only convenient. Perhaps another opportunity will come when he may tell me a bit more of the truth – if I dare ask! I want to tell Tim – I must tell Tim about Oscar."

Chapter Two

Under Fire

Later that afternoon, Inonge phoned a friend in a clinic in town to be told that the riots had started again. Crowds of people, men, women with babies on their backs and children had gone running up the main street. They were in a cheerful mood and laughing. People had started breaking into shops and looting goods. So many items had been amassed by individuals that they couldn't possibly carry them all. They had to hide them away in order to collect them later. Men scrambled up scaffolding on building sites or hid their loot in doorways on side streets. The police had arrived finally and taken charge of the streets. Inonge's friend said that there was some gunfire which had emptied the thoroughfares for a while. Then the rioters began to use the railway line to gain access to the city. Minibuses and cars had vanished from the roads. People were trapped at the markets and in their offices until dark when most of the rioters went home. There was no information to be had from the local radio and television. The President was rumoured to be on holiday somewhere. That evening Enoch's radio picked up a very brief uninformative report on the BBC World Service news about some rioting in Chambeshi but nothing about the reasons or the political significance.

The next morning the sun rose in a clear sky. It was a beautiful day, warm and balmy. Early reports from the city said all was peaceful. It was certainly silent. There was no traffic and not even one minibus on the streets. Lara took Enoch's Toyota to the airport. Enoch insisted that it was the most reliable car to travel in if anything untoward happened. All along the route people were waiting hopelessly for transport to get into work. The road was littered with rocks and broken concrete bricks as far as the outskirts of the city. Lara passed several burnt-out shells of vehicles but after she reached the dual carriageway to the airport there was nothing untoward to be seen.

At the airport people were gathered in quiet and serious knots reading the papers. The Chambeshian press had reported extensively on the riots. There were even photographs of damaged properties. The city shop looters may have been opportunists but politically directed attacks had been made on police stations and government offices in the townships. Buildings had been burnt down. There had been some deaths, one was a policeman, and there were many injured. Well organised activists had arrived from the northern mining towns. They, it was thought, had been responsible for the well-targeted attacks. Again Lara's stomach hurt. Had Oscar had a part in organising transport for those men? She knew now for certain that he had seen the riots as a way to loosen President Chona's hold on power and that he planned to install General Miyanda.

If only Tim's bloody plane would land on time.

Once they got back to safety she would start to tell him what she had discovered.

The flight arrival was announced. At that moment a young Asian man accompanied by two armed policemen entered the hall in a state of high excitement.

"The riots have started again!" he declared with authority and an expression of pleasure.

Immediately the crowd stirred and began to move about quickly gathering up their possessions and glancing around to see what everyone else planned to do.

"We'll be heading a convoy back to the city." the young Asian said. "Follow my pick-up truck. I have more armed police with me. Collect all the passengers – all of them – as fast as you can and we'll get moving."

Lara had two options. One was to follow the convoy which was to go back to the city down the main road which had been targeted by rioters the day before. The other was to go home on her own via a long dirt road through farming country that went in a quarter-circle round the city. She had no idea what she would find on that road but it was unlikely that it would attract activists or rioters of any sort.

Unfortunately Tim was slow in clearing his baggage. It was the last item dumped on the slow carousel. When he finally walked through the customs door, Lara had no time for greetings or conversation. She grabbed his arm.

"Quick, Tim. We must leave now. The riots have started again."

She could see he thought she was panicking unnecessarily. Riots did not usually start early in the morning but there was no time to explain. Her place in the car-park was close to the middle of the convoy behind the police pick-up truck, but two white men, one with a rifle, in a second truck, refused to allow her the space to join the queue. Lara reversed to make for another exit and head for the country route home. By a curious fluke however, the convoy leader saw her and signalled that she join the line of vehicles at a point immediately behind his vehicle. As soon as she joined the convoy she realised that she was committed to the more dangerous town route.

The convoy moved at a terrific speed with all the vehicles following close behind each other. Every now and then a car from a side road made a desperate and dangerous attempt to join them in the belief that this was the best way to get into the city. Lara did not look at her speedometer. It took all her concentration to maintain a steady distance behind the car in front of her. Tim said nothing; he looked once at the speedometer, once at Lara, stretched his legs out to brace himself and held onto the car door with one hand and the back of Lara's seat with the other. The leading police vehicle signalled for the convoy to overtake it and continue on down the road. It then swung into the gates of the agriculture college checking on possible dangers from gathering mobs of students. Lara found herself temporarily leading the convoy. Minutes later the leading police vehicle once again overtook the convoy and Lara. It raced ahead as the convoy approached the main university down a long straight incline. As she passed the university entrance, Lara saw that it was crowded with students, their hands clutching rocks, bricks, stones and paving slabs. A group of them were busy dragging car tyres filled with burning grass into the middle of the road at the point where it dipped as it went through a vlei. Shots rang out from behind her. Presumably the white man armed with the rifle had started shooting or the students had thrown their missiles at the convoy. At the sound of gunfire the front police vehicle throttled back, screeched to a stop then and swung backwards around Lara's car, and reversed down the road at top speed its engine shrieking in protest. In it, armed policemen fired over the top of the convoy at the students. As the bullets hummed over their car, Tim covered his head with his arms and ducked below the dashboard. Without slackening the car's speed, Lara drove, her head level with her outstretched arms on the steering wheel. She could barely see the road or the car in front of her and yet somehow, she also saw, with the clarity of a dream, the students running away up the smooth green lawns towards the university buildings. In their bright coloured clothes, the boys with clean white shirts, the girls with pretty skirts, they seemed to dance and fall like flowers in a summer breeze.

It was all behind them in a moment. A taxi oblivious to the situation appeared in front of the convoy. Lara swung out and around it as if she was a practised getaway driver with a procession of vehicles on her tail. The police car was in front of her again. When it reached the main street traffic lights it slowed down almost to the speed limit and the convoy following it swiftly dispersed leaving the streets empty of traffic once more. The Toyota drifted on gently through the peaceful city suburbs till it reached the Njobvus' home and an anxious Enoch and Inonge.

"We heard that the riots had started again." Inonge said. "Was the plane delayed – you took so long?"

"Took so long!" Lara giggled still in shock. "Twenty minutes to get from the airport! Twenty minutes! It's usually three-quarters of an hour!"

Tim was also grinning with relief.

"Lara was amazing! She should drive stunt cars in movies after that demonstration of skill! We had to join a police convoy that averaged over 100 mph all the way here."

Tim and Lara looked at each other properly for the first time since they had met at the airport. They both realised how upset they were by what they had seen on the drive.

Tim said, "You should have heard Lara swearing at the police – they were shooting at the university students. It was awful to see."

"Did I swear?" Lara had not heard herself shouting.

"Tim!" Lara she said grabbing at his arm. "We have to talk! I have to tell you things. Now! Come with me!" She pulled him towards the veranda where they could be alone."

"There'll be coffee and breakfast in the kitchen when you are ready!" Inonge called after them.

Chapter Three

Confession

"I don't think you'll want to see me any more after I've told you what I have found out." Lara said.

Now she had started she knew that she would be able to finish what she had to say. Those last few sweaty nights when she had lain awake uncertain and indecisive, dreading the outcome of this confession, were proving to have been a waste of time. There was only one thing to do and that was to tell Tim and then to tell Enoch and then to go to the airport and take the next plane to England, though that might prove difficult in the current political unrest.

"Okay – go ahead then." Tim frowned. "You are going to marry Oscar and have a white wedding – is that it?"

Lara was taken aback by his bitter tone but she shook her head firmly.

"No! Listen! It is nothing like that. Yes I have been – was – Oscar's – lover – but – ."

The words always sounded so crude stated in that way. Sleeping with someone never explained either the profundity or the shallowness of a relationship or how it worked.

"It's over between Oscar and me. I don't even know if it's safe for me to see him again – and that man Natan – he's the really dangerous one I think! Oscar is involved with the rebellion in the north in some way – because of Natan perhaps, though I'm not sure which of them is the actual instigator. I don't think Enoch and Inonge have a clue about what Oscar is really up to – and I don't know if they'll believe me when I tell them – I'm going to do that next – after telling you I mean."

Tim's face was very still and expressionless. His eyes fixed on Lara's face.

"I'm so sorry, Tim! I can't bear this – I am so ashamed of being taken in by Oscar – and I can't stand the idea that anyone would think I was connected with what Oscar does – but I know what it looks like."

All the time Lara was speaking she could see Oscar in her mind, looking back at her over his shoulder with that warm, humorous and loving look that he kept only for her. She squeezed her eyes shut to try and block out that memory and replace it with the last cold and hard stare she had seen on his face. The story must be told. Lara shrugged herself free of the memory of Oscar and looked up at Tim. She began her account of the ambush by the rebel gang and how Oscar had seemed so friendly with their leader, Njoka. It was always curious how talking over something with another person enlightened her understanding of it rather as the process of working on a painting increased and improved the artist's understanding of the purpose and beauty of their own work

"I think at first Oscar only wanted to keep control of his illegal gemstone trade but then he found out that Natan was helping to fund the rebels and destabilise Chambeshi. He had to take account of Natan's actions and include them into his own plans. On top of that, as President Chona was becoming increasingly unpopular, Oscar thought he would try and keep in with both the President and with the coup plotters so that he would not be a loser himself."

Lara looked straight at Tim. He was still looking at her and that gave her courage. Even if he never spoke to her again she hoped he would not think she was entirely bad.

"Oscar supported me and my art as a cover for his business

somehow. Yes – I was completely sold on Oscar – that's my fault entirely. I think he used me though – but I should have seen that. I have no excuse. He has also used Enoch and Inonge and their safari camp to hide his illegal operations and that has been going on longer than I have known Oscar. I have to tell them now. I don't know if they'll believe me – Inonge may, but not Enoch! It will hurt him so much!"

Lara ducked her head as her eyes filled with tears. Crying was not going to get her out of this mess. She must carry on. She straightened herself again.

"When I started to realise all this stuff – only a few weeks ago – I wanted to run away. Just leave Chambeshi and start somewhere else but the political trouble had already begun and I didn't want to leave Enoch and Inonge on their own in such a mess. I was afraid that if Oscar's payments to the rebels up north and to the disaffected army officers down here gets known about then Enoch and Inonge – and Enoch Junior will all be caught up in it and – well – God knows what might happen – anything – prison – or worse! Death sentences maybe!

"When you said you were coming – I thought you were the most important person to tell because if it is reported – if you believe me – that is – that might help protect people and most of all – save the Njobvus. Everyone needs to know the truth."

In spite of herself, Lara found herself crying.

"I don't really want to get Oscar into trouble – I don't want revenge or anything – but maybe he deserves it – I don't really know anymore – but Natan – yes! He is a bad man, a very bad man! Most of all Tim – I didn't want you to find out about me and Oscar and have you think I was involved with any of his horrible business. I am so sorry Tim!"

Tim was silent. He stood looking at Lara as she cried. After a while he gave her his handkerchief and put his hand on her shoulder.

"We need that coffee first." he said. "Then we'll talk more."

As she sniffed and blew her nose into his rumpled handkerchief, he led her into the kitchen.

"It fits pretty much with what I've been told in Harare." Tim said. "In fact it's the other part of the picture and helps to explain it all."

They were sitting opposite each other at the kitchen table with mugs of coffee. Tim had helped himself to a large bowl of cereal. Lara was breaking some biscuits into crumbs.

"Some of my information comes from various riff-raff in the Station Road bars. Guys who claim to be refugees or in the know or on their way to sign up with some or other mercenary group. The overall picture is that Chona is out of touch with his people, his advisors are sycophants, his army generals are ambitious, the poor people of Chambeshi are very dissatisfied and also hungry. The feeling is that a coup is likely and should be easily successful. There are stashes of weapons all over Chambeshi left by the freedom fighters when they returned to their homes in Zimbabwe and South Africa. There is easy money to be made by finding them and selling them on.

The political attachés at various embassies agree on one thing, that there is a Israeli who was with Mossad – you know, the Israeli Secret Service – maybe even the Kidon – the Mossad section responsible for assassinations – he was keeping tabs on various possible terrorist groups that might be training in Africa – but it's said this man has gone rogue and is happily stirring up small rebellions any place where there are sources of valuable gemstones – diamonds – emeralds – that kind of thing. No one can pin anything on this man. He is a bit like Kurtz in Conrad's book 'The Heart of Darkness'. He uses tribal conflict – pits one tribe against another so that he is always in control."

Lara nodded hopelessly. She had taken Conrad's famous book off Oscar's shelf and reread it the last time she went to the Tin Heart Mine.

"That's definitely what Natan is doing. I think he arranged the death of Njoka because Njoka had stopped obeying him."

"Where is he, do you think? Natan, I mean. Do you think Oscar is with him? Are you suggesting that Natan is the boss and Oscar does what he is told?"

Lara realised that Tim was thinking like the reporter and journalist he was and had put aside his personal feelings about her. It might be a wry thought but she preferred Tim this way to a Tim who might not like her any more. At least he trusted her enough to ask her questions.

"What I know about Oscar makes me think he wouldn't take orders from Natan unless he had no choice." Lara said. "I think perhaps that Oscar had been carrying on the same trade as Natan – that is acquiring illegal diamonds and gemstones – for even longer than Natan. I think he operated on a much smaller and more secret scale though and he didn't kill his competitors and threaten his suppliers. Maybe Natan muscled in and Oscar had to join him or quit. It doesn't make any difference, though, because I think that Oscar started doing the same terrible things as Natan."

Lara looked directly at Tim.

"If I had known that Oscar was into illegal diamonds when I met him I would never have wanted his friendship or his help and I wouldn't have become -" Lara hesitated, then blurted out, "I would not have become his lover! The trouble is that it is easy to say that now with hindsight – and I don't suppose you'll believe me – I would have been too scared to get involved with a criminal but also I do believe in doing the right thing – I do!"

Tim considered Lara for a long moment.

"I don't think you would have either, Lara. I don't think that you are a natural gangster's moll." Tim smiled at Lara briefly then, serious again, he asked. "Lara, do you think Oscar cared about you or do you think he deliberately set out to attract you and use you as a cover for his illegal deals."

Lara was racked once more with utter misery and self-doubt. It was hard for her to speak. Finally she did.

"I think he did both. I think he did care – does maybe still –

care for me but he can't separate out what suits his agenda and what is right. Or what and who he does care for – well – look at the way he has used – and is still using Enoch – I know he really does love that man."

Lara was afraid Tim would next ask her what her present feelings for Oscar were. He almost spoke and then was silent. After a while he suggested that they both should go and talk to Enoch and Inonge. Lara agreed. The moment she dreaded was upon her, but as they got up to look for Enoch they heard the sound of rifle shots and helicopters. The sounds seemed be from every direction, all around the house.

Inonge and Enoch were on the veranda looking up at the sky. Police helicopters were circling overhead. Inonge kept shaking her head, her hands covering her mouth. Enoch watching the helicopters said after a while that they needn't worry.

"Well – they are following groups of rioters – probably picking off the leaders. They are not far from us but if you watch you can see that they are over the main roads into town and to the President's house. We'd be mad to go anywhere today. We'll just have to sit here and wait for things to settle down."

Inonge rushed to the phone to make sure that her son was safe. She returned shaking her head even harder.

"Junior is at the hospital of course – I expect he'll be very busy – there must be many wounded – do you think he'll be safe, Enoch?"

"I doubt that either the rioters or the police will attack the hospital." Tim reassured her. "Do you think I can go out and have a look at what's going on? Can I borrow a car please?"

Everyone shouted out simultaneously that Tim must not on any account go out. Lara, knowing that sooner or later Tim would go out, even if he had to walk, suggested that perhaps Tim should spend the time phoning his contacts to see what they knew first.

"Okay everyone!" Tim said. "I'll cool it for a while. But – Enoch and Inonge, please let's sit down and talk. Lara and I have some bad news to give you though – not unconnected with all the present trouble. Lara do you want to begin?"

Lara made an instant decision not to start with her suspicions that Oscar had used the Tin Heart Camp Safari Camp as a cover for his illegal trade, but simply told Enoch and Inonge what she had heard Oscar and Natan say about their support for the riots and the coup.

"I don't think Oscar ever intended to support the Njoka gang – he just had an arrangement with them which meant they gave him no trouble until Natan forced his hand – or blackmailed him into it."

Enoch's face was averted. His expression grim. Once or twice Lara thought he was going to stand up and march out of the room but Inonge kept a restraining hand on his arm.

"This is what I discovered only days ago. Tim says he heard the same things in other places." Lara looked towards Tim but before he could explain what he had learnt, Enoch turned back to Lara with a vicious look.

"Where are you in all this Lara? Still Oscar's concubine? Maybe Natan's whore too? Why should we believe you? Why are you telling us this now? Is this a trap to get us into trouble with the President?"

Lara swallowed hard. She gave Tim another desperate nervous glance.

"When I realised what was going on, I wanted to tell Oscar I would have nothing more to do with him. I didn't want to have anything to do with treachery and crime but Oscar said no one would believe me. It wasn't possible that my paintings were used to smuggle out diamonds and gemstones without my knowledge."

"Lara's afraid that Oscar may try and shut her up or even kill her," Tim said. "Lara is going to leave Chambeshi to get away from Oscar but she wanted to warn you first – she thinks you are in danger too – and Junior. First let me tell you what I know."

After Tim had finished speaking there was silence. Like Lara, Tim did not as yet mention all their suspicions. They needed to see how Enoch took the information first. It was Inonge who spoke.

"We also suspected this. Junior came to warn us last week. He has been speaking to Pascal and Chimunya – they each have different information but together it points to Oscar's complicity and guilt. Chimunya's father is still in the government but he told her about the threatened coup and the 'white' businessman who gave money to the cause. She identified this businessman as Oscar. Of course she supports the government. Pascal, who knows what the word is on the street, said there are similar rumours in all the bars. He would love to see the government brought down. People think a change of government will make food cheaper – little do they know!"

"Since Junior told Inonge and me about these plottings, I have been checking all the business accounts that I can get my hands on." Enoch reluctantly admitted.

"I've checked Oscar's office too – Oscar's been importing dollars from his offshore accounts – in some cases converting it into cash – US dollars that is – then moving it on very fast – I don't know where to or why but he has also used our joint business accounts without telling me – it looks as if he expects the Wall Street crash to happen here – it is not how I do business."

Enoch still would not look at Lara or speak to her but Inonge reached out her free hand to touch Lara's shoulder.

"You are good to think of us and try and help, Lara. Sometimes us women just pick a bad man without knowing – we too thought Oscar was our friend – he was Enoch's hero. Hmm! No! No!" Inonge clamped her lips together in disapproval; her eyes closed while she shook her head, and swayed her body in distress.

"Now we need to work." she said collecting herself, "We must clean up the accounts, Enoch – I am not going to prison with Oscar when the coup fails!"

"If it does fail." Tim said.

"We'll probably all go to jail if the coup succeeds!" Enoch said.

Chapter Four

Curfew

The President was back in Chambeshi City the next day. He appeared on TV announcing the imposition of a 36-hour curfew while saying that there would be no reduction of maize meal prices. The TV showed damaged buildings and burnt out cars and police stations. Rioting was to be dealt with severely. Almost immediately arrests were made and the football stadium filled up with people caught with looted goods. No food was given to those who were imprisoned and they were held for days. Juveniles were taken to court and many were rumoured to have disappeared. Bodies were disposed of secretly – or so it was said. Helen's Cypriot ex-husband turned his shopping centre into an armed enclave. Unprotected supermarkets were looted at night one after the other. A crowd of rioters set off to attack the President's house but came across a very large battery chicken farm and stopped there to share out the poultry until the police caught up with them. The dusk to dawn curfew gave the populace an enforced holiday. Getting to work and back in time for the curfew to start was impossible for people who walked several hours back and forth to work each day. There were long queues at petrol stations, banks were shut, shops closed, food could not be bought. By misfortune and bad planning the riots had begun before pay-day and no one had any cash or money. Tim was out every possible moment and spent the curfew hours talking to anyone who had any information, otherwise he was on the phone and fax machine to his head office in London. They were only just beginning to take an interest in the story.

Lara went down one morning to the Umodzi Gallery and spoke briefly to Helen.

"No one's tried to loot any contemporary artworks." Helen said, with a grin. "If they take anything it will be the ritual objects and dance masks from the Chambeshi museum – those that have magic and power." She was going home to lie by her walled swimming pool with a bottle of wine. There was nothing else to do.

Inonge was busy seeing that her workers who came briefly to the house in the hope of food had, as usual, something to eat and this time also some provisions to take home to their wives and children.

"It's not like they weren't out looting and rioting with the rest!" Enoch said with irony. He was however, sympathetic to their plight.

By the end of the week the informal traders were back on the streets cleaning shoes, and selling sun-warmed, expensive imported apples. The state shops opened with sacks of maize-meal at the new raised price. It was also available on the black market, no cheaper, but in kilo packets that were more affordable.

The university remained in uproar. After the first day of rioting there wasn't one staff car that had not been set alight. Eventually the university was closed and the hungry students were sent home to their hungry families. The airport was open but flights in and out of Chambeshi were uncertain. Those that were outward-bound were full and tickets for future flights were hard to get. Lara had already booked herself on the earliest flight she could get, in 8 days' time.

It was still difficult to move around the city though life appeared to be returning to a version of normality. Enoch and Inonge had continued to work through Oscar's office files and felt that they had almost completed the task. After the first day Enoch asked Lara to help them. It was distressing work but it kept her mind occupied. There was no sign of Oscar. No messages, faxes or phone calls.

Chapter Five

Return to the Gold Mine

It was after midnight by the time they had finished clearing out Oscar's office.

Enoch said, "I want to drive to the Tin Heart Mine. We must make sure that everyone is safe and see that they have food and maize meal. We will leave before sunrise as soon as the curfew lifts."

He and Inonge had just finished packing up papers and putting boxes of files into the strongroom. Lara had been delegated to take down all the prints and paintings in the study, wrap them, box them and stack them in the strongroom in their dedicated storage space with all their relevant paper work attached. They had all worked as fast as possible without speaking while the local radio played rumba ceaselessly. It had been rumoured the day before that the radio and TV stations were under attack again from rioting crowds. Though the President had returned to the city his position wasn't at all secure. Announcements of a coup were still expected at any moment. So far however, there had been no new developments overnight.

Lara hoped that she was putting the documents where they would be safe from break-ins and looters. She finished sorting out the paintings and went into the office. There she found Inonge and Enoch frowning over some folders and letters from Oscar's desk.

“Does this mean anything to you?” Inonge asked Lara.

“No, Lara doesn’t know about this!” Enoch said frowning, “I am the one who should have realised this – I should have guessed what was going on. This is huge.”

“What are you talking about?” Lara asked, but she already knew without being told. Inonge and Enoch had uncovered final proof of their long-standing betrayal by Oscar. Now they knew that their beloved project had been exploited as a front to cover Oscar’s dealings. Real dread, hard and fierce, clamped itself around Lara’s middle, squeezing the air from her lungs and making her stomach churn.

“Oh God – what have you found – don’t tell me – is it what I think? What has he done?”

Enoch looked up, his face twisted into a grimace of hate and disgust.

“Oscar!” Enoch was choking as he spoke as if he could neither swallow nor spit out poison. “Oscar – you fool! You bastard piece of shit! What are you doing? – are you mad? – you evil fuck!”

Inonge and Lara recoiled staring at each other wide-eyed. They had never seen Enoch angry or foul-mouthed or – as he was now – afraid and shaking. Enoch folded up in stages. First he sat down at the great wooden desk, then his hands crushed the papers he was clutching, his head went down and then up and he banged it again and again on the leather padding. Then he cried and beat his fists on the desk and then on his head, turn and turn about. Inonge bent over him, holding him, hugging him and trying to soothe him. Lara rushed to the kitchen in a panic and came back with yet another pot of coffee but this time also a bottle of Oscar’s favourite smoky whisky which Enoch first pushed away and then grabbed at. He gulped down a mouthful with another curse at Oscar.

Eventually Enoch explained. He had found export permits for gemstones that purported to come from the Tin Heart Gold Mine and carried official-looking, but faked government stamps. Lara told the Njobvus what Tim had tried to tell her which she had refused at first to believe or accept about Oscar's secret dealings. Enoch's first thought had been that Oscar had taken their money for himself and run. Now he realised that not only had Oscar recently taken the money and given it to General Miyanda to fund his coup, but that for years Oscar had been dealing in illicit gems and building up funds for just such an event. The evidence was incomplete. Bernie had done a good job of covering things up for Oscar. Lara recounted the conversation she had overheard between Natan and Oscar about Njoka's rebel group. Enoch nodded.

"He's trying to pay off both sides so he'll be okay whoever wins, I think." Enoch said as if he wanted to prove to himself that Oscar was motivated by something other than self-interest. Lara found herself wanting the same thing. Again and again she had to force herself to remember finding the gemstones in the frame of her painting. A feeling of coldness overcame her.

"I blame myself." she said "I should have known – I should have guessed." The tears started from her eyes. "I thought he loved me – I thought he loved me."

"He did love you – he does love you!" Inonge said looking directly at her with a surprising calm, "You and Enoch are the only people he ever cared for – apart from his sister, I think – but don't doubt it – it may not be – perhaps it is a bad thing to know – but he does love you – I have seen it. I don't think he knows *how* to love you but he *does* love you."

"What does this mean for us – now – what do we do?" Lara asked, still tearful. "Where is Oscar? Do you know what he is doing know? Can you guess? Enoch – what do you think? What should we do?"

"I'll have to warn Junior immediately – tell him to leave Chambeshi at once – he may be in danger if Oscar gets found out – I think this is what Oscar meant when he rushed away – he wants me to hide all this stuff – or destroy it maybe – I can't believe that he could think I would go along with him -" Enoch picked up the phone and started to dial his son.

"He knew you wouldn't go along with this." Inonge said to Lara, "That's why he didn't tell you about it. He must have decided that because Njoka's rebellion was over, he would have to backtrack in case Colonel Miyanda's coup also failed."

Enoch was speaking on the phone to Junior telling of what he had uncovered and advising Junior to leave the country at once.

"Remember Inonge and I love you." he said as he handed the phone to his wife, "Take care!"

While Inonge and Junior exchanged a few words Enoch began to plan what actions they needed to take.

"Junior says that there may not be a coup. The army have taken charge of the television station and say they support President Chona. They keep saying that the President will make a statement to the nation in the morning. Junior says it isn't clear at this stage if the army will make the President their puppet or reinstate some degree of democracy. Everything is still uncertain."

"And what about us? What do we do?" Lara asked.

"I am setting off at dawn for the Mine. First I must decide what to do with all this incriminating evidence here. I can't tell at the moment if it implicates me or makes it clear that only Oscar is involved." Enoch replied, "As soon as I have got this sorted I will have to go and see what other evidence is still in existence at the Mine because that will probably need to be got rid of too or kept as evidence. If, as seems likely, the remains of the Njoka Gang are in retreat – it should be safe enough to go and I must make sure that all our people there are okay and have some basic supplies."

"I'm coming with you!" Inonge said, "No! Don't argue. I am!"

"I can't stay here alone." Lara, at first hesitant, decided, "I don't ever want to see Oscar again – I would be terrified to see him again. I'll have to come with you – I want to come with you! I have nowhere to go anymore but first I also must remove everything of mine from the camp too otherwise I will also be implicated." For a moment Lara stopped breathing, unable to speak as the terror of her situation became more apparent to her.

It seemed only yesterday that Oscar had been the centre, the axis of her world. Today she was in free fall in empty space with nothing to hold her anywhere.

"Enoch, where do you think Oscar has gone?" she asked, anxiety gripped her. "What about Natan? Do you think they are together?"

"Natan?" Inonge looked up from the papers she was reading through. "Do you know anything about him, Lara?"

"Same as you, I think. Tim said he thought that Natan was once Mossad, an Israeli secret service agent who had become a loose cannon, or turned traitor or was just wandering around Africa wheeling and dealing anyway he can. Oscar didn't talk about him but he did turn up in odd places all the time as if he was checking up on Oscar."

"I haven't seen Natan for a while." Enoch said, "Oscar went off in the Land Cruiser – his plane is still in the hangar. He might have gone to the airport or driven out of the country. Whatever he's done we can't know. We must just do what we think best and I think that is going to tidy up the Tin Heart Mine."

Enoch had burnt some of the letters and put others into a metal document box that he hid in the underfloor safe in the strongroom. They were on their way to get some sleep sometime after midnight when the phone rang. It was Junior telling them to listen again to the radio.

They heard American pop music, inappropriate and cheerful. A few clicks, a silence that lasted seconds and a very young-sounding, rather inarticulate voice, not very proficient in English, was heard. He was a soldier he said, a supporter of General Miyanda who had organised the coup and who was now in charge of the country of Chambeshi. He sounded incompetent and uncertain. Enoch listened.

"We must still go – first thing tomorrow."

Lara tried to phone Tim but his phone was busy. She sent him a brief fax telling him that she was going to the Tin Heart Mine very early the following day, Wednesday, with Enoch and Inonge to sort out 'business' there and take food supplies to the Tin Heart Camp. They would be back in Chambeshi City on Thursday, the second evening. "We'll radio back to the house on Wednesday evening as usual. Take care of yourself," she ended.

By the time they were ready to leave they were still all tired. They had twice been disturbed in the night by brief bursts of gunfire. In spite of it, Enoch had managed to grab some sleep during the night as he intended to drive the first half of the trip. Inonge and Lara had organised food and supplies and packed them into the Land Cruiser. Lara was to drive the second half of the trip if Enoch became too tired so she lay down on the back seat and dozed for the first part of the journey. It was hard to sleep properly. Lara found herself caught in a hallucinatory state between dreaming and waking. She was reliving the four past years of love and sex with Oscar, the hard work with Inonge and Enoch making the camp at the Tin Heart Mine into a paying safari business, the struggle to keep her creative life meaningful and her painting selling. Her body had changed, hardened, toughened, darkened and her hair and skin had lost its glow. Twenty-eight seemed a significant age to have attained but what had she achieved? What did Oscar mean to her now? Was she able to walk away from her relationship with him and what would she take with her from her time at the Tin Heart Mine? What had been the cost? What was lost? Could she start over again and where would she go? She supposed she would never see Tim again once all this was over. He had warned her again and again about Oscar. Now he knew what had happened she would have no worth in his eyes. She would never be able to claim his friendship. Lara's mind kept circling around the idea of Oscar. As soon as she started to think of him she felt herself losing control and panicking.

Would Oscar let me walk away from him when I know so much about him? Do I miss him? Did I ever really love him?

They scrambled out of the Land Cruiser at the Safari Camp soon after midday. They were stiff, tired and uncertain. They had met two road blocks on the way and the police manning them had been jumpy and aggressive and insisted on searching the vehicle thoroughly. Fortunately they had had enough provisions to successfully bribe their way through in each case. They had learnt little at either halt except that no one knew really what was happening in the city but had heard all the rumours and feared the worst. The police had shaken their heads when asked about the remaining soldiers of the Njoka gang but the consensus was that they were in retreat and would cross back over the border to Northern Angola very soon.

The Tin Heart Camp seemed deserted when they first drove in but after Enoch had hooted a couple of times, announced his name and called out the name of his manager, Mainza, and his foreman, Tembo, his staff made an appearance. They were, not surprisingly, keeping a low profile but were delighted to see Enoch and the supplies of food and fuel that he brought. Their safari camp was apparently safe. Another safari camp fifty kilometres north had been burnt down by the retreating rebels but no one had been there at the time and so nobody was hurt. Joseph the cook organised a meal for them of steak, sweet potatoes and rape leaves. Kimu, his 14-year old son, helped him cook and then served the food with a big smile that showed how relieved everyone at the camp felt at their arrival. Enoch explained that they still did not know the outcome of the rioting in the city and suggested that they might return to their villages for a few weeks until it was more certain what was happening. After eating, Enoch and Lara went through the safari camp office but all the paperwork was as they had left it; all above board and in order. Inonge sorted through the distribution of the supplies they had brought and organised the lock-up of vital equipment in the camp store.

"We'll have to go down to the Mine workings and see what is there." Enoch said, "Do you have any idea what is kept down there, Lara?"

"Oscar always insisted that there was nothing there." Lara replied, "There is the store room where he said he kept diesel locked up and the necessary equipment to keep the pump machinery going. That is all that was needed for the mine. I've always hated the place –it's cursed and ugly. The mine manager's cottage was almost empty but both places Oscar kept locked up."

"Well we'll break into the cottage and the storeroom." Enoch said, "I need to be sure that there is nothing incriminating there. It is also time to let the workers leave and go to their villages if they want to – and that means turning off the pump and allowing the mine to finally flood I think. Perhaps we'll come back one day but who knows? We'll sleep tonight at the safari camp and head back to the City in the morning very early – provided it seems safe."

"There are two camp vehicles here in good nick – your small jeep, Lara, and the Land Cruiser used for sight-seeing but I don't plan for us to drive them back to town. If they get stolen there isn't much we can do."

Enoch, Inonge and Lara climbed back into Enoch's Land Cruiser together with Joseph, Mainza and Tembo and bumped down the narrow uneven track to the defunct mine. Its rusting head-gear rose up black against the red scarring of the mine tip, balancing on what was apparently a heap of rock debris. It was an ugly monster of metal that stared out across the river. Hidden in the tree line behind the mine were the cement block shacks that made up the one-time mine manager's cottage and the mine storeroom. Two squat buildings crouching among long grass and the rubbish heaps of abandoned machinery and broken equipment under pale broken-edged asbestos roofs. Enoch ordered Joseph and Tembo to break the chains and padlocks holding the metal doors shut. The heavy shuddering clang of the great mallets as they attacked the locks made the echoes crash around the bare, stripped and damaged space below the mine. Lara cringed at each blow. Someone must hear them. The noise was tremendous, much louder than the mine pump. Would the departing bandits turn around and come back?

At last the doors were open and the three of them went inside, first of all into the old cottage. It was almost empty except for an ancient iron bedstead, a table and a couple of rusty and decrepit garden chairs. In one corner was a metal cupboard of the sort that old files were kept in but the doors were hanging open. There was a room that might once have been a kitchen and off that was a bathroom containing a stained toilet and a ceramic wash basin without plumbing. All the windows were barred with heavy thick gauge iron bars. It would be difficult to get in or out of the building if the heavy metal door was locked. Feeling momentary claustrophobia Lara looked up at the roof to see if that was also impenetrable. She saw to her surprise that the ceiling was made of solid iron sheets embossed with flowers and patterns, obviously recycled from some older and more elegant colonial house and put in here for extra security.

Next they went to the storeroom. It was an almost windowless space and very dark inside so Enoch sent Tembo back to get the torches and spotlights from the Land Cruiser. It took a few minutes to back the vehicle up close enough for the spotlight leads to reach into the hot dim space. Tembo and Mainza stood by the door each holding up a light and Enoch, Inonge and Lara went in. and immediately stood still to stare. Inside the storeroom was a rudimentary but well-organised mini-laboratory with a powerful microscope. Lara did not know what it was for but she had guessed by the time Enoch explained what it was to Inonge.

"It is a laboratory for testing gemstones!" he said, a quiet horror in his voice. "This is where the work was done to smuggle them out."

"Oh my dear Lord and God!" Inonge was not swearing but praying in a loud whisper.

Lara, full of guilt, noticed empty picture frames against the table waiting to be loaded with their illegal cargo of gemstones. Then they all three, at the same moment, saw piled in the corner of the store the smooth gleam of asymmetrical giant ivory tusks. Lara saw Enoch's face, stunned, grieving, his mouth fallen open.

"It's the Old Chief's tusks!" he said hoarsely, "My Old Chief!" and the tears started to pour down his face.

"My poor Enoch, my poor husband." Inonge's hands covered her face.

Tembo and Mainza stood still, open-mouthed in disbelieving shock.

It was then they heard the shouts from outside and turned around bewildered.

"Come out! Come out! Come out with your hands in the air! Come out!"

Lara recognised the deep, thick voice of Natan. Afraid and mesmerised by what they had seen, they all obeyed. In a semi circle around the entrance to the store were six men, two white and four black. Opposite the door and facing them as they re-emerged into the hot bright sunlight stood Oscar and Natan each holding a hand gun. The four Africans armed with Kalashnikov automatic sub-machine guns, knelt or crouched behind protective oil drums, and piles of rubble to the left and right. No one moved or spoke. The mine pump rattled, spun and spewed dirty water into the sludge of the gulley below the pit.

It was an eternity of 30 seconds.

"Lie down, Tembo. Lie down, Mainza," ordered Oscar. Both men dropped instantly to the ground, the spotlights in their hands burning up the beetles and ants in the soft dry earth beneath them.

Enoch stared at his old friend. He took one steady step forward, raised his fists and with a great shout of rage leapt towards Oscar. There was a bang and Enoch jerked backwards and sideways to fall in front of Inonge. Natan had killed Enoch.

Part Twelve

Escape 1989

Chapter One

Telling Brendan

"I don't know why I am telling you about Liseli at this particular moment."

Lara frowns at Brendan. Brendan looks back – silent, reassuringly serious.

In a rush Lara explains herself.

"I didn't understand what she was going through – I didn't help her – and now I don't understand myself. Why – why now – am I as mad as Liseli – as sad as Liseli – why am I so desperate now?"

A bitter thought comes to Lara but she laughs.

"I don't really think that fate is paying me back for being a naïve schoolgirl -but why can't we escape the past – why does the past lie in wait for us in the future – why are we its prisoners? "Why can't I forget everything and just move on? All my friends think I should stop being – so self-indulgent."

Brendan is firm. Usually he doesn't make statements.

"Lara – you know now that Liseli's depression was an on-going psychiatric illness for which she was sectioned. Your depression is a natural reaction to the events of your life. It is quite different. You will recover."

Lara sips her glass of water and sniffs into her tissues. She is relieved by Brendan's reassurance but if her feelings are natural or even normal, then she must find other answers or ask different questions.

"I don't want to recover!" She is being obstinate. "I deserve to feel like this."

Brendan raises his eyebrows in mild irony.

"You find it easier to live with your feelings of guilt and shame?"

Before Brendan reverts to his usual silence, he puts a quiet question to Lara.

"Is it only the bad in the past that comes back to hurt us? Can the good in our past also make traps for us?"

Lara is surprised. She remembered Liseli as she was for most of her school days – happy and laughing.

"Do you think Liseli will survive, Brendan? Do you think she can be happy some of the time? I so want her to be okay."

"Liseli is intelligent and motivated. We all make adjustments in our own way. It's good that you care about her, Lara," Brendan approves.

"I suppose that Liseli made me see things differently – she opened my eyes."

Then, without thinking, Lara looks at her hands and starts inconsequentially, to talk about sex.

"It's such a simple act really – sex that is – you bring nothing to it but your naked body. Nothing so natural and so basic and human gives so much pleasure – why doesn't it work out better and more happily?"

Brendan is silent. Lara glances up and catches Brendan's eyes focussed on her.

Oh God! He's imagining me naked and I am doing the same about him!

She stares down again trying not to grin with embarrassment.

I hope I'm not right.

Brendan saves her. "Do you want to talk about how you and Tim got together after the riots and the attempted coup?" he asks.

Lara breathes in. She starts at the end of the story because it's easier than the beginning.

"It was chance, I think – just lucky for me. Tim had been

trying to find out where I was and what had happened to me but all he knew was that I had gone with Enoch and Inonge to the Tin Heart Mine. Tim had arranged to leave Chambeshi on the same flight I was booked on. It wasn't safe to stay and his editor insisted – I arrived at the flat as he was packing to go. It was a lucky chance for me – a miracle."

The story is long and Lara has only begun to tell it. She hesitates and stops.

After a while Brendan makes a suggestion.

"Tell me what you feel you can – and only if you want to."

Lara breathes out. This is the moment. No more delays. It's time to tell the story of her escape from the prison at the Tin Heart Mine.

"It was after – afterwards – well anyway – I was lying there on the bed when I heard Oscar's plane fly overhead."

"I thought it must be his plane, but even that I couldn't be certain of – from the mine house you can't hear planes take off from the airstrip unless the wind is in the right direction. That must have been at least two hours after Oscar had left me."

Lara stops and turns her head away from Brendan. She thinks that she can't and won't talk about what happened before Oscar left but after a few moments she continues.

"I think the plane flew off northwards towards the Congo – that frightened me."

"It was late afternoon – where could Oscar have flown to in the dark? It was the wrong way. It seemed very quiet outside – too quiet – not right. I thought that Oscar had left us locked up and would come back when we had starved to death." Lara falters and swallows hard.

"I had no idea what had been happening in Chambeshi while we were prisoners – while we were locked in the mine house. We had been there less than a week – I did keep a record of the time then but now I can't remember it as a specific number of days. It was about 4 days I think. I didn't know if the coup had been successful – didn't know anything – so I got up and went to the door and banged on it in desperation. That's when I realised we weren't locked in any more." Lara shakes her head in disbelief at the memory.

"I couldn't understand why Oscar hadn't killed me before he left." Again she shakes her head. "I couldn't understand why the door was not locked. I had heard the padlock click but that must have been when it was clicked in place to stop the bolt closing us in permanently."

"The boy was there outside – Kimu they called him. He was crouching just outside the door and looked so terrified." Lara had felt so sorry for him that it had stilled her own fear for the moment.

"He kept saying Madam, Madam – you must go quickly – you must not stay – it is very dangerous."

"I went to rouse Inonge. She no longer moved from her bed or spoke and she had refused to eat for days. After the last – after Oscar had left me – I also felt unable to move – I felt I should give up like Inonge. When I opened the door Inonge was asleep – so deeply asleep I thought I might have to carry her to the car. I threw water at her and made her sit up. When she saw the door was open she got up and staggered outside and knelt on the ground outside the storeroom at the place where Enoch had died."

"Kimu was holding the keys to my old silver jeep and trying to push them into my hand. I didn't understand that we were free to go – I thought it was a trap and that we would be shot as soon as I started the engine and that they would pretend we had been killed in a robbery – though why bother out there with all the trouble and fighting that was going on – anyway I didn't understand what was supposed to happen to us and I didn't know if I could trust Kimu. He kind of tugged me and pulled me to the jeep. Then he went back and started to drag Inonge to it too. He kept saying we must go and I could see that he was desperate to leave us and run away somewhere."

"I asked him 'Where is everyone?' 'All gone!' he said 'Everyone is gone to hide. The rebels are coming tomorrow to kill us all. You must go now – back to Chambeshi city. The boss says so." That made me frown – it was so strange. Felt so unlikely and so untrustworthy coming from Oscar."

"I could see that the jeep had some stuff in it – a jerry can and a cloth bag and strangest of all – the portfolio of my drawings stuffed behind the seat."

Chapter Two

Escaping

At this point Lara's mind began to work again very fast. It appeared that she and Inonge were meant to escape. If so, she must make sure they could get all the way to safety. She tried to lift the jerry can – it was full. She tested the cap to see if she could open it herself. She could, after a struggle. "Where is the water?" she demanded of Kimu. He pointed to two 5-litre plastic bottles in front of the passenger seat with a blue plastic mug tied to the handle of one of them. The jeep had been packed with Oscar's thorough efficiency. Lara tore at the soft bag's opening. Inside was some bread, boiled sweets and a large stick of dried salted antelope biltong. Under the food was a full magazine of bullets. There must be a gun hidden in the car. Lara glanced swiftly at Kimu. She didn't think it would be wise to let him see that she had a gun. He might think he needed it more than she did. For a moment she was ashamed. Perhaps he deserved it more than she did. Briefly she wondered if it would be a protection for her if she persuaded him to accompany her. Lara had to get Inonge into the passenger seat. She gripped Inonge's hands and put her face close to Inonge's.

"We have to get back to see if Junior's okay – we have to tell Junior about Enoch. You have to help me – you have to wake up!"

Inonge raised her head slightly, her eyes blinked in a brief recognition.

"We must get back to Enoch Junior! Enoch Junior, Inonge – he needs you! You must move – Enoch wants you to be with your son! You must get in the jeep. Now! Come!"

Inonge moved stiffly at last, and awkwardly clambered into the car.

"Are you coming with us?" Lara asked Kimu but he backed away nodding his head and waving his hands wildly. 'No!' he said, 'No! Too dangerous! Go! You must go!"

Lara looked at the sky. The sun was almost setting. It was not normally advisable to drive in the park at night-time. It had been forbidden in the days when there was a government in Chambeshi except for registered night safaris with armed game guards. She had, of course, on several occasions had to drive in the dark but she had never been without company and she was not sure if Inonge would be of much help. It was a very long drive back to Chambeshi City – at least 4 and maybe 5 hours mostly over very rough dirt roads through places where buffalo and elephant abounded. There was a small town to go through, a couple of road blocks and the gates at the entrances to the park. Who would be in control of any of these places? Njoka's rebels? The city rioters? The army? A maverick bunch of villagers looking for revenge? They were all to be equally feared especially by two women on their own at night in a small open jeep.

"You go!" she said to Kimu and then called after him as he ran towards the bush. "Thank you, Kimu!" but he was already out of earshot.

Swiftly Lara twisted her hair up and hid it under the baseball cap she found pushed under the dashboard. She must try and look like a man or at least a boy. Inonge would be okay. She was slim, her hair was short and she was wearing bush trousers and a bush shirt. Too bad Lara was white. She scuffed up some soft dirt from under the car but it was hardly going to make her skin dark enough so she dropped it again. A quick look around to make sure no one was watching and she poked about, under, and into the driver's seat. The gun was tucked up exactly where she expected, wrapped up in a worn out bush jacket and a length of oily fabric under the passenger seat. The bush jacket would be a disguise of sorts and it would hide her breasts. She tied the oily fabric across her body in a sling to hold the gun out of sight under the bush shirt, but at an angle where she could grab it if she needed. Next she had a long drink of water and then crouched down in the lee of the jeep door for a pee without letting go of the safety of the car door handle. At least there had been no recurrence of her diarrhoea since midday. She asked Inonge to keep her provided with sweets and biltong while she was driving and to see that they both had water and did not need to stop the jeep in order to drink.

The jeep started perfectly. Lara checked the fuel gauge. It registered full. She had plenty of time to work out when the car would need more diesel. She would need to pick a sensible place to stop and refuel it. When the vehicle jerked forward Lara thought she was going to vomit. She was sick with fear and very tired. She would never make it to Chambeshi. She would fall asleep with exhaustion and crash the car. The long drive ahead with all its dangers and the nightmare company of her recent experiences was an ordeal which she could not hope or expect to end well. She would have to drive with her mind focussed on the journey and not on the end. If there were people anywhere near the road they could not fail to hear the jeep approaching from a distance away. Was it good that it was small with a light engine? Would that embolden any attackers or, with luck, might it make it possible that she would not be noticed soon enough for any enemy to make decisions? Unarmed and frightened villagers might run and hide. Armed gangs might just shoot blindly. If there were road blocks she was as good as dead and maybe she was better dead than being taken prisoner again. She would make the journey stage by stage and not think beyond the first stage until she had accomplished it. The first stage through the wildlife park needed her to concentrate only on the road and the animals. Herds of *puku,* impala or buffalo would hold her up and she would have to negotiate the jeep past them slowly. Elephant might be the biggest danger but they would probably move away from the sound of the car. The road itself was rutted and in places rocky. She must not risk damage to the car or to the tyres. She must set off slowly as if she were on a night time safari drive. She must only think of the wild creatures and the road; even a creature as small as a porcupine might damage her small jeep.

The first quarter of Lara's journey was the road out of the park. It seemed to go on and on forever. She had to manoeuvre the jeep slowly over its ruts and tree roots. Enoch's men did the work of repairing and maintaining the road and even of deciding where it would go. It curved up hills by the easiest slopes where there were small sharp fist-sized rocks ready to punch holes in her tyres. It crossed valleys and streams at the flattest and the shallowest fords where the road surface consisted of hard-baked ridges of black clay. The park entrance was manned by guards with old-fashioned rifles in the day and closed by a light wooden barrier at night. Lara intended to drive the jeep as fast as possible through or around the barrier but when they arrived it was pushed aside and the post deserted. The next section was a fairly straight dirt road through forest and sparsely populated subsistence farms. Occasional huts and small cement block houses stood by the road but the villages were away from the road among trees. Lara could drive much faster here as the few farmers and their free-ranging goats and cattle would not be around in the dark. The river crossings were the main problem. Heavy rain meant the rivers had flooded hungrily across the road and eaten rough gullies around the bridges. Though the gullies were filled in with earth and rocks; an awkward ramp and shelf had to be negotiated to gain the crest of each bridge and to climb down on the other side. When Lara was driving fast she had to concentrate on controlling her vehicle over the bad surfaces. Whenever she was forced to slow down her heart began to pound and her stomach went into cramps. That was when armed men might step into the road and order her to stop.

The place Lara worried about most was a small scruffy town with a pot-holed road and a garage that occasionally had fuel. If there was a road block, the police or soldiers would probably be drunk. Road blocks consisted of oil drums and branches. The bull-bar on the jeep should batter through those if she aimed the vehicle at the weakest spot but again there would be guns – could she – should she talk her way through? There was no way Lara could trust any man while she and Inonge were alone at night. Lara had never felt so vulnerable before and her relief when she found the town silent and empty was so tremendous that she almost cried.

Ahead was a long straight tarred road so Lara drove flat out down it. If there were troops or armed bandits that was where they might encounter them. The road went through mupane forests and its surface was broken by wide and deep potholes. Lara hoped she would remember where they were from her last daytime trip. It was almost impossible to see them at night. Hitting a pothole could roll the jeep or damage its axle. As long as there were no abandoned and unlit trucks on the roadside. Crashing into one at speed would kill both her and Inonge.

Chambeshi City was likely to be the most dangerous part of the whole drive so Lara didn't let herself think about its problems until she reached the outskirts. Would rioters or the army be in control? Maybe both would control different parts of the city. There might be road blocks set up by opportunistic robbers and thugs. What safe place or reliable person did she know who lived on this side of the city? It would be mad to pull off the road and try to sleep. A parked vehicle would probably attract attention from every passerby. In any case the jeep was open sided and canvas topped. She couldn't even lock herself and Inonge safely inside it. Lara told herself that exhausted as she was, she must keep on driving in spite of the curfew in the city.

The moment I begin to relax my guard and imagine I'm safe will be the moment of greatest danger – that's when the unexpected happens and when things go wrong.

Chapter Three

Tim's Flat

"We survived." Lara tells Brendan. "We saw no one. No one tried to stop us. There was nobody at any of the road blocks or even at the game park entrance. There were even times when my accelerator foot ached from being held steady at such a constant speed for so long. Inonge helped me – she kept offering me something to eat or drink. She rubbed my neck and shoulders as I drove. She reminded me about places where there were bad potholes and she watched out for animals on the road. It was a long five hour drive. Inonge's wristwatch said it was after midnight when we reached Chambeshi City.

When we reached the city outskirts I slowed right down and went as carefully and quietly as possible ready at any moment to accelerate away or turn around if necessary. I was aiming for Tim's flat and my studio. That was the first, the closest and the safest place we could reach and it had a phone. We, of course, had no idea what had happened in Chambeshi while we had been locked up. Tim might have already left – I didn't know if he would still be around but I knew I had spare keys to the flat attached to the jeep ignition key. I would be okay if the security guard on the building recognised me and opened the gate. It would be pitch dark of course if the curfew was still in place. There was no one on the streets, however, and we reached the yard around the apartment without incident.

Getting out of the jeep was difficult – I was stiff and clumsy from the drive – I took the pistol from inside my shirt and looked around for anything odd. There was no guard I could see. I started to try and unlock the heavy padlock and slide the bolt open – of course it scraped noisily. The next minute there were shouts – I had woken the guard up and he leapt out at me with home-made club in his hand. I screamed back at him and fired the pistol towards the gate. It made a helluva bang and the guard ducked down then ran off somewhere. Next the flat window opened. It was Tim! He said later he recognised my scream though I don't think he had heard me scream before."

Lara shook her head in wonderment.

"God! It was good to be inside the apartment. Inonge collapsed immediately and started crying in this terrible way. I had to explain some of what happened and my voice wouldn't work properly. Tim phoned Junior. Then Tim told us that the coup had failed – the President was back in power but promising elections soon and that things looked as if they were going to work out okay, for the moment at least. Junior organised some policemen and a truck to accompany him and he came to fetch Inonge. Perhaps that was the worst bit of all – telling Junior what had happened to Enoch while Inonge wailed and wailed – she was beside herself – in such an agony of grief. Junior looked at me at first as if I was dirt but Inonge kept holding onto me and saying I had saved her life and brought her back to Chambeshi. Then I think I fell over. Junior took Inonge away. Tim gave me some whisky which made me thirsty – then sugary tea which was disgusting after the whisky – I just asked him to hold me and never let me go and he did."

Chapter Four

The Legacy

"There are still things that you are avoiding aren't there, Lara?" Brendan says after the long silence that began Lara's next session with him. "It's clear from what you have told me that you are a survivor and a competent person. You can be very proud of yourself and what you have done. What is it that troubles you so much?"

"It's so complicated." Lara says. "I have trouble working out what action caused what reaction and where my responsibility lies. Tim and I had a terrible row before he left for Uganda, over the Otto Dix paintings. They arrived in London at Oscar's bank. A gift to me apparently, with all the correct papers proving their provenance and my ownership. Just the paintings – not even anything illegal hidden in their frames." Lara's face wears an ugly bitter expression.

"I wanted to sell them and save the money for Adam's university education but Tim said that nothing of Oscar's must ever be used for Adam's benefit. He alone would provide for his son. I felt so helpless and compromised. At first I left the paintings in the bank vault where the lawyers had put them for safekeeping."

Brendan tilts his head sideways.

"Reasonable for Tim to feel that way, don't you think?"

Lara nods hard.

"There was also some money from the sale of Oscar's ranch house but that was in Chambeshi and devaluing very fast along with all of Chambeshi's currency. That was easy to get rid of – I signed it over to the educational trust school that Inonge started in Enoch's name."

"You're still in touch with Inonge and Junior and still close friends with them, aren't you?"

Lara nods again.

"Inonge is a very dear friend to me. She has visited me in London twice and so has Junior, though now we just call him Enoch. Inonge and Junior went back to the Tin Heart Mine and recovered Enoch's body from where it had been thrown down the mine shaft. Enoch is buried next to his father, Samuel, near the family village. Inonge runs the safari camp as a training centre and school for the local community. It is called the Enoch Njobvu School. Junior visits regularly to give maternal and paediatric clinics. Someday I would like to go back to visit with Adam but again I don't know how Tim would feel about it.

"I don't know if Tim is ever coming back to me and Adam again. That's the trouble. I'm so afraid of losing him!"

"I could have given the paintings to an art museum on loan anonymously but that felt as if I was just putting off the problem. I didn't want to see them anyway. I decided to start the process of putting them up for auction. I could give the proceeds to the Enoch Njobvu Trust along with the money from the ranch but would I be able to stick to my plan? If I ended up with a lot of money would I be able to let it go? If Tim was going to leave me anyway why shouldn't I be rich? The thing is I want Tim back with me and Adam. I don't want the money but if Adam finds out in years to come that he is Oscar's child – won't he feel that the money was his anyway? Or – do I never tell him and do the lies just grow and grow?"

Chapter Five

Hostages 1997

Lara's mobile phone has been switched off throughout her session with Brendan. Outside Brendan's consulting room she switches it on. It flashes red at her. A voice message from Tim's editor asks Lara to call back at once. Lara has the sensation of falling fast into the cold wind of a dark mineshaft. Fear clutches at her throat. She can't stand in the street for this phone call. She might fall over, or cry or scream. She waves at a taxi. She must get home fast. Adam is with Hilda and Lester. For once Lara doesn't stop to collect him first. Fumbling with keys and locks and phones, she flings herself into the chair at her worktable and calls Tim's head office.

All the voices who answer her are calm and reasonable and reassuring. They all know who she is and they all expected her to phone. The telephonist puts her straight through to the editor's office and the editor's secretary puts her straight through to the editor.

"Is that Lara Weston? May I call you Lara? Are you at home now? Can you come and see us? I am afraid we have bad news but almost no information as yet."

"Two journalists have been taken hostage – one of them is your husband, Tim Weston – we have witness accounts of the kidnapping so there is no doubt about it. The other hostage is an Australian cameraman, Rod Gardner. We don't know where they have been taken and we have not heard from the hostage-takers yet. Apparently Tim and Rod were away on an unexpected assignment on the Kenyan/Somali border investigating a piracy story. The Foreign Office is informed and so are all the relevant embassies and High Commissions. We suggest you get directly in touch with them yourself as well. We have already done so. We are here to help with any contacts you need and will do anything that we can to help. Call us any time. We can arrange a meeting tonight if you want."

The phone call leaves Lara as empty as a squeezed tube of paint. She is in an airless void. Nothing around her has any meaning or significance except that she thinks she can hear the sound of Adam's voice and laughter, as if there are no rooms or walls between where she sits and the flat down the corridor where he plays with his friend Lester. She doesn't want to bring him into her world of fear and shock, as she must soon. It can't be kept from him for long. It will be on the TV and radio news this evening if it isn't already. She sits very still hardly breathing. There is little to be done but wait and wait. She knows how these things go on and on. She knows how they are most likely to end. There is time ahead of her that will need to be filled somehow. There's Adam to protect.

What of Tim? Where is he? Is he even alive? Please God let Tim have hope and time and life. Tim doesn't believe in God and she doesn't think that she does either but she will still pray. Let Tim endure. Let Tim come home.

Lara phones Hilda rather than walk the few metres to her flat. She knows her appearance at Hilda's door in a state of shock will upset Adam. She needs to be calm or at least a little calmer before she tells Adam about Tim.

"Can you keep Adam from hearing the news till I can speak to him myself please? I'll be so grateful, Hilda! I am going to meet the editor and someone from the Foreign Office now. Then I'll probably go and see Tim's parents. I need a bit of time to get myself sorted out and calm again, then I'll be around to collect Adam and tell him what's happened. I'll try and come tonight but it may be first thing tomorrow. At any rate it'll be before he gets to school and hears about it from someone else."

"You know me." Hilda answers. "I don't watch the news on telly. I've got a video for the kids and I'll feed Adam and put him to bed. Come when you're good and ready Lara. It's all the same to me – you poor dear!"

"These black bastards!" she adds.

Lara blinks. What has she just heard? She hopes Lester is not within earshot of his Nan.

Chapter Six

Adam and Lara

Lara receives a message from Brendan a day later offering to arrange another appointment or cancel her next one as she wishes.

"Your circumstances are exceptional." Brendan says. "I can be available whenever you need or not at all as you wish."

Lara thanks him but she wants to keep her regular appointment. She collects Adam from Hilda's early the day after the phone call from Tim's editor and tells him as simply as possible what has happened to Tim. Few facts are known anyway. Adam pretends at first to be grown up about it. He puts his arms around Lara and says he'll look after her until Tim is freed. Then he bursts into tears and the two of them sit on the studio settee and cry and talk their way through a whole box of tissues together.

"We'll have to make plans." Lara says to Adam a little later. "We'll have to keep writing to Tim and also keep a diary for him and -"

She can't think of anything sensible to do. She knows that Adam won't be fobbed off indefinitely with vague hopes and promises that might never be met. They might both need professional help from Brendan. Their daily life will have to continue in as normal and ordinary a way as possible for as long as needed. That might be years and years but that is not today. School is out of the question that day and for several more days. Lara takes Adam off to meet Tim's editor. They are both photographed for the paper and filmed for television while making pleas to the kidnappers or hostage-takers even though no one had yet admitted to the act. It would have been a greater mystery if there had not been witnesses who had seen Tim and Rod stopped at gunpoint by tall thin men in head-scarves who bundled them into a four-wheel drive vehicle and drove off firing automatic weapons. The day is exhausting but necessary. Tim's parents also appear for the press conference. Afterwards they offer to help by seeing more of Adam at weekends.

"Only if you promise never to be negative or downhearted about Tim in Adam's company," Lara says, feeling brutal and ashamed of it.

"What about you then?" Tim's mother, Gwen, asks defensively. "How will you avoid that?"

"I probably won't always but I will try." Lara answers. "That's why you mustn't be. Adam has to have all the breaks he can get. Forgive me – I know it's terrible for you both – the only useful thing we can do for Tim is not to let our worries weigh too much on Adam. I don't want the school to single him out for special treatment, either – there have to be places where he can just be a small boy and lead as normal a life as possible."

"Fair enough." Tim's father agrees. "We'll do our best around Adam."

"Thanks." says Lara. "Sorry. We can be miserable together when Adam is not around. We will be, I am sure."

"There doesn't seem to be anything to do but wait." Tim's mother says tearfully. "Can we trust the newspaper and the Foreign Office to do everything they should do?"

Lara shakes her head. "I don't know."

"I expect we will have to keep at them all the time, don't you?" Tim's dad suggests.

"I don't know." repeats Lara. "I am sure we will drive them mad and go mad ourselves but we will have to just keep on reminding everybody that we want to be kept informed and to have results."

Lara's parents offer to fly to London. They offer to pay for Lara and Adam to fly to Cyprus. Lara agrees to every suggestion but asked them to wait for news before buying any tickets

"We have to carry on as if nothing has happened. There is nothing to do yet." She says.

"We will pray for Tim." says her father. Lara had never considered that her father might believe in God. She doesn't think it will help much but has a few seconds comfort from the idea.

Chapter Seven

The Empty Room

Lara recalls the drive that she and Inonge had made from the Tin Heart Mine to Chambeshi City ten years before. She had had to keep her mind focussed on the journey and not the wished-for end. In fact she had had to give up any hope that the journey would end. She acknowledges with a minimal mental shrug and smile that it was perhaps a little like being in labour. When she was giving birth to Adam every contraction had demanded her total concentration. Only in the last stages had she begun to believe that she was actually producing a child. Well, there was no predictable end to the wait that lay ahead for Adam and herself. Tim might already be dead. He might be killed at any moment. He could be held a prisoner for months or years. It might be so long that if he ever did come back all three of them would have changed beyond recognition. They would be different people. Adam certainly would have changed physically. Without Tim's presence, how would they remember him? Perhaps it would be better to let Adam gradually forget Tim. To let the pain of Tim's loss slowly dissipate and disappear. Was that likely or possible? Or best? It was possible to consider all these awful possibilities without getting too upset if she did not think of Tim's face, his smile, or the way he liked his coffee in the mug Adam had given him.

Lara thinks how lovely it would be to give up remembering

Tim, just to shrug and turn away and get on with a new life and maybe even a new partner. All those women – it was most often women – who kept alive the vigils for the disappeared, for the prisoners, for the missing lovers, husbands, fathers and sons – how did they do it? How it must distort them and embitter them. Did they ever smile again or have pleasure in life? How long could their hopes survive – a whole incredible lifetime.

I'm not capable of this! Lara tells herself. She feels iron bands of sorrow tighten around her chest and her temple. She wants to scream out.

Let me go! Let me be free! I don't want this!

She doesn't want to care about the fear Tim must be enduring, or his suffering or any horrible death that waits for him. She wants to take Adam away to a new place and feed him a narcotic that would make him forget Tim.

Couldn't she just find a replacement for Tim who would make Adam happy? Someone so like Tim that he wouldn't notice that Tim had vanished. Like a kick in her belly, the memory of Oscar thuds into her flesh. He has no part in her life any more or in Adam's life either. She wrenches the image of him out of her thoughts in order to discard it but then she remembers her own imprisonment. What had helped her to survive? Somewhere inside herself had been the knowledge that Tim cared about her. The certainty – or had it been the desire – that her trust in Tim was justified. Her knowledge – or was it just a hope – that Tim would look for her – was looking out for her.

Lara stands up and walks across her dark sitting room to the window above the bright shiny street with all its rushing traffic and scurrying people. She knows in her heart that she had to be the candle that does not burn out. She has to keep trust and hope alive in her heart for Tim. She must conserve all her energy and direct it towards him always so that he knows he is loved. The phone won't ring any time soon with good news, but she must not give up. She must keep going and she must do the same for Adam. He is sleeping now in the bed that was hers and Tim's. It gives him some comfort to be there. It gives Lara comfort too. She will snuggle up to him soon and listen to his breathing even if she can't sleep herself.

Strange, she thinks. *I'm not in the grip of the same black depression that I was in last week. Is it because life is so much worse that I can't afford to be indulgent and preoccupied with myself? Thank God for Brendan. Someone to talk to and confess my faithlessness and doubt. This journey is not going to have an end that I can see – but I must keep going on and on.*

Chapter Eight

Gillian

Once again Lara takes Adam with her to see her new studio in the old warehouses near Victoria Park now renamed "The Art Factory". Adam has already met Gillian and is fascinated by her nose and eyebrow studs.

"Why do you have them? Don't they hurt? Don't they hurt you when you're kissing?" Adam asks.

Gillian laughs. She likes Adam and very little embarrasses her.

"I am weird aren't I? I like the feeling they give me when I do kiss – and they are like a decoration don't you think? Your Mum has pierced ears – it feels about the same to have these put in. Are you going to come and share Lara's studio? Perhaps you would also like to make art?"

Adam shakes his head in doubt but Gillian takes him on a tour of the other artists' studios and he meets two sculptors and three printmakers and Elaine, a woman who makes art from fabric scraps that she collects from fashion and clothing factories.

"I get them from the *schmutter* trade," she says to Adam.

"That is a *mysterious* word," Adam says, pleased by the sound of it.

The strange chaotic nature of the studios and the weird names for objects fascinate Adam and make him curious. He says that maybe he will come back one day and try out some of the techniques for himself.

"You can try them all out during our Open Studios week." Gillian tells him.

Lara already has been invited to take part in the Open week and exhibition for all the Art Factory inhabitants that is to take place at the month's end.

"It's good timing. We are building quite a good reputation here." Gillian tells Lara. "We have started to attract some of the talent spotters from the new East End Galleries – some have moved here from Cork Street and Mayfair because the rents here are lower. It could be your big opportunity. What new work are you planning to do, Lara?"

Lara has plenty of paintings – quite a number unfinished. In the larger space of the new studio she is able to reconsider what she is doing. She finds that she has new ideas and for the first time the space to experiment more playfully. It's easier to pull out her planchest drawers and spread her work around to study it all. Old drawings from the Safari Camp appear; notes and plans and ideas fill her sketchbooks. She feels re-motivated. She will be able to pull a reasonable exhibition together in the month before the Open Studios dates.

Back at the flat the front room is even more dreary and empty. Lara gets Adam to help her make decisions about how the room should be redecorated and reclaimed as a sitting room. She plans to do it very slowly but she doesn't explain her reasons to Adam.

"We will have to get this room in shape for Tim's return." she says without adding that there is no need to hurry. "First we'll clean up again – then patch the walls and then paint – what colours do you think we should choose? We'll have to put down a carpet too to hide the paint stains."

In spite of the cheap protective plastic sheeting Lara had put down on the floor, paint had seeped and leaked and splashed onto the floor and the walls.

"It will be a Penelope room," she explains later to Brendan. "You know how Penelope waited for the return of Ulysses from the Trojan War and each night unpicked her tapestry so that it would never be finished and she would never have to succumb to a new suitor. I won't undo the work I do but I will really do it little by little. When I do finish it – and Tim still isn't home – we will be quite used to his absence."

It hurts Lara to be so negative but she has a new reality to get accustomed to and saying negative things out loud where Adam can't hear them seems best.

Brendan smiles, raises an eyebrow and asks Lara how her life is to be financed from now on.

"That'll be the other reason why the living room will take so long to redecorate and furnish." Lara says and her lips twist downwards.

"Tim's newspaper will pay his salary for the time being. Some of that comes automatically into my account for household bills. The paper will also help me with discretionary payments if I ask, but I hope not to have to ask for that. What I earn from my part-time teaching certainly won't cover Adam's and my other expenses, but I will, with luck, get something from selling my own art though, of course, I have got to pay the rent of the studio."

"Oh – this is important – I had already decided to sell Oscar's paintings – the Otto Dix and the Käthe Kollwitz. It's a slow process and there's auction fees and tax to pay as well. I don't know what the outcome of that will be at all."

Brendan's eyebrows shoot up and this time he doesn't hide his surprise.

"Gosh, Lara!" he says. "How do you feel about that?"

Lara isn't sure how she feels about anything at the moment. Her strongest emotion at getting rid of Oscar's gift is relief but she does have reservations.

"I hate the idea of them being bought as an investment and put into a vault – they might as well have been taken by the Nazis.

The auction house thinks that perhaps they might go to a German art museum because they have provenance and weren't stolen. I do want them to be seen. I could give them away but then – I didn't think Tim had the right to stop me capitalizing on them. I felt that was – well – unfair."

Lara sometimes feels curiously light as if she is suspended in space and has to make very delicate movements to stay afloat. It is all right as long as she doesn't get tired, which of course she does. Of course she crashes into depression. She has to 'pick herself up and start all over again' just like in some song or other. It's odd, but her thoughts at the moment all seem to end in snatches of songs like 'I Will Survive'. Perhaps if she was religious it would be prayers that she would recall but all that does come are fragments and refrains of songs about grief and woe like 'Nobody Knows the Trouble I've Seen.'

"There's Tim and there's Adam and there's my art and there's today. That's all. No future. Just now. Just one day at a time."

Brendan considers her quietly for a while.

"Good," he says. "I'm always here."

The first object that Adam and Lara buy for the empty sitting room is a lava lamp. It's Adam's choice and Lara's suggestion. She first thought of leaving a symbolic candle alight in the window for Tim but then she decides it isn't safe or sensible. Together they visit the lighting department of a big store and choose the lava lamp. Lara had to draw the line at the red lava lamp. A woman further down the block of flats keeps a *red* light in her bedroom window and Lara doesn't want that lady's clients to confuse their establishments. Blue or green, she suggests to Adam, are the colours that Tim prefers. In the end Adam settles on the orange light.

"I think it will be seen from further away. Don't you, Mum?" he says and Lara's heart cracks again.

Tim's parents, Sidney and Gwen, come around once again to discuss the latest news, of which there is very little. The group who held Tim and Rod have been identified as Somalis, most probably Muslim, but without very strong political or religious affiliations.

"Brigands or pirates of some sort, they think." Tim's father says. "A random chance that they encountered Tim and Rod – just very bad luck."

"There's no question of the Foreign Office paying a ransom and the newspaper won't either. They say it increases the risks both for Tim and Rod and for future hostage cases. They are searching at the moment for people who have contact with the group or for someone who can negotiate with them," adds Gwen.

"I think Rod's family feel that not enough is being done but for the moment we don't have much choice – that's what I told them," again it was Sidney.

Tim's mother looks very pale and worn. Tim's father is a quiet, grey man so indeterminate in appearance and age that it isn't likely that any change of fortune will have much impact on his person. They had always seemed so neutral and indistinct to Lara that she finds it hard not to think of them as shadows rather than three-dimensional humans. She feels for their pain and anxiety but also wants to guard her own reserves and she really doesn't know how to help them. They aren't very huggable. Even Adam is inclined to be more formal with them, shaking Sidney's hand and kissing Gwen's cheek without putting his arms around her. Gwen and Sidney offer Lara money in case she is finding life financially difficult. They suggest that she move into their house if it would help. She replies that she is grateful but she doesn't need money and she is determined that Adam's life should continue as before if possible. They nod and agree and then surprise her.

"We thought it might be nice for Adam to have a pet, Lara." Gwen says. "We know it is difficult to keep an animal in a flat and we felt that hamsters and gerbils aren't necessarily what a boy would like so we wondered about sharing a dog. We could look after it during the school week and if Adam likes the idea he could have it at weekends."

Chapter Nine

The Sex Shop

Lara and Gillian stand in the middle of the sex shop basement holding mugs of tea.

"I don't believe this place!" Lara says with a huge grin. "It's run by women. They offer you tea and in the basement downstairs there's a forest of black dildos and pink rubber penises. It's totally surreal."

"There are educational booklets and gay woman's magazines." Gillian points some out.

"So you're not shocked are you, Lara? I didn't think you would be but you can never tell how someone will react." She is smiling too. "It's actually all awful kitsch isn't it? Everything's plastic and the colours are hideous. If you want quality sex toys in leather and steel you have to go to the very expensive places nearer Covent Garden."

"What is it about sex that links it to masks and whips and bondage, domination and sadism, Gillian?" Lara asks in wonder. "I can't pretend it isn't a turn-on in some way but I also can't imagine using many of these instruments successfully."

"It does take practice – and a sense of humour." Gillian looks wicked. "It's fun trying but in the end – well, it's easier to give up and use what God gave us – fingers and tongues.

"Some sex toys are good when you're alone you know – be free – have a look round."

So Lara does.

"Thanks, Gillian – it's cheered me up. I don't know why exactly. Maybe I feel less crazy and less of a pervert."

"Because you're not gay?" Gillian sounds surprised.

"No! Definitely not that – it's because this place – in its own bizarre way – helps me to recognise both my need of sex and the necessity of sex.

"You should read Angela Carter – my favourite novelist – she says that '*there is a striking resemblance between the act of love and the ministrations of a torturer*'."

"Does she indeed? My God!" Lara stares around her.

Chapter Ten

The New Studio

Lara stands in the middle of her new studio and spreads her arms wide. She tilts her head back. The grey concrete ceiling is high above her. She spins around in a stamping circling dance. The space is freezing cold even though it's already the end of April. The studio Health and Safety team had decided long ago that paraffin heaters and gas bottles were too dangerous in a space where there were so many flammable materials but the artists largely ignored rules that involved them in unnecessary expenses. Gillian had lent Lara a bottle gas heater and she also had a small two-bar electric heater to huddle over when she stopped work to have coffee. One of the artists has erected a plastic sheet tent in his space as a refuge from the cold but for the most part people just pile on layers of clothes. Gillian wears a charity shop ski suit and another artist paints in a duffel coat. Lara intends to go and get herself ski boots as soon as the discarded ski gear appears in the second hand shops. It's her feet that become numb first. Sometimes they're so cold that she thinks that she has stumps instead of toes and heels. Right now she has on two sweaters under her boiler suit and two pairs of Tim's socks. Dancing around helps warm her up but it also makes her feel damp and sweaty. She thinks that she is so well padded that if she tumbles over she will probably bounce right back again.

Her paintings and canvases are ranged around the walls.

Yesterday it had been liberating to spread them around and get a sense of what she had done and how the paintings related to each other. Today they look like a rather small selection of work both in regard to size and number. Lara suffers that diminution of purpose and loss of self-worth that comes to all artists as they review their intentions against their achievements. No matter. There's work to be done. She starts on the task of rearranging and sorting them – colours, categories, styles, subject matter, and size even. She won't manage any significant new work in a month but it will be important to turn her studio into a showcase for her work if there's even a small chance that a gallery owner might come by and look at what she had done. The studio is large, high windows go all down one side and there are steel girders above. Paintings hung under the window would be in shadow. Unless those opposite were large they might be dwarfed by the studio itself. It will be easy for visitors just to stroll through without spending time looking at them. Nowadays it isn't paintings that interest the public or the galleries particularly. Installations, videos, giant photographic prints, performance art – this is the art of the moment. Lara and Gillian spend hours huddled over mugs of instant coffee discussing the kinds of art that would bring them to the attention of the galleries and reviewers.

"It's who you know as well. It always has been." Gillian says.

Lara agrees.

"I had a special market and a reputation in that market. It was relatively easy for me for a time – well, until I wanted to develop in a new direction and I began to experiment. Trouble is I don't want to do installations really – well – I need to sell and I don't want to have to go through the whole business of competing for commissions or looking for funding for projects that have to have a high profile and take up a lot of space. I reckon all the well-known artists spend most of their time hob-nobbing with celebrities."

"Arse-licking more like." Gillian doesn't waste words. "Thing is you're a painter and that's just not fashionable at the moment unless you are painting corpses or bovver boys."

"Why would I do that?" Lara thinks of the Otto Dix paintings and Enoch's bloody body with Inonge crouched over it screaming. Imagine making money from such a personal tragedy? Yet that is what artists do. It would be therapeutic to express that horror and that pain in her painting but exploitative to sell it unless, like Otto Dix, it was all of one's life experience and not an experience that really belonged to other people who were also her friends.

"You're right about me – I am a painter more than anything. It is the process of creation through the medium of paint that seems so important for me. Something happens when I play with colours – it is a kind of visual music – only it happens when I do that physical organisation of coloured pigments into relationships."

"You make it sound like it should be a performance art and people should watch you working. We're starting to do that with film and video aren't we? – You know, you are a kind of Stuckist, Lara."

"A what? A Stuckist? What is that for goodness sake?"

"It just means that you are 'stuck' in what some people think is an old style of making art – that's all. It's another label that critics find useful. Some artist used it to slag off her boyfriend when he decided he was a painter and she decided she was an installation artist. Maybe it was Tracey Emin. Probably meant they split up as well. I am an installation artist too of course. My installations are supposed to challenge ideas about femininity and sexuality."

Gillian's work had been bought by a national gallery of modern art and she had been able as a result to sell to other national galleries in other countries.

"I still love painting – you are right about the process, it does magic things to one's soul." Gillian continues

"I don't see why paintings can't be installations too." Lara says thoughtfully. "I love your work, Gillian. It's just not how I want to make things – I mean paintings don't have to be framed and on easels do they – or even only two-dimensional either."

"Sounds interesting – you obviously aren't thinking of murals, are you?" Gillian acknowledges smiling. "Is that what you'll do for our Open Studios then? Better get on with it! We've loads to do."

By the first day of the Open Studios, Lara's workspace is transformed. First she had selected paintings of the same size and subject matter then she had secured them back to back and suspended them from the overhead iron girders in the studio across its width, but each on a different girder. There were doors at either end of her room and it was necessary to walk through her space to get to the next studio. Lara has arranged the paintings to appear like a continuous barrier across the room. They are in fact staggered across the space so that it was possible to walk around and between the paintings to reach the opposite door. Returning from the other side the same process has to be repeated, but this time the paintings will be seen differently and they will be in a new relationship with each other. It is a maze. Not a very complex arrangement but it allows many possibilities of varied viewpoints and combinations of image. Lara has also mapped the studio floor under the paintings with painted numbers, images, compasses, suggested viewpoints, footprints in an elaborate version of hopscotch to guide visitors through her space.

"It's fun, don't you think? I wanted people to enjoy my work – if not for the subject matter and content then for the colours and textures. I hope it doesn't look like walking through hanging curtain fabric and that it has a bit more to please and challenge visually. It will force people to look at the work and decide what they want to see in it."

"It's great – really different – an unstuck Stuckist explosion." Gillian walks through the space smiling. "Hey – you can put some coloured transparencies on the windows to catch the afternoon sun and add more coloured patterns on the floor and walls. You could use a few more lights to illuminate the paintings on the darker side – I'll lend you some. Don't forget to put up lots of personal information too – that's essential these days. Fake it that you're a minor celebrity!"

Are the wives of hostages minor celebrities? Lara wonders sourly remembering the press conference that she, Adam and Tim's parents gave when the news of Tim's kidnap first broke. For a couple of weeks she had been harassed by journalists outside her flat but that hadn't lasted. The breaking scandal about Monica Lewinsky and Bill Clinton made much bigger headlines and she was left alone. *Would it help our case if I flag it up here? I paint using my maiden name not my married name. Let's leave it that way – or would it help Tim? Don't see how.*

Working at the studio and putting up her exhibition was the most pleasure that Lara had had since Tim had left months ago. It had been pleasurable in spite of the constant presence in her mind of the horror of his kidnapping. Lara is sobered every time she focuses on Tim's situation. He is always there in her thoughts. As she set up her exhibition she was mentally explaining to him what she was trying to do. An account of it will go into her letter to him tonight. Adam also writes a paragraph or draws a picture every day for his father. Each week Lara addresses the letter to the Foreign Office to forward to Tim. She had been told that very occasionally hostages do receive letters from family. It may form part of the process of negotiation for his release that she hopes the Foreign Office is actively pursuing, though they never disclose anything about what they are doing or if they are succeeding or failing in it.

At the moment Adam's letters to Tim are all about his new weekend companion Lucy, the elderly ex-guide dog that Sidney and Gwen have adopted. Lucy is a creature with a sweet nature who is more than happy to lie around the flat for the greater part of each weekend. Each night Lucy sleeps on Adam's bed and Adam sleeps better for it. So does Lara. It is much more restful not to be woken at night with Adam kicking her in the back or clutching her tight around her neck. He's a restless sleeper always moving around the bed, constantly throwing off the duvet and even sometimes ending up with his feet on the pillow. If Adam is spending time with his friends, Lara brings Lucy down to the studio where she is provided with a warm bed in front of the gas fire and lots of attention from the artists.

Part Thirteen
1997

Chapter One

Ransom

"I want to tell you what happened to me at the Tin Heart Mine." Lara says at last to Brendan. "I think about it all the time in a confused way because I am always thinking of Tim and I have no idea what he is going through. All I am sure of is that what he is going through is much worse than what happened to me."

Brendan's raises both eyebrows, making such sharp creases on his forehead that Lara almost laughs aloud. She has become used to the multitude of ways that Brendan signals questions and comments with his eyebrows. This time he also speaks.

"Honestly!" he says, "I don't know how it might be possible to categorise and rate such experiences but tell me about it and why you think like that."

"Oh – I don't want to make comparisons at all." Lara's own brow becomes lumpier, "I just need to get it out of the way and as much as I can – out of my head. I need to concentrate on Tim."

Again Brendan indicates his acquiescence and Lara begins her story.

Chapter Two

Imprisoned

In the immediate and shocking moments after Enoch had been killed, time seemed to become elastic. Inonge had flung herself on top of Enoch's body and Lara knelt, holding Enoch's outflung hand, knowing there was nothing to be done but thinking that it must at least be attempted. The sound of the bullet, Inonge's screaming, the shouting of the men, all of those noises seemed to continue for hours, yet within seconds Inonge and Lara were pulled upright and dragged into the mine manager's house. The iron door clanged as it resisted the men's attempts to close it. There was thick grass clumped around the frame and trapped by the hinges. Eventually the men used a machete to hack at the grass roots and the door once again shut solidly into its frame. That did not stop the men giving it several reverberating kicks. Lara heard the broken padlock clunk into place. It would hold the door shut against any force they might exert on it from the inside. The room they were in was hot and very stuffy and airless but a sensation of such icy coldness rose up from Lara's belly to her heart that she was locked in position, frozen and immobile, her instinct only to wrap her arms around her body. For several moments she forgot to breathe. Inonge stood in the middle of the space rigid and silent. There was blood on her face, hands and down the front of her clothes. Outside Natan was giving orders. They could not hear Oscar at all. It gradually became clear to

Lara and Inonge that the men were now lifting Enoch's body and carrying it away. Inonge gave one terrible cry and fell to the floor. Lara found herself panicking. She was convinced that Inonge was also dead. That somehow she had also been shot and killed when Enoch was shot and killed. She knelt beside Inonge crying and pleading incoherently with her not to die, but to come back and not leave her alone, yet she also knew that Inonge was not dead, only deeply unconscious. Inonge's mind had fled to a dark and quiet place away from any acceptance of the fact of Enoch's death.

The sun would soon set and the mine manager's house was already filled with a dull gloom. When daylight ended it would become pitch black inside. Lara turned Inonge onto her side in the recovery position and she began a frantic search of the house. There had been electric lights once but they no longer functioned. She found an old storm lantern with a slosh of paraffin in the fuel chamber but nowhere could she find matches. Water? The single tap above the sink made a hoarse wheeze then a sucking sound and a tiny dribble of water collected on a spot of lime scale. Lara grabbed at the nearest container which was an empty tin can and placed it under the droplet. There was a half an oil drum standing next to the toilet. It had water in it but Lara could see mosquito larvae floating it and dead flies. It looked green and she thought there was mud in the bottom of the drum. It was probably river water brought up to flush the toilet and unfit for drinking. There was not even any way she could boil it. Lara kicked the drum. She must come and scoop out the larva so they didn't hatch out. There were enough mosquitoes around without any more. She was crying loudly now and panting and shaking. It was ill-judged of her, but at that moment she was more afraid of spending the night in the unrelenting dark than of anything else that might happen to her. Lara tried to force herself to stop being hysterical. She needed to decide what was the most important thing to do, but she did not know if there was any point in making any effort. Surely Natan and his men would come back and kill her and

Inonge? Was it impossible that Oscar would come back and let them both go? She could not believe Oscar wanted her dead but she also believed him easily capable of killing her and Inonge. After all he had minutes ago allowed his best friend to be killed by his business associate. Nothing seemed likely or sensible but anything was possible. Her most pressing need was to find some form of lighting and whatever she did must be done immediately because once it was dark she would not see her hand in front of her face. She needed to care for Inonge. For that she needed water and light. Food was unimportant and maybe unnecessary if their lives were soon to be terminated. The bed had a couple of rough blankets flung over the top of a stained and cheap foam mattress with a torn cotton cover. Insects, snakes, vermin, fleas must be everywhere – the house was most probably infested. Lara pulled at the blankets, banged at the mattress. She must lift Inonge onto the bed somehow. Inonge was a dead weight. Lara spread the blanket on the floor beside Inonge and rolled her onto the blanket. Then she pulled Inonge's inert body closer to the bed and lifted her onto the mattress, first raising her head and upper body and then her legs. She must pace herself. She might have lifted Inonge's body on her own but then she might have hurt herself or even dropped her. She must stay focussed and practical. If she could she would find a way of cleaning the blood from Inonge. Right now the smell of Enoch's blood was fresh and strong and intimate. It made Lara sob noisily again. She continued, however, as she cried, to look around for anything she could use to kill a snake or scorpion that might have taken up residence in the empty house. In the kitchen she found an old broomstick with a wobbly moth-eaten brush on it and she hurriedly pushed it around the room starting with the cobwebs on the ceiling and the spaces behind and under cupboards and furniture. That done she must see what she could find that they could use to drink out of and then once again try the taps in a hopeless attempt to get water. The ineffective broom disturbed wall-spiders, ants from under the sink, cockroaches from the empty cupboards, droppings from a rodent on the table, a couple of fortunate geckos that slid away into the outside world through the ill-fitting windows. There wasn't much to worry about considering that the place had been empty for years. Or had it? A strong pervasive, familiar, and unfamiliar smell tickled Lara's nostrils. A gradual awareness of it had been growing on her as she swept, then with a shock, she recognised what it was. It was the smell of the men who had been with Oscar and Natan. She had encountered similar odours in the crowded market in Chambeshi City and when she had travelled in the back of the pick-up with the labourers who had been digging the foundations for the camp kitchen. It was the smell of men. Familiar and not unpleasant in those earlier contexts, here it was oppressive. It was the smell of hot dry-skinned muscled workers overlaid with the acrid sourness of sweat and then again with the smoke of cheap tobacco rolled in newspaper. Here in this space it made Lara choke. The men who had been with Natan and Oscar must have been barracked inside this house. Inside the space that she and Inonge were now imprisoned. Lara bent over holding herself together with her arms. She couldn't breathe, she was gasping for air, she was hyperventilating. What possible chance did she and Inonge have against these people?

They might not just be killed.

She must not allow herself to think of what else might happen.

Lara went over to Inonge. She was so quiet and still that Lara once again checked her pulse and listened for her breathing. She stroked her forehead and spoke to her gently. She was desperate for company but it would be cruel to wake Inonge if she slept. Did she sleep? Was she unconscious? Was she safe? A mosquito whined past Lara's ear. There would be hundreds of mosquitoes once it was dark though ten would be enough to make their lives miserable. The insects, naturally attracted by sweating bodies, would also be attracted to the smell of blood on Inonge's clothes. Though it was hot Lara drew the blanket up and over Inonge's body. She lay down beside Inonge, her hand by Inonge's head ready to wave away any flying creatures and realised that she was exhausted but so agitated that sleep would not be possible. For a moment she closed her eyes.

The door banged. There was a peremptory knock, then a second, and Lara heard the voice of Natan.

"Lie down on the bed both of you. Lara! Inonge! Lie down. I am going to open the door. If either of you stand up or come close to the door I will shoot you dead. Do you understand? Lara?"

Lara's first attempt at a reply was a wordless croak then she managed to say yes twice. The second time loudly enough for Natan to hear and acknowledge.

The padlock clunked and banged and the door opened with a reverberation that shimmied in Lara's ears. Lara could see the outline of a man in the doorway against the fading evening light. It was not Natan but one of his men. Lara saw the shape of a shoulder and the muzzle of a gun poking from behind the door. That must be Natan. The man who entered was loaded with some bags which he left inside the room. He returned once more, this time with a saucepan, a large bottle of water, and two lanterns. Again he backed out. The door shut again. Lara found her voice.

"Natan!" she yelled, "We must have our malaria prophylactics and the first aid box." She heard a grunt from Natan. Perhaps it was laughter.

"Why?" he replied, "Do you think you'll live long enough to benefit from it?"

"Yes!" Lara yelled. She could hear him moving away as the other man replaced the padlock. This time the hasp clicked into place. It was a new padlock. "Yes!" she yelled one last time and then she sobbed again. "Yes! Yes!" but now she was whispering. Still crying she got up to examine what had been delivered. There were two rucksacks; those that they had brought with them from Chambeshi City. Each had been opened and roughly examined before being brought to them. Lara remembered with gratitude that her pen knife was still in her trouser pocket. If it had been in her rucksack they would have removed it. The rucksacks contained only their clothes for the trip and their toilet bags but Lara's had in it a small, but very useful, aerosol canister of anti-insect spray, a little torch, and, thank goodness, her malaria prophylactic pills. Her contraceptive pills were also there. God knows why she still continued to take them even after she knew that she would never ever want to go to bed with Oscar again. It was probably from a sort of superstition and fear that even months later, she might find herself made pregnant by him. Lara saw with sorrow that Inonge's rucksack had Enoch's belongings in it too. Perhaps it was as well that Inonge was still unconscious but even so Lara did not think it would help if she took Enoch's clothes and hid them somewhere.

Most important was the large 5 litre bottle of water. How long was that supposed to last? There was also a small camping gas light, a paraffin lantern and matches. Their captors were obviously not worried that they would try and burn their way out of the house. In any case only the mattress and possibly the blankets were flammable and the fumes from the mattress would choke them before they began to blacken the concrete block walls. Lara tested the weight of the gas bottle in her hand. It seemed pretty heavy for its size and the paraffin lantern was full. Again she had no way of knowing exactly how long they would last though she could make a good guess. Neither did she know for how long she would need them. Lara lit the paraffin lantern. The gas light would be brighter and for that reason she would save it. Once again she did a circuit of the little house with the paraffin lantern and her small torch and this time she found some stubs of candles and a pyrethrum mosquito coil. The saucepan that had been brought along with the water bottle held some cold and unappealing maize meal. There was some greenish oil and a few shredded vegetables in the bottom of the saucepan. Lara sniffed it but could not think how to warm it up. Inonge would not eat and she was not hungry. She put the lid firmly down on the pan and hoped that no insect would find a way in.

She returned to Inonge's side with the light and a tin dish into which she carefully decanted a little water. She would gently wash off as much blood as she could from Inonge's face and hands and then ease her out of her stained shirt in order to replace it with a clean one from the rucksack. Though she wanted Inonge's company very badly, she was careful not to disturb her. She didn't know, but guessed that Inonge needed to be as far away in her mind from all that had happened for at least, the time being. There was nothing to do but lie down on the bed next to Inonge and try to rest. She was certain sleep would be impossible. Instead she concentrated on the sounds of the bush around the house trying to identify the creatures and locate far away or how close they might be. She heard hippos on the river, hyenas not far away, owls hooting and the strange cry of a bush baby. She was very tired. The night that seemed so endless had become a cold grey morning. She must have slept after all but with the dawn pain and fear swelled up inside her so that she thought she might burst open with the agony of it.

There was nothing to do.

Waiting and waiting for what? She tried to listen again to the sounds outside. To see if she could distinguish the sounds of human activity, she tried to remember stories she had read, to plan paintings that she might do one day, she tried not to think of the people she knew. She tried to keep her mind from inventing scenarios where Enoch Junior and Tim arrived with an army – or the police force – what army? – what police force? Was there still some kind of government in Chambeshi? No – it was better to try and remember the words of songs that she liked. She made herself take her anti-malaria drugs and her contraceptive pill and even the Omega 3 pill that she took to counter the effect that working outdoors all day had on her skin. She looked again at Inonge, used a little more water to clean her a little more and tried to see if she would drink a few sips of water even in her unconscious state but though Inonge murmured a little and then licked her mouth, she did not swallow enough to stop her becoming seriously dehydrated. Lara also worried that she felt too hot and dry and that she could not make her take her anti-malarial prophylactic. She sprayed some of her lightest shirts with the insect repellent and placed them around Inonge's recumbent form. The smell made Lara sneeze and for a brief moment she felt awake and not drugged with worry. Her boredom was indescribable but her fear was worse. She was surprised and yet not surprised how soon she was overcome by hopelessness and lethargy.

The next evening once again there were the knocks on the door. This time it opened without any warning. Two Chambeshians stood there, one with a gun and one with more water and another saucepan of food. He made to take the first bottle of water away but allowed Lara to pour its contents into odd containers in the kitchen first and hand it back empty.

The man with the gun waved it around the room and in the direction of Inonge.

"Is she dead?" he asked terrified by Inonge's catatonic state..

Lara shook her head.

"No. She has gone to be with the spirit of her dead husband." she said, "He is coming back to take his revenge." She hoped that this would scare them without provoking them and it did. Inonge's trance was dangerous for them. The spirits demand revenge for any unjust killing. She heard them talking excitedly as they walked away. Where they went she could not tell for sure. Back to the camp perhaps.

There was so much time and it was stretched out so thin. Nothing to do. Nothing but think. And remember. Remember the story that's Fred's wife Monika, his old trout, had insisted she listen to – such a long and slow and painful story about Hanne. About Hanne, Oscar's sister – and about Oscar, and about Oscar's mother. Lara hadn't wanted to listen to the story when Monika recounted it. but she remembered every word.as it replayed again and again in her head.

"Listen, *meine Liebe*, such suffering, such a story. Hanne always lived with this trauma – it gave her cancer – so she died young.

They travelled with all the refugees from Dresden; Hanne, her mother, Oscar – first by train – then walking – walking – the gunfire getting closer – louder – believing Berlin would be defended – or surrender – or be safe. The Russians behind them – coming closer – such an army – so ragged – so angry – full of revenge. Their mother took them to the grandfather's farm. He was hiding in the cowherd's hut – he left his big farmhouse empty for the armies.. There was no food, no fruit, no animals, it was early spring and it was very cold. They were hungry – always hungry – very hungry. The Russian soldiers marched – they stopped – they raped – they marched – they stopped – they raped all the women and the girls. Hanne was thirteen years – thin and small – her mother cut her hair off with a kitchen knife – rubbed dirt on her face – hid her under the bedding." Monika mimed Hanne's hair tugging against the knife: imitated the scratchy scrape of the knife blade with her raisin eyes squeezed shut. "One soldier came – he found them – he raped the mother. Another soldier came – and another – they were going to rape Hanne – to humiliate Oscar with his sister's nakedness – he was a boy – nine years of age only – the mother was screaming at them – trying to stop them. The Russian soldiers shot her. They killed her in front of the children – left her bleeding on the floor in the dirt. That was the life of Hanne and Oscar as children. Gott bewahre!. God forbid!"

Sometime in the night or possibly the early evening, Lara became aware that Inonge was conscious once more. She did not move and her breathing did not alter much but somehow even though it was dark, Lara knew Inonge was present and alive. She turned on her side and touched her gently on the shoulder and spoke to her.

"Inonge – hello – Inonge – do you know where you are? Do you know what has happened?"

She felt rather than saw, Inonge's eyes focus briefly, heard her shuddering gasp and the convulsion of pain as she became aware of her surroundings, then she turned away folding herself up into a foetal position. After a while Lara persuaded her to drink some water and she lit the lantern and helped Inonge find her way to the toilet. Inonge shuffled like an old woman, doubled over and stunned as if she had been beaten. She refused to eat any of the unappetising mealie pap and relish that the men had brought for their supper. Lara made herself eat but soon afterwards her stomach began to churn and she was overcome by nausea. She spent an hour in the bathroom, vomiting and emptying her bowels which had turned to liquid, grateful for the scummy water nearby that allowed her to flush it all away. She suffered again in the morning and lay down feeling tired and weak, to doze a little. Inonge also was still in a drugged sleep though she did drink slightly more water and ate a very small ball of mealie pap without any of the sauce. The heat in the enclosed room increased steadily all day. There was nothing to do. Lara had a sketchbook in her bag. At first she had drawn objects in the room, even some of the creatures who carried on as if life was quite normal. But the stultifying afternoon forced her to give up and rest. Flies buzzed, sweat trickled between Lara's breasts, she was almost asleep and then she heard Oscar's voice outside.

"Lara – I must speak to you. Tell Inonge to go and wait in the kitchen. I must see you alone."

At the sound of Oscar's voice, Inonge rolled over and sat up. Her hair stood up around her head in rough spikes. She put her hand over Lara's hand and spoke for the first time.

"I don't want to see him but Lara – will you be okay by yourself?"

Lara's throat contracted. She nodded at Inonge.

"Go – I think I'll be okay. Go!" but she was afraid. Oscar had proved a monster. What form would he appear in when he came through the door? He must be changed.

When he stepped through the door, bright sunshine behind him, drifting dust motes in the slanting beams of light, Oscar seemed diminished. He was both shorter and slighter than Lara remembered him to be and his face looked older and weary, his skin darker and harsher in texture. Lara had risen from the bed and they stood facing each other. It was a familiar meeting, strange and yet expected. Then Oscar smiled at Lara. That personal, intimate, only-for-Lara smile that she knew so well and had loved so much.

"Lara! Oh Lara! I have missed you!" he said and reaching out his hand he stepped forward. Lara felt time and place swept away in a rush of hope. Perhaps it had all been a dream and now it was over? Then almost at once there was a sensation of falling fast into the hard reality of her concrete prison. She felt the prickle on her cheeks of shock. She had almost smiled back at him. Lara struggled to speak, lost and stammering for words to say what she knew – to tell Oscar what he was – crook – criminal – evil – bad – the vocabulary eluded her. All she said sounded childish and inadequate.

"You killed Enoch! I hate you! You are a cheat! A liar!"

"It wasn't me!" Oscar said with an involuntary glance over his shoulder. "It was Natan – he will pay – I will make him!"

Lara heard the catch in his throat. If he cries for his friend I will kill him, she thought. Stupid of her. How could she do that? The penknife in her pocket was shut; it pulled open with difficulty, and would close on her fingers before it went into Oscar's ribs.

"Lara please understand – please – I didn't know what Natan was doing – when I saw – then it was already happening – I wanted to keep Enoch out of it."

"You lied to us all – you tricked us – now Enoch is dead and you do what you are told – you do what Natan tells you to do!"

Oscar shook his head.

"Please sit down Lara – please I need you – I am going to get rid of Natan – we'll start over again. I can make it work again. All Natan wants is the diamond trade – I'll get out of that -" Oscar sat down on the bed indicating that Lara should sit down too. He laid his gun at his feet, first removing the bullets and turning the muzzle down safely. It was his favourite hunting rifle, not a Kalashnikov.

"Natan's men are still here." he said. "Not for long though – come with me Lara. I love you. You care for me" There was no doubt in his gaze, "I know you do! I need you. With you I can put all this behind me and we can start again – maybe somewhere new – maybe Chambeshi – there's an island off Mozambique."

"What about Enoch? What about Inonge? You can't put things right."

Lara was still standing but Oscar sat still. Her head swam and a spasm gripped her stomach for a moment so Lara sat down warily an arm's length from Oscar. This was an insane discussion. Where was it going? How would it end? What options did it give her?

"I don't want to come with you, Oscar. I want to go back to Chambeshi with Inonge. I want to go back to England. I don't want to see you again – ever!" Was she endangering herself even more by saying what she felt? "Do I have a choice?" she asked.

Oscar regarded Lara steadily. She saw the skin under his eyes crease and his mouth twitch as if he could not contain his feelings. Was he going to plead with her? No. She saw his jaw harden.

"You have a choice Lara. Natan wants you and Inonge dead. He will walk away and leave you with his men if you like. He can't let you go back to Chambeshi and tell stories about what he has been responsible for, can he? You can die – or you can survive. You can come with me. I know we can make it work between us."

"And Inonge? Your best friend's wife? Enoch's wife?" Lara's eyes blurred with tears. Was there a trade she had to do? Would Inonge be all right if she left with Oscar? Where was trust? She put a hand up to her face to wipe her eyes and dug for a handkerchief in her pocket. In that instant Oscar had her in his grip. For comfort? Or to kill her? Lara's hand was trapped in her pocket as his arm encircled her shoulder. He held the hand she was using to wipe her eyes and he searched for her mouth, pushing his face close to hers and kissing her roughly. Lara tried to turn her head away but unbalanced she fell backwards onto the bed.

"Lara – I know you love me! Lara, we must be together!"

In seconds Oscar was on top of Lara. The weight of his body pinned her down and left her breathless. He forced her hands together till he could hold them above her head with one hand and use the other to pull at her shirt and bra so that he could reach her breasts.

"No! I don't want this! I don't want you. No please Oscar – no!"

Oh God, Lara thought, *he believes that if he makes love to me that I will have to give in to him and go with him. He thinks this is how I will know what is in my heart. He thinks this is a demonstration of love. He can't? He must?*

She stopped fighting to free herself. It was hopeless and she was helpless. He was whispering in her ear, then kissing her mouth, her throat, behind her ears, he was making love to her, stroking her nipples, making them hard. Her body forced her to make those sounds, those gasps and little cries but she hated doing it. It was torture to be stretched out on a rack between arousal and humiliation and fear. Desire she did not feel at all. Pleasure was absent even when he forced her trousers down to her ankles and began to caress her vulva and clitoris and she felt herself moisten and tingle. She could not get enough air to cry but her tears flooded down her face.

Oscar entered her and the thrusting began. Lara opened her eyes wide trying to understand what it all meant. She felt her head rub back and forward, her hair pulled and knotted, and she closed her eyes wanting it to finish. Wanting the end. Aware of Oscar's body, the bones of his elbows, the flesh of his neck. She felt the jerking of his climax and then Oscar pulled himself out of her and stood up freeing her to roll over and to weep and weep. She had not had the orgasm he had hoped to give her. She had refused it. He zipped up his trousers and tucked in his shirt watching her. She knew he was surprised and disappointed. Did he feel shame as she did?

"Lara."

It was all he said. He turned, picked up his rifle and bullets, and walked out of the room. Lara heard the iron door close and heard the padlock scrape and click. She sobbed aloud unable to stop.

When Oscar had gone Inonge came back quiet as a shadow into the room. She knelt by Lara and stroked her forehead with a soft hand. Her eyes were wide with compassion and horror. After a while Inonge climbed back onto the bed next to Lara and again she fell into a coma of apparent unconsciousness and grief. Lara too half-dozed, half-slept for an hour or two till the sound of a small plane overhead woke her up and she found their prison door unlocked.

Chapter Three

Brendan 1997

There is a long silence in Brendan's room. Lara sits, sips tea and thinks of nothing much. Telling Brendan had been like riding a storm and it is pleasant to float in still water for a while.

"Oscar raped you." Brendan says.

"Yes, he did. At first I couldn't see it that way. It wasn't what I understood rape to be. I hadn't been beaten or hurt."

"You were frightened and a prisoner and you thought you might die even if Oscar didn't kill you. What do you think of Oscar now Lara?"

"I don't hate him anymore – I feel sad for him – is that pathetic? Should I hate him? I don't think he realised that he was raping me at first but he knew he had when he finished. I think he must have felt shame and guilt. Perhaps that's why he died as he did? Guilt about Enoch – and some about me and also Inonge. Sometimes I think his plane crash was suicide, though I'll never know.

"That horrible experience is over for me – it was only days – Tim has been a prisoner now for over a hundred days – my experience is nothing compared to his – it only gives me a little more understanding."

Chapter Four

Barry

Brendan promises that they will talk again about the rape on Lara's next visit if she wants, but by that time Lara has news for Brendan. She has had a phone call from the brother of Rod, the Australian cameraman held with Tim as a hostage. At his request she invited him to come to the flat to talk.

Barry, Rod's brother, is fed up, he says, with the way things are being dealt with under the management of the Foreign Office. Oh yes – he is sure they are doing their best but he doesn't think they can produce results. The kidnappers don't fit any of the criteria that might make for successful Foreign Office negotiations. They are a bunch of pirates on dry land, just robbers and bandits. They say they have a cause but they don't really have any support, or political aims or demands to be met. There are no prisoners belonging to their organisation, such as it was, who could be swapped for Tim and Rod. There is only one way to go about this, Barry insists, and that is to pay a ransom – as small a ransom as possible obviously – that means hiring a negotiator who works in this way, and he won't come cheap either.

Barry explains that he had raised quite a lot of money from various sources – he and his family have borrowed, begged and re-mortgaged – there are organisations and charities ready to help and there are individual people too. At this point he casts his eye around Lara's sitting room, still unfurnished and in the process of being painted and unable to help himself, he makes a wry face.

"I don't suppose you've got any money yourself have you? – family – no?"

"How much are you thinking we will need?" Lara replies and surprises Barry into silence when she says yes – she can find quite a lot of the million dollars that he reckons will be necessary.

"The Otto Dix paintings and the Käthe Kollwitz raised a considerable sum at auction." Lara explains to Brendan at her next session with him. "Now we wait again to see if it will be of any use to Tim and Rod – I don't know how long we have to wait for and I don't get any better at it either."

"I will be poor again too." Lara smiles, "No regrets – if it works – but I won't tell anyone and especially not Tim how the money was raised."

"Do you think he won't guess?" asks Brendan. "And Barry? What does he have to say about the experiences you both share?"

"Hmm." she says. "Barry is so Australian – I mean he has a very strong accent – but he's nice – very practical and down to earth. He reminds me of Bill who ran the game lodge back in Chambeshi– but -" here she frowns. "Barry says that people who have been held hostage are traumatised and sometimes their relationships with their wives and family break down afterwards."

Lara looks questioningly at Brendan.

"Yes, he's right." he replies. "We'll talk about that whenever you want."

Chapter Five

A New Strategy

Barry speaks in a measured way, his strong Australian drawl adding emphasis to his words. He seems to listen to the sound of what he said and to consider it carefully, but without self-consciousness. Lara likes both him and the sound of his voice. He contemplates her with calm reassuring eyes.

"Our dad's a rancher – sheep farm." he said. "Quite a big place – he's influential, luckily – he's taken out a mortgage to help Rod but lots of our friends have chipped in to help raise the ransom."

"I'm giving my time – I am on unpaid leave right now. That's why I've come here – to see what can be arranged and see what you wanted to do about Tim – and can do, of course."

The first time they meet Barry requests that it should be when Adam isn't around.

"Upsetting for the kid." he says. "Just knowing that this kind of business is being discussed."

The next time he comes he suggests that if Lara agrees, they could both take Adam on a boat trip up the Thames from Greenwich.

"That would be great." Lara says. "It was Adam's birthday a week ago and he refused to celebrate it because Tim hadn't come back as he had promised. I didn't know what to do and I couldn't make him change his mind."

"Let's do something that his Dad would like to do with him." Barry says. "We won't talk business unless you think he would like to know about my brother Rod being a mate of his Dad and also a hostage."

"I think he'll ask you himself." Lara smiles. "He's pretty astute for a kid."

She is right.

"Where you from? You have a different way of talking to us." Adam asks Barry as soon as they met.

"I'm Australian." Barry answers.

"So's my Dad's cameraman, Rod – the one who's a hostage with him." Adam is right on target.

"Yeah. Rod's my brother – that's why I came to see you and your mum. It's tough having such a big worry about people you love isn't it?"

Adam nods slowly looking at Barry.

"What are you doing about rescuing Rod?" he asks finally. "Mum says we just have to wait – and wait and wait. If we wait any longer I'll be grown-up and then I'll go and get Dad and just kill these people – dead!"

So much for all my rationalising with Adam. Lara thinks. He feels as *violent and angry as I do about it all.*

"Oh yeah! That would be good wouldn't it?" Barry agrees with Adam. "But we don't want to wait till you're grown-up if we can find another way. We'll have to make a plan, don't you think?

"Tell me about your Dad, Adam. My brother thinks he's a good bloke to hang around with – says he's got a sense of humour – and he's a good journalist."

"Yeah!" Adam imitates Barry and looks pleased at the praise for Tim.

"My Dad said your brother takes good photos – he showed me some he took of child soldiers in Uganda. Dad says that cameramen are braver than journalists because they carry on taking pictures when the journalists are running for cover – Pow! Pow! Pow!"

Adam acts out the gunfire as he had for Tim before his departure and Lara tries not to cringe.

The weather is grey, rainy and windy. It's bitter on the outside deck as the ferry takes them past Tower Bridge and up to Bankside Power Station, the site of new Tate Modern Gallery. The boat will have to fight the high tide on the downstream leg but is swiftly carried upstream passing under bridges that seem dangerously low. The Thames is struggling with itself, heaving and slapping and swirling. Lara is struck by how dark and dangerous it is and how impossible it would be to survive for long in its cold, rough waters.

London has trapped the river but not made it safe she thinks. Does anyone ever have a safe life?

The day is, however, a pleasant success. By the evening Adam and Barry are brothers-in-arms and Adam has been able to vent his feelings and his fears while Barry skilfully steers him away from any false hopes or dreams that a quick rescue can be easily achieved.

The next time Barry visits Lara, she arranges for Adam to spend the weekend with his grandparents as the two of them plan to talk about how the ransom is to be negotiated and paid.

Lara has made a beef stew and Barry has brought around a bottle of wine.

"Not the best Aussie plonk." he says. "Wine's bloody expensive here."

"I don't have any problem with the morality of paying a ransom in Tim and Rod's case." Lara says over their meal, "The Otto Dix paintings have been auctioned. The money is now an accessible liquid asset held by the bank. They will make a big fuss if they suspect money-laundering. They and I need to know that the negotiators' credentials are pure gold."

Barry laughs. His eyes have white crinkles at the corners and Lara can see how the sun had darkened the end of his nose and cheekbones.

"Yeah!" he agrees. "You really need to be sure that I don't

sell Rod and Tim down the river and buy myself a desert island somewhere."

"Here – this is how it's done and who we will be using. We'll have to arrange a meeting together with these chaps at their office. There are no guarantees it will work, you know. The kidnappers may manage to take the ransom and still kill Tim and Rod."

"I know." Lara is sober in spite of the wine. "What else can we do? It's probable Tim and Rod may come home badly traumatised. Tim may not want to be with me anyway. I know he'll always be a good father to Adam but I don't know about us staying a couple."

"You want him back with you?" Barry looks straight at Lara.

"Oh yes!" she says. "I love Tim. I love him very much."

Barry nods then sighs.

"Life's a bitch!" he says.

Lara and Barry talk the arrangements through until they are both satisfied that they have considered every possibility. Barry says he has chosen to use negotiators recommended by senior army sources in both Britain and America.

"It's two men with personal experience – I don't like to ask too much but I reckon they're ex-Special Services. Could be the one bloke has also done some work as a mercenary in Central Africa. They're really savvy about the people on the ground, their lingo, why they do this stuff and kidnap people, and what they want the ransom for. It's good the kidnappers are in it for money not politics. They'll cop that a dead hostage means no money. They're naïve though – it makes them unreliable. These negotiator guys have to use intermediaries. These intermediaries say they're humanitarian but people have a different idea of morality especially when there's lots of cash in the game. It's not just us who has to trust them – it's the kidnappers too. Anyway we're paying all these guys – the negotiators – they're no charity, but they keep accounts – the intermediaries – hopefully there aren't too many of those but they get greedier every day. There'll be other opportunistic thieving bastards around. Then there're the kidnappers – the bad guys."

"We have to act fast before another bunch of kidnappers arrives, pays the kidnappers enough to hand over the hostages, and then ask us for more cash than we've got – that's why we need the best. These blokes have ace knowledge about the Horn of Africa where Tim and Rod are being held."

"What's fast?" Lara asks holding her breath.

"Weeks only, I hope." Barry replies. "The kidnappers have had Tim and Rod for four months already. It was six weeks before they got in touch, as you well know!"

"Weeks would be good!" Lara doesn't dare hope. So much may go wrong.

"There are so many dangers to their safety." Lara feels dismal. "I know that Tim and Rod will have been beaten. I hope they haven't got malaria or dysentery. They won't be eating much. At least Tim speaks Swahili and some Somali and he does know the Koran. I kind-of hope that they won't have been imprisoned in a place without a window – or if they are, I hope they aren't kept chained."

Eventually Lara and Barry come to the end of what could be said about the situation and they fall silent.

Abruptly Barry asks about the paintings that Lara had sold.

"So how come you have these assets? You haven't faked them have you – I am joking – and I rather think you didn't buy them. You and Tim have art patrons for parents? What is your story, Lara?"

Lara hesitates. She doesn't want to talk but neither does she want Barry to go. Now that they had agreed to pay the ransom she had nothing to do but wait and Barry's presence was a comfort.

"It'll take some explaining and some time."

"Fire away." Barry encourages.

Lara gives the shortest account possible of her connection with Oscar and the Tin Heart Gold Mine and explains Tim's anger over it all. They sit together quietly for a while afterwards.

"Best get on, then." Barry says. "We'll head on next week to meet these negotiators and sort out money with the bank. The negotiators will keep us personally informed along the way but in the final stages they'll bring in the Foreign Office and nearest British High Commission and the last arrangements will be made with them."

A fortnight goes by. Barry phones Lara and they go out to a pub to talk about how things are progressing. There isn't much to report and neither of them wants to keep speculating about what may or may not happen. Barry talks about his life in Australia, about his work, about his wife Geena, and how much he misses her. Barry and his wife are both social anthropologists who work with aboriginal people. Geena's mother was part aboriginal.

"I guess we have done a lot of questioning of ourselves and our roles with regard to our work." Barry says. "God – I miss Geena."

Lara and Barry meet again a week later but both find it a strain meeting in a café or a pub without privacy.

"Come and have supper next week." Lara says and Barry does. Once again Lara cooks and Barry brings some wine. Adam is with his grandparents. They talk till it is almost midnight. Barry stands up to leave and then sits down again on the edge of his chair.

"I shouldn't say this Lara – guess I've had a drop too much. You're a really attractive woman, Lara. Hope you don't mind me saying this – if it wasn't for these circumstances I would really like to have asked to go to bed with you and make love to you."

Lara laughs. A delightful, lightening bubble of mirth floats up inside her.

"Barry, I think I would have loved that too. It would have been fun – and good for us too. Now I guess we have other things to focus on."

"Yeah!" Barry stands up, comes over to Lara. First they hug each other, then they kiss each other's cheeks. They think that they are taking enough care for their lips not to brush against each other by accident but it is the hug that undoes Lara. Her body has been rigid and tense with worry for so long that the warm firm pressure of Barry's hand on her back makes her shrug her shoulders with relief.

"Oh that feels so good – I am so knotted – are you the same?"

Barry holds Lara away from him keeping his light grip on her shoulders. He looks into her eyes.

"Yes, Lara – we are both the same – both stretched to the end of endurance."

Lara blushes. She has forgotten what it is like for her cheeks to warm and colour and for her to feel shy. She recognises her pleasure in Barry's reassuring touch, her need to be held physically, but she draws a deep breath and looks away from Barry's quizzical gaze.

"Shall we comfort each other – would it seem so wicked to you?" Barry asks with surprising gentleness, relaxing his hands.

"I wouldn't for worlds want to hurt your wife!" Lara answers. "I don't want to hurt Tim, either. I don't know what will happen between Tim and me but I'm afraid, Barry."

Barry turns Lara's face upwards so she can see his expression. He smiles at Lara.

"Humans are sexual creatures, Lara. We are made to give each other physical pleasure and comfort. It has never been only about marriage and children or jealousy and morality. All the same there is no pressure on you – I am not even sure that I am up to performing well sexually at the moment – worry gets me like that – but I should really like to cuddle you and have you do the same to me."

Lara frowns.

"Oh God – If I let go for a moment and stop being faithful something will go wrong for Tim."

Barry laughs but he looks tired and sad too. "Oh yeah! Does God work like that? I don't think so – but we fear it. It's important not to suffer guilt though – that is damaging."

Lara thinks for a moment then she leans up and kisses Barry gently on his cheek.

"Barry." she says. "I want you to hold me – I want not to think

– I want to be oblivious for a night – I tell myself that this would be a kindness to each other and only one night and would be our secret – but I can't do it. I can only think of Tim."

Barry slowly let go of Lara and she feels that her unsupported bones will soften and she'll fall over. She tries to ease the moment for them.

"I am tempted, Barry – you have so cheered me these last few weeks and I'm so grateful to you but – I can't."

"Damn." Barry says with a self-deprecating grin. "You don't mind that I tried – do you? It's a long way back to the hotel and it's so comforting to sleep with a woman. But you're right – it's not what we are here for is it?"

"Oh, Barry – I am flattered – and sorry – but please – it's time to go."

Lara shuts the door gently behind Barry as he disappears into the night. She still feels his lips against her cheek. She is so tired and so hopeless. Wouldn't it have been kinder to sleep with Barry? Does her refusal really help Tim or anyone else? What if Tim is never released? What if Tim arrives back and cannot forgive her? At least he would be alive, but what would her life really be like without him? How can she be sure of anything?

Chapter Six

Making Art Again

Adam is back at school. It is over three weeks since Barry had taken Lara to make the necessary arrangements with the banks and the negotiators. Lara is working at the Victoria Park Studios. It's one of her non-teaching days when she is free to paint.

She sits on her work table swinging her legs and contemplating her latest canvas. Sometimes she narrows her eyes, sometimes turns her head sideways as she studies her preliminary brush strokes. She is experimenting with a series of new paintings.

I'm going to take a huge risk.

I am going to make autobiographical paintings and drawings. I am going to mix up large paintings of emotional landscapes in wildly intense and saturated colours together with black and white charcoal drawings of mythical monsters and heroes. They'll be creatures of my own invention even if I draw on all kinds of stories and legends.

I'll start with the ugliness of the Tin Heart Gold Mine and the beauty of the wilderness and its animals. I'll paint Oscar and Enoch and myself and Inonge and Tim and Liseli – I'll paint riots and wars and crashing planes but I'll re-invent them. They'll be giant mechanical birds not the fish eagles and osprey which exist in our wonderful and beautiful world.

Whatever happens now – or happens tomorrow – whatever the outcome of the ransom payment – good or bad or tragic – I will paint it. I shan't care that it won't be for sale. I want to tell the story this way – my way. The monsters and the heroes will come from Manga, from Marvel comics and Greek and Inca myths. I'll use every idea I can borrow and steal and invent and create to tell all the stories I know of love and of war – of terrible things and – of cruel and kind people – of people who only want to live and not to kill. I'll tell the stories of people who want to live for freedom and beauty and die to tell the truth. I'll paint these stories for myself, for my past lovers, for my friends, for Tim – and most of all – for my son Adam.

Lara jumps down from her seat, stretches and yawns. So much concentration, so many ideas whizzing around in her head. She needs to make a pot of black coffee and to give her energy level another jolt upwards.

In the end this is all I have and all I can be – the Lara who works to make art.

It's never easy – it's not meant to be easy – it is just how it is.

As Lara moves over to the kettle by the sink, she feels the phone in her boiler-suit pocket vibrate against her thigh. The screen comes up with Barry's name.

"Hey, Lara." Barry says when she answers. "It's on, I think – there's still no guarantees as to the outcome. Don't hurry Adam off to school tomorrow – maybe keep him home. You won't get news from me first. Whatever happens, the British High Commission in Kenya will call you. Stay cool girl! It won't be easy but try and get some sleep tonight. Keep on hoping."

"Thanks Barry." she answers. "Will I see you? Are you also in London?"

"Yes. Maybe – probably – I think so!"

Barry doesn't sound as much in control as usual.

I'll finish here first. Lara tells herself but she can't focus on her painting any more. She starts sorting out her paints and cleaning brushes instead.

Mindless work is good.

It doesn't last long enough, however. She walks slowly home stopping to stare in shop windows but without being fully aware of what she is seeing. She realises that she is staring into a café when an annoyed man taps on the glass and with a rude jerky gesture suggests that she should shove off. Lara is humiliated and furious both herself and with him. Her rage is out of proportion to the incident. She must collect Adam. Lara tries to concentrate. She grits her teeth while raising her eyebrows into her hairline and makes some school kids approaching her giggle and duck as they pass her. Her mind and her body have separated at some point in the day and she is detached from them both. It was probably just as well because she isn't able to feel or think and if she could feel or think what might happen to her?

C'mon Lara! Make a plan. A beefburger restaurant and a Disney film tonight? Adam will think something is up if I suggest that midweek. Shall I just go home and try and switch off in front of the telly? I must phone Gwen and Sydney and warn them – but if they don't know why should I make them worry?

In the end it's easier to sink into a zombie-like state and put on a DVD for Adam. Adam is tired enough not to notice that Lara is distracted. When he finally goes to bed, Lara finds herself alert and agitated. She fails to become involved in a novel, opens a bottle of wine and drinks most of it while watching a repeat of an American movie in which all the cars spin out of control, every villain dies in mid-air flight from an explosion and the hero spends the last two minutes of the film hanging from a high building by his fingertips. Lara takes a sleeping pill too late and ends up checking the time on her alarm clock every 10 minutes.

I should be preparing myself to cope with the worst possible news and deal with Adam's grief tomorrow. God knows I have played through these scenarios often enough in my head. What if -?

But Lara can't permit herself to think these thoughts and her mind slides off in another direction and circles round and around.

At 2 o'clock in the morning the telephone rings. It's the man from the Foreign Office.

"Your husband has been released. He is safe and well at the High Commission in Nairobi. We'll send a car for you at 9 o'clock this morning to take you and Adam to RAF Brize Norton in Oxfordshire. Will you both be ready? Yes – similar arrangements have been made for Tim's parents. They will be there too. So will Rod's brother."

Lara climbs back into her bed and hides under her bed covers. She tries to scream or cry or feel anything but numb and exhausted. Adam is still asleep. After a time she finds that her face is wet with tears and she can feel that she has arms and legs again and a body.

Tim is alive. Tim is safe.

Lara repeats that again and again. It sounds even now like a prayer.

She goes into Adam's room and lies down next to him.

He breathes, he lives, he sleeps, he smells of boy, of child, of warm bed sheets, of life. He is Tim's son. Soon he will wake and yawn and complain sleepily that he doesn't want to get up.

Lara will tell Adam that Tim is coming home and Adam will smile and give her a hug as if she had managed to make it happen by magic.

Lara will find his clothes. They will have breakfast – perhaps. The chauffeured car will arrive and take them to Brize Norton where they will wait for Tim to step down off the plane and come and greet them.

Lara and Adam will hug Tim and tell him how much they love him.

After that, who knows what might happen?

EPILOGUE

Oscar 1945

The old man woke them early.

He whispered that there another group of refugees had arrived in the night. They had taken shelter in the empty cowshed and were sleeping on the small amount of flattened and mouldy hay that was left there.

"Don't go outside," he said, "Better no one sees you. They are afraid out there and hungry."

They too were hungry. Yesterday the young woman had collected nettles by the empty pigsty and the four of them: the old man, the young woman and the girl and boy, had had soup for supper with some wrinkled sprouting potatoes that had been hidden in the earth near the empty chicken coop. There were no animals on the farm. Not even one chicken. There was nothing growing outside either. It was early April, too soon in the year for any fruit to have developed on the plum and apple trees, let alone for it to have ripened. No crops had been planted. The old man's tractor had disappeared a while back and his winter vegetables had been uprooted and stolen. He had piled up all the hazel nuts and walnuts he could find, some he had even salvaged from the pig sty, but the hazel nuts were wormy and hollowed out and the walnuts black and bitter. The refugees in the shed did not even attempt to scavenge in the fields. They knew it was hopeless. They were not the first to pass and they would not be the last.

The old man had lost his dog. At first he had helped the skinny creature look for dry white bones in the midden but after a while he shut the dog outside and let him wander off, a sacrifice sent on a fruitless hunt. The cat still came into the cottage with a rat or mouse but no human could get near enough to remove its catch from its claws.

The gunfire was no longer to be heard behind them but out in front to the west. The woman with her children had left their comfortable apartment in Dresden after Christmas and finally reached the old man's cottage a few weeks ago. At first they had hoped to get all the way to Berlin but the train from Dresden had been halted by bombing and not started again. Instead they headed for the old man's farm which was off the main road a short distance south-east of Berlin. They ended their journey by walking just ahead of the sound of the guns. The first day the guns had been a faraway, distant booming. The second day they could distinguish the different sounds that different guns made. The third day they had seen flashes and the rifle fire was so close that they had sometimes run for short distances. The old man was the young woman's father-in-law. He had abandoned his large house on the nearby hill. It had attracted the retreating Wehrmacht and would now attract the advancing Russians. He was living in his absent cowherd's tiny and sparsely furnished cottage. He had wrapped his family's most prized possessions and his brother's painting collection in canvas flour sacks and hidden them in a pit which he had dug under the shed. The night his niece had arrived with her children, the main bulk of the ramshackle artillery of the Russian Army had overtaken them but passed by the farmhouse a few miles to the north. Today the noise of the battle was loud and remained at a constant distance.

"It's as well you did not reach Berlin." the old man said. "First the British and Americans bombed it and now the Russians will lay siege to it. They will encircle it first and then attack. They are shelling the centre and waiting for all their troops to be in place."

The young woman shrugged. Dresden had been bombed by

the British the previous year and then the bombing had stopped for a while. That was when she decided to take the children and leave for the old man's farm. Since then stories had reached them of the total destruction of the city. It was obvious that the Russian advance was not only inevitable but gaining ground at a rapidly increasing pace.

That morning, after the old man had spoken with the refugees outside, he took the young woman to one side and they spoke quietly together. Afterwards the young woman took her daughter to sit by the cold stove and cut all her long blonde curls off with a kitchen knife. The boy never forgot the stritch of the blade against his sister's hair and the way she squeezed her eyes and face up against its tug. Then his mother made the girl take off her frock and put on a pair of the boy's trousers and one of his shirts. After inspecting her for a moment longer, the woman rubbed some ash from the fire place into her blonde tufts and smeared a little on her cheeks. The girl began to look more like her brother's younger sibling than his older sister but also considerably dirtier. At midday the old man reported seeing soldiers of the Russian infantry on the road. The refugees in the cow shed became very quiet. The woman and the disguised girl lay down on the cottage floor and pulled the rough bedding they had slept on over themselves. The floor was very cold. The boy was inadequately hidden at one side of the fireplace. They waited.

The screams started in the early afternoon. There were a couple of gunshots and a lot of shouting. Men shouting. Men shouting in Russian. Then the sound of children wailing and again the sound of screams but this time also terrible groans and exclamations of pain. The old man was grey-faced, his hands clenched. The boy could not see his mother or sister but he heard his sister whisper and his mother say 'Shush'. He was shaking helplessly, tremors of cold running up and down his body. His teeth chattered uncontrollably.

Outside was a young Russian officer who looked as ragged, as lined and as hungry as the old man. He had once been an idealist, a student of Lenin and Marx, and he did not like to watch the mass rapes of women and children by his men. He could not stop his men from taking their revenge. They had been at Stalingrad and eaten rats. Some had eaten dead bodies. He had been told that another officer who had objected to his troops' behaviour had been arrested and would one day end up in Siberia if he lived long enough. They said that this other officer was some fool of a poet. The idea of sex however, aroused the young officer and he scratched at his uncomfortable, distended balls. He also wanted to have a woman. Next to the cow shed in which his men were occupied, he saw a one-room peasant's cottage. He would make the necessary search for any hidden German soldiers. He burst open the door, waited a moment, then strode in with his bayoneted gun at a proud angle in front of him. In a moment he pulled the old man to his feet and then knocked him down again with his gun butt, he yanked the shivering boy from his hole and turned to spear the bedding on the floor with his bayonet.

The old man cried out a warning to his niece and she rolled out from under the bedding just as she had always meant to. The officer kicked at the old man but moved towards the woman.

"Here I am!" she cried, in the Russian she had learnt as a child. "Take me! Let me be yours – keep me for yourself."

"I will be good for you!" she said.

The officer was already unbuttoning his flies. He swept the room with his gun.

"Lie down!" he hissed, "Lie down all of you!" and in a moment he was tearing at the woman's clothes. Pulling her legs apart, he forced himself into her. It did not take long before he jerked several times like a stuck pig, made a sound that was half-animal, half-howl of a baby, and then pulled himself up. He was finished.

"You can be mine." he said, "You are mine."

He stood looking at the woman. At the white skin of her legs and the white flesh of her belly, her pale hair spread around her head, her eyes staring, shocked. Then the door scraped again and two more soldiers burst in. The officer knew them far too well. One was just twenty and had been fighting since he was sixteen. His eyes were those of a dead fish. The other, an uneducated and brutal peasant who was older than the officer, had several times tried to challenge his authority.

"Good work!" said the brute, "She's ready for me." and he knelt on the bedding, his hand at his gaping trouser opening. The officer frowned helpless. The second man was erect for a second time. He had just finished raping an old woman outside.

"What's this?" he said, he had knelt on the hidden girl's leg and she had gasped in pain. He pulled her from under the cover roughly and flung onto the floor.

"Bloody kid! Watch what I do to your mother!" he said, and grabbing at the woman's hair to hold her down he carried on.

The third soldier pulled the thin child upright by her ear and looked at her more closely.

"Hey!" he said, "We have a little virgin here! Let's have some fun!

"Hey boy! This your sister in disguise? Do you know how to fuck? We'll show you what to do!"

Keeping his grip on the girl he reached for the boy and then he casually stripped the trousers off each child.

The boy was in the grip of long shuddering convulsions of absolute terror. For the first time in his life his penis was upright and distended in an automatic spasm of agony and fear. His sister kept slipping into and out of a faint.

"Hey! Look at this!" The Russian was laughing in incredulous mirth. "The little bastard is ready too! Let them get to it!" and he made to force the boy onto his sister.

As the second Russian climaxed and momentarily relaxed his grip, the children's mother tried to struggle to her feet, beating at him and screaming.

"Leave my children! Leave my children!"

The second Russian pulled out his pistol and shot her in the throat.

There was a sudden quiet. The girl was unconscious, the old man collapsed onto his knees.

"Get out!" screamed the young officer, blinded and maddened with rage, "Get out! Get out!" and he struck at his comrades with the butt of his gun.

Surprised into obedience, they did as ordered and left without a glance backwards.

The boy looked at his mother. She lay on her back, naked from the waist down, her eyes and mouth wide open, and a red flower blooming out from her neck. Her hands were up, her fingers curled. She reminded the boy of the cat at home whose tummy he had stroked and who had stretched out her paws in pleasure at his touch.

Acknowledgements

The Tin Heart Gold Mine owes its existence to the unforgettable days and nights I spent in the African wilderness with people who love it, understand it and share their knowledge of it. It is inspired by the passionate and generous artists and painters I know, from Africa and Europe, who give of themselves too often without much or any financial gain.

The story is driven by my anger at the depredations caused by the Cold War in southern (sub-Saharan) Africa.

As to the mine itself, my imagination was caught by a tin heart fastened to a tree in a tiny 1914-1918 war cemetery in Marondera, Zimbabwe. The physical aspects of the Tin Heart Gold Mine are based on an old copper mine close to the Hippo Safari Camp in the Kafue National Park in Zambia which is now a Zambian National Monument and my father's stories of an ill-spent youth prospecting for gold and working briefly on the Phoenix Gold Mine in Zimbabwe.

I am also deeply indebted to John Corley for his patient and efficient editing, to Emma Darwin for her advice, to Colin Carlin for his expertise and to friends including Lesley Bower and Claudia Naydler for reading and commenting on the novel. Terry Compton has once again made me a superb cover design. My thanks to everyone who simply allowed me to be anti-social and to write.